the things they didn't see

# the things they didn't see

*a novel*

## angela shaeffer

Published by Wander Lane Press, Holladay, Utah

AngelaShaeffer.com

The Things They Didn't See

ISBN 979-8-9928252-1-3 (paperback)
ISBN 979-8-9928252-0-6 (ebook)

Cover art by Shelly Coleman, shellycolemanart.com
Publication managed by AuthorImprints.com

# dedication

To my mom, who always believed I was a writer.
And for my dad, who gave the best flannel-shirted hugs.

# 1

# lake koda

WHEN JILL WAS TWELVE AND her mom moved out, her dad bought a boat to make everything better. Every five years or so, the ruby-red speedboat was swapped for a newer model, and Jill learned to tow a skier long before getting behind the wheel of a car. She never outgrew her love of Lake Koda, and boating days never stopped making things better.

Once she married Matt and they became parents, her dad added wakeboards and tubes and all the latest gear, and her three boys now loved the lake as much as she did. Many of their best memories were made on the water—first time getting up on skis, first time to slalom. First wakeboard backflip. Worst backflip. That time Matt lost his swim trunks.

Kicking off summer with a boating day was a tradition they'd been keeping since Jill was a teen. Now her own kids woke early to wait by the window and watch for Grandpa Roger and his wife to arrive in their black Suburban. The jubilant sound of the brothers laughing together as they remembered past boating trips and made plans for today's adventure filled Jill's heart with joy.

This past year, Jill's eldest, Jake, had developed a prickly personality, creating tension in their home. But for the next three months, she wouldn't need to bug him about homework, chores, or being on time. Instead, she could entice him with sunny lake days, and if all went according to plan, she'd trade eyerolls for laughs and they'd return to their easy, friendly relationship that had vanished a year ago when he started high school. She was confident that carefree boating days would be the reset they both needed.

The sun crested the mountains just as they drove into the state park. As they rounded the final bend in the road, they came out of the trees and into the open, where majestic Lake Koda sparkled in front of them. They unpacked the car and the three boys raced ahead of their parents and grandparents, their sandals slapping against the wooden dock and their shouts about who would get there first echoing throughout the marina.

The family worked together, prepping the boat, stowing towels and blankets, and filling the cooler with drinks and a picnic lunch. Finally, Grandpa took his place behind the wheel and slowly steered his family out of the no-wake zone and into open water.

He brought the boat to a puttering stop at the deepest part of the lake and spread his arms wide, as he always did, as if onstage presenting an opening scene to his audience. "It's a little bit of paradise," he exclaimed.

"*Practically* paradise," Jill responded with a wink, as she always did.

"Paradise" because the lake transformed from black to navy to a glittering royal blue as the sun rose in the sky. Tall pines surrounded the banks, obscuring roads and civilization. Sandy beaches beckoned as a quiet place to rest with bleached driftwood crisscrossing their shores.

"Practically" because by the end of the day, everyone was tired, at least one person grumpy, and something always happened that required an apology. Not that they ever got around to saying sorry. In their family, you avoided uncomfortable confrontations by getting over it and moving on. "Give 'em the benefit of the doubt," her dad was fond of saying.

He put the boat into gear and it surged forward. Jill closed her eyes, letting the wind blow her short brown hair away from her face and the sun warm her cheeks. Gratitude filled her heart, grateful to be in her favorite place with her favorite people. As they skipped across the glassy water, the rise and fall lulled her into a meditation. Almost. Until everyone needed her all at once.

"Mom, did you pack my hat?"

"Jill, where should we store the extra drinks?"

"Babe, can you hand me the sunscreen?"

"Mommy, sit by me!"

She rummaged through towels to find the hat, stashed the extra sodas behind the captain's chair, found two types of sunscreen in the glove box, then collapsed next to six-year-old Henry, pulling him into a hug and kissing his blond curls.

Too often she was preoccupied with keeping the family organized and on schedule, hoping one-word responses to her children's questions would suffice, so she wouldn't have to look up from her to-do list. But today, brimming with optimism and the endless possibilities that summer promised, she committed to rediscovering her fun-mom side. She'd revive Old Jill. The easygoing, smiling, funny woman she was when she and Matt first married. The mom she imagined she'd be before the busyness of having three children made her disappointingly serious. Of course, she'd always be type A because that's how you got things done. But she'd also tease and laugh and not worry so much.

A year ago, she'd believed life was at a turning point when her youngest entered kindergarten and she chose to go back to work, teaching Spanish, like she had before the kids were born. But it had been harder to adjust than she'd expected. She was stressed, which caused her to be rigid, and Jake had become crabby. Thankfully, the other two boys had seemingly survived unscathed.

Summer break would be her chance to right the wrongs of last year. She would say "yes" to her children's requests more often. Starting now. Today. *Can we go cliff jumping? Sure! Can I have a soda with lunch? Why not? Can I have one more turn on the wakeboard? You got it!*

As long as they didn't get sunburned. "Henry," she said, pressing her six-year-old toward her stepmom, "let Grandma Gina put sunscreen on you. Connor, you get over here." Jill patted her knees.

Eleven-year-old Connor bounced on his toes while she shook lotion from the bottle. It was nearly impossible to get her middle child to stand still. She rubbed a white dollop over his thin shoulders and down his arms as he wiggled his backside. "Where's your life jacket?" she asked, massaging his neck because she knew he loved it.

"It's way too small. I couldn't get it buckled," he said, bopping to an internal rhythm.

He was almost as tall as her—when had that happened? "You're growing up too fast," she said, playfully tugging his ear. "Let's see if dad can find you a bigger one."

Her husband sorted through the boat's storage compartment. "What do you think of pink?" he asked, tossing them a black jacket with a wide pink stripe down the back.

"Cool!" Connor said, giving him a double thumbs-up.

"It's a little big," Jill said, tightening the straps, "but next summer it'll be perfect."

"Will I be big enough to drive the boat next summer too?" Connor asked.

Her dad answered before she could. "Let's get you behind the wheel today!"

"All right!" Connor shouted, fist-pumping the air.

Jill almost intervened. *Isn't eleven too young?* Her dad was never one for following the rules. Then she caught herself. She was saying "yes" today. She wouldn't let her dad be the only fun adult. She smiled at Connor and he cheered again, hugging her neck. Her radiant middle child's unabashed affection was one of her favorite things about him.

She turned to Jake who was stretched out across the white bench seat, hands behind his head, dark curls peeking out from the ball cap pulled low over his sunglasses, listening to his ever-present earbuds. His legs were muscular from his many after-school soccer workouts. They'd become the legs of a man, but he was only fifteen. Why did it always seem that just as she was catching up, her children were speeding away from her? She tapped him on the shoulder with the sunscreen bottle. "Slather up."

He waved her away. "I'm tanning today."

Pressing the bottle back to him, she insisted. "The last thing we need is to start off the summer with you sunburned and miserable."

Jake rolled his eyes. "I'm not five."

His pout looked very much like a five-year-old's.

She tugged the brim of his hat, trying to be playful, but he turned away. This was another development over the past year—his resisting her attempts to show him she cared. She knew it was normal at his age to start pulling away, she'd been a pill as a teenager. But she blamed her sassy tone and mild rebelliousness on her parents' divorce. When she was at her dad's house, he was so laissez-faire that it was shocking she and her two siblings ended up in one piece. And their mom was so strict that being at her house was no fun at all.

Jill had felt such enormous pressure to be a happy kid—so her parents would be happy—that when she occasionally snuck out, the freedom was pure ecstasy.

But she was raising her children totally differently than she had been raised. Her marriage was loving. They ate dinner as a family. And Jill volunteered at her kids' schools and sports. She thought if she parented perfectly—well, at least better than her parents had—she'd avoid having disgruntled teenagers. But this year had proven her wrong.

Arriving at the far side of the lake, the motor's roar softened as they slowed, and the white, frothy wake dissipated into gentle ripples. Her dad killed the engine, and everything was blissfully quiet for exactly four seconds until Connor pointed out a fish and Henry screeched when he saw it.

"Let's get this party started," Grandpa sang. "Who's jumping in first?"

They waterskied, wakesurfed, wakeboarded, and tubed. As the sun moved higher, the lake became busier, a carnival of boats in greens, blues, yellows, and reds, speeding and slowing, seemingly in sync with one another. By early afternoon, with the lake at its most crowded, they were ready to leave the melee and find a quiet beach to eat lunch and stretch their legs while the boys ran around on the sand.

Their favorite cove was hidden by a rocky outcrop and they had the small beach to themselves. The boat's prop, like most of the new ski boats, was on the bottom of the hull—far safer than the old outboard motors. But this meant they couldn't beach the boat on the sand like they used to in the old days.

They threw in an anchor and everyone waded through knee-deep water to get to shore. Matt and Jake helped

Grandma Gina, while Jill and her dad ferried Henry on the extra-large purple tube along with the towels, a blanket, and everything else they wanted to keep dry.

Henry squealed as Grandpa bounced the tube back and forth, joking about sending him overboard. Until suddenly Grandpa yelped and lost his balance, pulling the tube to its side. Henry slipped to the edge and then into the water, bringing the towels and blanket with him.

"Henry!" Jill shouted, reaching for him as he sputtered.

Her dad got to him first and lifted him onto his hip.

"Geez, Dad!" Jill said. "He didn't want to get wet."

"We're in a lake, Jill. He's been wet all morning." Her dad winked at her, but she rolled her eyes as she hauled the soaked linens into her arms.

"It was fun, Mom!" Henry assured her, grinning.

Her dad laughed and tickled Henry until he giggled.

After lunch, Jill and Gina relaxed against a fat, weathered log, watching the boys play football. Henry was on Jake's shoulders, both arms pounding the air, celebrating a touchdown. They were all so happy that it was impossible to tell which team missed the tackle.

Gina watched Jake, her eyes soft with affection. "He's so sweet," she said. Gina had never had children of her own, but because she was so kind and gentle, her nephews, nieces, and grandchildren worshipped her. Jill's kids loved having sleepovers at Grandpa and Gina's—Grandpa the tease, Gina the saint—and Jill and Matt got the house to themselves for a night.

Her dad had married Gina when Jill was a few years out of college and too old for a stepmom but open to a friend. To her delight, Gina came with many endearing traits. She was a good listener, for one.

"Sweet, yes, but becoming challenging." Jill sighed. "Always irritated when I remind him to do his chores or ask about his grades. I walk into the room, and he acts like it's the most annoying thing in the world."

Gina laughed. "It's about time. He's a teenager after all."

Jill twirled the thin band on her right ring finger. Silver with three small stones—purple, green and blue—a birthstone for each of her boys. Matt had given it to her when Henry was born. After six years, the soft metal had developed a tiny mar, a pit in the silver on the back of her finger, hardly noticeable. But an imperfection nevertheless, and she often caught herself mindlessly scratching at it with her fingernail.

"I'm sure my dad's told you stories about my rebellious moments," Jill said, watching Gina's face for any sign of judgment. Jill and her brother had taken full advantage of their newly single, distracted parents—sneaking out, telling smooth lies when they got caught, covering for each other when their dad got suspicious. She hoped her traits as an involved, engaged parent were passed down to her children rather than the karma she'd earned from her teenage years.

Gina tightened her ponytail and simply smiled, not giving anything away.

Jill continued, "I try to ignore Jake's eyerolls, deep sighs, and 'whatevers.' But I didn't realize how much it hurts when it seems like your kid doesn't like you."

Before Gina could respond, Henry bounded toward them, hollering, "I made a touchdown!"

They both gave him high fives and then another round because his wide smile begged for a celebration.

Jill brushed the sand from her shorts and called after him as he started to run away, "Can you tell everyone it's time to get back on the boat?"

He stopped. "Do we have to go right now? I want to build another sandcastle."

"Sorry, bud, but we agreed to break for only a couple of hours."

"I could stay with him," Gina said, taking Henry's hand in hers.

"Are you sure?" Jill asked.

Gina held up her paperback. "I've got a book and I love building sandcastles."

"Connor!" Henry shouted. Connor was filling a bucket with sand. "I'm staying with Gina! Will you stay too?"

Connor looked from Jake, who was tossing a football in the air, to Henry, and back again. "Maybe."

Henry started chanting, "Stay! Stay! Stay!"

Connor grinned. "Okay! Let's make the sandcastle really huge!"

As the boat pulled away, Jill blew kisses to her two youngest boys who were waving and jumping up and down. A gust of wind ruffled Connor's hair as Henry grabbed his hand and pulled him up the beach.

An hour later, Jake landed a backflip on the wakeboard and flashed a Hawaiian shaka to cheers from the adults onboard. Jill whooped the loudest.

When he was a little boy, he would crawl into her lap and tell her everything about his day, starting from when he first woke up. "I really liked the blueberry pancakes you made for breakfast. And Sam brought gumballs on the bus, even though we're not supposed to. We played kickball for PE, which I'm super good at..." Even as he got older, he loved to tuck his head under her arm and later, as he grew, rest it on her shoulder while they talked.

Then last year, after fourteen years of being a stay-at-home mom, it seemed serendipitous when Jake's high school needed a Spanish teacher. Finally she'd use her talents for something beyond the PTA, and she imagined she and Jake having lunch together occasionally and getting some one-on-one time.

But their paths hadn't crossed as much as she'd hoped, and when they did, he avoided her, behaving as if the entire school was his personal space, and she was an intruder. This year she would try again, with a better plan to create connection.

She rubbed her shoulders as building clouds hid the sun and the air became chilly. "It looks like our day is ending early. Should we head back to the beach for Gina and the boys?"

Her dad tipped his cap back to check the sky. "You're right. It looks like rain. Why don't you call Jake in."

Jake already had his feet in the wakeboard boots, ready for another run. "Time to come in," Jill shouted. "The water's getting rough."

"It's not that bad," he called back. "And now there are hardly any other boats! Dad, come in with me! We can double!"

Matt didn't hesitate. He had his life jacket on in two seconds and tossed a board into the water. "Jill, clip on another rope; we've only got a few minutes."

Jill hated being the bad guy. If she pulled the plug on Matt and Jake's fun right now, Jake would be surly with her for the rest of the day.

"I'll look for smoother water," her dad said, laughing.

She was overthinking it. She reminded herself that she was trying not to be a control freak. Jake and Matt were having a blast. So she made the best of it, throwing on a sweatshirt and grabbing her phone to take videos.

Her dad found an inlet where hills protected both sides of the channel. But, even between the cliffs, the water was choppy, and Matt and Jake were bumping over whitecaps.

The sky was darker—or did it just seem that way in the narrow ravine? Pines swayed as they sped past, their branches waving like arms, urging them to head home.

Suddenly, lightning cracked in the distance. Her dad immediately killed the engine. "Pull them in. Fun's over."

As Jake and Matt hauled themselves up the short ladder onto the platform, it started to sprinkle. Jake was shivering and rubbing his arms. "Are there any dry towels?" he asked.

Grandpa tossed him the one he'd been sitting on. "You'll have to share with your dad."

With another flash of lightning across the darkening sky, the four of them jumped into action, storing the ropes and boards just as the rain unleashed. Roger moved to the captain's chair and put the boat into gear. "Hang on! It's going to be rough getting back to the marina!"

Jill dashed to his side, holding a towel over her head, more to keep the rain out of her face than to stay dry. They were already soaked. "You mean the cove, right? To get the boys."

"We need to get off the water," Matt said, slamming the hatches shut.

"We can't abandon them," Jill said, turning to Matt. "They'll be so scared. This is why I wanted to come in earlier!"

"We're not *abandoning* them. We're playing it safe," her dad said, standing to see over the rain-splattered windshield. "Gina will take good care of them. We'll shelter at the marina and as soon as the lightning stops, we'll go to the cove. If these waves get bigger, it'll be hell to maneuver anyway."

As if for emphasis, the boat hit a swell and keeled to the side. Losing her balance, Jill grabbed her dad's wet arm for support, inadvertently yanking his hand off the wheel. He swiped her away. "You need to sit down."

"Go to the beach!" she pleaded.

"We're going to the dock."

Jill didn't budge. The rain needled her back as she stood defiantly at her dad's side. Just as he'd predicted, the waves grew, and as the boat lurched over each one, crashing into the trough was like landing on concrete.

A rush of cold water poured over the bow and another flash of lightning cracked across the sky. Leaving the boys on the beach until the storm calmed really was their only sensible option.

Giving in, she squeezed onto the bench between Jake and Matt, ducking her head to shield herself from the rain slapping her face. As they dropped into another trough, she gripped Matt's wet knee, taking deep breaths to calm her racing thoughts. Henry was afraid of storms.

At least Connor was with him. Connor would turn it into a game, encouraging Henry to count the seconds between lightning and thunder. They could shelter in the trees up the hill—except trees aren't safe when there's lightning. She took another deep breath and brushed her dripping hair from her face.

Finally, they arrived at the marina. Rows of boats banged against their slips in a steady percussion of distress.

"Get ready to hold her!" her dad called.

Matt secured two bumpers port side to cushion the impact as they hit the dock with a dull thud. He leapt off and dropped to his knees near the bow, gripping the boat's edge. "Jake, help me hold her at the stern. Jill, throw us a rope so we can tie her up."

She picked up the rope, then looked at the sky. Sometime during their drive back, the lightning had stopped. Now that they were away from the open water, the feeling of danger ebbed, and her anger at her dad and Matt for not listening to her earlier pleas emboldened her. "I'm not staying," she said. "I'm going to the cove to get the boys." She widened her stance as the boat rocked.

"No," Matt said, his voice breathless as he tried to hold the boat still. "It's too dangerous. Wait until the storm stops."

She was the mom, dammit, and she wanted her boys. Jill turned to her dad, touching him on the shoulder. "You said we'd go after the lightning stopped. The rain could continue until dark. We can't leave them there that long."

With a hand shielding his eyes, he searched the sky for any indication of a break in the storm.

Jill held her breath, her heart as unsteady as the heaving boat. When he turned back to her, she continued her plea. "Please, Dad. We can do this together."

"Matt, push us away!" her dad called.

"What? No!" Matt shouted.

"We'll be back in less than an hour. I think the worst of it is over."

Triumph surged through Jill at the thought of holding her boys safe in her arms. But as they pulled away, the look on Matt's face gave her goosebumps. He wasn't angry; he was terrified.

Suddenly, both Jake and Matt were shouting and pointing, and she had to cup her ears to hear their words over the wind.

"What are they saying?" her dad shouted.

Jill stepped to the back of the boat, then returned to her dad's side, handing him a black vest. "That we should put on life jackets."

The rain had lightened, but the wind was still fierce, especially in the widest part of the lake. As they crashed through the waves, water poured over the bow and pooled around their feet. She was chilly, but the boys would be freezing. Gina had to be panicked, wondering where they were. They were doing the right thing.

The boat struggled forward as Jill strained to see the shore, but it was as if the whole world had vanished and only the steely, tumultuous water existed. She'd heard stories of surprise storms. Of close calls and desperate runs for safety. She never understood how people missed the signs. Dark clouds, whitecaps, rain—she'd believed only someone careless or inexperienced would get caught in a storm. *Had one been predicted in today's forecast? Did anyone even check?*

Water streamed into her eyes. Wiping it away was futile, and yet she persisted, squinting desperately, until finally the cove came into sight. Her dad gunned forward, bucking over another wave.

Her heart skipped as she scanned the empty beach, but then there they were, the two boys huddled with Gina against the log, already wearing life jackets, a bright green towel over their heads. As they spotted the familiar red boat, they jumped up.

Jill waved, pretending confidence, hoping to chase away their fear and suppress her own worries. "What's the plan?" she asked her dad.

"I'll drive in as close as I dare. You pull the kids over the front."

The turbulent waters pitched the boat from side to side. It was only ten feet at most from the beach to the open bow, but what was a calm, knee-deep wade only hours ago, now required swimming through chest-high waves.

Holding the boys' hands, Gina rushed into the water and managed to push them to the boat, but with both clinging to her arms, she was struggling to lift them toward Jill. The wind was blowing the boat sideways, and they were drifting dangerously close to the rocks.

Jill gripped Henry's life jacket and easily pulled him to safety. She kissed his cheek and turned for Connor. His life jacket was so loose she nearly pulled it over his head, but catching the waist of his swim trunks, she hauled him over the side and they fell into a heap on the deck. While they were still righting themselves, her dad shouted to Gina, "Swim back to shore—I've got to pull away from the cliff!"

Jill looked up and gave a strangled cry. The massive boulders loomed over them. Her dad hit the throttle, spinning them around. Then suddenly they were flying, boat and all into the air, then falling, falling into the frigid lake.

# 2

# *flipped*

ROGER FLAILED UNDER THE CHURNING water, fighting for air until finally breaking the surface, only to have a wave slam his head against the great white hull of the upturned boat. The bottom was where the top should be and he palmed the smooth sides, feeling for anything to hold on to. Nothing. His life jacket choked him as he splashed in panicked circles, searching. "Jill!"

The thrump of the rain pounding against the capsized boat made it impossible to hear anything else. And then, a faint "Dad!" His heart jumped.

"Here!" he cried, desperate for her to hear him above the cacophony.

When her voice found him again, it was impossible to tell whether she was screaming to be heard or screaming in terror, and he fought to stay calm. They were both worried about the same thing. "The boys?" he shouted, the hull a lurching mountain between them. He thrashed about, trying to see above the waves. Then in the distance, a bright pink object caught his eye. Without hesitation, he launched into the chaos, his powerful breaststroke propelling him toward his grandson.

"Connor!" he heard Jill shout.

"I have him!" he called, struggling toward the pink stripe. Rocked by a wave, he coughed, then yelled again, "I have him!" But in that moment, Connor was lost from view, hidden by the turmoil. Roger frantically spun around until, just as suddenly, he reappeared within arms' reach.

Lunging forward, he grasped Connor's limp body and pulled him on top of his chest. Bearing the weight of his grandson, he battled toward shore.

Roger exercised often—not only swimming, but strength training too. His legs scissored furiously and his heart pounded, his effort at an ability he didn't know he still had, but he managed to keep his voice calm. "I've got you, kid. You're safe with me."

Arriving in shallow water, he cradled Connor in his arms and splashed onto the beach. Jill ran to meet them and the three fell onto the sand. "Henry?" he asked.

"He's safe," she replied.

Roger pinched Connor's nose, pressed his mouth to Connor's blue lips, and visualized warm breath filling his lungs and heat moving through his veins. He unbuckled the pink life jacket and covered the small chest with his large palms, channeling love with each compression. *Please, let it be enough.*

Jill counted. Roger alternated with rescue breaths. He checked for a pulse and started over. Jill began counting again.

He was lost in the repetition until registering a hand on his shoulder. A man hovered in his peripheral vision. "We saw the accident. We'll get you back to the marina."

Two women were already helping Henry and Gina into a yellow ski boat pulled all the way onto the sand. An outboard motor, thank God. He hadn't even heard them arrive.

The boat seemed to crawl through the rough water. Roger continued CPR but couldn't tell if he was keeping time correctly. He second-guessed where his hands should be. Was it rain or his tears that fell onto Connor's cheeks? Finally they slowed, the motor stopped, and the boat slammed into the dock. Blue and red lights flashed in the distance. Two EMTs jumped aboard and Roger let them take over. A third peppered him with questions: "How long have you been doing chest compressions?" *I don't know.* "Has he ever had a pulse?" *I don't know.* "What time did the accident happen?" *I don't know.*

Roger searched the gathering crowd until he saw Matt pushing through and heard him shout, "Who is it?" Roger couldn't form the words. Jill's hand weighed on his forearm. He could smell her coconut sunscreen.

"Who is it?" Matt called again.

Roger turned to Jill, but she remained silent, a shaking hand covering her mouth.

"Who is it?" Matt wheezed, his voice breaking.

Only Gina managed to whisper, "Connor."

Wrapped in blankets and secured to a backboard, his grandson was lifted onto a gurney and raced to a waiting ambulance, with Jill and Matt sprinting right behind.

Roger stood frozen in place, shaking from cold. Or terror. Someone pressed a dry towel into his hands and he held it in front of him, not understanding what it was for. Feeling something heavy at his feet, he looked down. Henry was huddled against his legs. Dropping the towel, he picked up the boy and crushed him to his chest.

# 3

## *frozen*

JILL GRIPPED MATT'S HAND AS they raced after the team wheeling Connor through the hospital's automatic doors. They'd both jumped into the ambulance, and she'd squeezed against Matt, trying to make herself as small as possible, not wanting to be in the way. Wanting to make sure the medics had all the space they needed to revive Connor. Ten minutes seemed like hours—had she held her breath the whole way? Finally, finally—they were here. Here at the hospital where doctors performed miracles. Where doctors brought people back to life.

An edge of yellow blanket fell loose, and a nurse tucked it under Connor's leg as they pushed through a second set of doors, but she stopped Jill and Matt from following any further. Jill wasn't angry about it. She was eager to obey their instructions, to do everything they asked of her. To be perfect to earn her miracle. *He's in good hands,* she told herself as she bent over, trying to catch her breath. The doctors would save him.

The nurse came back, offering blue scrubs and warm blankets, encouraging them toward an empty room where they could change. Jill shook her head. "We'll stay here if that's okay. So the doctor can find us." She balanced on one leg, pulling off her wet shorts. "We have bathing suits on, so we'll just change here. Thank you for these." She pulled the pants on in the middle of the hallway and smiled to show her gratitude.

"If you follow me," the nurse repeated, "you can sit down while you wait, and I'll get you a bag for your wet clothes." The purple cats decorating her shirt danced across her chest as she spoke.

Jill read the nurse's badge. "Thanks, Pam. You've been so helpful." She wrapped the blanket around her shoulders, shrugging to show how comfy it was. "If you don't mind, we'll wait here."

Jill took a deep breath as Pam walked away without further comment. She needed to get her emotions in check. Calm the frenzy she'd felt over... How long had it been? A clock on the wall read 6:00, the red second-hand tick, tick, ticking forward. Three hours since the storm started? It felt like they'd been picnicking in the sun on the beach just minutes ago.

Suddenly the blanket was smothering her and she dropped it from her shoulders. How soon would they be able to burst into Connor's room and kiss his sweet cheeks? Brush the brown bangs from his forehead. See his smile. Hug him tight. That turkey. He'd given them quite a scare.

A woman pushing an oxygen tank crept by and Jill realized Connor may be hooked up to machines. An IV. Maybe even a breathing tube. She needed to be prepared. His condition could be serious. She took another shaky breath. What if he was in a coma? As she shuddered, Matt wrapped his arm around her, but she couldn't bear the weight of it. She turned to share her thoughts with him, but when she saw his face, her blood ran cold. He was shattered.

She blinked, hoping to clear the image and instead see his strength. But his face was a mix of misery and despair. "Don't," she whispered.

He took her hands and held them to his chest, his tears falling onto their knuckles.

"Stop it," Jill said, stepping back. "Whatever you're thinking right now, stop it!" She thrust his hands away.

"Jill..."

She held up her hand to stop him from speaking. "No." Her breath caught as her own tears started. "No! Matt, don't think it." She leaned over, gasping, hands on her knees. "It's not going to happen. It's not." She tried to stand tall, pushing her shoulders back. "He's going to be okay. He's our son. It's Connor!"

The metal doors swung open, and they both jumped back to avoid getting hit as a doctor walked out. His face was somber. It was not the jubilant face of a man who had performed a miracle. "Mr. and Mrs. Miller?"

She froze.

His voice was soft with sympathy "The EMTs warmed Connor and gave him three doses of epinephrine in the ambulance. When they arrived, we administered oxygen and defibrillated him, but we couldn't get a pulse." He touched Jill's elbow. "We weren't able to revive your son."

Jill reached for the doctor's hand but grasped his coat instead, clutching it in her fist. Her voice was hoarse. "He's in a coma?"

Wrapping his hand around hers, the doctor let her cling to him. "We did all we could to bring him back. I'm so sorry..." Her nose was running but she couldn't wipe it because her hands were caught in his.

"Your son has died."

She shook her head, not breaking his gaze, waiting for him to change his mind. Behind her came a whirring and a cold blast as the automatic doors opened. The voices of her dad, Gina, Jake, Henry. But she kept her eyes locked on the doctor until he tilted his chin, gently squeezed her hands, and pulled away. With no more hope to cling to, her knees buckled and she dropped to the floor, gulping for air. She was suffocating, as though back in the lake, drowning all over again.

Arms encircled her and she was squeezed so tight it made her choke. Pulling back, Gina's dark eyes pierced hers. She muffled her face into Gina's soft shoulder and screamed.

An eternity passed while sobs racked her body. Eventually Gina gently lifted her up and led her down a hall into a small room. Matt was there, standing over a child in a bed with a blanket tucked under his shoulders. He looked nothing like Connor, yet she threw her body over his because her heart knew him. She cried onto his chest, then harder when she realized she'd been expecting him to hug her back. Without his arms around her, she felt as bare and cold as if she were naked. Her beautiful boy was gone.

Matt held her up when she crumpled into him. He gripped her waist as if welding it to his and helped her walk, an awkward shuffle, as they followed a nurse down an endless hall. They entered a tiny, dark room and found Jake wrapped in Grandpa's arms. Henry nestled on Gina's lap, hugging his knees to his chin. The boys leaped up and barreled into her, collapsing her with their need. As she folded them to her, the room started to spin and she fell into a chair, her too-small family strangling one another as they embraced and wept.

# 4

## after

AT THE FUNERAL, PEOPLE WERE at a loss for words. Jill's friends—even those she wasn't close to—said they felt her pain. Every mother has imagined a tragedy of this sort. It's impossible not to. Because, as the saying goes, nothing could be worse.

She overheard whispering that had it been them, they'd be curled up in a ball, not able to function. She wondered if they were also whispering about how careless it was to boat in a storm. And their theories on who was to blame. Out loud, many commended her for her strength, as if it were a talent.

But they had it wrong. Here, with her chin up, in her best dress, accepting condolences and nodding at attempts to sympathize, she was merely a ghost of her old self. This wasn't the real Jill. Real Jill was trapped in a never-ending howl, screaming, screaming, screaming, "Give me back my son!"

After the service was over, the flowers wilted, and food stopped appearing daily on their doorstep... After the steady flow of texts and phone calls slowed and then stopped altogether... After people realized she was never going to answer their notes, texts, and calls... After all of this, Jill found nothing was worse than life continuing and realizing she was expected to be a part of it.

For weeks Matt valiantly took on the bulk of home responsibilities, letting her sleep at all hours of the day while he fed the boys, did the laundry, bought milk. He never complained that she wasn't carrying her weight. Didn't huff or roll his eyes. But still, as he got up in the morning when they heard Henry stirring and she rolled over and pulled a pillow over her head, she felt a measure of guilt. Sometimes she almost forgot that he'd lost his son too. But she avoided imagining how he was feeling because, even though he'd never said anything, she wondered if he might blame her for more than not getting up in the morning.

As the summer dragged on, so did she, easing back into the motions of what moms do—making breakfast, folding laundry, listening to a six-year-old's chatter, chauffeuring her kids to day camps. Even becoming accustomed to kissing two boys goodnight instead of three. But all the while she surreptitiously looked at her watch, clocking the hours until she could climb back into bed and let the weight of her blankets hold her while she faded away.

⚊

One August night, they'd finished washing up the dinner dishes, but it seemed like hours before the sun would finally set. Hours of emptiness that Jill needed something—anything—to fill until she could make her nightly retreat into grief. Her eyes fell on a casserole dish that had been on her counter for weeks—from a meal brought by her dad and Gina. Usually, when an unexpected dinner showed up, Jill would scrawl out a thank-you note and return dishes after dark when she could leave without being seen. She just couldn't bear to fake a smile and talk about how she was feeling.

That included her dad whom she'd successfully avoided since the funeral. She'd ignored her dad's calls and requests to see her, responding only with clipped texts that she wasn't feeling well and not available. The truth was, she didn't know what she wanted from her father. Sometimes she wanted nothing more than to have him hold her while she cried. Other times she wanted to scream in his face and shake him for not saving Connor. Tonight, she just wanted her kitchen counters clean.

"Want to go for a drive?" she asked Matt.

Yellow primroses bordered the neat lawn and brick path that led to her dad's front door and Jill inhaled the spicy summer fragrance. Friendly Adirondack chairs welcomed visitors to stay and chat. But Jill was planning a quick getaway.

She placed the glass Pyrex on the red, white, and blue doormat—the smiling firecracker screeching *Welcome!* at her even though the holiday was long past. As she stood, the door lock clicked. *Ugh.* Jill's knees cracked in complaint as she bent back down, but she mustered a smile as cheery as the seasonal doormat when Gina peeked out.

"Oh, Jill! Come in!" she said. "I saw the car pull up from the window." Dressed in pink silk pajamas, hair pinned up, no makeup, she called over her shoulder, "Roger, Jill's here!"

Jill shook her head, "No, I'm not staying, we—Matt's waiting in the car—we just wanted to return . . ."

Behind her the car door slammed. She turned to see Matt raise his hand in greeting as he strode across the grass toward them.

Damn her compulsive need to keep her kitchen tidy.

Her dad stepped forward, arms open, and she thrust the glass container into him, deflecting his hug. "We really can't stay. I was just dropping this off. Thanks for the meal."

Gina reached towards Jill's shoulder, but Jill leaned back. Matt put his arm around her and she shrugged him off as well.

The four of them stared at one another.

Breaking the silence, Jill pointed at their feet. "Cute mat."

Her dad opened the door wider. "Come in and sit down. We're so happy to see you."

"No, it's almost Henry's bedtime." She waved her hands in front of her as if protecting herself from their enthusiasm. "I was hoping not to disturb you."

Gina touched her elbow. "We were just talking about your upcoming trip. We're still planning to have Jake and Henry stay when you go."

"The trip?" Jill searched her brain for any recollection. August. Their anniversary. A trip they'd planned ages ago. Before. She freed her elbow by putting her arm around Matt's waist. "We've decided not to go." She looked at Matt for confirmation, but his eyes narrowed in confusion. She turned back to Gina with what she hoped was a smile. "It's such a busy time getting ready for the start of school."

Her dad's zeal was undeterred. "How about letting us take the kids to dinner and a movie? A sleepover!"

As Jill shook her head, he backpedaled. "Or just a late night? We'd really like to spend some time with them. It would be nice for us."

Jill retreated down the porch, pulling Matt's hand, who thankfully took her cue that it was time to go. "Henry's been very attached. And Jake . . . Well, he wants to be with friends all the time. You know, teenagers. Thanks for your gracious offer."

"Jill, it might be good for you and Matt to have some time . . ." her dad called after them.

She pulled her car door closed.

Matt shifted his red BMW into gear, revving as he waved and pulled away from the curb. "Did you actually just say 'Thank you for your gracious offer' to your dad?" he chuckled.

She leaned against the leather seat, squeezing her eyes shut. Her dad had a lot of nerve. As if he knew what was good for her. She hated the idea of leaving the kids. She imagined locking her family in their house and never going out again. They'd watch movies and play board games every night, all together for the rest of their lives. She could homeschool. And teach them to cook. Move to a ranch in the middle of nowhere. She pulled her phone from the pocket of her shorts and Googled *Ranch in the middle of nowhere.*

Matt rolled down his window, but the day still hadn't cooled and the hot air was stifling. "Why did you say we're not going on our trip? We never discussed changing plans."

Looking up from her screen, she studied him. His elbow rested on the frame of the open window, and she knew he'd be tapping a beat on the roof with his fingers. He had a freckle on his temple. It wasn't large, but it was part of her definition of him—blond, curly hair, blue eyes, a freckle on his temple. There was a smooth spot on his jaw where his whiskers didn't grow. It was part of what made Matt, Matt. After twenty years she knew him so well. All their adult years together. "Do you really want to go?"

"Yes, I would like to get away. With you."

She looked past him. Toward snug homes with well-tended yards, basketball hoops at the end of driveways, kids' bikes lying on front lawns, chalk art on the sidewalk. Signs of how families should be spending summer days. Did they appreciate what they had? Who they had?

"It seems wrong," she said, her voice subdued, "to sunbathe on a beach when your child has died. To abandon our boys when their brother has died."

"Maybe the best thing for the boys is for us to take this chance to reconnect."

They passed the middle school where Connor should've been starting sixth grade this year. A purple ribbon, visible in the glow of the streetlight, was tied to a tree out front, put there by friends to honor him after the accident. There were others on mailboxes and fenceposts around their neighborhood. After eight weeks they'd grown limp and dingy and seemed ready to be retired. Who would take them down? Was she supposed to do it? How could Matt even think about leaving their boys behind when she didn't want to let them out of her sight? What if something happened to another one?

"It doesn't feel right." She stared at her phone's bright home screen—a picture of her three boys. She caressed the cheek of her middle child. "I'm just not up for it."

Matt's voice softened. "I don't think there's a right or wrong way to . . . deal with what we've been through. But it seems healthy to have a break."

Her head snapped up. "A break? From being sad?"

He didn't flinch. "Maybe."

She was aghast. "Being somewhere else isn't going to change that. It's a physical pain that encompasses me. Even the rare times I think I feel fine, three minutes later I'm sobbing."

"I feel it too, you know," Matt said. He tapped a finger on the steering wheel. "What about a break from all the *how are yous* and the sad faces?"

She pondered how nice anonymity would be as she tried to see into the houses they passed. She recognized the home of one of her students, Vanessa Stuart. She had younger brothers who went to school with Connor and Henry. Their family was watching *Star Wars*. She could see Darth Vader through the window. "Why don't we take the kids with us?"

Matt glanced at her. "I'd really love time with just the two of us. Time to talk."

She sighed. She didn't want to talk about her feelings. Didn't want to hear how Matt was feeling. The thought of him confiding in her was overwhelming, not to mention the words that were lying in wait—that he blamed her. She was used to seeing his misty eyes and a lone tear. But if he broke down, she didn't have the energy to make him feel better. Her own emotions left her fragile. She couldn't take on his, too. She preferred to be numb. "I'll go if we take the kids."

"But your dad is willing to watch them, and they love being with Grandpa." He pulled into their driveway and waited for the garage door to open. "We haven't been out together since . . . Before. I miss our weekly dates."

"Jake would hate it."

Matt pulled to a stop. "Are you trying to keep the kids from your dad?"

Jill scoffed. Orderly garage shelves held dozens of blue storage bins, keeping the physical contents of their home life organized. Anything messy could be hidden away in an extra-large Rubbermaid, a lid popped on top and stashed away where Jill didn't have to think about it.

"I'm serious. Why don't you want them to be with your dad?"

"Do you?"

"Sure, I think it would be great."

She settled back in her seat. "You trust him? You're fine with him driving our kids?"

"Yes," he said, drawing out the word. "They've done it a million times."

She wouldn't back down even though Matt was becoming annoyed. "I'm not fine with it." She folded her arms across her chest.

"You *don't* trust him? Since when?"

Her heart started pounding but she met his eyes, trying to keep her expression neutral. She tightened her lips, determined to hold back her emotions.

"Since when?" he asked again, irritation creasing his face.

"I'm not saying it."

"You're basically saying it. So, say it . . . with words."

She glared, daring him to keep at it.

He spoke slowly. "What exactly did he do that proves he can't be trusted?"

"You know what he did."

"No." His focus didn't leave her. "I don't."

She looked away. "Stop it."

"No!" He smacked the armrest. "You stop it! Did something happen I don't know about?"

"It's what he didn't do!" she yelled. "He could have swum harder. He could have been more cautious driving the boat." The shadows that had been scampering through her mind turned into words. "He should have told me he didn't have Connor so I could help. Don't pretend you don't feel it too!"

Matt's voice rose. "Your sixty-five-year-old father was able to swim to Connor despite the wind and waves and get him back to shore. Yet you're saying *he's* the one to blame?"

Jill fought back tears of indignation. "I've watched it all my life. He always thinks he's right. And this time he was wrong. And the worst thing happened. The very worst." She climbed out of the car and maneuvered her way around bicycles and skateboards. Helmets dangled on the handlebars of each bike. Except for Connor's, which was still hanging on hooks where it had been stored out of the way last winter.

She was at the door, one hand on the knob. Matt covered her hand with his. "We don't have to talk about it. Anything but," he said.

Searching his eyes, she paused, wishing desperately once again that they could go back to Before. Her chest grew warm, and her eyes filled with tears.

"What if we leave them with someone else?" he persisted. "Your sister? Your brother?"

She shook her head. "I'm sorry."

He let go. "So, we're never leaving them until they're grown?"

"It's such a short amount of time."

"Henry's only six!" He pushed the door open and threw his keys into a wooden bowl on the small table just inside. Two photographs sat next to the bowl. One of their family from their Christmas card the previous year and the other of Connor on his own. He was sitting in a crabapple tree full of blossoms, grinning from ear to ear. It was the one they'd displayed at his funeral.

"You're just walking away?" Jill asked.

"I think you've said everything that needs to be said." He didn't look back.

"Let's take the kids."

Matt stopped and sighed but didn't turn around. He flicked his hand in the air. "Sure. Whatever."

Relief surged through Jill along with the buzz of having a project. Something to do. She called after him, "I'll check for tickets and get another hotel room!"

His voice from the kitchen was laced with sarcasm. "Are you sure you're comfortable with them in a separate room?"

She stayed up late browsing flights and activities. She needed this distraction. Something to focus on besides the memories of that day, of the storm, of thinking about what they should have done differently. She could fill the black hole of regret by making lists—packing lists, touristy options, and daily schedules. If she could fill her time with to-do's, she'd be able to get through tonight, tomorrow, and then the day after that.

The hotel reservation form asked for the number in their party. Without thinking, she entered "five," then whimpered when she realized once again that they were only four. If only she could leave a note of explanation. They were a family of five. How awful it was to say anything different.

# 5

## beach vibes

THREE WEEKS LATER, THE FOUR of them lounged oceanside under fluttering blue umbrellas, she and Matt drinking piña coladas garnished with pineapples, at a plush beach resort on the other side of the country. And they were hot, sticky, and miserable. All four of them. She had no one to blame but herself. When she and Matt originally planned their anniversary getaway, it was February, when it seemed winter would never thaw. They fantasized about hot sun, turquoise water, and green palms swaying in a light breeze. Umbrella drinks, reading, napping, repeat.

Jill thought it wouldn't be much different with the boys in tow. They would play in the waves, build sandcastles, and search for shells and sea glass together. Matt would teach Henry to body surf and the three of them would toss a football. She might open her eyes from time to time to watch, then happily drift back to sleep. When she'd finally agreed that a break would be good for all of them, somehow a sunny beach resort didn't seem remotely close to a stormy lake. Until they were surrounded by so much water.

Henry slumped on the edge of her lounger, complaining about the heat. Below them on the sand, Jake lay on a striped towel, scrolling on his phone. Jill was attempting to read, but the glare of the sun made her squint, even with sunglasses on. Her head pounded.

She summoned a patient voice. "Henry, why don't you go play? You'll feel better if you do something."

"It's too hot," he whined, laying his sweaty chest across Jill's bare legs. He twirled his foot in the sand and then abruptly kicked it toward Jake.

"Hey!" Jake slapped Henry's shin.

She turned another page, trying to ignore them.

Henry kicked again and this time sand flew into her face, the grit adhering to her lip balm. "Henry! That's not okay! Cut it out or we're going back to the room."

"Good," said Henry, "I want to go back."

"So do I," Jake said, standing abruptly.

Jill dropped her chin, trying to take calming breaths. A plane droned overhead, pulling an orange sign. There was a time she could defuse contention by enthusiastically pointing out the biplane. All three boys would forget their complaints and start jumping and waving, believing the pilot would see them. In an instant they'd be laughing together, playing tag, running with arms stretched wide, pretending to be airplanes. And now . . . "Fine. Let's go back."

Matt cracked open an eye. "Stay with me."

She grabbed the boys' T-shirts from the back of her chair and shoved them into her bag, then tossed in the sunscreen, her book, and her magazine.

"Let them go and we can be alone." Matt reached for her fingers.

She hesitated. Did she trust Jake to make sure Henry got back safely? If Henry kept bugging him, would Jake take off by himself? What if Henry got mad and ran away from him? She massaged her neck. "I have to make sure they find the room."

"I guess I'm coming too."

An hour later they were in their two-room suite, a fan whirring above them. Jill was reading with her heels on the coffee table, sipping a cold Diet Coke, while Matt snoozed in the chair next to her. Jake stretched on the couch, earbuds in. Henry had been drawing, but now his coloring book and crayons were scattered around him. "Play with me, Jake," he intoned in a robot voice—something he'd done a lot two years ago, when he was four. He hung his head above his brother's face.

"You're breathing on me," Jake said without opening his eyes. "Get away."

"Please," Henry pleaded.

"No. I'm relaxing."

Jill hated to see Henry disappointed. "I'll play with you, bud. Go grab your cards."

He plopped on the floor, elbows on his knees, fists smashed into his cheeks. "Jake's not even doing anything." He lifted his leg into the air and hit it against the cushion, inches from Jake's feet. Alternating leg slaps, he chanted, "Play. With. Me."

"Cut it out!" Jake said, pushing Henry's feet away.

"You're mean, Jake." He started beating his fists on the couch. "I hate you. I wish Connor was here!"

Matt and Jill sprang from their seats. Matt wrapped Henry's flailing body in his arms, tight enough to control his thrashing limbs. "Shh . . ." he whispered as he rocked him. "I've got you."

Suddenly Matt shouted and grabbed his arm. "He bit me!"

Henry wailed as Matt scooped him up, carried him to the bathroom, and slammed the door. "You need a time-out!" He held the door shut while Henry bawled and tried to yank it open. Matt's hair had gone frizzy in the heat and it looked like he'd just been electrocuted. "What is happening?" he mouthed to Jill.

For the millionth time, Jill realized coming on this trip had been a horrible idea. *Her* horrible idea. Again.

Within a few minutes, the door pounding stopped, but Henry was still sobbing on the other side. Matt collapsed onto the couch next to Jake and put his arm around him. "Hey, you know he doesn't mean that, right?"

Jake shrugged.

Matt stood, pulling Jake up with him. "C'mon, let's go explore." He glanced at Jill who nodded her support.

Soon after they left, Henry had seemingly exhausted himself and his cries died out. Jill let herself into the bathroom and picked him up. "Let's lay down for a nap, okay?"

Henry's cheek was wet but warm on hers, and he wrapped his legs around her hips as they walked to the bed. She tucked him under the thick white comforter, pulled him close to her, and they both fell asleep.

Later, when she awoke, she slipped out of bed and into the living room where Matt and Jake were watching a Marvel movie. She sat between them and laid her head on Matt's shoulder. She'd been asleep for two hours. "What did you guys do?"

Matt kissed her forehead. "Drove into town and got ice cream. Explored the resort. Just hung out," he said.

Jake turned the volume up so Jill lowered her voice. "I'm starving. Should we eat dinner here at the hotel?"

They roused a rested and more amiable Henry from his nap and twenty minutes later they crossed the lobby, live music filling the air. There was a time she would have grabbed Matt's hand, and he'd have done either a triple-step in time with the music or the running man, depending on the company, pulling her along with him. He could dance better than any other guy she'd dated. Connor had good rhythm, too, and was learning to play the drums. *Had* been learning.

"How many?" asked the host.

Jill was prepared for this. "Four," she said, twirling her ring with the three birthstones and silently chanting, *Five. Five. Five.* Her eyes found Matt's, a slow current passing between them. It would never feel right.

The next morning, all frustrations from the day before seemed to have evaporated. Jake helped Henry with his word search and his tenderness toward his little brother brought Jill renewed optimism. She suggested they visit the aquarium and afterward shop for souvenirs on the boardwalk. When everyone cheerfully agreed, she breathed a sigh of relief.

At the aquarium's starfish exhibit, Jake picked up a fat orange one from the shallow saltwater pool so Henry could feel its prickly spine. While waiting for lunch, they drew funny pictures on the butcher paper table covering, laughing at each other's renditions of a crab. Jake chewed with his mouth shut and nobody teased Henry for ordering spaghetti at a seafood restaurant. Matt took Jill's hand as they strolled past shops with bright awnings, crowds of tourists bustling beside them.

For the first time in a long time, it actually felt good to be around other people. Especially with her family by her side. Yesterday's meltdown was to be expected, right? Obviously, Henry was still processing feelings about Connor's death, so it was good he could get it out of his system. Jake had been as patient as one could expect from a fifteen-year-old. Plus, they'd all been tired.

Today had been a good day. Maybe her maternal instincts weren't so off after all. As if to confirm they were all in a better place, on the way back to the resort, Jake suggested they go back to the beach and Henry cheered.

But as the attendant set up chairs and an umbrella close to the water, Henry's demeanor changed. Jake tried to get him to play in the waves. "I'll race you," he said. But Henry pulled away.

Jake kept trying. "Okay, then let's build a sandcastle."

"No, I just want to stay here by Daddy." His unruly blond hair curled around his ears.

"C'mon! It'll be fun!" Jake gently tugged Henry's arm to encourage him, but Henry pulled back and stomped on Jake's foot. "Ow! What'd you do that for?" He shoved Henry's shoulder.

Henry flopped to the sand and started to cry. Jake looked at his mom and rolled his eyes. "I barely even touched him!"

"You're so mean!" Henry sobbed. "Connor wasn't mean!"

Jake threw up his arms. "I was actually trying to play with you!"

"No, you were going to make me go down to the water! I just want to be by Daddy!"

Jake blasted his heel into the ground, spraying sand everywhere; then turned and started walking away.

"Jake, where are you going?" Jill called.

"I have no idea." He kept walking.

She turned to Matt, her eyes silently asking if she should follow him. He shook his head. Her heart ached watching Jake walk away, knowing he was upset. It felt wrong not going after him. Not trying to make him feel better.

When he was almost out of view, she turned to Henry. His tears had dried as quickly as they'd started and now he was silent, also watching Jake leave. "Do you want to build a sandcastle with me? Or turn me into a mermaid?" she asked. "You can bury me in the sand!"

"If Daddy will help me."

They buried Jill's legs, but when they started on her chest, she began wiping off the sand as fast as they threw it on her. "Let's just do my legs, okay?"

Matt laughed, "C'mon! You gotta do the whole mermaid experience."

"No, I'm serious. I don't want my whole body covered." She was starting to hyperventilate. Trying not to panic, she turned on her sing-song voice. "Hey, guys, that was so fun! Now it's someone else's turn."

"Mommy, we have to make your legs a tail to turn you into a mermaid!"

"Not this time, Henry. Mommy's all done. I need to get unburied." She pushed the sand from her legs as fast as she could, her breath coming in short bursts.

"Are you okay?" Matt asked.

"Yep, great! I just want to get the sand out of my suit! This has been so fun! Yay! Henry, do you want Dad to bury you now?" She was spewing words, channeling unicorns and rainbows for Henry's sake, but really wanting to run away from the beach and the water.

Henry's small voice pierced through her panic attack. "Will I be buried like Connor?"

Jill startled. Taking a deep breath she knelt to peer into his big, green eyes. "Not at all like Connor. This is just a game." She plastered a grin on her face. "You and Daddy get started. I'll be right back." She avoided Matt's questioning look.

She jogged up the grassy slope to the bathroom and sat in a stall trying to catch her breath. She never did like getting buried. But just now, when she closed her eyes, she saw her dad carrying her little boy from the water. Purple skin. Blue lips. Sand smeared across his cheek and chest. He'd been so still. Rain had dripped from her wet hair onto his forehead as she leaned over him, cradling his head in her hands, willing him to wake up.

She thought she saw him move and her heart leapt, until she realized it was Gina, massaging his feet, trying to rub circulation into them. Her precious son was gone. Why had they come to the beach, of all places? What had she been thinking?

When she returned, Matt and Henry were sitting on loungers, neither speaking.

"Dad got sand in my eyes on purpose," Henry grumbled.

Matt touched Henry's shoulder. "You know I would never do anything to hurt you."

Henry scowled and pulled a towel over his head. "I want privacy."

Jill lay next to Matt, and he tucked a loose lock of hair behind her ear. "I shouldn't have insisted we come," he said. "Somehow I thought being in a new place without old memories wouldn't be so hard."

Jill sighed. "I didn't realize being close to the water would be so difficult." She stared at the clouds and the blue sky over his shoulder. She closed her eyes to let her mind clear, but Connor was there, always with a fresh wave of pain. "What do we do about..." She moved her head to indicate Henry who was still hiding under his towel, "And also..." She pointed toward where Jake had walked off, hoping Matt would have an answer.

"Give them space. We have to be patient with each other. Everyone says the first year is the hardest."

Jill closed her eyes, processing that thought. A year. Would Connor be only a memory a year from now? Instead of relief, it made her want to cling to the hurt.

# 6

## who would care?

JAKE'S THOUGHTS WERE CLOUDY AS he trudged across the manicured lawn, past the family pool where a dad tossed his child into the water amid cries of delight. A kid who looked about Jake's age was stretched out on a chaise, sleeping. What Jake had hoped to be doing on vacation. Not babysitting his little brother. Anyone could see that Henry was totally freaking out being close to the water. Were his parents clueless? What was his mom thinking dragging them on vacation? Read the room. No one wants to be here.

He stopped to look around. Where was he? This place was too big. He wished they were at the hotel they normally went to, the one where they had good memories. He followed a path leading away from the havoc of the main pool until he came to a gate with a small sign: "Adult Pool. Must be 18." Behind the fence was a small rectangular pool and a few old people reading or sleeping. No kids, no noise. He nervously glanced around looking for ... what exactly? Pool police? Could they tell he's only fifteen? Would they kick him out? There was a guy in white shorts and a blue polo serving drinks to a couple under an orange umbrella. The glasses clinked as he set them on the side table.

As Jake entered, he wondered if the guy would ask him for ID. He tried to look confident as he walked past a gray-haired man with a green-striped resort towel covering him like a blanket, but his stomach seized with worry. He lay down on an empty chair, turned up his music, closed his eyes, and prayed to be invisible.

But he couldn't squeeze his eyes tight enough to slow his racing thoughts about what Henry had said. It was true. Connor *was* the nicer brother. The whole reason he'd stayed back on the beach that day was to be nice to Henry. He doubted Connor preferred to build sandcastles over wakeboarding, and yet he cared about Henry's feelings. Of course Henry liked him better.

Jake had been tempted to shout that he liked Connor better too. Connor had finally been old enough to listen to good music and play video games with him. It had actually become fun to play soccer together because Connor was finally good at defending. And on their last family vacation over spring break, when their mom said, "I've signed up the two big kids for surf lessons," Jake had been ecstatic. Not about surfing— *the water was freezing, geez, Mom*—but because finally there were *two* "big kids."

Now who would he hang out with? Vacations were ruined forever. Clearly no one was having any fun on this one.

Smelling a musty perfume, he peeked through his eyelashes. An old lady had sat down next to him and was rubbing lotion on her legs. She was tan and wrinkled with huge red sunglasses and a wide-brimmed hat. Could she tell he didn't belong here?

He wondered what would have happened if he'd been the one who'd died instead of Connor. While Henry and Connor happily buried each other in the sand, their parents could read books and sleep with no one to bug them. They'd probably think, *Who knew it could be this great? No bickering, no teasing. We should go on more vacations!*

His phone chimed and he picked it up to see who'd texted. Kevin. A new friend he'd made at the skatepark this summer. A friend Jake was sure his mom wouldn't approve of just because he had long hair. And a pierced ear. And smoked. If she bothered to see past that—which she wouldn't—she'd learn he had a sister who died when he was little. He was the only person who actually got what Jake was going through.

hows the beach

sucks hate my family

when do you come back

3 days everyone fighting brain exploding

Three dots blinked on the screen then disappeared. Jake waited and worried. Maybe he'd said too much. Kevin probably thought he was annoying. Finally:

I have something that can help

Jake's thumbs hovered over the screen. What did that mean? Did he mean drugs? *Play it cool, Jake. Don't be lame.*

I wish

hit me up when you get back

Jake bit his lip as he stared at the screen, wondering. Finally, he tucked his phone under the towel and fell asleep.

When he woke up, he was alone. The nap had lifted his mood, along with the thrill of getting away with his crime. *Was it a crime to sneak into the adult pool?* On his walk back to the room, he had the idea for the four of them to play cards together. Snap was a game even Henry could learn. His stomach was rumbling and when he opened the door to their suite, the smell of hamburgers put a smile on his face.

A room service table was next to Henry at the couch, with a desk chair and ottoman pulled up for his mom and dad. When Jake walked into the room, his mom smiled. "Perfect timing! We ordered you a cheeseburger and salad and fries for you and Henry to share. Where'd you go?"

"The adult pool." He shrugged like it was no big deal.

"Was it nice to relax?" his mom asked, reaching out to rub his arm.

But he saw her wink at his dad. She was laughing at him. He pulled his arm away and all the goodwill he felt vanished. She'd been locked in her room, crying for two months, ignoring the whole family, and now suddenly she's winking and smiling at his dad over how *adorable* it is that Jake thinks he's an *adult* now. It was like she'd totally forgotten about Connor. Come to a nice resort and poof, everything's all better. Well, it wasn't all better for him. He wouldn't forget Connor.

When he was seated at the table, his mom announced, "We've decided we're leaving tomorrow."

Jake choked on a mouthful of burger. "What? Why?"

"I think we'll be more comfortable at home," she said. "This was a long trip to take so soon after... before the beginning of school."

"Were you going to ask us what we think?" Jake asked, trying to swallow. True, he'd been dreading the upcoming days until just a few hours ago. But it's not like things were any better at home. And he was a little afraid of seeing Kevin again. What did he want to give him? He'd rather not find out.

Now that he'd found a good retreat at the adult pool, he wanted to go there every day. Listen to music, sleep, not think. Get a break from all his other so-called friends. Sam, who wanted to talk about Connor all the time. And all the rest who never called him anymore, just filled his texts with group chats about inane things. Right when he's finally able to relax, his mom wants to cut the trip short.

"I don't want to leave! I want to stay, like Jake!" Henry said.

Jake watched his parents' silent signals to each other. His mom always bit her top lip before she said something no one would like. Sometimes she'd close her eyes and sigh as if being a mom was the hardest job in the world. This time she did neither. But his dad raised one eyebrow. The goofy one. The one that said he was on Jake's side.

Turning to Jake and staring at him as if her eyes were lasers mining his brain for information, his mom finally said, "Let me and Dad talk about it tonight."


The next morning, Jake walked ahead of his family on their way down to breakfast. Behind, Henry yammered on about last night's dream while his mom and dad held his hands and pulled him into the air, a game Jake loved when he was little. So it caught Jake by surprise when his mom was suddenly by his side. "We've decided we'll stay, but I don't want you wandering off on your own," she said.

"Why?" His heart began to pound. "It's not like I'm going to get lost! The whole reason I want to stay is I need time to myself."

"The reason we came here is to have time together. Before school starts."

He clenched his fists. "You have noticed that Henry hates me, right?"

"Jake, he doesn't hate you. He looks up to you."

He hated when she said his name like that, "Ja-ake." Like he was being ridiculous. He sped up to get away from her. "Don't blame me when I finally hit him. He's asking for it."

She matched his speed. "I know you wouldn't do that. He's little." They arrived at the entrance and she grabbed his arm. "Never hit your brother."

Jake yanked away as a chipper woman in an aloha shirt greeted them with a big smile. "How many?"

His mom brushed her skirt and smiled back. "Four."

She acted like she had it all together. Like they were the perfect family. Like they hadn't been fighting the whole trip. When they sat down, Jake was seething. He pressed his fingers to his temple. "You say 'four' so easily."

She raised her eyebrows. "What did you say?"

He knew she'd heard him, but he repeated slowly, "I said, you say 'four' so easily. It doesn't even bother you." He didn't break his gaze from hers. When her look turned to a glare, he smirked.

"Jake, you know that's not true," his dad said.

His mom gripped the edge of the table. Then with a deep breath, put on another of her fake smiles. "Okay. Let's do the buffet. Grab your plates and go see what looks good."

Jake ignored her. "Why did you even want to come on this trip? Are we celebrating? If you haven't noticed, no one is in the mood to have fun."

"Jake, that's enough!" his dad said.

She held up her palms as if to quiet them both. "Jake, I thought you wanted to stay. Now you want to go? What is it? What else can we possibly do to make you happy?"

The angrier she became, the calmer he felt. "Leave me alone, for one. Also, I'm not your babysitter. If the only reason you want me around is to watch Henry, you should pay me. I've got a long list, in fact. Should I keep going?" He actually didn't have a list. He was making this up as he went. But it felt good. Good to let her know she wasn't the perfect mom she thought she was.

He expected her to start lecturing, get angry, maybe even make a scene, but instead the chair scraped against the tile as she scooted away from the table. "Yes, I'd like to know what's on your mind. Why don't we go somewhere and talk?"

She looked like she meant it, but that was the last thing he wanted. A big heart-to-heart with his mom. Her telling him he was feeling things he actually wasn't. He crossed his legs and leaned back in his chair. "I'll talk to Dad, not you."

His mom's shoulders slumped as she turned away. He wondered if she was going to cry right here in the restaurant. She was always crying. He hated it.

Just like that, his dad was up. "Okay, let's go."

Jake panicked. He didn't actually want to talk to anyone. But it would be worse to let his mom win, so he stood. As they started walking away, Henry called out, "Wait! I want to be with Daddy too!" Jake spun around, scowling, daring his mom to try to pawn Henry off on them.

"No," she said reaching out for Henry's hand. "They're going on a walk while the two of us have breakfast." Henry started kicking the underside of the table, the orange juice glasses rattling in response. When she scooped him up, he started howling and twisting away from her, "No! I don't want you! I want to be with Daddy!"

She threw her purse over her shoulder, wrangling Henry as he kicked, and walked past Matt and Jake without looking at them. "We'll be in the room. Go. We're good."

From around the corner, Jake heard Henry screech, "Don't leave me, Daddy!"

As the sound died out, Jake grinned. "Well, should we go somewhere and get breakfast?"

# 7

# riding the bus

JILL SAT ON HER BEDROOM floor, finally folding the post-vacation laundry—bathing suits and T-shirts that still held a hint of coconut even after being washed. Working through the pile of clean clothes gave her time to think. As she folded T-shirts into neat squares, the scene of Jake and Matt leaving breakfast together at the resort ran through her mind. It was common for her and Matt to tag team. Good cop, bad cop. When one of them was tired, confused or simply not in the mood, the other stepped up. Over fifteen years, their parenting strategy had worked pretty well. She attributed it to her talents for organization and keeping a schedule and Matt's playfulness and spontaneity—they were perfectly complementary.

But reflecting to a week ago, when Matt and Jake had come back to the hotel suite, something had changed. She'd caught them sharing a look when she said she wanted to plan the next day. And she was sure Matt winked at Jake when she mentioned she'd made an early dinner reservation so they could get a good night's sleep before traveling home. And finally, when she told Henry he couldn't watch a particular movie on the flight, she purposely watched Matt from the corner of her eye. And sure enough, there it was. Not the narrowed eyes when he was frustrated with her, or the silly grin she expected when he tried to talk her into being more flexible. No. Each of the three times he shared a smirk with Jake.

Making a connection was a good thing, but ganging up against her was going too far. She clicked her tongue. Then realized it sounded exactly like her mom. The trip had been stressful for all of them, and it seemed in the few days they'd been home that things were back to normal. She should let it go. Tomorrow was the first day of school, and the new year was always like a reset.

She tucked two matching socks into each other and dropped them onto the pile. A reset. Something she'd always looked forward to in the past—new school years, new calendar years. Even Mondays. But now a reset would never be enough. She tugged so tightly on her short ponytail that the elastic grabbed her scalp.

What she desperately wished for was a redo. To wait for the storm to end before going back out. She would race to her boys with warm towels and hold them while they cried and yelled at her for leaving them freezing and scared and alone. She would squish them into her, kiss their cheeks, brush their wet hair, and say over and over that she was sorry.

Collapsing into the pile of clothes, she cried into the comfort of Downy and cotton until, only a minute later, she heard a bedroom door open and footsteps in the hall. The kids were awake. She wiped her eyes, swallowed her tears, and added another folded T-shirt to Jake's stack.

With everyone back on a schedule, they'd prioritize family dinner and stick to bedtime routines. Structure and more sleep would help them all cope better. Her principal offered to get her a sub for as long as she needed it. But Jill wanted to be busy. She needed the distraction. With her principal's encouragement, they structured the four classes she taught to midday periods so she could arrive late in the morning and go home early, if needed.

"What are you most excited about for first grade?" she asked Henry after breakfast. He was skipping around the kitchen, his blond curls bouncing.

"Me and Cole are walking to the bus stop by ourselves! We're big enough, right, Mom?" His green eyes exuded such confidence now that he was six and a "big kid."

Jill focused on the soapy dishrag and the pan she was washing. "Actually, I'm going to drive you to school this year. I'll drop you off on my way to work." She bit her lip, knowing this idea may not go over well. But she really would feel better making sure he got to and from school safely.

Henry smiled, his tongue sticking through the gap of his two missing front teeth. "You're teasing! I always ride the bus to school. I've done it all my life."

Jill didn't let his scrumptious six-year-old chubby cheeks and version of "all his life" deter her. "You know what? We'll take Jake with us, and I'll talk to Cole's mom and tell her I can take him, too."

Henry jumped down from the stool and stomped his foot. "No, I said! I have my own plan!" As he ran out of the kitchen, he dodged Matt, who had stopped to listen at the doorway.

"What's going on?" he asked, taking a seat at the counter.

She opened the cupboard to put a stack of plates away. "He'll like the idea once he gets used to it. However..." Jill paused, picked up her phone, and scrolled through the calendar. "I have a faculty meeting every other Wednesday. Can you take him on those days?"

Matt poured milk on his cereal. "Help me understand why he's not riding the bus."

She didn't want to admit she was nervous—she realized it sounded irrational. "Henry's been so clingy lately, I thought if I took him, he'd feel better. Frankly, I thought he'd be excited."

"But now that you know you were wrong..." he said, in the slow, know-it-all voice she despised.

She folded her arms. "If you're busy, just say so. But it's fun driving him and his friends and hearing them talk about their day."

Matt raised his eyebrows. "Yes, Jill, I know. I've had that *fun* chance lots of times. As you know, I often drive him and his friends places."

This was new, Matt being sarcastic. New since the accident. Jill began vigorously scrubbing the counter. "It's so funny listening to those two. It's like they don't even realize you can hear them!"

"You don't need to do this."

Jill looked at him. "I'm asking you to drive one day every other week. I'll drive all the rest." Tossing the rag into the sink, she muttered, "You'd think you could shorten your workout just one day so you could spend a second with your kids." Matt's spoon halted midway to his mouth. She'd hit a nerve. It was unfair because Matt always made time for their family—especially these past few months. He'd taken on everything without her even asking him to. She tried to meet his stony stare but had to look away.

"I am happy to change my schedule for our family," Matt said. "You know that. But why are you dead set on driving him? Henry wants to take the bus—like his brothers did—and it's easier for all of us."

Jill pursed her lips and took a deep breath. Then another. Once again, the anger at losing Connor boiled up inside her.

"I'm trying to take care of my children. I don't want Henry riding the bus with a million chaotic kids in a giant vehicle manned by a perfect stranger. I'm not sure if I can trust the driver, and I've decided that I don't have to. I'm taking responsibility for our family. And I would appreciate your support."

"It would be helpful if I knew exactly what I'm supporting." Matt's tone had a bite to it that was unfamiliar coming from her husband. "Is it us getting more time to hear about Henry and Cole's day? Or supporting you suddenly deciding the bus isn't safe?"

Jill started scrubbing the sparkling counters again. "Me, Matt. You're supporting me." The noisy way he slurped cereal really would kill her one day. She glanced at him, and her heart faltered at the grim look he returned.

The next morning, when she tried to take the annual first-day-of-school photo, Henry's eyes were red and puffy. He'd been crying throughout breakfast after hearing that Cole's mom preferred that Cole ride the bus—"he's really looking forward to it"—and that Jill would not back down from driving Henry herself.

Jake had scoffed. "Let him ride the bus if he wants to! Why are you making such a big deal out of it?"

She set their traditional first-day-waffles-with-strawberries in front of him. "You know what? Because I'm the mom. I think it's best and I don't have to explain myself to everyone." She looked at Matt. "Your dad and I decided this is a good change for our family. Right?"

Matt nodded, satisfying Jill with their unity, until he added, "If this is what your mom wants, we're going to support her. Got it?"

Jill blinked, trying to keep her face neutral even though inside she was reeling. Matt had made her the bad guy. They were supposed to be a team.

Matt squeezed Jake's shoulder and ruffled Henry's hair. "Thanks, bud," he said, wiping a tear from Henry's cheek.

Both boys gave Jill withering looks.

"Hey, guys," Jill said, trying to stay calm, trying to be a good parent. "Let's just give it two weeks. See how it goes, okay?"

They hit every red light until finally they pulled into the elementary school drop-off point, just behind the school bus, a big yellow reminder of her decision they all hated. Henry jumped out of the car, planted his feet wide, and used all his six-year-old force to slam the door.

"You're not always right, you know," Jake muttered just loud enough for Jill to hear. She ignored him. If she'd been driving on her own today, she could have driven past the middle school to spot Connor's friends and imagine him with them, bouncing as he walked, hands flying as he described his summer vacation, a new back-to-school haircut spiked up in front with too much gel. Her perfect boy.

The next three days were terrible. They didn't even make it one week before Jill finally gave in. Driving Henry wasn't keeping him safe; it was just making everyone mad at her. She wondered if flip-flopping her original plan made her a bad mom. Wasn't she supposed to stick to the rules she made even if her kids didn't like them? She was second-guessing her parenting decisions all the time now.

Henry was so happy to be riding the bus that he didn't even complain about her "keeping him company" as they walked to the stop. When the bus doors opened, Jill waved to the driver. Dolores, same lady as last year. Same lady as all the years. Henry and Cole climbed the stairs, their full-size back-packs outsizing their small bodies. Dolores greeted them with a fist bump. "I've missed you, Henry! Glad to see you back!"

Jill scanned the windows until she saw Henry clambering over Cole to get to the window where he waved at her with his toothless smile. She waved back, her other arm hugging her body, wondering if everyone was staring at her.

Three other women were there, all kindergarten moms dressed in workout clothes, two of them pushing toddlers in strollers. She didn't really know them. Their animated conversation had stopped as she and Henry walked up. Their smiles turned somber as they greeted her in a sad monotone: "Hi, Jill."

With school starting, she was out in public again for the first time since the accident. She hadn't seen her friends in ages and ignored their calls and texts. Most had gotten the hint and stopped trying. She had nothing to say, nothing to give anyone anymore. But just now she'd felt a natural reflex to smile at these ladies until the voice in her head reminded her just in time that Connor had died and that she should never smile again.

She was the visceral reminder that everyone should hug their kids a little longer and not sweat the small stuff because you never knew. You never knew. And yet, she did sweat the small stuff. Lately, she was angrier at her family and hugged them much less. Out of everyone, shouldn't she have learned her lesson that time was valuable and she should appreciate every moment of every day?

At the swoosh of the closing doors, she backed away from the group. As the bus merged into traffic, her heart began to pound. Her breath turned shallow. Pressing her fingers to her lips, she tried to steady herself. She tucked a lock of hair behind her ear, trying to act natural.

Why were the moms still standing around? Were they waiting to whisper about the accident? That she'd demanded they cross the lake in a storm? Did they know it would have been fine if her dad hadn't rushed to pull the boat around so fast? She glanced behind her. No, no one was staring. They were just talking. Ignoring her. Ignoring that her son had died. Connor.

She jogged home so she wouldn't be seen crying at the bus stop, then dashed into her house and up to her room so she could weep in private.

# 8

## support group

THE FOLLOWING SATURDAY, AFTER HENRY'S soccer practice, Jill suggested they visit Connor's grave. They'd only been once before, last month, and the memory wasn't a good one. The argument had started because she didn't know what was appropriate to wear. Probably not black, she'd supposed, so she put on a blue pencil skirt and blouse.

That summer day a month ago was sweltering, so when Matt was dressed in shorts and a golf shirt, she shouldn't have been surprised. But she looked from her low heels to Matt's tennis shoes. "It seems like we should dress up."

"Why?"

"I don't know. Out of respect?"

Jake and Henry pounded down the stairs, also in T-shirts and shorts. Jill tried to keep her voice light. "Jake, you need to put on a different shirt. You too, Henry."

"It's hot outside," Henry said as he slipped on his flip-flops.

"You can't go to the cemetery dressed like that."

"Says who?" Jake asked, looking genuinely confused.

"Okay, guys," Matt said, "Go change your shirts. Mom's asked you to."

Jake pleaded with him. "It doesn't matter. I'm fine with what I'm wearing. This shirt is new." Henry nodded his endorsement.

Jill softened when she saw them lined up together, matching. The three of them looked so handsome. But just as she was about to give in, Jake snarked, "Connor doesn't care, Mom."

A fire flared inside her at bringing Connor into their quarrel. "You get more dressed up to play golf. Just go put on a damn collared shirt."

"Nice," Jake said, stomping upstairs to change. "You're swearing at your kids right before we visit Connor's grave. I wonder how that makes him feel?"

That August visit had been a tortured affair, and at the time Jill wondered how she'd ever go back. But today would be different. That first time their hearts were still raw. But now she had more control over her emotions. A touch of cool was in the air, the sun was bright. It was the kind of day that invited you to be outdoors.

"Can I drive?" Jake asked, always begging to get behind the wheel. "I've only got five more months to get my practice hours in before I turn sixteen."

"Of course," Jill said, sitting next to Henry in the back so Matt could sit beside Jake, gladly letting him take over the teaching responsibility. But when Jake missed a street on the route and made a sudden U-turn in front of a honking, oncoming car, Jill gasped, Matt grabbed the wheel, Jake shouted at his mom to stop freaking out, and it all went downhill from there.

When they finally arrived at the cemetery, Henry was sucking his lip and Jake swatted at him to cut it out. Crossing the lawn, Jill caught Matt's eye, rolling hers heavenward—an attempt to unify them against the kids—but he ignored her, instead lifting Henry onto his shoulders and wrapping a free arm around Jake as they walked ahead. Normally, Jill would have snapped a picture to remember the tender moment. Instead, she slowed, falling further behind.

When they arrived at Connor's grave, Jake put his arm around his dad, Henry rested his chin on Matt's head, and she stood on the opposite side of the gray stone.

The last time they were here, she wanted to talk about Connor, but Jake had said, "Can we just be quiet for once?" So this time she stayed silent, grateful not to talk. But right away Matt pointed out a car in the parking lot and he and Jake were guessing the model.

"Guys," she said, "let's take a minute to think about Connor."

"We were thinking about Connor," Jake said. "We were saying that green Porsche was one he would have really liked."

Matt touched his shoulder. "If your mom wants to have a minute, let's give her one. We can talk about Connor after."

Her heart sank. Was Matt intentionally turning everything into "us against her?" She spun around and started walking back to the car. She missed the feel of Connor's hand in hers. How he'd pat her on the arm whenever he wanted her attention. "Mom, look. Look at that!" He found wonder in everything. Helped her to see joy through his eyes. And now she would never have that again.

The ride home from the cemetery was subdued and Jill ached to hole up in a place where she could escape and let the silence continue. When they entered the house, Henry slammed the door, sending reverberations through her aching head. The framed photos on the table also clattered in protest. She was so used to seeing the large photo of Connor flanked by one of the family that she hadn't properly looked at it lately. Were they so used to him being gone that cars in a parking lot distracted them and his picture no longer stood out? Was his being gone becoming normal? She trudged upstairs to her room.

She collapsed into the large blue chair in her bedroom. Outside the window, a few trees were changing color, their yellow leaves glowing in the afternoon sun. Why had she believed that visiting Connor's grave would bring her peace?

A car honked in front of the house and Jake ran out the front door. She listened for the sound of it closing, but never heard the click and knew it was now slowly easing back open. Tires screeched as they pulled out of the driveway. Who was he with and where was he going? She never knew anymore. She imagined he couldn't wait to get out of this sad, depressing house.

That first week after the accident they'd often cried together. Matt held her as she sobbed, his tears falling into her hair. They gripped hands, strengthening each other as they walked through the mortuary choosing a coffin. Just forty-eight hours after losing her child, she was expected to get dressed, put on makeup, and go shopping—for a casket. Choose a wood. Consider price points. Ivory or white interior? How about an add-on: a guest book, audio recording, flower arrangement? Did she want a flower spray to cover the lid? Or on an easel next to his picture? "You have a large, framed picture, right?" They even offered an option for a ribbon sash with his name on it. *Like a prom queen?* She wanted to scream.

At the funeral it was as if their four bodies were fused together, an architectural wonder holding them upright. She and Matt leaned into each other. Jake's head rested on her shoulder. Henry straddled both their laps.

But now, their proximity was like being tangled in a net, bumping and banging into one another, pushing each other aside, trying to escape the claustrophobia of being four in a house built for five. They peered past each other as if always looking for the person who was missing. Except for Henry. Everyone drank his naiveté like it had healing powers. If he gave you a hug or crawled into your lap, you felt chosen, and for a moment, you were the winner.

Henry talked about the accident more than anyone else. In fact, he was the only one who did talk about it. "Grandpa tried to save Connor, right, Mama?" He didn't wait for an answer. "Grandpa tried to make his breath come back. Did you try to give him his breath back?" No, she hadn't given him mouth-to-mouth—her dad was doing it. Then the paramedics took over.

Henry didn't remember that after the boat flipped, she had immediately grabbed him. He was screaming and choking but she kept his head above water as the waves washed over her, trying desperately to remember what she'd learned in a high school lifesaving course. Henry's arms were like a vice around her neck, but she kept swimming. She didn't slow or stop.

She expected her dad to appear by her side with Connor swimming next to him. Once they were onshore, her dad would hug her and tell her everything was going to be okay. He would say he was proud of how levelheaded she was in a crisis. Of her strength.

But instead... even though her dad tried "to give him his breath back," he hadn't saved him.

Her phone rang, and as if she'd conjured him, a grinning picture of her dad with his arm around her stared up from the screen. He'd continued calling to check in on her, leaving frequent voicemails. If she answered, would he apologize again? Or not apologize? Or act as if everything was fine, inviting them to dinner or a game night? Or say hello with his quiet voice—the one that meant he might cry? What if he wanted her to confide in him? She wouldn't give him the satisfaction. What if he said he understood? No. He would never understand her pain.

She let it go to voicemail. She couldn't deal with him right now.

Matt walked into their room. "Ugh, my dad called," she said.

"Did you answer it?" he asked, leaning on the doorframe.

"I couldn't deal with whatever he was feeling today. What if he cried?" She scrunched her nose.

Matt didn't take the bait to join up against her annoying dad. "So? He probably does cry. I cry. You cry. It would mean he was feeling sad."

She changed the subject. "I feel like you and Jake are making fun of me all the time. Like you're gathering the boys around you and pushing me out of your group. You did it at the cemetery just now."

"I'm just trying to keep the peace. You know, good cop, bad cop. You and Jake are always at each other."

"Are you sure that's it? Are you sure it doesn't have something to do with ... the accident?"

He sat on the bed and took her hand. "Life was good, *before*, you know? It was perfect. And now everything's different."

"Do you blame me, Matt?"

He sighed and looked over her shoulder. "Blaming won't bring Connor back."

*He blames me.*

He choked up. "I wish we talked about him more. I miss him."

She couldn't look at him. She didn't want to see him cry. "Every time I think about him, I want to cry," she said. "So

I just... I try to think about him only when I'm alone, you know? I'm doing the best I can to move forward. Trying to survive without crying all the time."

He squeezed her hand. "But you and I... At least when it's just our family, we can talk about him, can't we? Remember all the good stuff together, even if we cry."

A picture of the two of them with broad smiles on their honeymoon in Barcelona stared at her from his nightstand. "Someone needs to be strong. Two people can't be sad at the same time," she said.

Matt squinted as if he were trying to make sense of a picture he'd never seen before. "Two people *are* sad at the same time. Our whole family is sad."

Jill swallowed, trying to be matter-of-fact. "Yes, but we're sad to ourselves so we don't pull other people down. We're trying to be strong."

A tear fell from Matt. One. He swiped it away. "But no one else gets it. We're the only ones. Wouldn't it feel good to understand one another?"

Jill felt lightheaded. A minute ago, she asked if he blamed her. And thank God he avoided the answer, because some things were better left unsaid. She took a deep breath to regain her composure. Matt was right—blaming wouldn't help them heal. And talking about it would do nothing but get their pointer fingers wiggling. And that was even if they could talk without weeping. "We can't sit around crying together for the rest of our lives," she said.

Matt caressed his wedding band, then stood, running a hand through his blond curls and staring at something out the window.

She turned to see what he was looking at but only saw the golden tree.

"I wasn't talking about the rest of our lives," he whispered, as he left the room.

A minute later she could hear the TV in the family room and Matt and Henry's voices. Jake was with friends. Everyone accounted for, no one needed her. Had anyone shut the front door?

She slipped down the hall to the emptiest place in the house. She ran her finger along the shelves in Connor's room, lined with collections of rocks, shells, sea glass and snow globes, and took in his neatly made bed and the green furry beanbag chair. Moving to his closet, she slid open the door, lifting the sleeves of shirts that hadn't been touched in three months. Carefully, she took a blue T-shirt down and held it to her nose, breathing his spirit into her soul. She ducked behind the hanging clothes and slid down the wall to the floor, comforted by the depth of the darkness. Bundling his shirt, she pressed it to her face and wept.

# 9

## sports clips

MATT LAY AWAKE THAT NIGHT worrying about his relationship with Jill. After twenty years of marriage, she had still been his favorite person to hang out with. Until now . . . He'd fallen in love with her because she not only made him laugh but also laughed at his jokes. He loved the way she took charge when she was passionate about getting things done, and how she supported his ideas one hundred percent and was psyched about them right along with him. And now she essentially tells him she expects them to grieve separately?

Before, he loved that she always had a plan. But now her plans were frenetic. He never knew what was coming next or why. It was hard to find his bearings when they were together. He would never intentionally cause friction between the boys and her. But they needed someone they could rely on.

The strain between her and Jake was tugging at all of them. In reality, the tension between those two had begun long before the accident. And now it seemed even Henry was unsure if he could trust her. A week ago, after dark, Henry remembered he'd left his bike outside. Jill offered to go with him to move it to the garage, but he said, "I'll ask Daddy." And when there were monsters under his bed, it was Daddy he wanted.

He wasn't trying to be their favorite. He was just trying to be a dependable parent.

The next morning, he couldn't get his hair to lie flat. His blond curls hung over his ears. The back almost touched his collar. It had been months since he'd gotten a trim and he was starting to feel out of place at his accounting firm where all the other partners had short, professional cuts. At breakfast, Henry showed everyone how he could almost get his hair in a ponytail and Jake said he had to pull his into a topknot during soccer practice. Matt said enough was enough and on Monday night after dinner, the three of them headed to Sports Clips.

They sat in the lobby, flipping through sports magazines and watching *Monday Night Football* while they waited for their regular stylist, Trish. Henry climbed into Matt's lap. "Hey, buddy," he said, hugging him, "Are we giving you a mullet today?"

"No!" Henry giggled, leaning his head against Matt's chest.

Matt wondered at how Henry laughed and smiled so readily. At home he even talked with ease about Connor. Not with the usual catch the rest of them had whenever mentioning him, which was rare.

"It's nice, isn't it?" he'd commented to Jill a few nights prior. "He doesn't seem to mix memories of Connor with sadness that he's gone. What's the difference?"

Jill was thoughtful. "Because we're his parents, we miss Connor right now, but we also miss his future—not seeing who he's going to be. I don't think Henry comprehends that."

"Do you think he gets sad but doesn't tell us?"

Jill bit her nail and shook her head. "No. Henry would tell us. He's fine."

Trish walked to the lobby, winking at them while her previous client paid. "No Connor today?" she asked, motioning for them to follow her.

Henry stopped wiggling. Matt's smile froze and his heart sank. Jake elbowed him. His mind went blank trying to figure out how to say it. He found himself wanting to let her down easily and felt like he should whisper, like he was revealing a dirty secret. Was he actually feeling embarrassed? That his son died?

Henry broke the silence as he climbed out of his dad's lap. He looked at Jake, as if hoping for backup. "Connor died."

Matt carefully put his magazine in the nearby rack, avoiding Trish's reaction. When he finally turned to her, her brows were scrunched in confusion. "I'm sorry. Is Connor not here? Sorry, what did Henry say?"

For some reason it was easier now that she was caught off guard. He didn't like upsetting people. He preferred making people feel better. Words came to him as he reached for Henry's hand. "Connor was in an accident. He passed away in June." Matt tried to put an arm around Jake, but Jake dodged him.

Trish's hand flew to her mouth. Matt could see there would be tears. This was going to be a long hour. He could wait for a haircut another week. Just Henry and Jake today.

The bells on the door behind them chimed as the previous client walked out the door. He must have been listening. Matt glanced back and saw that the customer who had been sitting next to them had his mouth open. At Matt's look, he quickly dipped back into his *Sports Illustrated*.

Matt guided Henry in front of him, walking past Trish who was still in shock. "I'm sorry to have to be the one to tell you," he said. *The world's biggest understatement. C'mon Trish, let's get this over with.*

"I'm just so sorry... I don't know what to say." Trish gulped, pulling Henry's hair through her fingers as he sat in her stylist's chair.

Could she even see what she was doing through her tears? She held up a chunk of hair with one hand, scissors in another, and with no free hands to dab her eyes, she hunched a shoulder and wiped them on her arm. She sniffled, but her nose began to run anyway. Matt was fascinated. He wondered what she was going to do about the snot running onto her lip. Would she keep cutting or take a second to clean herself up? He glanced at Jake who was also enthralled.

Finally, she put her scissors down and grabbed several tissues to blow her nose and mop her face. After blowing a second time, she got back to work. Henry seemed oblivious, playing a game with the animal designs on his cape. Probably doing his best to ignore Trish.

"I hope he didn't suffer," she said. "Was he wearing a seatbelt?"

*You've got to be kidding. Just stop talking, Trish.* Matt looked at Jake, who was studying his shoes. Matt hadn't ever told anyone, in front of the boys, how it had happened. Should he be brief with the details? Would it be uncomfortable for them?

"We were boating at Lake Koda. A sudden storm arose and the boat flipped. Unfortunately, Connor drowned." This, of course, sounded like the entire family had been flipped out of the boat. Did he need to explain that some of them were safe on the dock? That his wife had insisted on plunging into a storm instead of waiting at the marina? That she and his father-in-law also fell into the water? That they were supposed to rescue Connor but didn't? Couldn't. Didn't.

While still circling the animals on his cape with his finger, Henry said, "I fell in the water too. But Mommy saved me. Grandpa tried to save Connor, but he was already dead."

They all peeked at Trish who wheezed and grabbed more tissues. Finally, she brushed Henry's neck and unclipped the cape.

Seeing an out, Matt took it. "I think we'll come back another time. Thanks so much. I'm so sorry." He hated apologizing for his son dying. Without waiting for a response, he handed her two twenties, squeezed Henry's shoulder and directed him out the door with Jake close behind. They drove home in silence.

When they walked in the house, Jill was sitting at the kitchen table working on her laptop. Jake headed to his room without a word. Henry crawled into her lap. Matt set his keys on the counter and let out a long sigh.

"What? What's wrong?"

"She hadn't heard. She bawled throughout Henry's cut and I made an excuse and we left. It was hell. I think Henry probably has boogers in his hair."

Henry's hand flew to his head. "Do I, Mommy?"

"You'll want to take a bath to wash the hair off your neck anyway. Why don't you get it started?"

"We need to warn people ahead of time," Matt said after Henry ran upstairs.

"How do you expect me to do that?"

"I don't know. It was horrific. I hated having to tell her. I hated that I was apologizing for sharing sad news when it was my son who died! She sees him for fifteen minutes a few times a year and I had to figure out how to make her feel better."

"Did you?"

"Did I what?"

"Make her feel better?"

He rolled his eyes and shook his head. "It was like watching a train wreck." He put his hand to his face, trying to rub away the memories, then rubbed his temples. "I have the worst headache. I've got to lie down."

With a washcloth over his eyes, he tried to push away the memory of Trish's snot and tears. This must be why Jill avoided going out. Up to now, he didn't really mind it. People were kind. Yes, they asked how he was doing. Yes, he lied and said they were "getting through it." And then they talked about work or cars or sports.

But this. Trying to explain what happened. Feeling responsible for someone else's grief. All eyes on him. He didn't know how to fix it, and it shouldn't be his responsibility to try. He wasn't cut out for that. He squeezed his eyes tighter, praying for sleep.

# 10

## the soccer game

SEPTEMBER WAS DRAWING TO A close, and Jill hadn't been to any of Jake's soccer games yet. Of course she wanted to support him, but the thought of seeing people who would inevitably want to talk about the accident, even old friends, drenched her in a cold sweat.

Each week Jake asked if she was coming. Each week she made excuses and Matt and Henry went without her. But this week was an away game and she wouldn't stand him up anymore. But she desperately hoped to avoid talking to anyone while there.

Matt came home from work early and they drove across town together. Jill set up three camp chairs under a fiery orange maple tree at the end of the field, far away from the fans in the bleachers grouped by the colors blue or green, depending upon which team they were cheering for. Jill adjusted the brim of her green ball cap low over her sunglasses.

While the teams warmed up, Henry and Matt kicked a ball to each other on the sidelines. Matt dashed after Henry, stealing the ball, then teased him by dribbling to the right, then to the left, dodging out of Henry's reach. Their smiles were contagious and Jill relaxed. She wished she could be playful again, which seemed to come so easily to Matt.

A touch on her shoulder took her by surprise. Marley. Old Jill would have enthusiastically greeted the friend she hadn't seen in several months. But having no warning, a fog encompassed her, and she couldn't think of a thing to say. She braced herself for platitudes.

Marley crouched down to Jill's level and grabbed her hand, her laser focus making Jill blink. "I've been thinking of you. Every. Single. Day. Did you get my text?" Jill paused. There were so many texts that she'd stopped looking at them. But Marley didn't wait for an answer. "How are you doing?"

Jill wished she could say, "Horrible." But a minute ago, she was lighthearted watching Matt and Henry play. Honestly, she didn't know how she was doing. It changed by the second. Jill managed a weak smile. "We're here!"

Marley laughed a full octave higher than her normal voice. She squeezed Jill's hand, made a pouty face that Jill took to mean "I'm sorry," then rubbed her back. "I'm here for you, Jill. We all are. I hope you know that. Whatever you need, just let me know."

Jill nodded.

As Marley made her way back to the bleachers, Jill could see the other parents in matching green gear lean forward in their seats, clearly waiting for a report. Marley made the same pouty face and the whole group turned toward Jill, who quickly looked away.

The blast of a horn signaled the start of the game, and a breathless Matt and Henry joined her.

"Marley came over." Jill sighed.

"What'd you say?" Matt asked, fidgeting to straighten his seat.

"We're here!" she said, imitating herself with air quotes. "Then Marley gave me the 'I'm-sorry-your-life-sucks face' and walked back to the group who were all eager to hear if we've recovered or not."

"Sucks to suck, right?" Matt said, surprising her with a kiss on her temple.

She smiled back at him, then grabbed his hand, intertwining her fingers in his. Henry crawled into her lap, and she kissed his sweaty head, wrapping her free arm around him.

*Two kids can't die, can they?*

Jake was on attack, running the ball up the field. He had a good pass. A steal. An assist. Parents shouted encouragement. A collective groan when the other team stole it. Raucous cheering when they scored. This game was everything to the families sitting here on a Thursday evening watching green and blue jerseys run back and forth trying to kick a ball into a net. Emotions so high and so low over digital points on a board.

Just six months ago, it felt like everything to Jill, too. But it was just a game now. Her son kicked the ball. She clapped. Matt even cheered. But her emotions didn't change. She didn't care about the outcome. She just wanted to watch her boy.

Now Jake was chasing the ball. Blue kicked a bad pass and turned it over to Green and a teammate crossed it to Jake. Jake deftly stopped it with his foot, then turning toward the goal, smacked straight into the defender and they both fell, Jake flat onto his back.

For a split second he was still, and Jill's breath caught. But he pulled his knees into his chest and rolled onto his side. She slid to the edge of her seat. When Jake finally sat up, his mouth gaped open as if he were screaming but without sound.

Jill and Matt jumped up. "It's only the wind knocked out of him," Matt said, grabbing her arm. It felt like he was trying to hold her back rather than comfort her. As if he feared she would break the rules and sprint onto the field.

But the coach was there. Jake's body melted into the man's knees, who held him for a second before helping him stand. Everyone clapped as they walked off the field.

The game resumed.

Jill wanted to run over to make sure he was okay. She could probably get away with it since she was the mom whose child had died. But she couldn't risk embarrassing Jake. She could only watch from afar as he buried his head in his knees and closed himself off from his buddies on the bench next to him.

She couldn't take her eyes off Jake. Pretty soon a teammate had his arm around him. Then an assistant coach knelt in front of him. Jill's heart began to pound. *Is he okay?* The coach shaded his eyes with a hand, scanning the spectator seats. Jill stood, tentatively raising her arm. He signaled her over.

"Where are you going?" Matt asked.

"Jake's hurt. The coach wants me there. Wait here with Henry." She walked as fast as she dared without drawing attention to herself. Jake would hate her forever if she humiliated him.

As she neared, his teammate ran to her. "He's crying, but he won't say what's wrong."

Jake was sitting on the grass, facing away from the game, head bent over his folded arms. She could hear him gasping. His coach nodded to Jill then moved away, giving them privacy.

"Are you hurt?" she asked, kneeling beside him, her hand on his back. He shook his head, his chest heaving as he sobbed. The tears that couldn't stop. How she knew this feeling!

She dialed Matt. "Pull the car around. We're taking Jake home." She threw his gear bag over her shoulder and helped him to his feet, wishing she could shield him from the whispers of his teammates.

The ride home was silent except for Jake's sniffles, and as soon as they stopped the car, he ran into the house, Henry chasing after him.

"Did he tell you what happened?" Matt asked, not opening his door.

"He said he wasn't hurt. But he couldn't say much else because he was crying so hard." She dried her own tears. "It hits at weird times, doesn't it?"

Matt rubbed his hands through his hair. "In the middle of a soccer game?"

"Maybe getting hurt triggered it?" She opened the door, wanting to get inside and check on Jake.

"He'll be embarrassed." Matt said, fingers massaging his temples.

"It's good for his friends to know he's still grieving. They'll look out for him."

Leaning his head on the black leather seat, Matt closed his eyes, "Will it ever get better? I mean, will we ever be normal again? I'm just so tired of being sad. Of everyone being sad."

Jill started to sit back down.

He waved her off. "Go in and find Jake. I'll be in in a second."

Jill had mac 'n cheese on the stove and Dino nuggets in the microwave when Matt came in. He'd been in the car for at least twenty minutes. "What can I get you to eat?" she asked as he sat at the counter.

"You know what? I'll have what Henry's having. Barbecue dipping sauce and all."

Jill smiled. "That makes three of us. Should we watch a movie during dinner?"

"Disney Channel!" cheered Henry.

As they were finding a show, the doorbell rang. A car drove off before Jill could see who it was. But on the step was a box of donuts and a note addressed to Jake. She took them upstairs, knocked on Jake's door, then peeked in before he could answer. He was under a pile of blankets. Sitting on the edge of his bed, she found his shoulder and gently massaged it. "Hey, bud. Someone dropped off a treat for you."

He hunched his body even smaller.

"Do you want to talk about it?" she asked.

No response.

"We're watching a movie if you want to join us."

She rubbed his neck and then his back. His body eased. After a while his muffled voice came from under the blankets. "I couldn't breathe."

"Did you get the air knocked out of you?"

"Yes. But I thought I'd broken my back, and I was going to die or be paralyzed or something."

"That sounds really scary."

"Do you think Connor was scared?"

Her hands stopped.

"Do you think he knew he was going to drown?" he asked.

Jill held her breath as her mind started spinning. She slowly exhaled. "I don't like thinking of him scared."

Jake was still talking from deep under his covers and she had to listen carefully to hear him. "Some people say when you drown, you fall asleep. But today, when I couldn't breathe, I didn't fall asleep. I thought I was suffocating. Wouldn't it be the same if you were drowning?"

Jill was relieved Jake couldn't see her tears. "I'm not sure."

"I started imagining Connor unable to breathe and afraid, and then I couldn't stop crying and I couldn't get it out of my head."

"I've felt that way before," Jill said. Her hand rested on the heap of fabric and fluff, but her heart felt her child underneath the layers.

"I don't like feeling this way," he said, choking up.

"I wonder if you had an anxiety attack. It's normal for someone who's been through what we've been through." She actually wasn't sure what an anxiety attack was and had no idea if it was normal or not.

His voice rose with emotion. "I don't want to be the kid with anxiety. I don't want to cry every time I get hurt!"

Jill started rubbing his back again. Then he mumbled, "I don't want to watch a movie tonight. I just want to be alone for a while. Will you shut the door when you leave?"

Jake didn't emerge the entire evening and when she checked on him later, he was asleep.

As she and Matt changed for bed, she asked, "I wonder if we should find someone for the kids to talk to? I think Jake had an anxiety attack today."

Matt tossed his T-shirt in the hamper like it was a basketball. "Jake doesn't have anxiety. He's sad. You said yourself, it hits at weird times." He moved into the bathroom.

She followed him and began washing her face. "I told him what happened today was normal for someone who's grieving. But I don't know if that's true." She watched him in the mirror as he brushed his teeth. His bedtime routine took two minutes and then he'd hit the pillow and be fast asleep. "I thought with sports and school and being on a schedule, it would be easier for everyone to cope. But I'm not so sure anymore."

Matt leaned against the counter. "I just don't see how a psychologist would be able to relate unless they'd also lost a brother or a child. If not, they couldn't understand. Do you really want advice from someone who learned about grief from a textbook? Or a *TED Talk*? They wouldn't get it at all."

Jill paused before putting her toothbrush in her mouth. "But what if they did? What if there was someone who'd been through this and could help us figure it out?"

Matt didn't answer right away. He rubbed his chin, fiddling at the spot where his whiskers didn't grow. "What if they make it worse?"

She spat and washed out the sink. "Like how?"

He walked to their bed and started removing the pillows. "Sometimes I have nightmares that we're back in the storm. And it's all I can do to push the memories away. A psychologist might force him to relive it. Like when I had to explain everything to Trish at the hair salon. It was the worst. I don't want him to go through that."

She climbed into bed and folded her body into his.

Matt continued, "I don't want him talking to a shrink. He can talk to us if he needs to. That's our job as his parents. We're the ones who need to be there for him."

Jill closed her eyes. She understood where he was coming from. She really did. But she had no idea how to help her kids. She didn't even know how to help herself.

# 11

## what we see

THE NEXT WEEK, JILL LINGERED at the door of her classroom, double-checking to make sure she was in the right room because Halloween decorations had appeared that weren't there yesterday. Beneath the cultural posters of Spain and Argentina, three large orange pumpkins sat on the bookcase. And next to her chart of basic Spanish conjugations, a skeleton perched, wearing a witch's hat. How was it October already? She could guess which of her faculty friends had done it, and she had to bite her lip to keep from crying. Her old friends were still doing nice things for her even though she avoided them as much as possible.

She held a yellow handout from that morning's faculty meeting, folded in half as if to hide what was inside. "Risky Behaviors in Teens" was the heading, followed by a long list of potential problems, arranged in categories: Abuse, Anorexia, Bulimia, Cutting, Drinking, Drugs, Pornography, Sexting... It was all so overwhelming.

Before teaching high school, Jill assumed "troubled kids" was synonymous with "bad parents" and could be spelled out in unwashed clothes and worn-out shoes. A kid on the fringes. Like Kevin, in her fourth period class. He missed a lot of school and smelled like smoke. Or Damien, from her own high school years, with his awful sneer and obnoxious laugh, who boasted about raging parties while his parents traveled the world. He wouldn't be on the fringes but smack in the center raising two middle fingers.

However, last year when she started teaching again, Jill was stunned by some of the kids who got caught with drugs. Perfectly charming, likable kids.

And now that Jake was in high school, she was realizing parenting was much easier to get wrong than she had originally imagined. Staying in your kid's good graces wasn't as easy as bringing the right team treat to soccer games and volunteering at the school carnival. Suddenly everything she said or did, or didn't say or didn't do, was potentially the wrong thing to say or do, or not say or not do, and could very possibly send her child into the welcome escape of drugged-up oblivion.

Jake wouldn't do drugs, would he? They'd taught him better. She paused. Had they? Was talking about it once a year enough? When was the last time she'd shared meaningful advice with him—or even given him a hug? To be honest, she thought about it a lot, but was afraid she'd say the wrong thing and he'd make her feel like an idiot. They really should have another talk at home. Sitting at her desk, she made a note in her phone's reminders so she wouldn't forget.

She organized her books and plan for today's assignment, then surreptitiously unfolded the handout and scanned the list of warning signs: Dark, sunken eyes, frequent need to use the bathroom, wearing long sleeves even in the heat, avoidant behavior—*Jake!*—drop in grades, frequent absenteeism . . . She felt like she was memorizing for a test.

Refolding the paper, she tucked it under her laptop before opening the grade reports and glancing down the screen. Four weeks into school and all but a few kids were holding steady. Her students were good kids. She didn't need to worry about them.

The bell rang and Jill called out, "Bienvenidos. Welcome," as she did at the beginning of every class. Last year she was a lot more creative, switching it up with "Hola clase! Que hay de nuevo? Hello class. What's new?" or "Buenas tardes, mis estudiantes inteligentes! Good afternoon, my intelligent students!" But this year she didn't have a creative bone in her body, and she stuck to routine as if it were a life preserver.

The classroom chatter died down as she passed out quizzes and twenty-four students focused on conjugating irregular Spanish verbs as Jill watched them from behind her desk. What was going on in those little heads of theirs? Beyond classes and tests and homework. Beyond wanting perfect hair and needing name-brand shoes. Beyond teenage crushes and driver's licenses. Those are the things they talked about with their friends. Maybe their parents. But what else were they worried about? What secrets were they keeping?

The storm came to mind. Although she would do anything to get Henry to shore, as she tried to swim while the waves tried to sink her, she desperately wanted to stop and breathe. A part of her, only for a split second, but a very powerful part of her, wanted to untangle him from her neck and let him float—for just a moment—so she could catch her breath. Even in a crisis, when her child's life depended on it, she could be selfish. But she didn't do it. She fought.

Had her dad stopped trying? Drowning in the waves, struggling for air, his grandson close to his reach, did he pause—just for a minute—to breathe?

A movement caught her eye. Vanessa's dark curly hair hung down to her desk, forming a curtain around her paper. She worked methodically on her assignment, a finger in her mouth, gnawing on her nails. The black sleeves of her shirt were pushed to her forearms with at least five Band-Aids on each arm. She looked up as if sensing Jill watching her and when their eyes met, she quickly slid her sleeves down to her wrists. Jill remembered driving past Vanessa's home last summer and imagining their perfect family watching a movie together.

More than once a week, Vanessa asked for a bathroom pass. She was a good student, so Jill tried not to let it bother her. But the frequency was annoying. Now all the Band-Aids. It was weird, right?

Every single one of these teenagers was stressed out about something. A breakup, a difficult class, a fight with a friend, a bad hair day. She remembered being their age. At sixteen, it seemed your whole future hinged on high school. If you didn't understand math, you might never get into college. If you couldn't afford the right shoes now, would you ever? And if even your friends didn't get you, would anyone? Were you destined to be lonely for the rest of your life?

They kept those feelings pent up, acting like nothing was wrong. And while some walked with a strut and others chanted "YOLO," she knew it was just a different way of covering up their anxiety. And it was no less real than the stress of those who scurried around with to-do lists and an all-consuming fear of getting less than an A-.

Jill checked the timer on her phone. They'd been writing for fifteen minutes with five minutes left before time was up. They were slowing down. Some kids were staring at the ceiling, racking their brain for answers. Others' eyes were skittering around, hoping clues would reveal themselves from somewhere around the room. Maybe the skeleton would tell them.

Was Jeff cheating? He was staring at something beneath his desk. She wanted to go over and expose him. But what if she was wrong? No, he just did it again. He was definitely cheating. Her heart sank. Teenagers. She didn't have the energy to accuse him. To hear him deny it or to watch him confess. She didn't have the grit for it today. Someday he'd have a conscience that caught up with him. If she called him on it now, she doubted he'd even feel bad about it, so what was the point?

The timer rang and her students sat up straight with a chorus of sighs, put their pencils down and turned to friends to commiserate. As she walked through the aisles collecting tests from each desk, she wondered if she was any different from her students. She dressed in an outfit that made her feel good. She earnestly taught Spanish vocabulary with a smile even though inside, her heart felt like it had been scraped with a potato peeler. The slice took her breath away when she thought about it, so she tried not to. Work was a welcome distraction to pass the time, bringing her closer to night, when she could crawl into bed and close her eyes.

Her students knew her son had died. Working in the same community where she lived and raised her family meant she rubbed shoulders with many of their families. During the first week of school, she received several cards and notes slipped onto her desk, appearing seemingly out of nowhere. Short messages expressing a teenage version of sympathy, beautiful in their youthful attempt to give comfort: "I'm sorry you lost your son." "We prayed for your family this summer." "I was sorry to hear Connor passed away. I hope you feel better soon." Some had been unsigned. It was endearing, really.

They had tried to be there for her. How could she do the same for them? Back at her desk, she scanned the classroom again, stopping on Vanessa. Only her fingers peeked out from her sleeves. She had a math book open and was scribbling in a notebook, flipping the pages, then biting at a nail until she wrote something down again.

The girl wouldn't have any nails left at this rate. Jill stood. "Por favor, abran sus libros..."

Jill was making risotto for dinner when Matt came home. "Want some help?" he asked.

She didn't. Risotto was easy, it just took commitment. Matt sat on a stool and opened his Diet Coke.

"How was work?" she asked, not taking her eyes off the rice.

"The usual. Nothing to report. You?"

"There's a girl in my third period. I think she's cutting herself."

"What do you mean?"

Jill stopped stirring to look at him. "Cutting her arms... hurting herself on purpose."

Matt looked shocked. "Why would she do that?"

She added another ladle of broth. "I'm not sure. She hasn't missed any class. She's got perfect attendance."

"Do you think she's on drugs?"

She shook her head, then waved the wooden spoon. "I had a 'type' in mind too. A drug-user—a troubled kid. But she doesn't fit that stereotype. She's a good student. Her parents are really put together. She has younger brothers Connor's and Henry's ages. Typical family."

"How do you know she's... cutting?"

"She always wears sweatshirts, even when it's hot. She leaves to go to the bathroom more than anyone else. One day when she came back, I noticed blood on her sleeve. Today she had like, five Band-Aids on her arms."

"Are you sure you're not jumping to conclusions?" He sounded skeptical. "It could be anything."

"Maybe. But I just can't shake the idea that she seems to be hiding something."

"Are you supposed to do anything?"

"If we think someone may be in danger, we're supposed to report it to their counselor. But I'm not sure I have any actual evidence. It's more of a suspicion. I'm going to keep an eye on her."

Late that night, after everyone else had gone to bed, Jill Googled *cutting*. She'd assumed it was like wanting a tattoo or wanting to look tough. But she discovered it wasn't that at all. Most kids who cut tried to hide it, even from their friends. Like so many other teenage issues, it was a symptom of needing to feel in control, a distraction from other hurts. The pain acted like a drug and was even accompanied by a high. And like everything else teenagers had to battle, it could easily become an addiction.

What were Vanessa's parents like? Were they emotionally unavailable? Jill started to imagine the worst-case scenarios. Was she abused? Was someone hurting her before she began hurting herself? Imagining what Vanessa might be dealing with, turned to ways Jill could mentor her—take her under her wing. It was just the distraction Jill needed to forget about her own problems.

# 12

## just a feeling

BY THE END OF OCTOBER, their golden fall weather turned cold, and when the front door opened, a chill blew through the house, reaching Jill at the kitchen table mindlessly surfing the internet for the Halloween costume Henry wanted. Was Jake home from soccer practice already? She looked at her watch—5:00. The time had gotten away from her. She'd planned to have hot chocolate ready for him when he got home. It wasn't something she normally did, but she'd been thinking of ways to show him she cared.

Evenings used to be so frenzied—Jill chauffeuring three kids to soccer practices, piano lessons, school events or birthday parties, then a mad dash home to get dinner on the table and, finally, homework.

With Connor's death, managing two kids' activities instead of three felt exponentially smaller. The busyness that was almost overwhelming last year, in retrospect, seemed lively and full. The calm she'd desperately craved just six months ago had been thrust upon her unexpectedly, and she found her day-to-day life depressingly quiet.

Jake set his backpack on the counter and opened the fridge. "Where's Henry?"

"Playing at a friend's house. Was it cold at practice today? Do you want some hot chocolate?" she asked. "I can make you some."

His brown hair was sticking out at odd angles, sweaty from working out. "I'm good." He took the carton of chocolate milk from the fridge and grabbed a bag of chips from the pantry cupboard.

"We'll be eating dinner in an hour, so don't snack too much."

He picked up a stack of Oreos as well.

Jill bit her tongue, not wanting to harp. And in trying not to annoy him, she turned the subject to the other person she hadn't been able to stop thinking about—Vanessa. The more she kept an eye on her, the more she was sure she was cutting. "Do you know Vanessa Stuart?"

He poured the milk into a glass, then sat on a barstool. "Not really. She's in my math class, but she's a grade older."

"Does she have friends?"

"Probably. She's on the girls' soccer team."

Jill watched him work to open the chips, the bag finally tearing down the center instead of across the top, and, although it nearly killed her, she refrained from commenting.

"Let me guess, she's getting a bad grade in Spanish." He took another drink, slurping as he drained his cup.

"She's actually getting a good grade in Spanish." Jill should have shut her mouth. She really tried. But the desire to show her son she was caring and sensitive, overpowered her reason, and she committed a major faux pax for a teacher: Sharing information about a student with her own child. "I'm kind of worried about her."

"So she doesn't talk to anyone or have friends to sit with or something? Or does she talk too much?" He wiped his mouth but missed a spot at the top of his lip.

"She has people to sit with in class and she's a good student." Jill didn't plan on getting into specifics, but she couldn't help digging for information.

"Well, that's everything that a teacher should care about." He crunched on three chips at the same time.

"Sometimes you can just tell," she said.

"That's creepy."

"To care about someone?"

"To care too much about a kid in your class. You probably should just mind your own business."

"Actually, kids need adults to care about them. If I see something that concerns me, I want to help. Or get her help."

He tilted his head back, emptying the crumbs into his mouth. "But you're saying you don't see something that worries you—it's just a feeling. That's what's creepy. You can't just assume something's off based on a feeling."

"I just want to help where I can."

"Mom, it's high school. Every single kid needs help."

She fixed her eyes on him. "What can I help you with, Jake?"

"Ha." He pushed the bag of chips away and jumped off the stool. "Why don't you use your *feelings* to figure it out?"

"I'm serious. Talk to me." She meant it. She moved to the counter to be closer to him.

"I'm not doing this. We're not suddenly going to become the family that talks about our feelings."

"Would that be such a bad thing? You used to talk to me all the time."

"It's weird. No teenager wants to talk to his parents about that kind of stuff."

"It's good to talk about *stuff*. You might find we actually know a thing or two."

Jake threw his backpack over his shoulder and headed toward the stairs to his room. "Then I guess it's good I don't have anything wrong with me. I'm all good."

Just when Jill thought he was gone, he called out, "By the way, I got an A on my math test."

"Hey, that's great!" she started to say, but his bedroom door clicked shut.

The next day, when the late bell rang for third period, Vanessa's seat was empty, and she was absent the rest of the week. *Kids get sick, no need to worry. Maybe her family went on a trip.*

During her lunch hour, Jill popped into the counseling office. "Hey, Ellis, one of my students, Vanessa Stuart, hasn't been in class. Did you get a call from her parents excusing her?"

Ellis put her pen down and folded her hands on top of her desk. "Not yet. Most often parents send excuses afterward."

Jill tapped the doorframe. "Right."

Ellis leaned forward. "How are you?"

Jill was so used to the concerned look people wore for her benefit that she saw the question coming before Ellis even asked it. Waving her hand in the air, she brushed it off with her prepared response. "Fine. We're good. Some days are hard, of course, but we're fine. Everyone's fine." She smiled to prove it.

Ellis wasn't deterred. "Have you found someone you and your family can talk to?"

Jill paused. "Do you mean, like a psychologist?"

She nodded. "Or a therapist. Someone who specializes in grief."

Jill didn't want to seem like an irresponsible parent. This was the school counselor after all. Jake's counselor too, actually. "I've definitely thought about it. I feel like it would be interesting to talk to someone. But we're muddling through. Matt's a typical guy—he doesn't trust 'shrinks,' his words, not mine. And you know kids, they're pretty resilient."

Ellis didn't comment, just silently watched her.

Jill felt obligated to fill the void and found herself diving into unchartered territory. "Sometimes I worry about Jake, but more typical teen stuff, you know?" Heat rose up her neck, and her heart started racing. She didn't really know Ellis at all. Why was she telling her this? She closed her eyes to recalibrate and took a deep breath, digging up her broadest smile. "What I'd really like is for a therapist to teach him to say 'please,' 'thank you,' and 'I appreciate you.'" She half laughed. "If you've got someone who can do that, sign me up!" She raised her hand as if volunteering and backed away. "Thanks, Ellis, for your concern. I appreciate it."

Ellis' face remained neutral, and her focus didn't leave Jill. "Let me know if you change your mind. I have some good resources."

Jill tried to force another smile, but quite possibly it was a grimace. She walked past staff offices, then stopped around the corner, reaching her hand to the wall for balance, squeezing her eyes shut. Just three seconds. That's all she needed to regain her strength. With a deep breath, she straightened, then headed back into the halls of high school.

*Ugh. Human interaction, amiright.* She dashed into the empty stairwell and took the stairs two at a time so she wouldn't be late for class.

The more she thought about Ellis' questioning, the more it bugged Jill that, while their family was the obvious choice for therapy, so many other kids were crying out for help and going unnoticed. What was the school doing to help Vanessa and everyone else who was struggling?

They were going unseen, and it wasn't right. If Vanessa needed help, it would have to be up to Jill.

# 13

## vanessa's story

VANESSA LIKED THE ADRENALINE RUSH of cutting. Her heart would pound, and she'd hold her breath, letting anticipation sweep through her as she touched the glass to her skin. Then, just as she had to gasp for air, she slowly sliced through the tension of her arm or her thigh or her shoulder, savoring the warmth that washed through her body and silenced her brain.

She was so relaxed as she cut, it almost felt like sleepwalking. Controlling the pain made her feel invincible. And overcoming her fear made her feel strong. Some people were squeamish about blood but not her. It was like she had a secret superpower.

≈

She'd started two and a half years ago, when she was fourteen and trying to do everything right, but no matter how hard she tried, she was never able to be perfect.

Privacy was nonexistent in her home. Five kids, two parents, a cat. They were living in chaos. Toys everywhere, a pile of shoes in the path of the front door, heaps of laundry by the washing machine near the back door, dishes in the sink, and homework for five kids spread across the kitchen table. It was impossible to find a place to think.

Her three younger brothers formed a little team, always loud, always wrestling. Or watching TV with the sound turned way up.

She shared a tidy room with her older sister, Sylvie, but never got to see her anymore. Straight-A-Sylvie was always studying, volunteering, or practicing the flute.

In the spring, when their mom was swamped with new real estate listings, and Dad was home late—like always, no matter what time of year—everyone was expected to do a little extra to pitch in. Vanessa was in charge of the laundry and getting the boys to clean up. She and Sylvie took turns making dinner. Vanessa just wanted quiet and to be by herself for five minutes. Was that too much to ask?

Then, at the end of eighth grade, when the weather warmed up and she and her friends could finally be outside in T-shirts and shorts, they sat on the grass and talked about summer and freedom, boys and high school, and all the possibilities their futures held. When the first notes of their favorite song started from their shared playlist, they jumped up to dance. Arms waving, bodies swaying, singing at the top of their lungs, pretending their glass bottles of soda were bottles of beer. They didn't have a care in the world until Amber's bottle slipped and shattered on the driveway.

The three girls immediately knelt to clean up, stacking the broken pieces in a pile. Where the driveway met the grass, Vanessa found a fragment imprinted with a large "V" as if it were specially made just for her. She slipped it into her purse as the song's chorus faded and noticed blood on her hand. She hadn't even felt it nick her.

That night she rested her special shard on her nightstand, balancing it against the lamp. A few days later, while she lay on her bed memorizing states and capitals for her US History final, her brothers ran through the house shooting Nerf guns, shouting, and banging into walls. When she slammed the door to drown out the noise, her little souvenir fell to the floor. She picked it up, cautiously touching the sharp edges.

With it hidden in her hand, she slipped into the bathroom and locked the door. She was just curious, that was all. Sitting on the edge of the tub, she pressed the flat side against her leg, the "V" leaving an indent. She tapped the jagged point onto her thigh, then spent the next several minutes lightly scratching her skin, mustering her courage. But soon one of her brothers was banging on the door, yelling to be let in. With a sigh, she hid the pale green glass in her hand, flushed the toilet, and walked out.

~

When she thought about it later, it seemed silly. Why would anyone want to intentionally cut themselves? But the next week she had more tests and couldn't concentrate with all the noise. Then a phone call that her mom and dad would both be home late, so would she please get dinner for the boys?

After a meal of warmed-up soup, she cleaned the kitchen, and when her parents were finally home and putting the boys to bed, she tried to focus on the X's and Y's of algebra, but her sister's flute scales in the next room made Vanessa's head ring. Closing her books, she went upstairs to change into her pajamas. By ten thirty, the boys were asleep, her parents were in their bedroom, and Sylvie was doing homework downstairs. Vanessa took her glass to the bathroom and locked the door.

As she methodically thought of all the things that she wished would be different—would just stop—it was easy to press down and break her skin, and just like that, calm flooded her body and her panic vanished.

She made another line perpendicular to the first, just to make it look deliberate. When she realized she hadn't washed her hands, she worried about giving herself an infection. She rinsed the shard clean, then dabbed her leg with toilet paper and trickled rubbing alcohol over the two lines, blowing until it evaporated. The sting was cool and healing. Finally, she poured the alcohol over her glass to sterilize it, and then a little more over her cuts, just to be sure. Wadding the tissues, she tossed them in the trash, put the alcohol back in the cabinet, washed her hands, and climbed into bed.

By the next day, they'd made only the narrowest of scabs. Almost imperceptible really. Just one more thing about her that was insignificant. But as the months passed, she was drawn back to the feeling of calm that had filled her.

〰

Now Vanessa was a junior. Her sister was away at college, and she had her own room and plenty of privacy these days. But now she wanted privacy so she could cut. She wasn't addicted, she just liked the way it made her feel. She chose to do it. She'd also chosen to start throwing up after she ate so she could fit into a size four. Cutting helped her realize she could do hard things—like make herself throw up. It wasn't that difficult, really, and it was much easier to hide than starving yourself. She ate with everyone else and then excused herself. It was perfectly normal.

She liked the way her body looked, how she could see its angles and sharp spots. But she kept this a secret too, concealed under her hoodies and soccer sweats. She liked having a part of herself that was all her own.

When her family sat down to dinner together, her parents made up for all the days they worked late by peppering her with questions: "Did you do your practicing? Is your homework finished? Have you done your chores? What do you want to be when you grow up? What colleges will you apply for?"

They wanted updates on her school day, what she thought about current events, and was she still enjoying soccer? After each of the boys shared about their days, they'd ask, "Vanessa, do you remember being their age? Any advice you could offer? Have you talked to your sister lately? It's important to let her know we're thinking about her. Include her in our lives."

Vanessa answered question after question, said "please" and "thank you," reported on her classes and homework and in the back of her mind tracked the minutes until she could be alone.

# 14

# the pep talk

A WEEK LATER, JILL WAS feeling cautiously optimistic about her relationship with Jake. He'd volunteered to take Henry and his friends trick-or-treating and even surprised her in her classroom, offering to help take down the Halloween decorations. Maybe Matt was right—they just needed time. She was also less worried about Vanessa, who had come back to class after only missing three days. She'd had a cold, proving Jill had worried about nothing. She scolded herself for seeing problems where none existed.

While things were on an upswing, it seemed like a good time for the family talk she'd been thinking about ever since the last faculty meeting, but with a different tack. Instead of talking about drugs and drinking and all the things the kids shouldn't do, they'd have a family pep talk. Like the ones her swim coach used to give in high school.

Matt believed the kids would confide in them if they needed advice, but Jill wasn't so sure. When she was a teenager, her dad knew almost nothing about her private life, and she never offered anything up. With her own children, she wanted to be proactive. This was an opportunity to not only unify their family but also instill confidence in the boys.

During her lunch period, she put her thoughts down on paper. Obviously, she wouldn't read notes as though giving a presentation. That would be weird. But she did want to make sure she covered everything that had been on her mind.

She tapped her pen to her lips as she considered the most important points. They can do hard things. In difficult situations, she and Matt could help them. Don't get discouraged. Life gets easier to navigate as you get older. Like sports. You need to practice at soccer to get better at it. At first, it's hard to kick a ball or intercept a pass. But with practice, you got better, and after years of practice, it came naturally. Someday Henry would be as good as Jake on the soccer field—if that's what he chose to pursue. She should mention he didn't have to do soccer just because Jake did. He might want to explore other things. And Jake might try something else as well. But whatever they chose, they should give it their all. She flipped to a fresh piece of paper.

*#1. Hard Things.* And *Soccer* as her keyword. After staring for a minute, she ripped off another piece of paper, deciding it would be best to write out her thoughts in full and use this short list as a reminder.

*#2. Life will give you choices. Sometimes you'll wish you made a different choice. But we'll be there for you, no matter what. And hard things often turn into beautiful experiences.* She paused. It seemed absurd to think that from Connor's death something beautiful would emerge. She crossed that part out and wrote, *You will get through hard things, and you will be stronger.* She underlined *will* in each instance. But that didn't feel right either. The pain in her sliced heart reminded her every day that she would never be unbroken. She crossed out *you will be stronger.*

*#3. It's normal to have bad days. It's normal to be upset from time to time. It's also okay to laugh and have good days.* Did she believe that? Had she laughed since Connor died? She never wanted to laugh again. But she wanted her kids to be happy. Of course she did.

*#4. If you ever need to talk—about sad or happy things—I'm available to listen.* She should also acknowledge, especially to Henry, that it might be hard to see Mommy crying. But she didn't want him to be afraid to talk to her, even if he thought it would make her sad.

With the pep talk's main points outlined, Jill's mind turned to dinner. She planned to make everyone's favorite—chicken enchiladas. Cornbread too. Good food would put them in the right mood to sit around the table a little longer and listen. And as insurance for good behavior, she'd serve dessert. It would keep them happy while she gave her speech—her pep talk.

On the way home from school, she ran into the store to pick up ice cream. Walking briskly through the frozen section, she selected Oreo. But at the end of the aisle, the chocolate syrup caught her eye. She stopped. A sundae bar would be more fun—ice cream and an assortment of toppings. Yes, that was a better idea. She turned back and swapped Oreo for vanilla. Then a carton of chocolate too. Balancing the two on top of each other, she grabbed the chocolate syrup with her free hand. Making her way to the cookie aisle, she placed the syrup on top of both cartons of ice cream, leaning all three against her chest to steady the tower, and added a bag of Oreos. She crossed the aisle to the candies for gummy bears and, with her last two available fingers, reached for peanut butter cups.

Willing her precariously positioned foods not to fall, she carefully approached the checkout, where she dropped everything onto the belt, breathing a sigh of relief.

"Looks like you're having a party," the cashier cheerfully commented as she examined the bag of gummy bears before scanning it through. Her name tag, adorned with a pink unicorn sticker, read "Paige."

"Let's hope my kids think so," Jill replied.

"You must have lots of them," Paige said as she held up both cartons of ice cream, raising her barely-there eyebrows. "Somebody's birthday?"

Jill scrutinized Paige, wondering why suddenly you had to have lots of kids to enjoy two flavors of ice cream and a few toppings. "Do you have lots of kids, Paige?"

"Three. But they're all grown. I'll be a grandma soon."

Jill swiped her card. "I've got seven." She picked up the bag and cackled as she walked away. She wasn't sure why she said it. It was none of Paige's business after all.

When Matt came home from work that evening, she followed him up to their room, and while he changed into casual clothes, she told him about her plan. Of course, she didn't use the words "pep talk." That was her own private way of thinking about it. "Family meeting" seemed more appropriate.

He hung up his jacket. "Are you sure we should do this all together?" he asked. "Shouldn't we talk to the kids individually?"

Jill chewed on her thumbnail. Speaking to them on their own did sound like a good idea. A chance for a conversation—what she was actually encouraging. But she'd already made the plan. And had ice cream. "I'm worried if we try to talk to Jake privately, he'll feel cornered."

Matt sat on the floor to tie his tennis shoes. "But Henry and Jake are such different ages. Any issues they have will be different. I think it's a good idea. I just wish I had more time to think about what I'd like to add."

She took his hand. "I've got this! I've put a lot of thought into it. We'll keep it light but also a real heart-to-heart." Just like the talks her coach gave before important matches back in her swim team days.

After dinner, Jill was prepared. She'd committed to memory the order of topics so she wouldn't leave anything out. As the boys cleared their dishes, she announced, "I've got ice cream for dessert. A sundae bar, in fact. Henry, get the spoons. Jake, will you get the bowls?"

"Yay!" Henry shouted. "Did you get Oreo?"

"What are we doing?" Jake asked, his eyes narrow with suspicion.

"We just want to talk to you about something important," Jill replied.

Henry and Jake shared a skeptical look and Jill strengthened her resolve.

After the boys scooped heaps of both chocolate and vanilla ice cream into bowls and doused the mounds with treats and chocolate syrup, Jill crushed two Oreos on top of vanilla for herself, then sat next to Matt and squeezed his knee. Black Oreo dust spotted his pants, and his soft groan flustered her for a second.

Nevertheless, she began. "We've been through something terrible this year. But even if we hadn't, I'd still want to have this talk."

Jake was shoveling ice cream into his mouth, eyes focused on his green bowl as if divining an important message in its contents. Henry pinched two gummy bears between each thumb and pointer, engaged in an imaginary conversation.

"When we go through hard things," Jill said, raising her voice just a bit, "it's important to know you can keep moving forward. Sometimes even getting out of bed can be difficult, but we do it. And everything will eventually become easier." This wasn't exactly what she planned to say, but close enough. She looked at Matt but couldn't read his expression. She continued, "As you get older, you get better at learning how to do hard things."

Jake was studying his bowl so intently that Jill wondered if there actually was something interesting inside. Henry popped one gummy bear into his mouth, then spat it out and stuck it on the rim of his bowl. Jill's mind went blank. She tried to remember the outline.

"Henry and Jake . . ." She waited, but they didn't respond. "Henry. Jake." Henry picked up his bowl and licked chocolate syrup that had dripped down the side. "Jake, I need to know you're listening."

He rolled his eyes. "I'm listening. You have a hard time getting out of bed. Your life is hard."

Jill faltered. "Actually, I was saying we've *all* been through something hard, but it will get easier. For instance, Henry, you practice soccer so you can get better. Jake's played for many years and with all that practice, he's really good now."

This didn't sound at all like what she'd intended. She racked her brain trying to remember what practicing soccer had to do with Connor's death. Certainly not practicing at getting used to dying. Her heart picked up its pace.

Thankfully, Matt intervened. "When you play soccer, or any sport, sometimes you win, but often you lose. No one likes to lose, but you can learn a lot from it. You learn what you need to improve on. And how to empathize with other people. You learn losing isn't the end of the world. The best players don't let it get them down."

"Right." Jill nodded, collecting herself and smiling at Matt. "And also, we're here for you. Both Mom and Dad. If you ever need to talk about anything, or you've made some choices you regret, you can talk to us. We can help you."

Jake's phone vibrated and they listened to his one-word responses to whoever was calling. "Yep. Yep. Right now. Yeah." He ended his call and got up from the table. "We're done, right?"

"Not really." Jill inhaled and smiled. "I still need a minute. Did you hear what I said before your call?"

"Yeah, you think I'm making decisions I'll regret, and I should talk to you about it."

She furrowed her brow. "No, that's not what I said. That's not what I meant at all." She took another deep breath. "We all make bad decisions sometimes, but that's okay. That's part of life. Mom and Dad are here to help."

Jake glared back at her. "What bad decisions do you think I've made? I'm actually a pretty good kid. No matter what you think."

She put her hand on his arm. "I do think you're a good kid. I'm not saying you've made bad decisions."

"Then why are we having this big talk?"

"Because . . ." She couldn't remember. Her mind, her notes, and her outline betrayed her, leaving her entirely speechless.

Henry stood on his chair reaching across the table for more Oreos. He smashed them in his fist and let them drop into his bowl. "Mom!" he shouted. "Can you find me a green and a yellow gummy bear? Actually, six of them?"

Jake pulled away. "I have to go. Sam's here. We're studying for a test."

"I'm just trying to let you know that if you ever want to talk, I want to listen."

As he strolled to the front door, Jake brushed off his arm where she'd just touched him as if wiping off her germs.

Jill turned to Matt, her shoulders limp. His eyes were wide, a silent "I told you so" while he shook his head. Jill slumped into her chair.

"Mommy," Henry shouted. "Green and yellow! Hurry! Before I finish my ice cream!"

She plopped the bag in front of him and pressed her fingers to her forehead. She did not know how to do this. Raising a teen. She was tempted to call her dad. Ask his advice. But she wouldn't. Wouldn't give him the satisfaction of needing his help.

# 15

## fast and furious

THE NEXT MORNING, MATT SLID a hand toward Jill's side of the bed, hoping for her comfort after a fitful night's sleep. But she was gone, up early even on a Saturday, and the sheets were cold. He sighed. Even the days she lingered, there was never heat between them anymore. Was this their new forever?

He stretched, then climbed out of bed and parted the curtains. Gray and cloudy once again, like it had been all week, ever since November began. Figures. He considered going for a run, but the cold and gloom crushed his enthusiasm. Instead, he trudged downstairs in his pajamas, where Jill was sitting on the couch with a book. Minutes ago he was hoping she'd still be lying next to him, but now that they were face-to-face, she was the last person he wanted to be with. Her paranoia about that student, Vanessa. The terrible family speech last night that made no sense. My God, was she *trying* to get Jake to hate her? She'd gone from practically comatose all summer to full tilt the last few months. It was exhausting.

She gave him a smile and he tried to muster up some compassion. Maybe he could get her outside and help expend some of that pent-up energy she was harboring. "Want to go for a run?" he asked.

"Not today," she said, tucking the book under a pillow. "I've got papers to correct a little later, but this morning I'm just reading." She reluctantly moved the pillow and motioned to the title on the cover: *Life After Grief.* "Someone dropped it off months ago. Thought I'd see what it says. What are you doing today?"

And without giving it a second thought, Matt lied. He told Jill he had to catch up on work at the office and would be gone for a couple of hours. He did need a day—or a week—to catch up. He was falling behind, which kept him tossing and turning at night. But today was not that day. He just wasn't up for it.

He kept up the ruse by putting on a dress shirt and jeans and tossing his computer bag in the car. He didn't know where he was going, but he had to get away.

After the accident, the other partners at Matt's accounting firm stepped in when he took a month off. Everyone had said, "Take as much time as you need. We've got you covered." But by the end of July, when he went back to the office and was desperate to be busy—to be buried in a mountain of paperwork—he couldn't focus and simply didn't care. He didn't worry about it in the beginning, his drive would come back to him in due time and his partners had been happy to help. But by October, when even looming tax deadlines couldn't motivate him, he recognized his lack of productivity might turn into a bigger issue.

Easing into the right lane, he veered onto the freeway, relieved to be alone. Jill was driving him insane, Jake was moody, and Henry talked non-stop. A year ago, Jill confided that Henry's never-ending dialogue was becoming annoying, and they laughed together as they strategized ways to pretend she was listening. They'd even practiced using her hair to hide her AirPods. He put them in his ears too, to see if they really blocked out all sound, and he kept them in the rest of the evening, smiling and nodding whenever she tried to get his attention. She laughed and playfully swatted at him.

If their life were a movie, he would have pulled her to him and kissed her passionately, grateful for their perfect life and affectionate romance. But it wasn't a movie. They'd had no idea their happy life was on borrowed time. Instead, he'd continued teasing her until she'd gotten annoyed and they'd both gone to bed angry.

The roads were still damp from the morning rain, coating his windshield with a fine layer of grime. He turned on the wipers to clear his view and realized he was headed toward the lake.

This jolted him as much as if he'd had a close encounter with one of the many trucks lumbering up the canyon. Did he really want to go back to the lake? It seemed both dreadful and cathartic all at once. Would Jill be mad that he went without her? He gripped the steering wheel. She hadn't mentioned wanting to go. He'd never thought of it himself, before now. Was it wrong not to share this together? Did he care?

For several weeks after the accident, whenever they opened their front door, flowers, notes, and meals were waiting for them, left surreptitiously so as not to disturb them in their grief. Which was thoughtful, he supposed, but not necessary. He wouldn't have minded talking to a friend and having a real conversation. And then suddenly, it all stopped. Summer was in full swing for the rest of the world, The Miller Family Tragedy safely in the past.

Matt remembered back to a morning about a month after Connor's funeral, when Henry had wanted milk with breakfast, but they were out. For the first time in weeks, Jill got dressed, determined to go to the store. But as soon as she slipped on her sandals, she became teary, which quickly turned to sobs. Matt held her while she cried, then took the keys from her hand, threw on a ball cap and went to the store himself.

Leaving with a gallon of milk and two boxes of cereal, he ran into his friend Blake. Matt waved, intending to keep walking, but Blake stopped him. He grabbed Matt's elbow and put his other hand on his shoulder. "Matt," he began, and Matt braced himself. His mind raced for how to respond to the inevitable "How are you?" But even as he flipped through his mental catalogue, the question changed from anything he'd heard previously. "How is Jill doing?" Just Jill.

"She's hanging in there," he'd said, nodding. "Thanks for asking." And he turned to go.

"Will you send her our love?" Blake called after him.

Matt lifted the bag of groceries in response.

He hadn't thought much about it until a day or two later, when his own mom called to check in, and her first question was, "Tell me about Jill. Is she managing?"

From then on, just one month after he buried his son, his name was dropped from the concern and sympathy flag. From then on, it was directed only toward Jill. They'd both lost a child. There was a gaping hole in their family, in their home, and in both of their hearts. The smash of grief broadsided him when he least expected it. But starting that month, he took the cue from neighbors, friends and even his mom—it was time to man up and be strong.

Recalling these memories made Matt's chest tighten, and he turned up the volume of his music to drown out the voices in his head until arriving at the gates of the state park. He slowed the car and killed the music as he drove the familiar road where pine trees lined the road and blocked any view until rounding the corner near the boat ramp. There the road widened, and the expansive lake appeared before him. However, instead of a shining blue, the water was gray and ominous. In late fall, fishermen who liked their solitude and weren't afraid of frosty temperatures could be sighted close to shore. But today, even the fishermen stayed home; the bark of the harsh wind warned everyone away.

Branches whipped as Matt pulled into the parking lot, just like Before. On that day, after Jill convinced her dad to go back into the storm, he and Jake waited inside the marina lobby. Bright green Adirondack chairs invited them to recline as if relaxing during a pleasant afternoon shower. But they perched uncomfortably on the edges, noses next to the rain-smeared windows, repeating one sentence: "Can you see anything?"

A police car had pulled into the parking lot. No sirens, only red and blue lights reflecting off the glass where they waited. They stopped talking after that. Boats rocked in their slips. The dock heaved.

Minutes later, an ambulance arrived and both he and Jake were out the door, running toward the dock, the emergency team beating them there just as a boat entered the no-wake zone. A yellow boat. Not Roger's. Five EMTs stood side by side as the boat got closer. Radios crackled but Matt couldn't make out any words. Someone placed bumpers on the dock's edge to soften the hit as the boat came in, and two paramedics jumped on board, blocking Matt's view. He stood on his toes and thought he saw Gina. When he sighted Roger, he pushed his way through the crowd but was stopped in his tracks by the appearance of a backboard with a white bundle strapped to it being hoisted onto a gurney. He'd called out—screamed out—asking who was hurt. But his heart knew who was missing. His brain had done the math, made the calculation, but was slow to upload the answer, giving him another second of life before everything changed forever. He locked eyes with Jill and soon they were sprinting side by side, joining the race to the ambulance.

Now devoid of both people and boats, the empty dock below him was in stark opposition to the commotion of that afternoon, and Matt wanted to think through everything that had happened, sitting in the spot where everything had changed. Alone.

Whitecaps covered the lake and debris blew across the parking lot. Raindrops appeared on his windshield. He zipped his jacket up to his chin. As he opened his car door, the wind grabbed it, as if trying to yank it away. He wrenched it back, slamming the door shut, furious at the wind for trying to take something that was his.

Enraged, he started the engine and revved backward, flipping the car around and squealing onto the road. He hated this cold, hollow place. He turned up the stereo, maxing the volume, feeling the beat reverb through his body—so loud the lyrics thundered into his brain, drowning everything else out. Once on the freeway, he stepped on the gas, quickly accelerating to ninety mph. Abandoning caution was exhilarating. Just because a road sign displayed a number didn't mean he had to follow it. In his euphoria, he took his speed over a hundred. He raced along, music blasting, weaving through traffic, feeling more in control than he had in a long, long time.

He dared a cop to pull him over and entertained the idea of giving chase. How fast could his BMW go? He'd never actually pushed it to its max. The speedometer inched past 105.

Singing along to a classic from his college days, he banged out the beat on the steering wheel, remembering days when he was young, drinking on a rooftop with his three best buddies, playing guitars and singing this same song at the top of their lungs, none of them caring that it was the early hours of the morning. They were twenty years old, anything was possible, and they were invincible. His best friend, George, jumped on top of a wooden picnic table, and they joined him, singing and pumping their fists in the air. Someone across the street yelled at them to shut up, so they sang even louder.

Ten years ago, George had gotten divorced after an overdose. After years of relapses, he was now sober. Devin was a lawyer in a small town, settled with a host of kids and even horses. Jon was a preacher who played music at a local church. He'd tried to recruit Matt to play guitar with him for the youth groups, but Matt had declined. *Would it kill him to step in a church once in a while to support his friend?* He slowed the car to a respectable eighty mph. The repetitious chorus and incessant bass were giving him a headache. He turned the stereo off.

He wondered if he would ever cry again. More than just the single tear that made an appearance at the most unexpected times. Sometimes he yearned for the gasping and heaving of those first weeks that he'd tried so hard to squelch. If he could just weep one more time it might clear the constant ache squeezing his chest. Just once more to release the knot in his gut. But trying to force tears left him feeling, well, lonely. Maybe he'd worked so hard to suppress them that he'd lost the power to soften his pain.

He headed home. His family needed him. He needed to save Jake from Jill. Really, Jake and Jill from each other. Was this what the rest of his life would look like?

# 16

## jake's room

AFTER MATT LEFT FOR THE office, *on a Saturday, no less,* Jill put her book away and started her own chores. Her rule was that if the kids brought their dirty clothes to the laundry room, she'd wash and fold them; the boys only needed to put them away. But when she dumped Jake's basket, two folded T-shirts and three pairs of folded socks tumbled out from underneath his dirty clothes. *Seriously? All he has to do is put the folded clothes away. It isn't hard.*

She marched into his dark bedroom—pitch black, even now at eleven in the morning. Still hurting after being so misunderstood last night at the awful family meeting—angry at how disrespectful he was—she threw open the curtains, not caring that he would get mad. She expected to see him in the jumble of blankets piled on his bed and was ready to deliver a lecture on gratitude, but he wasn't there. She stepped back into the hall and listened at the closed bathroom door. He was in the shower.

She scanned his room. Shoes and socks lay on the floor as well as a pile of clothes next to his closet. But other than that, it was surprisingly clean. Books and papers were organized on his desk beside a trophy from a winning soccer season back in seventh grade. A poster of the solar system hung above his bed with a planetarium bumper sticker thumbtacked underneath: "Failure Is Not An Option." Both had been there since he was in third grade.

Opening his dresser drawer, she put the clean socks and T-shirts away, then lifted the stack to look underneath, wondering if she'd find . . . what exactly? She'd only ever hid folded up notes in her bedroom drawers, wanting to keep her latest crush or her use of swear words hidden. But kids didn't have notes to hide these days. They just texted and sent Snapchats and TikToks and who knew what else. Parents had to read their kids' texts to find out any juicy gossip, and that was only if their kids didn't delete messages first. Had she and Matt talked to Jake lately about using social media responsibly? It was Matt's turn for the next parent talk. Last night was a disaster.

She lifted a T-shirt from the clothes on the floor and gave it the sniff test. Clean. Throwing it over her shoulder, the fire of her son's ingratitude flamed again. The whole pile seemed clean. But when she held up a pair of pants, it was easy to see they were way too short for Jake. They were two months into the school year, and she realized she'd never taken him shopping for new clothes. He'd probably outgrown most of what he owned. Just one more thing she couldn't get right this year.

Stooping over, she peeked under his bed, again not really sure what she was looking for. She reached for a half-empty Gatorade bottle and some candy wrappers and saw a neatly folded brown paper grocery sack tucked between his headboard and the wall. The placement was definitely intentional—out of sight but easy to reach. There was a book or a narrow box in it. She looked behind her, wondering if she dared to pull it out now, before he got out of the shower. No, she'd wait until he was gone. *What are you hiding, Jake?*

His low voice from behind startled her. "What are you doing?"

She jumped up. Jake had a towel loosely wrapped around his waist, his chin length hair dripping wet. "I . . ." she faltered.

"Can you leave? I need to get dressed."

"Do these things not fit?" She pointed at the heap of clothes.

He shook his head. "Nope. Go. So I can put clothes on."

She didn't move. "When you're dressed, do you want me to help you go through your stuff? We could clean out your closets and I could take you shopping." Shopping together and organizing closets was just the kind of project Jill liked. They could spend a little one-on-one time together and maybe he'd even open up about his feelings.

He adjusted his towel. "I have plans today."

Jill moved toward the door but tried again. "We could go later. Or tomorrow. Do you want to get some stuff for your room? Like a new poster or something?"

"Mom! Leave!"

As she shut the door, Jake's music exploded behind her.

While she folded clothes in the laundry room, she contemplated how she could regain Jake's trust—get him to confide in her. She'd always wished her mom was easier to talk to. The type who understood teenage concerns and offered advice. When she was young, Jill imagined lying with her head on her mom's lap, spilling about friends and drama, teachers she liked, the annoying things boys did. And sharing her goals for swim team, like beating the school record.

But when Jill and her two siblings—Todd and Cara— showed up every other week, her mom's initial joy—throwing her arms around them and holding them close the first day—diminished by day two to exasperation that they didn't know how to sweep the floor correctly and frustration by the third that Jill had borrowed her mascara and not put it back. Listening and sharing were rare and never therapeutic. By the end of the week, Jill couldn't wait to get back to her dad's house because he was so much more easygoing.

Jill reveled in holding her kids while they talked about their lives. She was nailing motherhood. But over the past year—even before Connor died—Jake had changed. He gave one-word answers and never offered up information. Before long, Jill ran out of questions to ask.

"Mom," Jake said, interrupting her thoughts.

She spun around.

"Sam wants to go to the skate shop. Will you take us?"

Jill thought about everything she wanted to get done today, including getting into his room to see what was in that sack under his bed. Shopping together for new clothes sounded fun. Chauffeuring him and Sam to the skateboard shop did not. She wanted time with Jake alone.

"When do you want to go?"

"Right now. Sam wants to buy a bunch of stuff. I want to look at a new deck."

"If Sam is buying a bunch of stuff, shouldn't his mom take you? And do you really want to spend your money on a new deck? They're expensive, aren't they? Isn't the one you have good enough?"

"You said . . ." He blinked instead of finishing his sentence. He was several inches taller than her now and his bangs flopped in front of one eye. She reached out to brush it aside, but he stepped back, adjusting a backpack slung over his shoulder. He turned away. "Fine."

"Before you go anywhere, let's box up your clothes that are too small. It won't take long, and your room will look tidier."

He didn't turn around. "I'll do it when I get back."

"I've got mad cleaning skills," she joked.

Jake shook his head and jogged down the stairs. "Nope, I'm good."

She swapped clothes between the washer and dryer. A penny fell onto the floor, tails side up. Unlucky. As soon as she heard the front door open, she dashed to his room. The sack was gone.

She bit her knuckle as she sat back on her heels. So, he *was* hiding something. But where did he move it to? The front door slammed, jarring her back to reality. He'd asked for a ride to the skateboard shop—literally handed her the opportunity to spend time with him—and she'd failed to see it.

"Jake!" she shouted as she ran down the stairs. She tripped on the last one, almost falling. Regaining her balance, she rushed to open the front door. "I'll take you!"

He was on the front path, almost at the sidewalk, his skateboard under his arm.

"I'll take you! I wasn't thinking back there."

He threw his board on the ground, and without looking up, said, "Sam's mom is taking us. Sorry I even asked."

As he skated away, she chastised herself, promising she wouldn't be so oblivious next time.

⚊

In an effort to make up for her flub with Jake, Jill determined to show Vanessa extra care—find a way to mentor her. And if she could do that for Vanessa, maybe there was someone in Jake's life who could make a special connection with him.

Another teacher, perhaps, or his soccer coach? Even another mom. Anyone.

When the bell rang at the end of class on Monday, Jill asked Vanessa to stay. Vanessa's friends gave her a look and nudged her on their way out the door.

"Hi!" Jill exclaimed too loudly and too brightly. She tried to tone it down. "It's nothing big, I just noticed you did really well on your latest test, even though you were absent that week. I wanted to say good job."

The ends of Vanessa's fingers were barely visible, nervously pulling her hoodie strings tighter. She was clearly confused at the extra attention. "I didn't cheat."

"No!" Jill blurted, again much too loud for a two-person conversation. "I didn't think you did! I just wanted to say keep up the good work!"

A wrinkle developed between Vanessa's dark eyebrows. "Thank you?"

"Yes! Well, again, good job!"

Vanessa's eyes moved toward the door.

"I shouldn't keep you." Jill sensed she was waiting to be excused. "I know you have to get to your next class."

Vanessa turned to go, and Jill made a last-ditch effort to show support, remembering Jake had told her she was on the girls' soccer team. "Good luck in your game tomorrow! I'll be cheering for you."

Vanessa turned back; her guarded expression now transformed with delight. "You're coming to the game?"

Jill hesitated. She'd meant she'd be cheering for her metaphorically. She was going to Jake's game which was also after school, but across town. But now she couldn't say no. Vanessa was clearly hoping she'd come. She could probably go to a few minutes of Vanessa's, then make it to Jake's before the end of the first half. "Yes! What number are you?"

A grin danced at the corners of her mouth. "I'm twelve. I don't play very much."

"That's okay. I'll be there."

Jill was smiling on the outside, but inside she was computing logistics, figuring out whose house Henry could play at after school since she couldn't meet him at home, and how long it would take to get to Jake's game. She had to time it just right so she didn't let any of them down.

# 17

## games everyone plays

JILL SAT ALONE AT THE top of the bleachers, experiencing a conundrum each time Vanessa's team made a play. Was it weird if she cheered? Was five months since Connor's death too soon to whistle and clap at a sporting event? Was it weird if she didn't? She looked at her watch. She'd stayed the whole first half and Vanessa hadn't left the bench. She calculated how late she'd be to Jake's soccer game if she stayed just a few minutes into the second half to see if Vanessa would play.

Matt called just as both teams took their places on the field, including Vanessa. "I just arrived at Jake's game," he said. "Are you almost here? They're starting soon."

Jill hadn't told Matt about her plan to get to know Vanessa better. He'd been distant ever since last weekend when the pep-talk night went awry. *You're failing to connect with your own kid,* she imagined he'd say. *The last thing you need is to take on another one.* She hoped the piercing sounds of refs' whistles and fans' shouts wouldn't give her away. "I haven't left school yet," she answered, which was truthful. "I've got something I need to do, but I won't be long."

"Just another few minutes, right? He'll only play the first half or the second. Not the whole game."

"I know. Yes, I'll see you soon." She hung up. Vanessa was looking toward the bleachers. Looking for her? Jill raised her hand and waved, and Vanessa gave a slight wave back. While the other girls played in shorts, Vanessa wore leggings and a long-sleeved shirt under her uniform.

Jill checked her watch again. It would take fifteen minutes to get to Jake's field. She really needed to leave. But she also wanted to tell Vanessa she saw her make a play. After ten minutes without Vanessa getting any action, Jill couldn't wait any longer and made her way down the metal stairs. And then Vanessa finally got the ball. She took it downfield and passed it to a teammate who kicked it into the goal. Without overthinking, Jill cheered.

She heard her name and turned toward a petite woman with straight, dark, chin-length hair and a brightly colored purse over her arm.

"Ms. Miller, I'm not sure you remember me, but I'm Gayle Stuart, Vanessa's mom. I just wanted to tell you she really enjoys having you as a teacher."

"Oh, wow!" Jill was taken aback. "Thank you for saying so!" She faltered. Should she confide her suspicions? No. That needed to be a much longer conversation than she had time for, and the soccer stadium wasn't the place.

Gayle smiled. "It's nice when kids see their teachers care about them. Teenagers can be hard—I don't have to tell you that. I know you have a lot of students to keep track of. But Vanessa talks about your class—and you. And I wanted you to know I appreciate you."

Jill touched Gayle on the arm. "She's a wonderful student and a great girl. Tell her congratulations on her assist."

As they parted ways, Jill looked at her watch. How had twenty minutes passed so quickly? She calculated her drive time and prayed that Jake was playing the second half. Instead of soaking in the praise she'd just received, she was annoyed with herself. She'd never meant to be so late for Jake's game. She should have been upfront with Vanessa. What was wrong with her?

Jill scooted into the bleacher next to Matt just as Jake's half-time ended.

He glanced at her. "Where have you been? Jake played the whole first half."

She moved close so their arms were touching. "That's great! How'd he do?"

Matt kept his eyes on the field even though play hadn't started yet. "Great. He had an assist and a goal." His voice was cool.

"Amazing! I'm so sad I missed it."

"Why did you miss it?" he asked, bending forward as if not wanting to hear the answer.

Jill kept her tone light but moved a fraction away so there was space between them. She couldn't tell him the full truth. He'd think she chose a student over her son—and it wasn't exactly like that. He wouldn't understand how complicated it was. "I had something I was finishing up and then a parent stopped to talk. Believe me, I tried to get here sooner."

As Matt had predicted, Jake was on the sidelines the whole second half. Matt kept the space between himself and Jill, exaggerating his cheers for the team, but only giving one-word answers when she asked him questions. Ironically, he'd missed a lot of the kids' games and school performances over the years. And it was rare when he was on time. Now he's suddenly Mr. Perfect Dad, and she's Ms. Thoughtless because she'd arrived late.

When the game ended, Jill and Matt waited for Jake on the grass, not speaking until he ran over. Matt gave him a high five. "That was so awesome! You were fantastic!"

Jill gave him a hug. "Congratulations!"

Jake was all smiles.

"Mom missed the first half, so she didn't see your goal," Matt said, "but I explained it to her play-by-play. She was super excited."

Jill swung around, her mouth open.

A teammate interrupted, patting Jake on the back. Then more encircled him, celebrating the post-game victory.

Jill narrowed her eyes at Matt. He smiled back, acting innocent.

"Excuse me!" she whispered. "Why did you have to say that?"

"Say what?"

"Tell him that I wasn't here. Bring it to his attention."

"Well, you weren't." Matt shrugged.

"Did you need to point it out, especially right now?"

"Were you planning on lying about it?"

More families walked past. She faked a smile as they congratulated one another. Matt good-naturedly slapped a friend on the back and shook his hand, chatting about the defense and various plays. Rolling up her blanket and then rummaging through her purse, Jill tried to look busy to avoid conversation.

"Jake," she shouted so he'd hear. "Do you have a ride home when the bus drops you back at school?" He gave her a thumbs-up while still talking with his friend. She watched them walk across the field toward the bus together, then she went in the opposite direction, toward the parking lot.

Matt caught up to her. "I'll see you at home."

She gave him a sidelong glance and shook her head.

"What?" he asked, seemingly oblivious.

"I'm angry, that's what."

"It wasn't that big of a deal. Don't be mad."

Jill dropped the blanket on the ground behind her car and fumbled for her keys. "It's like you're trying to prove to him that you're a better parent than me."

"Hey, you're overreacting. I was here, and you weren't, and I told Jake I'd filled you in. That's it."

"That's my point. You were trying to make sure he knew you were here, and also making sure he knew I wasn't." She opened the trunk and threw the blanket inside.

"Well, I care about Jake, and it hurts him when you're not there for him."

Jill whirled around and hissed, "So you pointedly made sure he knew I wasn't there. Which is what I'm saying. You know it hurts him and for some reason it makes you feel good telling him *I* hurt him, but you didn't."

Matt rolled his eyes and threw his hands in the air. "Oh brother. Why would I do that?" He turned away. "See you at home."

Jill slammed the trunk, the thud echoing through her body. Tears pricked at her eyes. Someone touched her on the arm and she jumped.

"Hey, Jill, it's good to see you." It was Priscilla.

Jill tried to blink the tears away, but some escaped, rolling down her cheek. Priscilla, who sent notes and often dropped by after the accident, even though Jill always ignored the doorbell. She quickly wiped her eyes.

Priscilla pulled Jill into a forceful hug. "Oh, Jill! I'm so sorry! Does it still hurt all the time? It must hit when you're least expecting it."

*These damn tears*! Jill's face was smashed against Priscilla's shoulder, and her arms were trapped between their two bodies, so she couldn't properly hug her back. She tried to shake her head but ended up rubbing her face back and forth along Priscilla's yellow cashmere sweater. "I'm fine, really," she said, hoping her muffled voice could be heard. She pulled back to send the hint that she was ready to be released, but Priscilla continued squeezing her close. Jill relaxed, whispering, "I guess, for the rest of my life, I'll never know if I'm on the brink of tears."

Priscilla grasped her shoulders so they could look at each other. "It will get easier. It will! It just takes time. We're all here for you, Jill. If you aren't up for coming to the games, we'll cheer for Jake! This team is a family!"

Heat rose into Jill's cheeks. "I think I'll be able to come. I just... I just got stuck at school which made me late. I really want to be there for Jake."

Priscilla grabbed both of Jill's hands, pressing them between her own. "He must be going through such a hard time himself. It's hard being the mom, right? Taking care of everyone? And no one takes care of you. Of course, Matt is amazing, I'm sure. You're a great team, the two of you. You're going to get through this."

Jill couldn't hold back the flood of tears that her words triggered. *Dammit! Why am I crying in front of chatty Priscilla?*

"Oh, I've hit a sensitive chord! You go ahead and cry!"

She clutched her again, but Jill's arms were free this time and she awkwardly grabbed a fistful of sweater as they embraced. Looking over Priscilla's shoulder, she saw Matt's car drive by and his head turn, watching the two of them as he passed.

Jill managed to break free. "Oh, Priscilla, I really need to go."

"I'm bringing dinner by this week." She touched her arm. "What night would be most helpful?"

"You don't need to do that."

"I'm doing it. Thursday night. I'll drop it off at five. Jill, we love you. Don't you ever forget it!" She kissed her cheek before leaving, her ankle boots clapping on the pavement as she walked away.

Jill sat in the car, locked the doors, and laid her head on the steering wheel. She hadn't been touched that much in five months. Priscilla's perfume lingered and she took a deep breath, inhaling the spicy scent. The smell was comforting, and while those hugs were awkward and originally unwelcome, if she closed her eyes, she could still feel their warmth.

⁓

Priscilla was true to her word, and two days later brought a lasagna, garlic bread, green beans, and another hug. Jill popped the meal into the oven to keep it warm, wondering where Jake was. He should have been home from practice already.

Over the past couple of days, she'd searched his room when he wasn't home, but never found the brown paper sack. Its possible contents preyed on her thoughts. Porn? Marijuana? What was he hiding? Just then the front door slammed, and she heard heavy footsteps jogging up the stairs.

"Jake!" she yelled, hoping to catch him before he was out of earshot. "Jake!" she shouted again as the slam of his bedroom door echoed down to her. She called his phone. "I need you in the kitchen, please."

"I need a minute."

Ten minutes later he appeared, hanging on the doorframe as if he didn't intend to stay long.

"Where've you been?"

"Practice."

"After practice?"

"With friends. What's the big deal?"

"Nothing. I think it's great you were with friends. I just need you to tell me where you are and if you'll be home late."

"Why?" His wide eyes and little smirk told her he thought she was being ridiculous.

She tried to ignore the look and took a stack of dishes from the cupboard. "Because that's part of living in a family. I worry if I don't know where you are."

"Why do you always think I'm doing something wrong?"

Jill rolled her eyes and handed him a stack of dishes. "Can you set the table, please?"

"I saw you roll your eyes," he said as he put a plate in each spot.

"I didn't."

"Yes, you did. I saw you. You know what? You have no idea what's going on in my life. You say you want to spend time together or support me or whatever, but you didn't even come to my soccer game."

She shook her head. "I was late because I was busy at school. Between you, Henry, Dad, worrying about a hundred kids at school, and getting dinner on the table, I'm swamped."

"You didn't even make this dinner, Priscilla did. You told us this morning she was bringing dinner. So why are you lying?"

"Jake, I'm not lying."

"You said making dinner was making you swamped. But you didn't make the dinner. That's lying. And maybe, if you weren't so focused on Vanessa all the time, you'd have more time to care about your own kids."

"Why are you bringing Vanessa into this? I care about you, Jake. That's exactly what I'm trying to say. And because I care, sometimes I worry. Especially if I don't know where you are."

"You're worrying about the wrong things!" He slammed his fist on the table, making Jill jump. "You're always mad at me." His voice was shrill, and Jill realized he was about to cry. But in an instant his tone changed to mimicking her own. "Jake, your room's not clean enough. Jake, why haven't you put your laundry away yet? Jake, are you sure all your homework is done? Jake, if only you were perfect like . . ." His voice trailed off.

Jill froze. Blinking. Breathing. Blinking. Breathing.

Jake stared as if daring her to finish his sentence. "You're not perfect either. I know you were late to my game because you were at Vanessa's." He nodded. "Yeah, I know about that. In math yesterday, she told me you came to her game. So you lied about that too."

Jill held her hands open as if welcoming his criticism. She would let him vent to her. But she needed him to understand her as well. "You're right. I tried to go to both of your games. I thought I could see some of hers before yours started, but it took me longer than I realized. I feel sick that I missed seeing you play and especially your goal. But Jake, it's really important that you know I'm here for you, even if I don't do it perfectly."

Jake shook his head. "Right. Sure. When I told you I was having a hard time, you didn't want to talk to me about it. You just wanted to send me to a psychiatrist and let them deal with it. Deal with me. So you don't have to."

"Oh, Jake. That's not what I meant." She moved to hug him, but he stepped out of her reach.

"You're on my case because I don't always tell you where I am. Where on earth could I possibly be? I'm literally here all the time. I lied when I said I was with friends. I was walking home from practice, by myself, like I've done all season. I have no friends, except Sam. He's the only one. Everyone else treats me weird. And you know what? It's fine. I like being alone. But whenever I'm home, you're always shouting at me!"

She could relate to friends treating you weird—it was almost easier not to have friends. Except she had Matt and Jake and Henry. She would choose her children over her old friends any day. But, of course, a teenager wouldn't. Jake was lonely.

"Oh, Jake, why didn't you tell me you needed a ride home from practice? I thought you were getting rides from your teammates. I would have come for you."

"That's just it, I like walking home. I like being alone."

She tried to take his hand. "Hey, I didn't know you were hurting so much."

He waved her away. "I'm not hurting! I don't want to talk about this. You wouldn't understand."

Suddenly Henry skipped into the room and handed his mom a piece of paper. "My Thanksgiving program is tomorrow, and we need to get everything on this paper for my costume. Jake, you're coming to watch me, right?"

Jake pulled Henry into an embrace, glaring at his mom over the top of Henry's head. "I sure am, bud. I'll be there the whole time. I wouldn't miss it for the world."

# 18

## family first

FORTY-TWO SIX-YEAR-OLDS smiled and waved to their adoring audience at the end of the first grade fall concert. Handprints made into turkeys with colorful feathers decorated the walls. Jake whooped Henry's name while memories of first-grade Connor brought tears to Jill's eyes. Or was it the joy of Jake cheering for Henry that caused the surge of emotion? Or was he still trying to make a point? Was she happy or sad? She never quite knew.

Earlier that evening, when she'd reminded Jake about the concert, she'd braced for another jab, but instead he chattered about his own performance, and did she remember his lisp at the time because he was missing both front teeth?

As they exited the auditorium, Henry ran to them with his own gap-toothed smile and jumped into Matt's outstretched arms as his family surrounded him. Caught up in the festivity, Jill asked, "Where shall we go to celebrate?"

"Ice cream!" exclaimed Henry.

"Drop me off at Sam's house," Jake said, keeping step with the family as they headed to the car.

"Can't you wait until after we get dessert?" Matt asked.

"No, we've got plans."

Disappointment oozed through Jill as their time all together was cut short. But she rallied with a burst of inspiration. "Invite Sam. We'll take him with us!"

"It's their family night and they invited me to join them. They're waiting for me. We're going bowling."

The idea of Jake having fun with another family filled Jill with jealousy. She told herself her envy was silly. Of course the kids spent evenings with other families—and their friends often came on outings with them. But that was Before. She tried to loosen the knot developing in her chest. "I wish you'd asked ahead of time."

"I did. I asked Dad this morning and he said it was okay." Turning to Henry he said, "You don't mind, do you, bud?"

Henry scrunched his eyebrows, his dismay evident. "That's fine."

"Why didn't you tell me?" Jill asked Matt as the boys walked ahead.

"I didn't realize it mattered. Most of the time you're not in the mood to go out."

Jill was quiet as she considered the truth of his statement. "It was just so nice being out as a family. I hate for it to end so soon."

Henry shouted to his friend Spencer, and soon Spencer's parents were walking next to them. "How are you?" they asked.

Matt glanced at Jill. She hesitated, then through a forced smile responded, "Good." At the same time Matt said, "Okay."

Spencer's mom put her hand on Jill's shoulder. "I'm sure some days are harder than others. I'm so sorry. I can't even imagine."

Jill hugged herself as Spencer's family hurried away.

Matt put his arm around her, but their steps were off kilter. He tried to grab her hand, but she resisted because she was cold. He tucked his hands into his pockets and sped up. She tried to match his steps, but the effort annoyed her, and she fell back.

As they loaded into the car, Jake and Henry climbed in back, discussing the concert and laughing about Andrew who turned the wrong way, and Annie, who danced a little extra. Jill was grateful for the distraction from the chill that had once again settled between her and Matt. As they drove towards Sam's house, Matt broke their silence. "I can't read your mind. I didn't know that being together was something you wanted to do."

In the back seat, Henry was telling Jake a knock-knock joke. This was every mother's dream—having her children getting along so well. Except, one of her children would always be missing out. "I just wish that every time we're finally having fun together, it didn't have to end."

⸗

On Sunday afternoon, Jill and Henry sat on the family room floor in front of the couch building Legos. Jake was doing homework and Matt was on his laptop. Jake closed his textbook. "Dad, will you take me driving? I need more practice hours."

Before Matt could answer, Henry said, "Jake, help me. I found four more wheels—we could build a car."

Jake ignored him, looking expectantly at Matt.

"Sure," Matt said, "Let me finish this and we can go in five minutes."

"Should we all go?" Jill asked. "Would you like to go on a drive, Henry?"

"Nope. I just want to build Legos."

Jake's smile grew bigger, if that was possible. "I'll grab the keys!"

Jill mindlessly clipped bricks together. They were so often moving past each other rather than spending meaningful time together. Sam's family was onto something. If they could do it, why not them?

Jill presented her idea when Jake and Matt came home a couple hours later. "Guys, let's make one night a week family night, like Sam's family is doing. We can take turns choosing the activity, like bowling or frisbee in the park or whatever we want."

Jake sighed. "I always have a ton of homework."

Jill wasn't deterred. "You can do it right after school."

"I can't. I have workouts."

She ignored his excuses. "Just once a week. If we plan ahead, we can make it work. It'll be nice to have fun together, don't you think?" She held up a pen. "Let's brainstorm. What ideas do you have?"

"Get ice cream! Go bowling!" shouted Henry.

"Be by myself," said Jake.

"If it doesn't snow, I could take the boys golfing at the club next Sunday," Matt said.

"Sounds great!" Jill said. "I'll come too—I can drive a golf cart with one of the boys." She ignored Jake's grunt, trying to think of something she knew Jake would like. "We could see the new Marvel movie."

"Dad and I are going to see it, just the two of us," Jake said.

She winked. "I like Marvel movies, and I won't even hog all the popcorn."

Jake tossed his hands in the air. "You don't even know the name of the movie!"

Matt changed the subject. "Let's add mini golfing. For Connor. He loved mini golf."

Jake became indignant. "This is so stupid! It's like Mom won't let me and you do stuff alone anymore."

Jill tried to be patient. "Of course I want you to do stuff together. But we need to plan family things too. What about a game night?"

Jake was playing with the cap of the pen, flicking it with his finger so it would spin around. "Why are we pretending we're this big, happy family? We're not, you know." He flicked the cap again, but this time it flew out of his hands and hit Jill on the cheek.

She banged her fist on the table. "You're right! We're not a big, happy family. We're a sad, broken family! When I try to do something special, you look at me like I'm so lame and Dad takes your side."

"Jill, I don't . . . we don't . . . ," Matt faltered.

"Do you think it doesn't haunt me every single day that I'm the one who made us go back to the beach? That I didn't want to wait? I know you all blame me. But believe me, I blame myself more." She couldn't see through her tears and sunk into her chair. "You know what else? I'm mad at Grandpa. I'm mad at Dad." She pointed a shaking finger at Matt. "Mad that he didn't have the right-sized life jacket for him."

She covered her face with her hands. "I wish we'd never gone on that damn boat trip. I'm just so angry." She seethed at how unfair life was. Instead, she took a breath and lowered her voice. "But you know what else? I care about our family. I love you all, and I want us to be happy again." She smacked her thighs. "We're doing this, and we're going to try it until we actually like it."

When she opened her eyes, all three of them were crying. Not just tears, but great heaving sobs. Had Jill raged so hard that the fragile hearts of her family were irreparably broken? In that moment, she hated herself for never being able to shut up.

She pulled Henry into her lap. He threw his arms around her neck and buried his face into her shoulder. She put a hand on Jake's knee, but he jerked away.

She caught Matt staring at her and expected him to look away, but instead, he moved next to her and took Henry from her. She was free to put her arms around Jake and she pulled him close. This time, instead of resisting, his head fell into her chest.

She rubbed his back until his sobs softened and he stopped sniffling—an innate gesture that began when she'd become a mother. She kissed his hair. When had she last held him? Had she finally broken through? She would do anything to have him love her again.

"Mom?" he asked.

"Hmmm..." She tightened her arms around him and his voice was muffled.

"What I want to do is go to the lake."

Her breath caught. *The lake? Please God, anywhere but there.* She swallowed. She tried to keep her voice steady. "Oh, Jake. I'm not sure that I can."

Jake pulled away from her and turned to his dad, pleading with a sincerity Jill rarely heard from him anymore, "Please? I really want to go."

Matt stood up and gave him a hug. "I hear you. Let Mom and me talk about it tonight."

Later, Jill turned down the bed. "I don't ever want to see that place again."

Matt shrugged as he fluffed his pillows.

"You'd actually be willing to go back?" she asked. "Why would you want to put yourself through that?"

He sat on the bed with his back to her. "To support Jake. We can't say no now. You just made a big deal about spending time together. If this is what he wants, we need to go. And I'd like to see it again when it's calm, without a storm. It's the last place where Connor was alive."

"That's exactly why I *don't* want to go. It's the place where Connor died." She closed her eyes, seeing her dad running up the beach, Connor in his arms. Holding Connor's head, brushing the hair from his face. She shuddered, trying to throw the memory to the back of her mind. "I can't go there again. Even if it's bright and sunny. I can't see other families with all their children."

He turned to face her. "It's November. No one goes to the lake this time of year. We'd be alone."

She picked at a loose thread on her T-shirt. "Matt, I can't. I'll do anything else. Anything."

For a minute they were silent, then he climbed under the covers. "Then I'll take the boys and just the three of us will go."

She was shocked. "Are you serious? You'd go without me?"

He scrutinized her. "You don't want to go, and we do. So . . ." He lifted his hand, palm up, indicating he was stating the obvious, then took a drink from the water bottle on his nightstand.

Jill had an urge to shove his elbow so he'd spill water down his front. He acted so calm. It was starting to make her feel crazy. "You're doing it again," she said.

"What am I doing?"

"Trying to be the favorite. Trying to win."

He screwed the cap on. "I find it interesting that you're accusing me of being the bad guy when you're the one holding everyone, well . . . hostage. You don't want to go, so none of us can go. I don't like it. Quite frankly, you're not the only one in charge here. I also get a say." He wiped his mouth. "Honestly, I'd much rather go to the lake to remember Connor than to the cemetery. The lake is special. We have so many happy memories there."

It should have been so easy to put her arms around him, to rub his back, his shoulders. To say that she was sorry, to give in and lay next to him. But now one more thing divided them—the damn lake. "No," she said, staring him down. "I'm holding firm on this one."

His face changed, resolve knitting his brows. "I want to go, and the boys want to go, so I'm going and I'm taking them with me. I'm sick of this, Jill. You're always laying down the law and expecting me to go along with it. I'm a nice guy and I guess after twenty years, that's what you expect. But I'm done. I lost my son too. You don't get to tell me how to grieve, and you don't get to tell the boys how to grieve either."

Jill blanched. "What do you mean 'you're done'?"

He shrugged. "I'm done with you telling me how to live my life. If I want to go to the lake, I'm going, whether you like it or not."

They stared at each other. His jaw was clenched, his eyes unblinking. The way he looked at her, so dismissive, so *done*, Jill knew he was leaving her. Maybe not right this second. Maybe not this month. But one day he would say he'd had enough. He'd leave and he'd take the boys with him—they'd choose to be with him. She collapsed onto the bed as a tear crept down her cheek. Her head pounded as her brain popped, trying to make sense of her world. She pulled a pillow over her head.

"Just wait," she whispered.

"For what?"

"Just don't go to the lake yet. Please. I'll try. But just give me a little longer."

The next morning, during breakfast, when Matt walked into the kitchen, Jill tried to catch his eye, but he avoided her. He sat on a barstool between the kids. "Hey, guys."

Jill held her breath as she slid a plate of pancakes in front of him.

"I forgot I have a commitment on Saturday, so I can't take you to the lake next weekend."

Jill caught his side-eye, and it wasn't friendly.

"But I do want to go, and I will take you soon. I promise." He kissed them each on the top of their heads as he stood up. "I'm so sorry. I love you."

Jill quietly exhaled. She didn't begrudge him walking out the door without giving her a kiss or an *I love you*. He'd waited for her, and she was grateful. Even though Jake's face was dark.

# 19

# jake at the lake

JAKE WAS DESPERATE TO SEE the lake. Just one more time. Sit in the sandy cove where he had last been with Connor. Climb the large outcrop of rocks where they'd gone cliff jumping. To understand where the boat flipped over and see how far they had to swim. If his parents wouldn't take him, he'd figure out how to get there himself.

Trying to envision the accident and how Connor died was occupying his thoughts nonstop, even waking him up in the middle of the night, his mind trying to play out the details. It plagued him when he was alone and glimmered at the edges of his consciousness even when he was with friends. Well, his one friend, Sam. He couldn't stand to be around anyone else. They just didn't get it. And Sam was impossible to drop, no matter how often Jake ignored his texts, which were really annoying half the time. Kevin would understand, but they hadn't talked since Kevin had given him the *gift* after he'd cried at his soccer game. "It will help," Kevin had said. Jake knew he was trying to be nice, but it made him uncomfortable.

And his mom almost found it, snooping around his room. He'd caught her just in time. So he'd put the paper sack in his backpack and moved it to the trunk of his car, stashing it underneath the blanket he kept for emergencies. It wasn't even that big of a deal, but of course she always thought the worst of him. It would kill her wondering what he was hiding. And he liked it that way.

Now he was kicking himself for telling her that he wanted to go to the lake. How could he have thought she might actually listen to him for once? He was furious that she shut him down. And this morning, when his dad sided with her, he wanted to punch the wall. She always ruined everything. After school, he locked his bedroom door, opened Google Maps and zoomed in on Lake Koda for the millionth time, a black splash on the satellite image, surrounded by dark fingers creeping away from the main body of water.

Enlarging the image, he examined the uneven shoreline. It jagged in and out, creating dozens of secluded coves around the perimeter and making it difficult to find the spot that was theirs. But there . . . a beach where he thought he could detect the rocky cliff jutting into the water.

He wouldn't wait around for his parents to eventually say no. He was going on his own. He wanted to walk along the water and be alone where he could think. The only problem was not getting caught.

He already had his own car, a used Subaru his parents bought last spring because they found a good deal. He didn't turn sixteen until February, but until then, he used it on practice drives with his dad.

He would have to ditch school so he could get to the lake and back while his mom and dad were at work. It was a forty-five-minute drive to the marina, he knew that. But he was following the road to the opposite side of the lake and hiking down a hill to get to the water. And hoping to end up at the right beach. One that his family—and anyone else—only ever accessed from a boat. He wasn't sure where he was going; he could only guess.

And, of course, there was the other small matter of not having a driver's license yet. And never having driven alone. And navigating the freeway.

On Tuesday, Sam wasn't in first period, which meant Sam couldn't pepper him with a million questions if he skipped class. So, despite all his planning, the actual *doing* turned out to be completely spontaneous. His heart was pounding, but after first period ended, he simply walked out the back doors of the school, through the parking lot to a side street, then jogged the mile home.

On Sunday afternoons when he practiced with his dad, driving up and around the lake was one of their favorite routes. Jake knew how to get there easily enough by now. But until Sunday, it had been almost six months since he'd been behind the wheel of a car.

Nervous that a neighbor would see him home in the middle of the day, he ran through the garden gate, letting himself in through the back door. Once in the house, he held his breath and listened. What if his parents were home? He tiptoed to the garage to check for their cars. Only his Subaru was there. Racing up the stairs to his parents' bedroom to get the keys, he wondered if parents could read minds. Would his dad hide the keys knowing Jake might try to steal them? Nope, there they were in the top dresser drawer, where they always were.

He inched out of the driveway, checking and double-checking over his shoulder to see if anyone would catch him disobeying the rules. The sidewalks on both sides of the tree-lined street were empty. Was anyone looking out of their windows? He pressed the pedal too hard, gunning too fast, and then slammed the brakes, jolting almost to a stop. *Don't be an idiot, Jake. You know how to drive! Act normal!* He took a deep breath, pressed the gas again, this time with more control, and turned left out of his neighborhood.

His arms were shaking by the time he made it onto the freeway. He hadn't expected to feel so panicked. He was only three months away from turning sixteen and getting his license, and he'd had a lot of practice. But driving alone was scarier than he realized—that and ditching school and stealing the car. He jumped as a semi whizzed by on the right. Then a red Mercedes sat on his tail, and he wasn't sure what to do. He was already going the speed limit—should he speed up or get out of the way? Just as he switched on his blinker, the Mercedes pulled out first, speeding around him and honking. Jake tried to relax his grip on the wheel.

Thirty minutes later, he passed their usual turnoff for the marina and followed Siri's guidance to the next exit that traversed the opposite side of the lake where he believed the cove was. The unfamiliar two-lane highway climbed a hill, and the water was now far below. He slowed as Siri indicated he was close. From Google Maps, he hadn't realized the road was so high above the lake. He would have to bushwhack through overgrown bushes and squat, branchy trees to get down to the beach.

He parked the car on the narrow shoulder and cautiously looked around as he locked the doors and stuffed the keys in his jeans pocket. He reminded himself he wasn't doing anything wrong—aside from driving without a license and ditching school. His heart skipped a beat. He hopped over the guardrail and began hiking.

The trees were bare of leaves, which aided his view, but sharp branches snagged at his sweatshirt as he made a path through the brush. He wasn't worried about getting lost. The lake was below him, the road above him. If he stayed up high, he could see where he was in relation to the marina, a speck across the water. He pushed hard, fueled by adrenaline, not noticing how steep and far he'd come. The effort eased the knot in his chest.

After wandering for almost an hour, he was close to giving up. Twice already he'd cut down a hillside to see if he was at the right beach. Both times he'd been wrong. He didn't know exactly where it was from this perspective, but he felt sure he'd recognize it when he found it. There would be a large log, pine trees, and of course, the rocky cliff jutting into the lake. The one that caused boats to crash.

But he didn't have much time left. He'd planned one hour for the drive each way and an hour to hang out at the spot, only skipping three classes and lunch. His graphics teacher wouldn't care if he missed, nor his PE coach—he'd just make up the work on another day. And his English teacher was easy. He'd tell her it had been a bad day, and she'd pat him on the shoulder and tell him not to worry about it. As long as he was back in school after lunch, no one would even know or care that he'd been gone.

However, he hadn't considered the time he needed to find the dumb place. Why had he imagined he'd walk straight to it? He was such a moron sometimes. He checked his watch, looked back up to where he'd started, then back to the water in search of any familiar landmarks. He only had a few more minutes to search.

When he came into a clearing on his third try, he knew he'd found it. It was all there—the weathered log resting on the sand, the grove of pine trees at the back of the beach, and the jagged cliff. He touched the log, palming the softness of the old wood. Grandpa had thrown a pass just over there and

Jake had made a great catch, then passed it to Henry who had made a touchdown. Everyone was celebrating.

After that, he'd asked Connor to go cliff jumping with him, but Connor wanted to build a sandcastle with Henry instead. Jake called him a chicken and intentionally dropped the football, crushing part of the castle, and pretended it was an accident. Henry threw a fist of sand at him, but Jake just laughed. Connor ignored him, rebuilding the part that had been smashed. So Jake picked up a long stick and poked Connor in the back of his swim trunks as he walked away, laughing when Connor shouted, "Hey!" Jake didn't bother to say he was sorry.

The recollection slammed into his chest, the tightness making him wheeze. He crushed his hands over his ears as if trying to drown out the sound of Connor's voice. He fell to his knees.

He held his breath and clenched his teeth until the pain of the memory of taunting Connor loosened its grip. Balling his fists, he hit the sand. They hit with a dull, cold thud. He let the feeling reverberate through him, then struck again and again. His rage was squelched by the shrill alarm of his phone, a reminder that he had to leave to get back to school.

He stormed up the hill, sliding on loose sand, grabbing at twigs for balance, desperate to get away from this place. His curiosity had been tormenting him for months but satisfying it didn't make him feel better at all, instead it made him angry. Midway up the hill he turned for a last look. He bent down, clutched a large rock at his feet and threw it as hard as he could. It landed at the edge of the slope and rolled to a stop. It didn't even make an impact. Turning back uphill, he vowed never to return.

As he ducked under low limbs and pressed through bushes that grabbed at his feet and tripped him up, instead of the mad seeping out of him, it grew. The eerie silence of the beach behind him was haunting, and he sped up, the sound of Connor shouting "Hey!" repeating in his mind. He broke a stick from a bush and swiped it through the air. "Hey!" he heard Connor say, over and over again.

Suddenly a mouse ran across the path. Startled, he lost his footing, falling onto a knee and scraping his hands. "Hey!" he yelled. He imagined Connor jumping up from the sandcastle and shouting at him. He imagined grabbing Connor and pushing him over. Wrestling in the sand. Connor rolling him over and hitting him back. Connor sitting on him and pushing his face into the sand. "Connor!" he screamed.

Tears came then, but after two loud sobs, he sucked the next ones down, using them to fill the empty cavern in his heart. He stomped forward until he reached the top of the hill, hopped over the guardrail, and ran to his car. He would be late to fifth period. But as long as he made it before class ended, the teacher wouldn't say anything. No one ever did anymore.

# 20

## checking in

ROGER WAS WASHING THE BREAKFAST dishes when his phone rang. Gina. He dried his hands and hit speakerphone. "Hello!"

"Hey, I'm rushing into my yoga class, but wanted to let you know I just saw something weird."

"Lay it on me."

"I just saw Jake driving. I was waiting at the light on Sycamore Boulevard, and he drove past in the black car Matt got for him."

Roger started washing dishes again. "That wouldn't have been Jake. He doesn't have his license yet."

"That's why I'm calling you. I'm sure it was him and I know he's not sixteen yet."

"But then how would he be driving?"

"Roger, he snuck the car out. He's supposed to be in school and he was going the opposite way. There's no way Matt or Jill would have let him drive."

Roger picked up the phone and collapsed into a chair at the kitchen table. He needed to sit for this. "Should we tell them?"

"I'm not sure. I wanted to let you know so we could both think on it. I've got to go, but let's talk when I get home."

"Okay. Love you."

"Love you too."

Roger hung up. He felt oddly unconcerned about Jake's taking the car. *Surely it isn't stealing when it's your own family car, right?* He remembered when he caught his son, Todd, stealing the car before he got his license. *Ah . . . it's "stealing" when you're angry and "taking" when you're not.* Todd and his friends snuck out at night and went for a joyride. Roger had heard the car pull out and was waiting for Todd in the dark just inside the garage door when he got home. He'd been furious at his son. Looking back, he understood he was more stressed than angry—stress from the worry of him getting in an accident or causing an accident. Stressed about what kind of kid he was raising. Worried about the type of person a kid who sneaks out, steals the car, and drives underage might turn out to be. *A hooligan at best, a criminal at worst. Surely not a murderer though.*

But with his grandson, he didn't feel that old sense of panic. Instead of worrying about all the bad things that could happen, he was more concerned with why Jake was behaving this way. Why was he skipping school and where was he going? He didn't think a group of kids would take a joyride in the middle of the day. It was too risky. They're sneakier than that. He tapped his finger on his nose and clicked his tongue. *What are you up to, Jake?*

Roger's thinking place was his woodworking shop. It was simply an extension off the garage, but had its own door so was a separate space. On one side of the room was a wood lathe next to a narrow table. On the opposite side, shelves lined the wall, packed with dozens of sizable blocks of wood. Some were thick round sections with the bark still attached. Others looked like firewood. Another shelf held blanks, uniformly cut twelve-inch squares, more refined than his other pieces. Turning wood bowls was a hobby Roger picked up after he'd gotten divorced, and he'd become quite proficient at it. Woodturning required patience. The slow methodical process of shaping and sanding helped him think. Taking a blank of rough beech from the shelf, he placed it on the lathe and tightened the tailstock.

If he told Matt and Jill that Gina saw Jake driving on his own, they would ground Jake. If he was already sneaking out and taking the car, getting grounded wouldn't stop that. It would make things worse. But if he kept quiet and something bad happened, an accident perhaps ... No. It wouldn't. It couldn't. He pushed the dark memories of the lake away. It was highly unlikely Jill would answer his call anyway. He was trying to let her have space, but he worried about her. And he missed her.

What did he really want for his grandson? He didn't feel responsible for teaching Jake about rules and consequences. That was his parents' job. Roger's only job, and he felt strongly about this, was to love him. He would ask him to dinner, wherever he wanted. Give him a chance to talk. No teen would pass up dinner.

He texted, hoping Jake wasn't stupid enough to text and drive:

> Haven't seen you in a while. Can I take you to dinner? I miss you.

He put the phone down and got back to work shaping his bowl. Five months had passed, and it still seemed impossible

that Connor had actually died. Even on good days he rumi-
nated on the choices he made the day of the accident, wrestling with what he should have done differently. He should
have driven the boat slower, stayed calm. In his effort to hurry,
he'd made it worse. The very worst. The haunting memories
began to hum with the vibration of the lathe.

Working in his shop was the best distraction from reliving
last summer. But sometimes it did just the opposite. Instead
of calming him, it turned on the "if only" thoughts, which
inevitably broke him with "it's all your fault."

His brain protested the idea that he had killed his grandson. When he talked it through with Gina, she would remind
him of the terrible conditions they were dealing with. But
it being unintentional didn't make him feel better. If he had
slowed down, taken his time, it would have made all the difference. Oh, Connor! How he missed him!

Roger had tried to apologize a few days after the funeral.
"It was an accident," Jill had said, cutting him off. But her lips
were pursed, and she was looking past him as if reading a cue
card when she said it. He knew that look and he knew her. She
blamed him. He blamed himself, so he didn't expect anything
different. But he did wish they could talk it through together.
Given all the other factors—the wind and the rocks and the
waves—might she ever forgive him? God knew he was so, so
sorry.

When his mind started the endless loop of reliving that
day, he stopped the lathe, sat in a cracked, green vinyl chair in
the corner of the room and put on his headphones. Mark, his
old college buddy who recently lost his wife, had introduced
him to a meditation app. At first Roger was skeptical that
simply focusing on breathing could be helpful. *The beauty of
breathing is we don't have to think about it, Mark!* But after just

a couple of sessions, he found he looked forward to this form of coping.

He set his breathing app for ten minutes and closed his eyes. Inhale four counts, hold for two. Exhale four counts, pause for two. Repeat. As ludicrous as it sounded, it did make his stress more manageable.

After the ten minutes were up, he went back to the lathe. This time, as he held the tool to the wood, he focused his thoughts on what he loved about Connor: How he would pause to think before answering a question; his deep brown eyes; the way he wrinkled his nose when he smiled. Then what he loved about Jake: His enthusiasm; that he took time to teach his brothers how to play soccer; that he always seemed genuinely happy to be with his grandpa. His laugh the first time they got a kite in the air.

Later that night, Roger's phone dinged with a text from Jake:

You know I love burritos. Tomorrow at 6?

The next night, Roger didn't have time to get all the way to the front door before Jake ran out of the house. "I've missed you," Roger said, as Jake fell into his embrace. "We've got a lot to catch up on." He held Jake away so he could look into his eyes. "I want to know everything that's going on in your life. Jump in."

As the car doors shut, Jake immediately started talking. "School's good. I like most of my teachers. The soccer season just ended. I played pretty well. Thanks for coming to some of my games."

They small-talked until their food arrived. As the waitress laid their burritos on the table, Roger asked, "How's everything at home?"

Jake bit his lip. "Kind of sucks."

Roger nodded.

"Mom's such a control freak, you know?"

Roger did know, but he kept that to himself. Instead, he said, "It's hard to be a teen, but it's hard to be a parent too."

Jake took a bite of his burrito. Roger did the same. A full mouth was better for listening.

Jake didn't mind talking with his mouth full. "Yeah, but Mom isn't like you. You're chill. She's always mad at me."

Roger laughed. "I wonder what my kids would say to that!" He was pretty sure all three would disagree. "That's the best part of being a grandpa. The rough edges from parenting have become a little smoother." He sat back in the booth. "Why would your mom be mad at you? How are your grades?"

Jake's eyes grew wide. "That's the thing. I do everything I'm supposed to! I'm getting good grades. I help out around the house. I could be so much worse—she's not even grateful."

"It's hard when you don't feel noticed."

"Right! You'd think since they already lost one son, they'd appreciate the two they still have. But they don't. It's like, 'We wish you'd died instead of perfect Connor.'"

The words crashed into Roger's sternum with the force of a boulder thrown from a cliff. He strained to keep his face neutral. "It must really hurt to feel like that."

Jake looked away, wiping an eye.

They both took another bite and Roger closed his eyes, smiling in mock ecstasy to hide the pain still reverberating through him from Jake's words. When he opened them, Jake was pushing his food around his plate.

"Have you tried talking to your mom about how you feel?"

"It would just make it worse. They'd just be all, 'We can never make Jake happy.'"

Jake still had the cowlick in his bangs like he had as a child, reminding Roger that even though he was almost as tall as him, he was still so young. "What about friends?"

"At first everyone was really nice. But if you're always talking about the same thing, your friends get sick of you. Like, 'We're sad for you, but it's time to get over it.'"

Roger understood. He even felt like that with his own friends. It's why, every time people asked, "How are you?" he simply replied, "Doing pretty good." If he answered honestly, it would be complicated because every day he experienced a different set of emotions. No one wanted a long, meaningful discussion; they were just acknowledging his tragedy and needed to get on their way. Fortunately, Gina found a therapist they both talked to on a regular basis. He was surprised at how helpful just talking was. "Does your family talk about the accident or about Connor?"

Jake shrugged. "I mean, it's not like we don't talk about Connor. We visit his grave and remember stuff he liked. But we don't talk about that day." Jake picked at his plate. "Some days I feel good, but on others I really, really miss him. I know I need to focus on the happy times and everything. It's just hard." Jake lowered his head.

"Do you know that its normal to have conflicting feelings when someone you love dies? There are stages of grief. That's why it's called a grieving *process*."

Jake bit at his thumbnail. He finally looked up. "Do you feel sad, Grandpa?"

He nodded. "I do. I really, really do."

"How long until we'll stop feeling sad?"

Roger wiped his mouth with his napkin, then moved to Jake's side of the booth and put his arm around him. "All I can tell you is it's going to take time and it's different for everyone. It might be painful for a year or two or more. But it will get easier to live with. I promise." He pulled his grandson close, loving that even though he was a teenager, he didn't resist. "Even though I still hurt, it helps being able to talk to you, right now. Someone who misses Connor like I do." He held him a second longer, then released him to see his face. "Have your parents talked about seeing a family therapist?"

Jake wrinkled his nose. "We don't need to see a shrink. That's weird."

Roger smiled. "Actually, it's not weird at all. A therapist helps you understand your feelings. But I realize it can feel uncomfortable talking to a stranger. I just thought I'd mention it. Hey, how much homework do you have tonight? Would you be interested in working with me in the shop?"

"Like making bowls and stuff? I don't have time tonight. I've got a test to study for."

Roger had brought Jake to his shop when he was young, but he'd lost interest within a few minutes. "Good for you. Glad to hear you're taking school seriously."

"I'm hoping to get good enough grades to get a scholarship. I can't wait to move out and live at college."

Roger smirked at Jake as they stood up to leave. "Go easy on your parents. They just want what's best for you."

Jake made a face. "I try! I swear!"

"I believe you. But I've also raised a few teenagers myself. It's not as easy as you may think." Roger held the door open, making sure he could see Jake's reaction when he said, "Hey, you've got a birthday coming up. I'll bet you're pretty excited to get your license so you can drive your car!"

Without any hesitation, Jake replied, "I can't wait!" his face as smooth as butter.

*Typical teenager—a good little liar.*

As they pulled in front of Jake's house, Roger turned off the car. "I think I'll go in and say hi since I'm here. But Jake, you know you can talk to me, right? I can tell you about that day. I've also been reading a lot about grief. I can answer questions about that as well. It's helped me a lot."

"I know. Thanks."

They both got out of the car, and as Roger caught up to Jake, he put his arm around him again. "I love you, kid."

"I love you too, Grandpa," he said, leaning into him.

Roger followed Jake into the house, discomfort suddenly seizing his gut. Before the accident, he'd often stopped by, and always felt welcome. Now he was unsure where he stood. If he stayed away, it would just make the tension between him and Jill worse. She blamed him for Connor's death, and he would let her. God knew he wished he could blame someone. If blaming him made her feel better, it was a gift he would give.

"Hello!" Roger called out.

"Hey, Roger!" Matt called from the kitchen. "Come in!"

Roger sauntered into the kitchen where Matt was drying the pans that Jill handed to him. "I thought I'd just come in and give a hug to my other favorite grandson."

Henry ran over and threw his arms around Roger's legs. "Hi, Grandpa!"

"Hey, squirt! I haven't had a hug from you in too long and it feels good! Can we plan a sleepover?"

Henry squealed with delight. "Please, can I, Mom?"

"We'll see," Jill said, drying her wet hands on a towel.

Roger put an arm around her waist and pulled her to him. He tried not to say it, but it just slipped out, "How are you?"

"We're fine," she said, pulling away and turning to pick up a serving bowl.

He wanted to kick himself for asking the worst question possible. "It's good to see you," he said. *That's better.* "How would you feel about Henry sleeping over this weekend?"

"Sure," Matt said.

Jill froze, arms in midair, still reaching toward the cabinet. She started rearranging the bowls in the cupboard, taking a surprisingly long time given there were just three. Finally, she said, "I don't know, Dad."

"Please, Mom?" Henry begged, folding his hands and bouncing on his toes.

Jill ruffled his blond curls and shared a look with Matt, who scooped Henry up and said, "Mom and Dad will talk about it. Right now, it's time to get your pj's on." He and Henry left the kitchen, Henry in giggles as his dad tickled his stomach.

Jill finally turned to face him. "Can you call me later this week so we can talk about it?"

Roger chuckled. "I can call you, but the question is, will you answer?"

Her tone turned icy. "What? I answer!"

He patted her on the shoulder, ignoring her protest with a grin. "Oh, Jill. Sure you do."

"You know I can't answer while I'm in school."

"I do know. That's why I always call after four o'clock."

Jill gave a resigned sigh. "It's hard to talk, sometimes."

Roger held on to her shoulder and looked her in the eye, making sure she held his gaze. "I care about you, Jill. I care about all of you. Why don't you walk me to the door?"

"I feel like I'm in trouble," she grumbled.

"We'd love for Henry to sleep over, but do you have some reservations?"

She hesitated. "For some reason, I just feel nervous about him not being home."

"Is it me?"

"No! No. I just . . . It's weird. I need to keep him close."

"A late night?"

"Maybe."

"To the movies?"

She shrugged. "I just need some time to figure out what I feel okay about."

"I get it. Think about it."

"Thanks for stopping by." She opened the front door for him.

It sounded like she really meant it, so he felt brave enough to ask what was really on his mind. "Jill, are you talking to someone? To a therapist?"

She shook her head. "I asked Matt about it, but he isn't interested. And the boys don't want to either."

"Henry said that?"

"Jake did. Henry is doing fine. He's so young. Young kids are resilient."

Roger tilted his chin, not sure if that was entirely true. "Well, if you change your mind, I can ask mine if he has any references."

"You see a shrink?"

"A therapist, yes."

Jill stared at him, her mouth open.

"Turns out you can teach an old dog new tricks. I'm reading a thoughtful book on grief, too. I'd be happy to lend it to you when I'm done."

"I have one I've read a bit. But I might look at yours. But I sort of don't want the boys to see it. So, don't drop it off on the porch."

"What do you mean 'you don't want the boys to see it'? It's okay to admit that everyone is grieving. It's actually an important part of the process."

"Thanks, Dad. I appreciate your concern."

He recognized the deflection in the formality of the phrase—an automatic response to unsolicited advice she had no use for. He squeezed her elbow. "Love you, Jill. I'm glad you're coming to Thanksgiving next week. Please don't worry about bringing anything."

"It's just mashed potatoes, Dad. It's no trouble."

"Well, everyone's happy you're coming. Todd's family arrives on Tuesday and Cara flies in on Wednesday. It'll be nice to be all together." He paused when he saw her wince. *No, not everyone will be there.* "I'm sorry. I realize what I just said."

"It's fine," she said, waving him away. "I'm going to shut the door so we don't let any more heat out."

He fought to swallow the lump in his throat as he walked down the path to his car.

# 21

## telling secrets

THE LAST THING JILL WANTED to do was celebrate Thanksgiving. Halloween had been so hard—photographing the two boys in their costumes, the third child very much absent. Looking for Connor's friends in every ghoul or sports icon that came to the door and feeling so angry that he was missing out. She wondered what emotional body-slams she'd have to brace herself for during dinner with her dad and siblings. She didn't want to have a special day. She just wanted a normal day, one where she could lie in bed and sleep. But instead, she showered, plastered on a smile, and mashed the potatoes.

She was the oldest of three. Todd was two years younger and the life of the party. In the past, she could count on Todd for slightly irreverent gut-busting laughs which drew everyone to him, including Jake and Connor. His sweet wife, Nicole, good-naturedly put up with all his antics, and their shy five-year-old, Sophie, was Henry's favorite cousin. Jill's baby sister, Cara, was eight years younger and quite the opposite of Jill and Todd—soft-spoken and wise.

Jill usually loved being with her family, but this year she felt so vulnerable. She couldn't hide anything from her siblings, and she didn't want to be exposed to the people who knew her best. The scars were still so raw. They'd be able to *see* she wasn't doing great. The tension with Jake. With Matt. What if they wanted to talk about it? What if they didn't talk about it? She didn't have the fortitude to open herself up to more pain.

When they arrived at her dad's front door, they were ambushed with hugs. Cara kissed her hair and wiped tears from her cheek. Todd picked her up, whispering in her ear, "Hey, big sis," then cracked a joke that she was crying because she missed him so much. Which wasn't too far off.

Gina had hung a small poster with pictures of Connor on the dining room wall and encouraged everyone to make time to add a favorite memory between TV parades, football games, and dinner preparations. Jill was leery, afraid that sorrow and pain from missing Connor would hijack the day.

When they sat down for their Thanksgiving meal, instead of their usual tradition of circling the table sharing what they were grateful for, they each took a turn sharing a memory. How Connor used to skip instead of walk. The way he said "Auntie Cawatt" when he was little. The time—when he was only six—that he told Todd and Nicole he was an expert holding new baby Sophie because "he'd become a *professional* with Henry."

"He really did know more than me!" said Nicole.

Mostly they laughed. And when they did cry, their tears weren't awkward—it was a Connor lovefest with her favorite people. For the first time since the accident, Jill felt emotionally safe, even light.

Throughout dinner, Todd made her laugh in a way she didn't realize she still could as he told stories about the people he worked with in his public relations firm. Often, she felt Cara's hand on her arm or her knee, it's warmth giving Jill strength.

Afterward, they moved to the family room where Jake sat companionably between Todd and Cara, both of them treating him like one of the grown-ups instead of a kid, and Sophie and Henry played a board game in the corner.

"How's life as a teenager in the Miller family?" Todd asked Jake. "Is your mom as strict and mean as our dad was?"

"No way Grandpa could be mean. He's so chill!" Jake said.

"Dad, how much are you paying him to say that?" Todd laughed, raising his eyebrows. "Jake, you do know you got the *chill* parents, don't you? When your mom was a teenager, if she got caught sneaking out, she was as cool as if she were breezing home from summer camp and Dad would be nothing but thrilled to see her!"

"Sneaking out? Tell me more!" Jake said, the shock lighting his face.

Jill shook her finger at her brother. "Todd, don't tell lies about me, I beg you."

He put his hands up. "My wife's a lawyer! I'm sworn to tell the truth, the whole truth, and nothing but the truth, isn't that right, babe?"

His wife mouthed, "I'm so sorry," as Jill kneaded her brow.

Todd barreled forward. "Here's the truth, Jake, now that you're old enough to hear it . . . It seems hard to believe because we're both such amazing adults, but growing up, Jill and I were loud, rambunctious, and always getting into trouble. You don't get into trouble, do you, Jake?" He asked, pointing at him.

"No! Never." Jake grinned, even looking at his mom and sharing a laugh. "But what about Cara? Was she with you?"

Cara shook her head. "I was six years younger than Todd, so I never got invited. Plus, I was an angel."

Todd's eyes practically twinkled. "I could tell some stories about Cara, but I think that's when chill Dad emerged, the one Jake's so familiar with!"

Roger winked at Cara. "You remember me as chill, right?" They both laughed.

"Okay, so when Jill and I were teenagers, I came up with all the ideas, like 'Let's throw snowballs!' But your mom would always want to go one step further, like 'Let's throw snowballs at cars!'"

"What!" Jill interjected. "It was definitely the other way around. All your deviant ideas made me a nervous wreck."

"Maybe that's true," Todd conceded. "But don't tell Sophie." He pretended to muffle his voice with his hand.

"I can hear you, Dad!" Sophie chimed in without looking up from her game of Chutes and Ladders with Henry.

"Well cover your ears, you rascal, this is grown-up talk!" He looked back at Jake. "If your mom suggested doorbell ditching, I talked her into toilet papering. And contrary to what she says, she was pretty easy to convince."

"I hated breaking the rules," Jill said.

"Yeah, but I could always talk her into it. And I needed her on my side because she was a damn good liar."

"Oh no," Jill said, burying her face in her hands, "I don't like where this is going."

"So, one time we stole the car."

"Todd, stop. I mean it." She threw a pillow at him, but he caught it and smirked at her.

"Relax. Okay, we didn't *steal* steal it. It's not like we were breaking into garages with ski masks and hot-wiring the neighbors' vehicles. It was Dad's car, so it wasn't that bad. And she knew how to drive; she just didn't have her license yet."

Jill wasn't sure if this was fun anymore. What would Jake think? "Jake, do not listen to him. It was wrong and not safe at all. Learn from my mistakes." Jake's smile looked suspiciously strained. Was he totally disappointed in her?

"I talked her into driving us to McDonald's after midnight. It wasn't far. We were simply having a little brother-sister bonding time. So that night when we got home, we were tip-toeing up the stairs and holding our breath to be as quiet as we could. It was pitch black, but when we got to the top, Dad was standing there! My thirteen-year-old heart nearly gave out! Jill, on the other hand, was superhumanly calm." Mimicking her voice, he continued, "Hey, Dad, did we wake you? I'm *sooooo* sorry! I left my backpack at Carol's, and Todd walked over with me so I didn't have to go alone in the dark."

The whole room erupted in laughter.

"Todd, you're such a blabbermouth," Jill said. "I'm going to write a book to share with Sophie when she's a teenager if you keep this up." She pointed at Jake. "I'm serious, don't ever take the car."

Jake's face was still frozen in that pained look. Was he angry that she'd insinuated, in front of her whole family, that stealing a car was something he'd consider? She vowed to make a better effort not to embarrass him.

"Do you remember that, Dad?" Cara asked.

"I do. I obviously knew they'd taken the car. And I was furious. The only entertaining part was watching Todd turn purple, about to pass out because he was desperately holding his breath!"

Todd nodded. "It's true, I was having a heart attack. So Dad, surely recognizing Jill didn't have a backpack, just says, 'Where's your backpack, now?' And Jill whispers, as if respecting how late it was and how quiet she should be with Cara asleep, 'I put it in the car so it would be ready for school tomorrow. Did you hear the garage door open? I'm so sorry we woke you up! Sorry, Dad. So, so sorry! Love you!' She gives him a big hug and dashes up the stairs to her room with me right behind!"

"You didn't get grounded or punished at all?" Jake asked, clearly dumbfounded.

"Listen," Roger interjected, "I knew it had to be Todd's idea. And I think he probably peed himself when I caught them. I remember wondering if I'd find wet pants when I did the laundry the next day. I figured he'd never dare to do it again, and I was right—at least for a few more years."

"Did you do it again, Todd?" Jake asked.

"Hell no! I really was scared straight. Anyway, Jill could drive soon after that and she took me wherever I wanted to go. And I would never be able to lie as well as Jill could, so I didn't have a prayer of getting away with anything."

Jill closed her eyes. "Okay, new topic. And why don't I go dish up the pie?"

∽

Why did the day after having fun feel like a hangover? For a full day they'd laughed and felt, well, normal. But the aftereffects wiped her out, and the next day a gloom settled over their home. Was it because with Thanksgiving behind them, now it was Christmas season? The long weekend wasn't even over and out of the blue they had copious amounts of neighborly attention, just like after the funeral. People started bringing treats, which, yes, happens at Christmastime, but this year it was more than usual. A friend of Matt's even offered to help put up their lights and said his wife could help Jill decorate—or would even do it for her.

That lit a fire under Jill. She could decorate her own home, thank you very much. And in fact, she would do something Christmassy every single day in December. They'd have Christmas spirit, dammit, and planning it all would give her a distraction to avoid the very big hole in her heart and in their home and under their tree.

In fact, she'd take a cue from Gina. It was so lovely talking about Connor with people who knew him—really knew him and loved him almost as much as she did—she wanted to do it again. But with just her own family this time. On the winter solstice, she traditionally served dinner by candlelight, just for the fun of it. But this solstice, she'd plan something extra special.

She'd already bought Connor a couple of gifts. She hid them on the top shelf of her closet, of course, because if Matt knew, he'd think she was losing it. But she wanted to wrap them in green and red paper. And write his name on a label. And tie a beautiful bow around a present for her son. She would donate them to Goodwill after Christmas. Or even next year. Sometime later, when she was ready to say goodbye.

# 22

## out of the chaos

AFTER HIS ESCAPADE TO THE lake, Jake didn't feel brave enough to ever go back. Sneaking out, driving, and lying had made him jittery for a full day afterward. And what was that story about his mom stealing the car? Did the whole family know what he did? Were they trying to warn him not to do it again? He was so nervous his mom and dad would confront him that he felt physically sick. He ended up sleeping most of Thanksgiving break to avoid them.

But at night he lay awake, and getting caught wasn't what haunted him. It was the pain of remembering how he had been so mean to Connor that last day. It was clawing a hole in his chest. The excruciating guilt hammered away at him as if being physically pummeled, which fueled his need to go back. Maybe, somehow, the lake held answers to how he could make it right.

He was also desperate for an excuse to get out of the house. His mom was going all out decorating for Christmas. She was obsessed, as if the magic would bring Connor back. She'd made a whole list of Christmassy things to do every single day of the month, and her unabashed Christmas cheer made him angrier than ever.

It was easy to slip out the first week of December. One morning he pretended to be sick, which wasn't a challenge since his mom had made a hot chocolate bar after dinner, complete with marshmallows, peppermint sticks, whipped cream, butterscotch syrup, and sprinkles. He told his mom he'd been up all night with a stomachache, which was kinda true, so before she left to work, she brought him Gatorade and a sleeve of saltines, which he packed in his backpack for a snack.

As he pulled out of the driveway, halfway down the block, Mrs. Fitzgerald, bundled in a coat and scarf, was walking her dog and pushing a baby stroller. Jake looked straight ahead. She wouldn't know how old he was—or wasn't. His heart was thumping, but he told himself everything was going to be fine.

He was still nervous driving up the canyon, but he congratulated himself as he arrived safely. He thought he'd recognize where to hike down to the beach, but he brought a pocketknife to mark some trees just in case. And he'd prepared for the cold with a coat and warm socks. Once at the beach, he spent an hour eating his snacks and carving on the log. He tried putting his feet in the water, but it was freezing, and pretty soon he was bored. He was home and back in bed by early afternoon.

The next week, he wrote himself an excuse note, pretending to leave school for a doctor's appointment. He forged his dad's signature, and no one even questioned it. This third time he felt far more confident driving alone. At the cove he sat on the log and actually did a reading assignment for English. He loved being on his own. With no one around to bug him, he had a clear mind for the first time in forever.

The third week of December was the last week of school before Christmas break. He counted the days to Wednesday when he'd leave after second period, planning to be gone all day. Tuesday night, he skated to the grocery store and bought a hoagie sandwich, salt and vinegar chips, and a box of powdered-sugar donuts. He packed a sleeping bag in the trunk of his car and an extra battery pack for his phone. At the lake he was going to watch a Christmas movie. Maybe even try to build a fire. It would be his own solitary party. He was so excited for days leading up to it that his mom commented on his good attitude. Said how appreciative she was that he was being so responsible with his chores. It was true. With the lake to look forward to and some space and time to himself, he just felt more relaxed.

But in the morning, he woke up to a blanket of white, and the forecast said it would continue all day. The first snowstorm of the season was usually something to celebrate, but now it was messing up all his plans. There was no way he could risk driving in a storm—he didn't even know how. It seemed the whole school was thrilled that it would be a white Christmas, but Jake was furious. Stuck in classes with everyone around him chirping about what presents they hoped for and where they were going on vacation, he scowled at the gray sky, watching the big fluffy flakes float down, resenting every single one of them.

That night, after their family activity of cutting out snowflakes—which actually went pretty quick because Henry was bad at it and Jake refused to do more than one—Jake tried studying for a final at the kitchen counter. His mom and dad were on the couch, heads bent over a laptop, talking about finances, and Henry sat near them, watching TV.

"Henry, can you turn it down? I need to concentrate," Jake barked.

"I can barely hear because Mom and Dad are talking!"

His mom asked, "Would you be more comfortable working in the office where it's quieter? Or in your room at your desk?"

Mumbling, Jake put in his earbuds instead. A few minutes later his mom walked over and tapped the counter in front of him to get his attention. "Can you concentrate if you're listening to music? What class are you studying for?"

He slammed his book shut. He couldn't stand to be in the same house with her for one more second. "Actually, I need to go to Sam's house so we can work on a project."

"So late?" His mom took the pack of chips in front of him, folded the top over, and placed them out of reach on the counter behind her.

"It's not late. It's just dark." He opened his backpack and pushed his books inside.

"I'll take you."

"I'll just skate," he said, standing up.

"Not in the dark. And it's wet."

"Can I take the car then?"

Her head snapped up. "What? No! Don't get any ideas!"

He shrugged his shoulders. "Why not? I'm done with driver's ed. I know how to drive. You did it and you were fine."

"Because it's illegal!"

"Technically, but I'll just be in the neighborhood. No cops patrol around here."

She rolled her eyes. "No. I'm obviously not letting you take the car, and I'm going to kill Todd for putting the idea in your head. I'll take you. Or Dad can."

Jake picked up his phone and pretended to look at a text. "Never mind. Sam said he's coming to pick me up." He stood at the front door for two minutes pretending to wait and listening to the conversation about nothing coming from the living room, then walked outside. The snow had melted off the streets and sidewalks. It was wet, but skating was doable. So he picked up his board off the porch, walked down a few houses until he was sure his parents couldn't see him, threw the board to the ground, and skated to a place where it would be quiet and he was sure he'd be welcome. Not to Sam's, but to Grandpa's.

When he arrived, Gina was delighted to see him and walked him to the garage, pointing him toward the shop. He quietly let himself in and waited by the door. His grandpa had a magnifier attached to his glasses and was using tweezers to press something tiny into a thin groove on one of his wood bowls. When he finished, he looked up.

"Jake! What a great surprise! Are you coming to work with me?"

Jake grinned. "Maybe just watch?" He pushed his hands into the pockets of his denim jacket.

"Sure! Pull up a chair, get comfortable. Placing these little stones is delicate work. I'd love an assistant to pick up any that drop onto the floor." He gave Jake a wink.

Instead of sitting, Jake walked to the shelves filled with organized rows of wood. "This is crazy. I thought all trees were brown, but there are so many colors here. Reddish and black and all sorts of different shades."

"Pick that one up," Grandpa said, pointing to a dark piece, about a foot square.

It was so heavy it took both of Jake's hands to heft it. "This weighs like twenty pounds!" he said, amazed.

"Now put that down and hold this one." Grandpa gave him a reddish piece about the same size.

"Wow! It's so much lighter!"

Grandpa smiled. "Every tree has a different density. Different coloring, different striping. Even sections from the same tree can turn out drastically different. See this here?" Grandpa pointed to a small bowl in the middle of the table with what looked like a giant bite out of it. "A knot created that gouge. Some people think it looks broken. I think it adds character."

Jake put the wood back and picked up a third piece. "Do you know what trees each of these are from?"

Turning the wood upside down, his grandpa showed him a little white sticker on the bottom—*Leon / Black Cherry / 2015*—written in Grandpa's neat small print. "Whenever I get a piece of wood, I make a label indicating the type, where it came from or who gave it to me, and any other special details. Then when I start shaping it, I think about that person, or where I was when I received the wood. I remember the conversations we had. When I'm making a gift, I reflect on the person I'm giving it to and their special traits. Memories we've made together, what I've learned from them."

Jake turned over a few more pieces, then held up an ugly log with a giant growth on it. "Can this be made into something too?"

Roger laughed. "Believe it or not, that's actually a really special log. My good friend Marty gave it to me, taken from an old Douglas fir tree he removed from his cabin site in Colorado. He passed away a few months after the cabin was finished. I'm planning to create something special for his wife."

"And while you make it, you'll think about him?"

"That's right. That wood is challenging to work with, so it will give me lots of time to remember the fishing trips we took together. How he was a great listener when I needed to talk. And how he always laughed at my jokes."

Jake ran a finger over the label on the bottom. *Marty / Douglas Fir / 2018.* "He gave you this a long time ago. Have you waited too long?"

Grandpa put a hand on his shoulder. "When you get to be my age, you realize it's never too late to let someone know you've been thinking about them. I'll get to it soon. Yes, a few years have gone by, but it might be even more meaningful because his family will know he hasn't been forgotten."

Jake pulled a chair close to the table. Grandpa uncapped a bottle of clear glue, placed a small dot in the groove on the bowl, then pinched another tiny turquoise stone with tweezers and fixed it into place. He gently pressed a finger against the greenish-blue stone for a few seconds. "Ten years ago I met Mike, from New Mexico, at a trade show and he and I traded wood. A few years later, with the block he gave me, I made a bowl for two friends, Joe and Nancy, as a wedding gift. I didn't know it, but Nancy spent her childhood in New Mexico. When I gifted it to them, I included a label with the details of the tree and where it came from, and she was delighted that the tree was from her home state. Life's pretty special that way."

"It sounds like choosing a wand in *Harry Potter*." Jake laughed. "You have all this wood to choose from, and magically, the block you chose matches the person you're giving it to."

"It sure seems that way. Perhaps that's how JK Rowling got the idea."

Grandpa winked at him and went back to his work. They sat in silence for several minutes.

Jake closed his eyes and rested his head on the back of the old green chair. The shop was warm and smelled of wood, and he discovered it was easy to clear his mind here too, like at the lake. He imagined bringing a sleeping bag and camping out on the floor. It would be a lot warmer than the lake in December.

"Is everything okay, Jake?" Grandpa whispered.

He opened an eye. "Yeah. Is everything okay with the bowl?"

"Yep." He showed him the progress he'd made. "Anything on your mind, son?"

"Not really. Can I just sit here while you work?"

"You got it. But while this dries, I'm going to use the lathe." He took two pairs of headphones from the pegboard and handed one to Jake. "Put these on. No better place to think than in the shop with headphones muffling the drone of the lathe to a pleasant white noise."

Jake slipped them on and then leaned back, closing his eyes again.

Thirty minutes later, Gina poked her head in. "Hi, Jake. Roger, I'm going to bed. Will you two be done soon?"

Jake stood, stretching his arms in front of him, cracked his neck, and then looked at his watch. "I need to go home. Thanks for letting me come over, Grandpa."

Roger put an arm around Jake's shoulder. "You're welcome here anytime, kid."

Jake walked the two miles home in the dark, his skateboard under his arm. It had started to snow again, and the warmth of the shop had quickly faded now that he was outside and freezing. If he wanted to spend more time in Grandpa's shop this winter, he'd need to figure out a warmer way to get there and back.

# 23

## made it through

THROUGHOUT DECEMBER, MATT KEPT THINK-
ING he'd like to buy a Christmas gift for Connor. But that
seemed weird, so he kept it to himself. His Christmas spirit
was further dampened by Jill's incessant planning for a candlelight dinner in Connor's memory on the twenty-first of
December. When she first mentioned it, he'd loved the idea.
They spent a family night brainstorming which food should
be on the menu and all four of them laughed as they remembered his favorites: Turkey with barbecue sauce, macaroni
and cheese, peppermint ice cream. Carrots and ranch. The
way they talked about Connor finally felt right. Natural.

But then Jill got to work planning and preparing, and suddenly Matt was bombarded with questions about what table
settings would remind them most of Connor—the Christmas
china or the everyday plates? Should she decorate with the
gold chargers because they're fancy and special, or a fun plaid
because it's more kid-like? What should the centerpiece be?

It took every ounce of control not to answer sarcastically: *The kid was eleven. I can assure you—he didn't care then, and he especially doesn't care now.* But he didn't say that. Just barely.

"Don't the green candles say 'Connor'? Because, remember, he liked green? But I guess he also liked blue. I know, we could do a blue tablecloth with green candles." What did Matt think about that? And did he think she should prepare a program? Henry could play a piece on the piano and Jake would play the clarinet.

It seemed to escape her that no one had taken piano lessons since the accident and Jake hadn't picked up a clarinet since elementary school.

Matt didn't feel like playing along anymore. Why couldn't they talk about Connor on a regular afternoon when they were just sitting around? Why did it have to be a whole event just to remember their son?

On the *special night,* they lit the green candles, but nobody played an instrument. They ate Connor's favorite foods and afterward Jill asked that everyone share some of their favorite memories. She had written notes; Matt could see her holding the paper under the table. But when Henry simply said, "I miss him and I like his souvenir collection," and Jake said, "He was getting good at soccer," Matt saw her fold up the paper with shaking hands and fidget as she put it in her pocket. In the end she just said, "I miss his smile."

⌣

On Christmas Eve, Jill agreed to Chinese takeout, something they'd joked about doing for years but had never "resorted so low." The best part of the meal, besides being an easy clean-up, was that beef and broccoli helped disguise the fact that it was actually Christmas Eve. But the illusion shattered as they filled the stockings after the two boys were in bed. Four were full of treats and surprises, but Connor's was limp and empty, and they were faced with the appalling decision between leaving it hanging—a screaming visual that he was gone—or taking it down and boxing it up as if they couldn't stand his memory.

Now, three days after Christmas, the tree was at the curb and everything red or green was stored away. The sparkle and shine had been shelved and in just one week, the boys would go back to school. Matt had scheduled two weeks of vacation so they could spend time together. Go sledding. See a movie. He'd even happily work on a thousand-piece jigsaw puzzle with Jill if he could get a glimmer of his old wife back.

But so far, they hadn't done any of that. Jake was always taking a nap and Henry had had a stomachache for the past two days. And Jill . . . she stayed busy. Holiday checklist busy. Not the spontaneous and playful *let's take a snowy walk at midnight*, like the woman she used to be, but the *in the morning we have to make chocolate chip pancakes because it's Christmastime* busy.

He'd hoped that with everyone home, things could go back to how they were before. Of course, not entirely, because someone would always be missing. But he hoped they would talk about Connor, remembering last Christmas when he was so excited about the binoculars. And imagining what he would have wanted this Christmas. Maybe they'd even watch old family videos. But no. Instead, they continued not talking about him, not really, which made it feel like he was not only gone but disappearing.

In the late afternoon, Jill and Henry were at the mall exchanging his new shoes for a larger size, and Jake was in his room, sleeping once again. Matt sat at the kitchen counter alone, snacking on a bowl of Cheerios. In four days it would be a new year, a time to make resolutions. He'd never been a goal-setter, Jill's lists were enough for both of them. But he wondered if there was something he could change, something he could do to make his family whole again. He'd tried being a buffer between Jake and Jill, but while it seemed to help Jake at first, it had hurt his relationship with Jill. It felt like he was being asked to choose sides in a fight between his two best friends.

Were he and Jill still best friends? They used to dance together, and when they did, she was sexy as hell. She was an expert behind the wheel of a boat, something he knew nothing about when they first met. But she had such confidence in him—teaching him to drive and making him feel like he was capable of anything. She also loved to curl up in the crook of his arm and let him take care of her, which was, well, an incredible turn-on.

He was a better person with her by his side because she used to make him feel like he was amazing. But now she was different. Just when he felt a hint of connection, he realized he was seeing things that weren't there. She was so damn independent and closed off; she didn't need him anymore and expected him to feel the same way.

He twirled the last two oat circles, spinning them in a lake of milk, the little one chasing the big one. And suddenly he had to get out of the house.

Opening the front door, he inhaled the crisp winter air, expanding his lungs so he could feel it all the way to his fingers and toes. Anything to fill the emptiness. And to his surprise, he did feel brighter. Maybe getting outside was just what he needed. When was the last time he'd gone for a walk? Or exercised, for that matter?

As he stepped off the porch, one foot flew forward, slipping on slick ice, both arms flailing as they tried to keep him upright. Icy patches from his poor shoveling job created a minefield as he cautiously made his way down the path. When a blue car like Jill's turned the corner, for some reason, he felt like he needed an excuse to be in the front yard. He raised his hand to wave and point to the mailbox, then saw it wasn't Jill's car after all. His hand stopped midair, scratching at his beard instead. He'd let it grow in over the break, but he hated it. He needed to shave.

The gray sky hung low, making his suburban neighborhood seem one-dimensional, like a depressing postcard. He could almost fool himself into believing the world was black and white. And months of this dreariness lay ahead of them. Going on a walk was a dumb idea. He was freezing. He turned back, but a streak of pale blue at the edge of the horizon caught his eye. It was far away, beyond the end of his street, but it was a reminder. Of what, he couldn't think. But the glimpse of color when everything else was leaden seemed to be a beacon.

Now he reconsidered. Maybe he would go for a walk. He opened the mailbox. Empty. He chewed the inside of his cheek. He was wearing a thin, long-sleeved T-shirt and tennis shoes. He wasn't dressed for it. But the blue stripe was widening, and with it his desire for something to be excited about, and he decided that yes, he was going, but he was going to do it right.

Dodging the icy spots, he dashed back to the house, retrieved his coat from the front closet, and laced up his winter boots. He found gloves in a pocket and pulled on a knit beanie, then a baseball cap over it, and headed down the street toward the patch of sky as blue as an Alaskan glacier.

At the edge of their neighborhood was a playground where he used to push Connor in the swings. The soccer field was next to it, and beyond, a trail through a small forest. He used to jog alongside the boys as they rode their bikes on this path. It seemed like he and Jake and Connor rode through here every Sunday for years. When had they stopped? He'd never run beside Henry.

In the dirt on the side of the forest walkway, a small crocodile-green rock caught his eye. When he picked it up, he saw another larger one, about the size of a walnut, with a rusty strike like a lightning bolt embedded in it. He imagined giving them to Connor, who was always excited about anything you showed him. Even if it was just junk, he'd see what you saw that made it special. Plus, he was always starting a collection. Rocks, pinecones, sea glass, pennies, and feathers, to name a few.

When he came out of the trees, the sky was now saturated with color. Like it didn't care that soon the sun was setting and dark would dominate again. Even if just for an hour, hope would make an appearance and dazzle whoever was looking.

He wrapped his fingers around the rocks, like talismans, in his pocket. Somehow, they would help him figure out a way to hold his family together.

Everyone was in the family room when he got home. The boys were playing with Henry's new Matchbox cars and Jill had started a puzzle.

"Daddy!" Henry shouted when he walked in the door. "Do you want to watch a movie with me and Jake and Mom? Jake wants to watch *Elf* and I do too. It's okay even though Christmas is over, right?"

Matt squeezed the rocks in his pocket, then sat at the puzzle table across from Jill. "I love *Elf*! Should I make spaghetti for dinner, just like in the movie?" His wife smiled at him as he helped her turn puzzle pieces color-side up.

That night, after the boys were in bed and he and Jill were locking up, she paused in front of a new, framed picture on the fireplace mantle and touched the toothy smiles. Gina's Christmas present to them was a framed selfie of the whole family on the boat, taken on Roger's phone just hours before Connor died—the last picture they'd ever have of everyone together. He and Jill had completely forgotten they'd taken it.

Gina hoped it wasn't too painful—it was why she'd waited to give it to them. But they assured her they loved it.

He stood behind Jill, resting his hand on her waist. She didn't squirm away or flinch. Instead, she leaned back into him and asked, "Do you like this picture, or do you hate it?"

"It depends on the hour."

"Yeah, me too." She laced her fingers through his, sighing. "This Christmas has gone really great." She tucked a lock of hair behind her ear. "I was dreading it, I really was. But with all the daily activities, we somehow made it through. Everyone really liked having so many fun things to do, I think." She turned to face him, wrapping her arms around him and resting her head on his chest. "And Jake, he's been good, right? He's seemed really happy the past month. It's been nice. Like we're all in a good place. Maybe it's a turning point, do you think?"

He didn't think so, given what he'd discovered two weeks ago, but he ran his fingers through her hair and lied. "I think you're right."

They held each other for the first time in a long time. She whispered into his neck that she loved him.

"I love you too," he murmured. His heart beat faster as he rubbed her back and kissed the top of her head. He could feel the weight of the rocks—Connor's rocks—in his pocket. They'd helped change the day from bleak to happy, like they really did hold some magic. It definitely wasn't going to be a turning point for Jake and Jill's relationship when she found out what he knew, but maybe it was a turning point for them.

Maybe starting today, they were finally healing and every-thing between them would begin to get better.

He took Jill's hand and led her upstairs. He knew the brightening sky held promise. He led her to bed and kissed her cheek, her neck. When their mouths met, she kissed him back with a desire he'd thought had faded forever.

She slid her hands down his back, and he pulled her to him. There was no way he would ruin this moment by reveal-ing that Jake had been stealing the car.

Three weeks ago, he noticed Jake's Subaru was parked much closer to the wall than usual. He actually wondered if it could have rolled there.

The keys were in Matt's dresser drawer, where he always kept them, so he backed it up to its normal spot—not too close to the wall or the garage door. But he put a small piece of shiny, silver duct tape where the back tire met the floor. A week later, the tape was black with grime. He took a picture of the mileage on the odometer.

He knew he couldn't ignore it, that he had a responsibility to talk to Jake. But not during the holidays that were already so hard. He was waiting for a better time and to figure out the right way to handle it. He probably should get mad or disci-pline him, but hadn't they all been punished enough this year?

# 24

## *pain like mine*

JAKE WAS KICKING A SOCCER ball against his bedroom wall when his phone rang. If he had to guess, it would be his mom yelling at him to quit. He ignored the ringing and continued using the wall as a rebounder. Sweat dripped down his temple and he had to push his long hair out of his face. The phone stopped, but a second later it started ringing again. He trapped the ball and glanced at the flashing screen on his desk. Grandpa. "Hello?"

"Hey, kid! How's the first week back to school been?"

"Pretty good."

"I'm going to the Woodworkers' Festival downtown this Saturday. Want to come with me? We can get lunch after."

Lunch, good. Early Saturday, bad. "What do you do there?" Jake asked.

"Look at other people's work, ask questions about their technique. Get new ideas. Trade wood. I'd like to go for a couple of hours, but we don't have to go too early. I assume you like sleeping in?"

⮑

When Jake and Grandpa arrived at the festival, Jake was surprised at how crowded it was. Rows of tables packed the
large expo center, each one displaying wood bowls in every
shape and size with various styles of finish. Some with wide,
rounded bottoms, others with sleek, narrow necks. Many had
metal strips inlaid or small stones added for color, like the
bowl he saw Grandpa working on last month. Some were tiny
dishes, just big enough to hold small rings or bracelets, but
others were huge, taking up half the table. And there weren't
just bowls on display, but also writing pens, boxes, vases,
bracelets, salt and pepper shakers, table legs, toy tops, and
cooking spoons, all made of wood.

A lathe was set up on a stage in the middle of the room
and a man with a microphone clipped to his denim shirt was
explaining his process as he worked. As they walked by booths
with tools for sale, Grandpa named them and explained how
they were used. He also stopped to talk to many of the crafts-
men and women to compare notes. It reminded Jake of a sci-
ence fair for grown-ups.

They stopped to talk to the millionth person—a woman
with blocks of wood a lot like those in Grandpa's shop, and
Jake tried to stifle a yawn. Grandpa pulled out his billfold and
gave Jake five dollars. "See if you can find some popcorn or
something. Can you give me thirty minutes?"

Holding a bag of kettle corn, Jake wandered through the
last aisles and discovered that not every artist used wood.
One bearded man displayed knife sheaths and wallets made
of leather. A short lady with pink hair hung painted metal
decorations in her area. And at the end of the final row, a guy
with tiny, dark, round glasses and a beret was surrounded by
colorful wind chimes made of sea glass.

Jake stopped, mesmerized by the delicate tinkling as the pieces brushed against each other. A few years ago, during a family vacation to Florida, he and Connor found a flat green jewel on the beach. Their mom said it was sea glass—a piece of broken bottle that had been polished smooth after years of being tumbled in the ocean. The rest of the trip, they'd searched the beaches together looking for more.

Henry was a toddler at the time, so their mom had let Jake and Connor walk up and down the beach alone while she played with Henry. He'd felt so old. Almost a middle schooler and trusted to be in charge of his little brother. Jake realized that if Henry had been two years old at the time, it meant he'd been eleven—the same age Connor was when he'd died.

In spite of searching every day, they'd never found anything other than broken shells. On the last day, Connor bought a jar of sea glass as his souvenir.

"What kind of projects are you working on?" the glass man asked as he threaded a thin wire into a hole on a smooth blue piece no bigger than a quarter.

Jake turned to look over his shoulder.

"No, I'm talking to you," the man said, looking up at him.

"Um ... I'm just a kid," Jake mumbled. "I don't do any of this stuff."

"Sixteen, I'd guess? Lots of kids have made some pretty cool art by your age. My name's Ethan." He stuck out his hand.

Jake wiped his hands on his pants, then shook Ethan's hand. "I came with my grandpa. He makes bowls."

"Are you thinking of making bowls too, or has something else caught your eye?" Ethan asked.

"I never knew there was other stuff besides bowls. Your chimes are pretty cool."

Ethan clipped the wire, then twisted it into a knot and began the process again, threading a white piece next to the blue one. "I've been making art since I was about your age. I made my first chime for my mom when I was eighteen."

"For Mother's Day?"

Ethan picked up a green piece and threaded the wire, then twisted and clipped it. "Nope, when my brother died."

Jake choked. "You had a brother die, too?"

Ethan put his work down and lifted his glasses. "My brother died of a drug overdose when he was twenty-one. Did you have a brother die?"

Jake suddenly felt tears burn his eyes, and he tried to blink them away. He picked the green piece off the table and turned it over in his hand. "Last summer. My little brother drowned."

"Ah, dude. I'm sorry. That's rough. It's so recent."

"Is last summer recent?"

"It is. It's going to feel 'recent' for the next couple of years."

"When did your brother die?"

"Eight years ago. I was eighteen. I thought he was the coolest guy in the world. I also thought he was a bit of a jerk. And I know that makes me sound like a jerk. But just because he died doesn't make him perfect. Or me."

Jake studied him. That made a lot of sense. But he'd never heard anyone say something unkind about someone who was dead. "And then what? I mean, what happened to your family after that?"

"We were all kind of screwed up for a while. It was just me and my brother, no other siblings. My mom slept all the time. My dad cried all the time. I started taking drugs, which is a shit thing to do when your brother has just overdosed, and I can't explain why that was my answer. Although... maybe you get it?"

"I don't do drugs," Jake said.

"I don't either anymore. You should never start because getting clean was the hardest thing I've ever gone through.

Worse than my brother dying. So, promise me, man, you'll never, ever start."

Jake's jaw hung slack as he nodded.

"Good. But you know what? We're better now. My parents are back to work, and they laugh again, and we have fun together. We miss him, but we talk about him without getting sad. We can remember without getting overwhelmed. I think we've made it through." He picked up the end of the wire and another piece of polished glass. "It took a while, but we're going to be okay. You are too. You may not feel like it now because it's really, really hard losing someone you love."

Jake's eyes filled with tears again.

Ethan sifted through his bowl of glass pieces, picked out a milky blue one, rubbed a cloth over it, and handed it to Jake. "Let me give you some advice. Be okay with telling yourself you loved him. And you miss him. The more you say it, I promise that ache will ease. And some day you'll be able to talk about it with a kid you just met at an art show without worrying about losing it." He gave him a fist bump. "It gets better, dude. I promise."

As he left to find Grandpa, Jake caressed the smooth glass with his thumb.

"Did you see anything that interested you?" Grandpa asked when he and Jake met at the exit and pushed through the doors into the bright January sun.

Squinting, Jake walked aimlessly towards the parking lot, fingering the glass in his pocket as he thought about the question. He was a few steps ahead when he felt a tug on his elbow. "The car's this way," Grandpa said, pointing to the row Jake had just passed.

"Do you think I could work on a project in your shop sometime?" Jake asked, letting himself be guided to the car.

"I'd love it. Do you want me to teach you how to use the lathe?"

"I won't need it," Jake said, dodging a slushy puddle. "I have an idea for something else."

# 25

## alone in the shop

MONDAY AFTER SCHOOL, JAKE LET himself into
Grandpa's house, calling out, "Anyone home?"

Grandpa walked into the hall. "Hey, Jake! To what do we
owe the pleasure?"

"I wanted to get started on my project. Is that okay?"

"Sure! Do you want company?"

"I'm good. I don't need help."

Pointing to the brown grocery sack Jake was carrying,
Grandpa said, "I'll take you back and show you where you can
store your stuff." They walked through the garage into the
shop and Grandpa flipped on the lights. He picked up a rag
and dusted off an empty shelf. "This space can be yours for
anything you want to leave here." Pointing to the large table
in the center of the room, he said, "If you're in the middle of
something, you don't have to put everything away when you
leave, but do tidy up. If you get cold, you can turn on the
space heater."

Jake thanked him and placed his bag on the table without opening it. He bit his thumbnail, willing Grandpa to leave without asking questions.

Grandpa glanced at the bag, then at Jake, his face relaxing into his affectionate grin. He patted Jake's shoulder and then left, closing the door behind him.

Jake took Connor's mason jar of sea glass out of the bag. He'd also brought a spool of fishing line he'd received with a new pole a few years ago, a pair of scissors, and Kevin's *gift*—but he left that wrapped up inside the bigger bag. He took off his coat and turned on the space heater.

Jake had never been in the shop alone before. The few times Grandpa had tried to engage him in a woodturning project, he'd quickly lost interest. Holding the small screwdriver-like tool steady against the rotating bowl was hard, and making ugly dents when he used too much force was easy. He knew he'd never be any good at it.

But today, the dusty smell of the space heater as it warmed the room, combined with the hint of freshly cut wood, gave Jake the feeling that Grandpa's shop was a place of possibility. Just being trusted to work there on his own made him think he was a person who could accomplish something.

He ran his finger across the workbench. A fine layer of dust covered everything. Sunlight streamed in through a small window, spotlighting particles that were still looking for a place to settle.

The table was topped with four wood bowls in varying stages of finish. Two had rounded outsides but were solid in the center; another looked complete, positioned next to a folded rag and a can marked "oil," neatly printed with Sharpie on masking tape across the front. The fourth sat next to the small jelly jar of turquoise that Grandpa was using the other night. Jake picked it up and held it near his eyes. Each miniature stone had black veins crisscrossing its surface, like rivers crossing little planets. He lightly shook the jar to hear them rattle.

Behind him was the lathe. He'd watched Grandpa situate a thick square block in the clamps, then flip the power to start the spin. When Grandpa used the tools, he made shaping a bowl look easy. Years of the tree's life curled and fell away as the metal glided across the wood.

Above the lathe, tools hung on a pegboard with an outline drawn around each one so you knew where it belonged. Three pair of clear goggles were organized on a shelf next to ear protectors, several dust masks, a cardboard box of rags cut from old T-shirts, and a metal can of turpentine. Jake unscrewed the lid and lowered his head, the sharp smell surprising him even though he knew what to expect. He leaned in again for another quick drag, smiling because there was no one here to see.

He spread a handful of blue, green, and white glass onto the table. He remembered Connor enthusiastically calling for him to *come and see* when he found the large jar for sale in the gift shop. Jake was envious he hadn't seen it first. When Connor offered to share with him, it bugged Jake even more. "Why do you want to buy so much of it? What are you even going to use it for?"

Connor shrugged. "I don't know. Maybe just look at it. They're cool."

"It's just junk," Jake said, pinching Connor on the arm as he walked away.

Undeterred, Connor bought it and placed the jar on his already full display shelf in his bedroom. He loved collecting stuff. Stopping at souvenir stores was his favorite activity on any family vacation. He wanted the clear bag of huge seashells. Snow globes from every place they visited. Anything tiny or patterned or in the shape of an animal cried to him like an abandoned pet that he had to bring home. Once he wanted a velvet pouch of polished rocks from the gift shop at the zoo. When his parents wouldn't buy them, he asked for a rock tumbler for Christmas.

On Christmas Day, Jake and Connor collected rocks in the backyard, anticipating turning them into the vibrant, smooth gems like the ones in the giant barrel at the zoo. But when their mom told them rocks from the yard would stay gray, and that they may crumble in the polisher, Connor was disappointed, but Jake was embarrassed. They never used the tumbler. Not even once.

Jake pushed the sea glass around, studying their differences and holding them up to the light. Some were as thin as a quarter, others thick and curved, and a few were oval, like stones. He stacked them into piles, then spread them out and sorted them by size. The container was still over half full, so he poured more onto the table. When they bumped against each other, they made music.

It reminded him of the rainstick he had as a kid. When you held it up, whatever was inside rattled to the opposite end and sounded exactly like rain. He never got tired of flipping it over and over.

Jake searched the shop for something to pour his glass into. Connor's glass.

On a high shelf, a few of Grandpa's wood bowls were covered in dust. He climbed onto a stool and found one with a large crack through the center but still intact, and placed it on the table. He tipped the jar and as the glass cascaded into the bowl, it seemed to sing.

He pretended they were priceless, precious jewels and buried his hands, letting the smaller fragments fill the spaces around his wrists as he wiggled his fingers.

Finally, he picked out his favorite five, each a different size and slightly different hue. He ordered them biggest to smallest, measured a foot of fishing line, cut it, and waited for the glue gun to heat up. He experimented with design and spacing as he glued and removed and reglued them to the almost invisible thin line, working until he was satisfied. When he was sure the glue was dry, he held the strand to the window and was delighted to see that it shimmered in the sun. He folded it into his pocket. His first masterpiece.

Jake scooped the rest of the glass back into the jar and put the jar in the brown paper sack, along with the scissors and spool. He didn't think Grandpa would care if he used the bowl, so he left it on the center of the table. After folding the top of the bag over a few times, he found a stapler and fastened it shut for good measure. Then he put it on the shelf.

He hoped to come back soon—maybe even tomorrow, his excitement reminding him of the feeling he had with Connor on the Florida vacation. Each morning, whoever woke up first would say, "Do you want to look for glass?" knowing the other would. Or in the middle of building a sandcastle, one of them would say, "Maybe a piece of glass should go right here!" And they'd both jump up to search.

The trick would be getting to Grandpa's without anyone else knowing. It wasn't enough to be alone. He wanted it to be a secret too. It made him mad just thinking about his mom asking about what he was working on and how it was going and treating him like a baby with a little art project.

She couldn't find out. He'd just have to tell her he was spending a lot more time with Sam.

# 26

## so they're not lonely

THEY WERE ALREADY A MONTH into the new year and Jill still hadn't bothered to set any resolutions. Usually, she liked reevaluating and imagining everything she could become in just twelve months. But now, what was the point? Who cared how many goals you achieved when a split-second decision could take everything important away.

It seemed like their family had slipped into a state of melancholy throughout January. No one was arguing, but no one was happy either. She and Matt hadn't spoken about visiting the lake again, and Jake hadn't mentioned it. She supposed she'd gotten her way, but she didn't feel very good about it.

Jake seemed to be gone from home more now than during soccer season. She was trying to let him have his space, like Matt suggested, but she just wanted to know when to expect him home. Every other day she'd casually say, "Hey, I need you to tell me if you're not coming home after school."

And he'd always respond with, "Oh yeah, I forgot. I was just with Sam."

He seemed better. More relaxed. So she let it go. "Just remember tomorrow."

"Sure," he'd say. And she truly believed he would. But he never did. She tried not to worry.

Jill carried a laundry basket down the hallway, moving it to her hip to free up a hand so she could touch a finger to a hanging portrait of Connor—to his cheek. She paused, blowing him a kiss. She lingered on the family portrait next to it. Henry was just a toddler then. The three boys' smiles were all teeth, and they clutched hands like little monkeys, Jill and Matt innocently happy behind them.

A voice came from Connor's room. Someone was whispering. She put the basket down and peeked around the corner. Henry was facing Connor's bookshelf, his head only tall enough to reach the middle shelf, where, instead of books, souvenirs were displayed—Connor's knickknacks from their family vacations. Henry was holding a miniature dog made of tiny shells.

"I remember you because we were at the beach and we wanted shells. Connor likes dogs, but I got a turtle. Someday I think I'll have a real turtle."

He touched another figurine next to it. "You can nod your head to say hello. I don't have one like you. Would you like to come live in my room?" He touched the head which bobbed up and down. "Okay. Do you want to bring a friend?" He turned it to face his companions as if the little animal were choosing. "Would you like this one? No. You want something better. Do you want this teeny tiny snow globe? No, because it's too small. But you want to look at the other snow globes? Okay. This one with the Statue of Liberty? This one from Grandma's house? How about this one with the bus? That's the one you like the best? Okay. You can come live in my room. Connor's going to be gone for a long time, so I know it's getting kind of boring in here."

When he turned and saw Jill, he jumped, and she tried to look like she had just walked up. "Hi, Henry. I thought I heard someone talking in here."

He hid his hands behind his back. "I'm just looking at stuff. I'm not touching anything."

"I'm so glad you come into Connor's room and keep his toys company. Did you find some things that you'd like to have in your room?"

Henry's shoulders relaxed and he held up the tiny animal and the snow globe.

Jill bent down, cupping Henry's hand in hers, examining the toys. "I bet Connor would be happy that you like his stuff. Is it fun to look through his things?"

Henry nodded enthusiastically. "I come in and talk to him and tell him that his toys are getting lonely, and they want to have a turn visiting my room. Everyone is getting different turns. Connor likes that I'm taking care of his toys."

Jill's heart fluttered. "Does Connor talk back to you?"

Henry wrinkled his nose. "No, Mommy, that's silly! I tell him what I'm thinking, and then my head tells me what Connor would say."

Jill knelt and pulled Henry into a hug, kissing his cheek. "I do that too. I like that he always says nice things."

Henry wiggled into her lap. "Except that I don't think he's very happy that his glass collection is gone. He liked that a lot."

"Is it?" Jill turned to look at the shelf, so full of "special things" that she wouldn't know what Connor had kept over the years, let alone if anything was missing.

"Yep. It used to be in the back behind the animals."

"Do you think Jake or Daddy wanted it to visit, just like the toys want to visit you?"

"Mommy, they don't play with toys."

"I know. But I'll bet everyone wants something that Connor loved. It makes us feel better when we miss him. I think if they're borrowing the glass collection right now, it would make Connor happy, just like it makes him happy that you're bringing toys to your room, so they don't get lonely."

Henry laid his head on Jill's chest. "But should we find out if Daddy or Jake have it?"

She breathed in his innocence, feeling that if she could sit here and hold him long enough, her heart would also start to heal. "If they're borrowing the glass, I think they might want it to be private. Did you want it to be private that you were looking at Connor's things?"

"No, Mommy, you can know."

She snuggled him into her lap, shifting so she was sitting cross-legged. "I love you, cutie."

"Do you like to borrow things from Connor's room too?" he asked.

"I like to come in here and sit on his bed. Sometimes I come in and read. And I like to look at his things just like you do."

Henry squirmed out of her embrace. "Okay, Mommy, I love you too." And he skipped out of the room.

Jill's knees cracked as she picked up the laundry basket and stretched. The afternoon sunlight made a yellow stripe across his carpet. She loved lying in the sunspot on her bedroom floor when she was a child. She would turn her face to the window, the brightness forcing her eyes shut, the warmth a cocoon, holding her until the sun slowly moved away. She wished she could lie on the floor in that light right now. But some things you can't do when you're old. When you're a mom.

That day's mail included Jake's report card from the most recent term. All A's and B's. But she was surprised to see several absences. She went in search of Jake and found him watching TV. She sat on the couch next to him. "Hey, Jake, what's this?" she asked, holding the paper so he could see it.

He looked at it and smiled. "Proof that I've been doing well in school."

"You have three absences in PE, graphics, and English. How come?"

Sighing, he paused the TV and looked where she was pointing at the attendance column. "I was probably just late and they marked me as absent. Did you want to comment on my good grades? Absences really don't matter if you're getting A's."

"Your grades are great. But I have to disagree that absences don't matter. Especially if you weren't sick. Jake, did you cut class?"

He rolled his eyes and unpaused the TV. "You're making a big deal out of nothing. It happens all the time. The teacher marks the wrong person absent."

She studied his profile. His brown hair was long, almost chin length now. His beautiful blue eyes. The way he was biting the inside of his cheek. Exactly how he did as a child when she caught him in a lie.

That night, when she crawled into bed next to Matt, she grabbed his hand and moved close to him. "I think Jake ditched a few classes last term. His report card had some absences in a few classes. He says he was there, but I'm not so sure."

Matt pulled his hand away and turned over. "I don't think you should be so hard on him. Cutting class occasionally is normal."

She rolled onto her side and fluffed her pillow. "I wasn't hard on him. He told me he was there, and I didn't say anything else. But I'm pretty sure he was lying."

Suddenly Matt was close, his voice in her ear. "I'm going to tell you something, but you've got to let me handle it."

Jill's heart started to pound. "This sounds bad."

"Jake's been taking his car."

She flipped to face him. "What!"

"In December I noticed it was parked closer to the wall than normal. I thought it might have rolled somehow." He told her about the tape behind the wheel. "Clearly someone—Jake—had driven the car."

She sat up. "I'm going to murder Todd."

Matt put his hands on hers. "Jill, listen. Todd ratted you out at Thanksgiving, but everyone made a big deal about your dad not overreacting when it happened. Things have been going well and Jake seems to be in a good place. I don't want to rock the boat."

"But where is he going? What's he doing? Sam has a car, so he wouldn't need Jake to drive anywhere. So who is he hanging out with?"

"For all we know, he's going to McDonald's, just like you did. Listen, I checked the odometer about two weeks before Christmas and it hasn't changed since then. I decided not to say anything because I think he's stopped. I don't want you to say anything either. We're just going to let it go unless it happens again."

"But what if he gets in an accident? What if he causes an accident? I can't . . ." Her throat seized as every worst-case scenario flashed through her mind.

"Well, you're going to have to keep a lid on it. I mean it. He's getting his license in a month. I'll talk to him if he does it again. But for now, let's just keep the peace. Please."

She lay back down. She wanted to storm into Jake's room and shake some sense into that smug kid. Her arms shook with anger—or was it fear?—as she thought of smashed metal, broken glass, and another lifeless body. She spooned her body into Matt's. She needed to feel grounded. Needed his weight to hold her in place so she didn't run screaming into Jake's room.

He put an arm around her, pulled her to him, and kissed her shoulder while she sobbed.

# 27

## memories

ROGER HAD LET JAKE INTO the shop several times throughout January. But now, the first week of February, he'd been over three times already. Sometimes he was there for less than an hour. Other times up to two. "What do you think he's doing in there?" Gina asked one evening after he left.

Roger was chopping potatoes for chowder. Fresh rolls in the oven filled the kitchen with the smell of "no place he'd rather be" while a light snow fell outside. Roger had offered Jake a ride home, but he declined, saying his friend was picking him up.

"I have no idea," he replied, attention focused on his precisely chopped squares. "He took down one of my old bowls. It's on the table, dusted up, but empty. And your glue gun is sitting next to it. But he cleans everything else up before he leaves. He has a large brown paper sack on a shelf—I assume that's where he's keeping whatever it is he's working on."

Gina put a pot of water on the stove, tossed in a couple of bouillon cubes, and turned the burner on high. "Are you tempted to open it?"

"I'm curious, for sure. And I'll admit that I did pick it up once, but it's stapled shut. So I'm not going to look. I think it's good for him to have a project, and I want to respect his privacy." When the water began to bubble, Roger pushed the potatoes into the boiling water and dumped a bowl of chopped celery and corn in too.

Gina leaned against the counter. "He's a sweet kid. Why do you think he and Jill are butting heads? He's perfect when he's here. Looks me in the eye when he says hello. Knows how to have a conversation. Cleans up after himself."

Roger washed his hands and laughed. "Teenagers can be angels to everyone but their parents—especially when those parents impose rules and expectations. We're lucky we just get to love him." He stirred the pot, then turned the heat to low and took his drink to the table.

"What do you remember about Robert?" Gina asked, her voice soft as she stood behind him rubbing his shoulders.

Roger exhaled. He widened his eyes and shrugged. Robert, his older brother whom he had no memories of. "Nothing." His gaze moved out the window to the snow dripping from the trees.

"Nothing at all?"

Roger shook his head. "I was only two when he was hit by the car. He was five. I was too young to remember him."

"Do you remember how it affected your parents?" She sat next to him.

He shrugged again. "They were fine. 'Right as rain,' as my dad always said in the worst English accent. I'm sure they had a hard year, but for as long as I can remember, they were fine. They didn't let it get in the way of taking care of me."

Gina put her hand on his knee. "Why do you say a 'hard year'?"

He caressed her fingers. He loved that she always touched him. "You know. A year. When someone dies, everyone says, 'You'll feel better after a year.'"

"Do you think you'll feel better about Connor after a year?"

He stuck out his lip. "I hope a little bit. That's what everyone says."

His wife raised her brows, her eyes boring into his.

He rubbed his chest trying to lessen the constant weight that now resided there. "It seems impossible, doesn't it? The pain is so consuming. Just when you think it's eased up, it hits you all over again. But Gina, it's gotta get better. It's hard to live like this."

She wiped her eye then looped her fingers through his. "I want to believe it gets easier with time. Did you ever talk to your parents about Robert?"

"They talked about him all the time."

"How did that make you feel?"

"To be honest, I felt special. I had a brother who was in heaven, and I told other kids he was my guardian angel who looked out for me. Other kids had imaginary friends, but mine had really existed. I used to pretend he gave me superpowers."

Gina's voice turned earnest. "But when you grew up and married and had kids, you had to have felt something different. You must have had concerns. About their safety. Understood better that something could happen to them."

Roger didn't say anything. He looked out of the window where barren trees stood stiff and cold, snow piled around them. There were times the kids had gotten hurt. And yes, there were behaviors he was concerned about. Todd drove too fast. He was sure Cara smoked pot. But Jill. He hadn't worried about her.

His ex-wife, Hilary, was constantly anxious. She was always imagining worst-case scenarios and bracing herself for disaster. But he didn't. It was life. The kids were ultimately going to be fine. He guessed being the strong one was part of being a man.

Gina squeezed his hand. "What are you thinking about?"

"I don't know. I think some people are worriers. I like to stay positive."

"I like to stay positive too, but I still worry," she said.

He cut her off. "Jill fell out of a tree once."

"Really?" Gina sat back. "When? How old was she?"

"About ten. She was such a little daredevil." Roger grinned. "Never afraid of anything. Got it from me, obviously. She could climb any tree. But her arms were so scrawny she'd have to ask for a boost to get her legs to the first branch. After that, she could climb to the very top. Hilary hated it. If it was up to her, she'd have kept the kids home sitting on the couch."

"What would Hilary say when they wanted to do things she considered risky?"

"She never said anything. She let them go and would keep her mouth shut, but later she would tell me how much it frightened her."

"It sounds like she was being a good mom. To keep her worries quiet, I mean."

Roger rolled his eyes at that. "One time we were at a park having a picnic. Cara was little and we were pushing her and Todd on the swings. Jill went to find 'a good tree.' Hilary wanted her to stay with everyone else. Swing on the swings, take her sister down the slide. Keep her close. But Jill walked off."

Roger chuckled. "She had a mind of her own." Taking a breath, he closed his eyes and massaged the bridge of his nose. "I heard her call 'Dad!' and just as I looked up, she screamed and there she was, falling out of a tree. It was a big pine, and it was like watching her fall in slow motion because she hit branches all the way down. Hilary and I left Cara and Todd on the swings and ran. When we got to her, she wasn't breathing. Hilary grabbed her shoulders, shouting her name, and Jill immediately opened her eyes. The wind had been knocked out of her, and she made a terrifying wheeze. But aside from having scratches and being covered in pine needles from head to toe, she was fine. Soon she started crying, then Hilary started crying, and I was just thinking, she's fine. There's no need to cry. She's just fine."

Suddenly Roger's breath caught. "Everyone was always supposed to be fine." His eyes filled with tears. "I was so sure." He began to heave as sobs overtook him. "I really did believe. I know it sounds stupid, but I really believed that Robert protected me. Us. Jill's fall proved it. Somehow, because my brother was lost, I didn't have to worry. Nothing bad could happen twice. Not to the same family."

# 28

## it's my job

A WEEK HAD GONE BY, and Jill was trying to keep her mouth shut. She really was. Jake's birthday was only a week away—by February thirteenth, he'd be able to drive legally. But her anxiety about him skipping class and lying and stealing the car was eating her up.

She'd compromised with Matt, agreeing that she wouldn't say anything if he made Jake keep his phone's location-sharing app on. Jake had thrown a fit, but Matt promised they would only use it in emergencies. Two nights ago, he'd walked through the door in the middle of dinner, and Matt didn't say anything. Just "Hey! Let's get you a plate!" Even Jake seemed surprised. Was it really a good idea to let their fifteen-year-old come and go as he pleased?

Yesterday, she'd run to the window when she heard a car door slam. Jake had his backpack over his head to protect him from the snow as he ran up the front walk. A small black car drove off. She was sure it was a woman driving.

"Who was that dropping you off?" she asked as he came in the front door.

"A friend. No one you know." Jake avoided her eyes as he slipped off his wet shoes.

"She looked old."

He just swaggered past her.

Tonight she was trying to prepare her lesson plan, but her heart was pounding as Jake sat twenty feet from her, watching TV. She wasn't going to say anything. She wasn't. Henry was in bed and Matt had run an errand. It had been a long time since Jake had kicked back in the same room as her without anyone else around to act as . . . a barrier, she suspected. She would appreciate the fact that he wasn't avoiding her tonight and be grateful. She refused to ruin it. She stopped biting her nail and got to work.

His phone dinged and he stood up. "I have to go," he said.

She gaped at him. "It's nine at night! Where are you going?"

"A study group. Do you want me to stay home and just fail tomorrow's math test?"

"Why did you wait until the last minute to study?"

"This was the only time our group could meet. So, can I go?"

"Who's house?"

"You don't know him."

"I actually probably do."

"Steven Larson."

She didn't know him.

He grabbed his backpack and was out the door while she was still debating whether or not she should say yes.

Matt walked in a few minutes later. "Did Jake leave somewhere? I saw him jump into Sam's car."

Jill's head was spinning. "He has a study group."

"So late? Why did you let him go?"

She tossed her hands in the air. "Because I've been forbidden to question him about his whereabouts, and I'm in an absolute panic that you may be correct that it's the right thing to do, and I have no idea what I'm doing anymore. Where have you been?"

"I was out of shaving cream." He held up a grocery bag as if proving he had indeed been where he told her. "Should we watch a show? Your turn to choose." He sat down next to her.

She threw her feet into Matt's lap. This whole *chill*-mom thing—acting like her son was an adult who could come and go as he pleased—did not feel right. She took a breath. He's studying. He's getting good grades. He's fine.

It was almost eleven when they turned off the TV and Jill looked up Jake's location on her phone. She knew they'd promised not to, but too bad. His location showed he was home. *Why would he sneak back in?* As Matt locked the doors and turned out the lights, Jill peeked into Jake's room. He wasn't there. The bathroom was empty. She trotted down two flights of stairs to the basement. No Jake. She dialed his number as she tromped back up. A familiar buzzing greeted her in the foyer—his phone was vibrating on the table. That little liar.

Just then, as if sensing she was searching for him, Jake walked in, whistling, of all things.

She held up his phone. "Why didn't you take your phone with you?"

He looked her in the eye. "We didn't want any distractions."

Jill narrowed hers.

Jake threw his hands up. "Well, that's what the adults are telling us all the time. *Stop needing your phone every second.* And then when I leave it home, you think I'm lying. 'K. Nice."

Jill turned away, but quickly spun back, gripping him into a fierce hug. She held him close for several seconds, then pulled away and looked into his eyes. Then she hugged him again.

Jake yanked his arms free. "Ew! Did you just sniff me? What is wrong with you?" He ran up the stairs.

She couldn't help it. He was lying and she had to know what he was hiding.

Climbing in bed next to Matt, she whispered, "Are you still awake?"

"Mmmm."

"I don't think Jake was really at a study group. He left his phone here so we couldn't track where he was."

"Can we talk about this in the morning?"

"Aren't you worried?"

"Not particularly. He's a teenager. I don't think we want to know everything he may be up to."

Jill pondered that. Weren't they supposed to make sure he didn't do any deviant stuff? Wasn't that their job? "I think he was with a woman yesterday."

Matt didn't answer.

"A woman dropped him off."

"Like a mom of one his friends? Or an older sister?"

She hesitated. "I'm not sure because it was snowing, and I couldn't see clearly. But she was definitely older, and he wouldn't tell me who it was."

"Jill, I don't think our fifteen-year-old is hanging out with older women. You need to back off him. He's purposely not giving you information because he knows it drives you crazy."

Jill rolled over, her thoughts keeping her awake. *I'm his mother. It's my job to keep him safe. If I don't, obviously no one else will.*

# 29

# *just wondering*

JAKE HAD TOLD HIS MOM he was studying at Steven Larson's house because Steven was a quiet, anti-social brainiac who studied all the time and had no friends. He took French, not Spanish, and he lived with his grandma. There was no way his mom would know who he was. Jake got the idea to use Steven's name as a "study-buddy alibi" from the seniors on the soccer team. Last fall he overheard them laughing about how all their moms thought Steven was a *wonderful* influence, helping their boys with their homework and encouraging them to study, when the truth was, none of them had ever talked to him before. If only the PTA knew what the kids were really doing when they lied and said they were going to Steven's house.

In reality, Jake was just hanging out with Sam because it was too late to go to Grandpa's. He didn't have to make up a story about being with Sam. Their families had been close ever since they'd become best friends in kindergarten. But there was no way his mom would let him hang out after nine without a purpose. In a week Jake would have his license and wouldn't need Sam to drive when he wanted to get out of the house. But for now, Sam was his ticket out.

Jake walked carefully down the path, cautious of slipping on black ice in the dark. His backpack, slung over only one shoulder, was pulling him off balance. It was freezing. He tucked his hands into his sleeves. Snow covered the lawn but had mostly melted off the sidewalks and roads. He wished he could be watching TV in his warm house right now, but his mom hovering over him made him crazy. Being alone with her was like having a noose around his neck. He couldn't breathe. So he texted Sam, then lied to his mom, saying he was going to Steven's.

"What's with the backpack?" Sam asked as soon as he climbed into the car.

Jake tossed it in the back seat. "I grabbed it off the counter without thinking. I'm an idiot." Lying to Sam was easier than explaining he'd lied to his mom about having a study group. Turns out he was really good at hiding the truth. His life had been public property all year—he was tired of it. "But my wallet's in my backpack. McDonald's? My treat."

Sam did a U-turn, heading toward the shops.

Minutes later they were each dipping fries in chocolate shakes as they cruised the quiet streets around their neighborhood. "Are you ready for the math test?" Sam asked, licking the drips around his cup.

"Yeah, it's easy," Jake said, shoving five chocolate-drenched fries into his mouth.

Balancing his cup between his knees, Sam turned a corner. "You're lucky you're smart. I don't understand any of it."

Jake shrugged. "Helps if you listen in class."

Sam slouched. "I'm so tired by seventh period, and it's so boring I can't keep my eyes open. You're lucky your parents don't make you have a job."

Sometimes Sam said the stupidest things. *Your life's not as hard as you think it is*, Jake wanted to say. *You didn't have a brother die, did you?* One time, right after the accident, Jake told Sam he was feeling sad. He surprised himself by actually saying it out loud. They were at the skatepark and something about skating just loosened him up.

Sam replied, "At least you weren't that close to Connor. Then that would have really sucked." Jake had to stop himself from shoving Sam off his board and slamming his head into the sidewalk. Sam was annoying as hell half the time because he didn't understand a thing.

But most times, neither of them talked about Connor or the accident, and Jake was grateful to just feel normal. Sam complained about his shitty life—math was so hard and working at Pizza Pie was so hard—but Jake would just nod and pretend to care, and then they would skate. When Jake was skating fast, he felt a rush that he'd started to crave. And when he fell and skinned his knees and his palms, for a few brief minutes, the pain would silence the scream that was becoming constant inside his head.

They finished their shakes and were now close to the elementary school, so Jake said, "Let's skate." They grabbed the two boards that Sam always carried in the trunk of his car.

An hour later, Sam said he needed to get home. They were sweating when they got back in the car, and their breath fogged up the windows. Sam rolled them down to clear the windshield, and the biting air on Jake's neck as they sped through the night made him feel invincible. He plugged in his phone and queued their favorite rap song—the explicit version. Jake turned the volume up. Sam turned it up a little more, then Jake reached over and maxed it out so loud that he knew Sam would worry about his speakers blowing. But Sam didn't say anything. They raced along the empty boulevard, the cold night air whipping around them, the sharpness a refreshing reprieve from how stifling home felt. Jake closed his eyes, hitting back against the headrest, thumping in time with the bass.

Arriving at Jake's house, Sam rolled up the windows but left the music loud.

"Do you ever feel like your head is going to explode?" Jake whispered, his eyes closed.

Sam turned down the music. "Did you say something?"

Jake took a deep breath. "No."

"Do you ever wish we could smoke pot?" Sam asked. "And just forget about everything for a while."

Jake's eyes flew open as he whipped around. "We're not doing drugs, Sam! God!"

Sam looked away, quiet. After a minute, he swung around and shoved Jake's shoulder, "I didn't say we *should* do drugs! I just said *what if!* Give me a break once in a while, Jake!" He turned the music up to a roar.

Jake's heart was racing. They knew each other too well. Had Sam read his mind? Jake had been thinking the exact same thing. About trying weed. It was one thing to fantasize, but if the two of them had the same idea together, there was no one to stop them from going through with it.

Sometimes he felt so shaky, his heart beating so violently that he was sure other people could hear it. Would know he was weird. Or worse, sometimes in the middle of class, he almost started to cry for no reason. That's when he wished for a drug to take it all away.

Some kids said pot made you relax. But in the movies, people who did drugs did really stupid stuff. The thought of being even more out of control than he already felt, made him sick to his stomach. Like he literally thought he was going to throw up. *Get it together, Sam. We're not going to become drug addicts.* He grabbed his backpack from the back seat of the car and leaned against the doorframe. Sam was staring straight ahead. "Pick me up for school tomorrow?" Jake asked.

"Sure."

# 30

# my new friend, kevin

THAT NIGHT JAKE COULDN'T SLEEP. He was still cold from skating with Sam and he nuzzled the comforter under his chin. He wished he could be in Grandpa's shop with the faint buzz of the space heater that warmed his feet while he worked. It's funny how the slightly burnt smell stayed with him, like a craving.

He couldn't believe his mom had sniffed him when he got home. She was checking for the smell of smoke. Or weed. She always assumed he was doing something bad. It kinda made him want to.

He knew he'd hurt Sam's feelings and yes, he felt bad about it, but Sam was always saying the stupidest stuff. Jake used to have a big group of friends. Mainly kids from soccer—whom he'd been playing with since grade school. But this year, they'd stopped calling him. To be honest, he'd stopped saying yes to their invitations.

It started in September, after their first win, when they all went for pizza to celebrate, just like they always did. Rico was being obnoxious, as usual, telling a story about his younger brother who wrecked his Xbox. He said he was so mad he could just kill him. Then Andre elbowed Rico, and everyone fell silent. Jake didn't even catch the slip until Rico apologized. At first, he couldn't figure out what he was sorry for and then finally he pieced it together. *Oh. He said he wanted to kill his brother and mine was killed, and now me just being here has made it awkward for everyone.*

After that, whenever the team got together, Jake made an excuse about needing to go home. Then there was the time he cried at the game, which was mortifying. Soon after, everyone stopped texting. Everyone but Sam.

Jake flopped onto his back and sighed. It was after midnight and he was wide awake. He grabbed his phone from the nightstand, turned the volume off, and checked Snapchat. No messages.

Last summer, right after Connor died, it seemed like the whole world was his best friend. Everyone was texting or going out of their way to say hi when they saw him. Girls he hadn't talked to since elementary school dropped off treats. One hot summer evening, a big group of kids, whom Jake didn't even know well, came over unexpectedly. His mom invited them in and called Jake down from his room. They gave Jake hugs and told him how sorry they were, then his mom ushered them into the backyard and asked them to stay. The boys found Connor's red-and-white basketball in the bushes and started shooting baskets while Jake sat with the girls who talked about all their summer plans.

Up until then he felt like a celebrity, but even acknowledging that made him feel like shit. What kind of person *likes* the attention he gets after his brother dies? But that night everything changed. These kids weren't even his friends. He knew who they were; he'd had a crush on one of the girls in seventh grade. But she sure as hell didn't give him the time of day back then. And now suddenly they show up at his house like they're close?

Pretty soon the girls started sharing sad stories—Ava's grandpa had Alzheimer's and was probably going to die soon, and Misty's dog ran away a year ago and she never saw him again.

Jake prayed that his mom would come save him. Tell everyone it was time to go home because Jake was tired and needed his rest. Like an invalid. The way moms in the movies took care of their kids. Just as he was wishing for this, she slid open the patio door, but instead of saving him, she brought a tray of brownies—he was pretty sure a neighbor had dropped them off the day before—and a pitcher of lemonade, like they were hosting a party.

Finally, they left, and that was the last he ever heard from everyone but Misty. She texted a few more times and he tried to be nice at first, but then he stopped responding. He just didn't give a damn about her dog. By that first soccer game, the celebrity status had worn off, and he was just the kid who was a bummer to be around because you had to be careful with what you said.

He pulled a pillow over his head. Should he text Sam and say he was sorry? Even if he didn't, Sam would still pick him up for school tomorrow and they'd act like nothing ever happened. Last summer, when Jake got sick of Sam being clueless, he'd tried to lose him too, but Sam kept texting and coming over—even after he'd ghosted him.

Should he text Kevin? He picked up his phone and his thumbs hovered above the keyboard. He typed his name and their past conversations appeared like a journal. He let his finger swipe across the screen, cringing, remembering how he had evaluated every word, trying to be cool. He thought of the package Kevin had left. Should he tell him thank you and that it had helped a little, even though he hadn't touched it? He didn't want to seem needy again. He put his phone down, then pulled off his sweatshirt and tossed it on the floor. He couldn't get comfortable even in his own room.

⟨⟩

Last summer, Kevin Anderson, whose clothes were all black, who wore black eyeliner, and whose jet-black hair had an ever-changing stripe of pink or blue or purple cutting across the front, approached Jake at the skatepark. He'd moved to their school in the middle of the previous year and, of course, Jake had never spoken to him. He was two years older and hung out with a group of kids who sat on the hill behind the school and smoked during lunch. Well, Jake hadn't actually seen them smoking. But he had seen them on the hill, and they did look a little scary. So when someone said they smoked, Jake believed them.

Jake was on the top of a vert, one foot on the back of his board, the other still on the ground, working up the courage to drop in, when he saw Kevin coming closer. He was already nervous standing at the ramp precipice, and now his heart began pounding. Was he going to kick him out of the park? Tell him their gang claimed it or something? Or maybe he was going to make fun of him. Jake was wearing wrist guards. Was he going to laugh? Were they going to have a fight?

"Hey, you're Jake, right?"

Jake bent over to pick up his board and cradled it against his chest. "Yeah."

"I'm Kevin. We go to the same school."

"Yeah." The rough grip of the deck sandpapered Jake's arms. He turned it over.

"I'm sorry about your brother. My little sister died of leukemia when we were kids. It's really tough, man."

Jake couldn't stop staring at Kevin's eyes, outlined with black makeup. It was distracting him from coming up with a response. "Thanks," he mustered.

Kevin held out his fist and fortunately Jake had the presence of mind to recognize the gesture and give him a bump.

"I'm here at the skatepark a lot. Hopefully I'll see you around."

"Yeah, okay."

Kevin hopped on his board, rode the ramp, and pulled up on the opposite side where his friends were waiting. He kicked the board into the air, and without even looking, grabbed it with his right hand. The group piled into an old blue sedan and drove away.

Sam ran over, not even bothering to skate or act casual. He was panting, like Jake had survived a fight. Or seen a movie star. "What'd Kevin say to you?" His round eyes were practically bulging out of his head.

Jake shrugged. "He heard about Connor and said he was sorry. His sister died when they were kids."

Sam's mouth gaped. "Oh man. Do you think that explains why he's so messed up?"

Jake smacked the back of Sam's head as he jumped on his board and flew down the ramp with perfect execution. He kicked up his board like Kevin had, fumbling a bit but still catching it with two hands, then sat on the hood of Sam's car just like Kevin and his friends had done.

Sam caught up with him. "What are you doing? Do you think it will hold us both?" He tried to climb up, but his foot slipped on the bumper. He tried again and smashed down next to Jake, so close their shoulders were touching.

Jake sighed. He looked to see if the hood had dented. Nope. It had survived Sam's onslaught. He moved away, putting distance between them. Sam kept yammering. "Pizza Pie is hiring. I'm going to apply. You should too, because you should probably stay busy this year."

*Eff you, Sam,* Jake thought, and scrolled through his phone, trying to find any info about Kevin Anderson.

The next day, while Sam was interviewing at Pizza Pie, Jake skated to the park, hoping to see Kevin. Eventually, the beat-up blue sedan pulled up. Jake tried to act casual, nodding at him from the top of a quarter pipe, then nervously avoided him, not able to think of anything to talk about.

Those last weeks of summer, whenever Sam texted to go to the park together, Jake pretended to be busy and went only when Sam was working. One day, he fell when Kevin was close by. Kevin gave him a hand up, then advice for positioning the next time. "Give me your number. I'll send you a link to a skating video I like. It's helpful."

It turned out Kevin was really nice. They never talked about their siblings or death or dying. Just skateboarding mostly. They shared skating TikToks and Snapchatted goofy pics.

Then suddenly it was the end of the summer and Jake was on the horrible beach vacation with his family. When Kevin said he had something to make his stressful family situation better, Jake assumed he meant drugs and it scared him. But it intrigued him too. Maybe he'd see what Kevin was referring to when he got home. It would totally piss his mom off if she knew, and he liked the idea of that.

But by the time he got home and school started, the thrill of the idea passed. Jake didn't have time to go to the skatepark since he had soccer practice every day, and soon he and Kevin stopped texting. They'd nod when they saw each other at school but didn't acknowledge each other besides that. Then a few days after he freaked out at the soccer game and couldn't stop crying, there was a brown paper sack on the front porch with his name on it. And he'd discovered what Kevin had had in mind when he said he had something to help.

# 31

## sweet sixteen

WITH JAKE'S LIE ABOUT STUDY group last night, on top of the fact he'd been taking the car, Jill knew Matt knew that even though she'd promised to let him handle it, trying to keep her mouth shut was going to be next to impossible. So he'd been burying her in obnoxious texts throughout the day, trying to distract her from the cliff's edge:

> Funny story . . .
> Guess what my boss did . . .
> Want to see a movie tonight?

But Matt's constant texts were becoming annoying.

> I said I wouldn't say anything and I'm not. Cut it out.

Matt responded with a winky face emoji and heart.

She needed a distraction. They hadn't been to the movies together in almost a year. Remember when that was normal? He owed her a chick flick:

Yes to a movie: Love Lately.

He sent her a screenshot of *Love Lately*'s reviews and had circled the headline that read: "Bring your wife, she'll thank you later."

How can I pass that up?

Her heart skipped a beat. Even now. Even sad. When was the last time she'd seen love in his eyes? The unabashed you're-my-everything look that never failed to melt her heart. She missed his blue eyes looking at her like that.

We're getting kettle corn.

On the drive home after the movie, Matt's left hand was on the wheel, the other holding hers. Like the old days when they were first dating. He'd driven a stick and would hold her hand and shift at the same time. A skip in her chest again. Tonight had been nice. They'd laughed together. And it felt okay.

Yellow headlights on the freeway rhythmically illuminated their faces like the pulsing lights of a club. Like when they were young.

Matt interrupted the quiet. "What are we getting Jake for his birthday next week?"

She'd been planning a surprise party, but she believed his gift was taken care of. "We got him the car."

"But that was almost a year ago. We need to get him a surprise."

Jill squeezed Matt's hand, trying to play off what she said next as a tease. "This is exactly why I said we should wait to give him the car until his birthday." She watched his reaction from the corner of her eye.

He grinned. "*I* remember we *both* agreed he should practice with the car that would be his."

"He's definitely made sure to get more than his fair share of practice," she mumbled. But she didn't want to ruin this night with an argument. "If you think of something he needs, let's talk about it." And just like that her mind began its shuffle, searching for a gift idea, unable to simply let Matt worry about it. "He always needs new clothes. Do you want to take him shopping? Hey, can you take him to the DMV on his birthday? He wants to go during his lunch break."

Matt shook his head. "I've got a full day on Tuesday. Can you get a sub?"

She pulled her hand from his, trying to keep her sigh internal. Typical. "It's not as easy to get a sub as you think it is. Can't you reschedule?"

He ignored her frustration. Or was oblivious to it. "I'm swamped until six. He'll just have to wait until you're done."

Jill let out a slow exhale as she tried to sort through everything she needed to do on his birthday and add in his driver's license test as well. "I'd hoped to decorate and have some friends over to surprise him after school. A cake. Pizza."

Matt's shoulders slumped. "Aw, Jill, why didn't you tell me so I could plan for it? I'd like to be there for a party."

"Obviously we'll be having a celebration for his sixteenth birthday. I shouldn't need to remind you of that."

He was undeterred. "What if you take him to the DMV after school, then keep him busy until I can be home. I'll cancel my last meeting and be home by five thirty. You could take him shopping for his present."

Jill thought about it. Jake hated shopping with her. But maybe on his birthday he'd have something he wanted to buy? He'd mentioned a skateboard a while back. Her brain started shifting pieces to make it work. She could get party supplies and drinks tomorrow, balloons on Monday (she'd hide them in the basement), and pick up the cake on Tuesday, right after school, before they left for the DMV.

"Will you order the pizzas?" she asked.

"Of course. I'll be there when his friends arrive and can organize the surprise."

They smiled at each other. This could work.

∽

Tuesday morning, Jill woke at five, an hour earlier than normal, to shower and have time to decorate (thankfully, the balloons were still floating), hang a birthday pennant on the front door, a banner over the fireplace, and set the breakfast table with the festive tablecloth and confetti plates. She whipped up a batch of waffles and sliced the strawberries.

"Happy birthday, Jake!" she sang when he came downstairs. He let her hug him and was all grins when Henry and Matt joined them around the kitchen table, happily repeating that "today was the day" he would finally be able to drive.

When her last class finished that afternoon, Jill raced to the bakery across town to pick up Jake's favorite chocolate cake. The bakery took longer than expected and by the time she pulled into her driveway, it was almost four—thirty minutes later than she'd anticipated. Jake had called three times to make sure she hadn't forgotten.

She was determined to be patient with him. This was the biggest day of his life so far. Of course he was nervous about being on time. When she opened the garage door, there he was, waiting on the back step, bouncing on his toes with pent-up energy.

"Mom, you're late!" he shouted as she opened the car door.

"I know, but they don't close until five. We'll be there on time." She reached to the back seat for the cake in the pink bakery box and whistled Happy Birthday as she sashayed past him toward the kitchen. "How was your day? Did you get lots of extra attention?"

He didn't answer and was hot on her heels. She set the box next to the cake plate. "Should we open it and see how it looks?"

"No! We need to go right now!"

Jill jumped. "Yes, you're right. Go get in my car."

"Can I drive my car?" he asked, jingling his keys in her face.

Oh gosh. When she was anxious, the last thing she wanted was the additional stress of her teenage son practicing his driving skills. Especially as traffic was starting to get heavy. But this was his day. She smiled. "Of course!"

He ran toward the garage. "Do you have my birth certificate and your driver's license?"

"I do." She patted her purse.

"And a checkbook for the fee?"

"I've got everything right here," she said, bending into the passenger's seat of his little Subaru.

They arrived safely at four thirty-five, and Jill silently congratulated herself for "enjoying" his music with him, even asking about different artists and songs. While they waited their turn, Jill suggested he take Henry for ice cream in the next day or two to celebrate "their" newfound freedom. Jake laughed and agreed that Henry would probably like that and said maybe he'd take him once a week. Jill squeezed his arm. He was glowing. And to think she almost let Matt be the one to bring him.

Ten minutes later, they were at the front of the line.

"I'm here to get my license," Jake announced, impressing Jill with his confidence. His hair had a slight shine and Jill saw he'd used gel to hold his curls just right for the picture.

The pencil behind the ear of the attendant wobbled as she shook her head. "I'm sorry, young man. All tests need to begin thirty minutes before closing. That was fifteen minutes ago."

Jill's heart heaved a wallop that couldn't have been more severe if she'd been shocked by a defibrillator. She glanced at Jake. His face was frozen. *No, no, no.* She jumped in, "We definitely were here before then, but we've been waiting for fifteen minutes. Is there any way you can fit him in"—she looked at the woman's nametag—"Darlene?"

Darlene frowned and seemed genuinely sorry. "All the instructors are busy until five."

Jake's head dropped, and Darlene reached across the desk to pat his hand holding the now useless forms. She gave Jill a stern look. "I recommend getting here no later than four o'clock tomorrow, then you'll have plenty of time to get through the line and take the test before closing."

Jill wasn't type A for nothing. She wouldn't let her son down. Not today. "Today is his sixteenth birthday. What can you do for us? We can wait and see if someone finishes early."

Darlene pursed her lips. Jill knew that look. It said: *Every single day, moms like you show up begging for mercy because they can't get it together enough to get their child to the most important appointment of their life on time.* Jill herself had given similar looks to parents at school. *You can blame me all you want, but it's not on me, lady. It's all on you.*

When Jill broke from Darlene's mind control, Jake was already pushing the doors open, heading into the cold February evening. *No, no, no.* As she briskly walked across the tiled floor, her tennis shoes squeaked, sharing the shame of being too close to the woman who failed her son. *No, no, no.*

The forceful bang of the car door echoed across the parking lot as Jake slammed himself into the passenger seat.

Jill ran to the car, climbing into the driver's side. Jake was hunched over, hands covering his face, shoulders shaking. She brushed his shoulder. "I'm so, so sorry."

"Don't touch me!" he screamed.

She yanked her arm back. Fortunately, he'd dumped the keys in the cup holder.

The silence in the car was thick as they made the slow drive home in rush hour traffic. If only she'd had Matt pick up the cake. Really though, he should have offered. She'd been planning Jake's birthday for weeks and Matt hadn't lifted a finger. Jake would forever remember that his mom ruined his sixteenth birthday. He'd also probably think it was his dad who saved the day with a surprise party and pizzas.

Jill pictured Henry and Jake as grown men sitting with their dad, laughing about it, probably celebrating birthdays with Matt's new wife, and talking about what an awful mom they'd had for so many years.

A tear leaked from Jill's eye.

*The party!* She needed to warn Matt. She texted:

Abort! Cancel party. No license.

The light turned green. She set her phone where she could see the screen.

Pizza here, friends here. You sure?

Her head buzzed. Would having friends over make him feel worse? Or better? If they didn't celebrate, would he feel forgotten? She hesitated.

Another text from Matt:

???

She fought back tears. *Why did all the hard decisions have to be up to her?* She startled when Jake spoke. "Who's texting?"

"Nobody."

"Did you tell Dad?"

She glanced at him, catching his eye before turning back to the road. "I invited your friends over. They were going to surprise you."

His hands flew to his face. "Mom! No! They'll know I've been crying!"

Suddenly she made a screeching right turn into a gas station and pulled up to a curb across from the pumps. Turning to him, she rushed to get the words out. "A surprise party right now is obviously the worst timing and I'm so, so sorry. But it will be okay." She pointed toward the station where two men in paint-stained overalls were holding the door for a mother and toddler. "Run inside to the bathroom and splash water on your face."

He looked at her, horrified. "No! All those people will see me!"

"Okay. I'll walk in with you." Opening the car door, she said, "You walk behind me and go straight to the bathroom. No one will notice you."

He pounded his head on the headrest, hissing, "I am not getting out of this car!"

She grabbed her purse sitting at his feet. "Okay. I'll be right back." She dashed inside, grabbed a bottle of water from the coolers, then grabbed a second. While the cashier rang her up, she texted Matt:

Nm. Keep friends there.

Back in the car, she handed him the cold bottle. "Open the door, dump some water into your hands, then splash it onto your face."

He followed her instructions.

Handing him another cold bottle, she said, "Hold these against your cheeks and eyes. Cool yourself off until we're home. First thing tomorrow, I'll take you back to the DMV. I don't have class until later and you can skip first period. We'll go as soon as they open."

Five minutes later, she pulled up in front of the house. The light skimming of snow wasn't enough to cover the dead annuals she'd never pulled up last fall. Two giant blue helium balloons—a "1" and a "6"—were tied to the front door. Not the ones she'd bought. Someone else had brought these. Several cars were parked at the far end of the street, just as she'd instructed back when keeping the party a surprise seemed like the perfect end to the perfect day—a double celebration: Jake turning sixteen and getting his driver's license. "They're expecting you to go in through the front door. You run in and I'll pull around to the garage."

He shook his head as more tears leaked from the corners of his eyes. "Who did you invite?"

"Just your friends. Sam, Rico, Jeff. I told them to let the other kids on the soccer team know. I didn't have all their numbers."

"Did they say they were coming?"

"Yes, of course. They may have invited some girls too. I told them to include anyone they thought should come."

"I don't even know if they're my friends anymore. I can't do this," he whispered, his voice hoarse.

She reached over to grip his knee. "Yes, you can."

He pulled down the visor and checked his face in the mirror.

"You look perfect," she said. "No one can tell."

He took a breath and held it for several seconds while Jill's heart pounded. She silently prayed that he'd have the courage to leave the car and go into the house. Finally, he climbed out, walked up the path, and tentatively opened the door before going inside. Lights burst on in the living room, happy shouts carried to Jill at the curb. Dark shadows of friends gathered around him were visible through the window. She imagined his smile. This was the right thing to do. He was going to be okay.

She pulled into the garage, exhaling as the car came to a stop. She needed to get inside and make sure the kids saw there were two kinds of pizza. Had Matt remembered to get the sodas from the fridge? The garage door lumbered shut behind her.

A heaviness cemented Jill to her seat. She'd scheduled everything perfectly for the past two days so she could make this day special for Jake. She was awake at five making waffles, dammit. And still she screwed up. She bit her lip. Why couldn't she ever get anything right for her boy? No matter how hard she tried, she wasn't enough. The dim light of the garage clicked off and still she didn't move. *I can't do this. I can't do this. I can't do this.*

# 32

# between the trees

A WEEK AFTER THE DISASTROUS day at the DMV, the
surprise party he absolutely did not want, and finally getting
his license a day late, Jake was able to sneak away to the lake.
Grandpa's shop was warm and had been a great place to think
and work for the past month, but he needed a wide-open
space. A place where no one knew where he was. Somewhere
he could scream and no one would hear him.

He slip-slided down the icy hill and emerged from the
brush into a world of white. The beach was snow covered and
the lake frozen, creating a brilliant glare. Jake's breath made
cloudy puffs as he tromped fresh tracks across the snow, feeling like an Arctic explorer. He walked along the edge of the
water, knocking his heel against the ice, trying to get it to
crack. No luck. He faced the cliff-jumping rocks that were
practically sparkling in the sun, wondering if he could climb
to the top. But ice dams filled the crevices, and the cold
burned right through his thin gloves. Not today. Rubbing heat
into his hands, he surveyed the landscape, disappointed that

he was out of things to do, until heavy snow dropped from the pines at the back of the cove, breaking the winter stillness.

He jogged toward the trees, fascinated that he'd previously never thought to explore that part of the beach. From the outside, the grove looked like an impassable jumble of branches, all jutting in different directions. But as he shimmied across the lowest ones, he entered an open space between the trunks of several trees, large enough for him to stand up. A secret fort, just for him, where he could quite literally disappear.

Welcoming the thought of vanishing, he relaxed onto the pine-needle bed, used his pack as a pillow, found a mellow playlist, and closed his eyes. He was almost asleep when a tap on his hand jolted him awake. Just a falling twig.

Sticks poked his shoulders as he wiggled to get more comfortable. He searched for a different playlist. Pop ... Rap ... He settled on rock. Topping out the volume, he let the music drum through him and tried to sleep again. Something brushed his cheek and he swatted it away. Then an itch on his leg he needed to scratch. Was something in his hair?

Wide awake now, he scrolled through his playlists until he found a song that Connor loved. A year ago, when their family went out to dinner to celebrate Jake getting his learner's permit, not only did he get to drive, but he also got to choose the music. That night, after they were supposed to be in bed, Connor snuck into his room and asked about a song. Lying next to each other, Jake introduced Connor to different genres, cool new artists and all the songs he should know, with the sound down low so they wouldn't be discovered.

Now alone in his new forest hideaway, Jake scrolled through his music again, finding so much more he wished he could share. He started a new playlist: "From Jake to Connor."

A text came from his mom:

Just checking in. Where are you?

Studying

He'd turned off location tracking after his birthday and his mom hadn't said anything about it. Guess that was one benefit of her screwing up and not getting him to the DMV on time.

Are you with Sam?

He shot off a quick text to Sam:

ru home

jeffs for math

I'm with you

He texted his mom back:

Yes doing math

Dinner at 6. Blowing a kiss emoji.

It was already after five. He added a bunch of songs to the playlist, then crawled out from under the trees and headed up the hill.

～

Three weeks later, on his last free day of spring break, Jake prepared to spend the whole day at the lake. Their family had had a "staycation" where his dad kept busy at work and his mom took Henry to the trampoline park and the zoo and wherever he wanted. Sometimes Jake gave in when Henry begged for him to go with them—he was trying to be a good big brother, and he actually loved the trampoline park. Who didn't? And there was still plenty of time for him to alternate between hanging out at Grandpa's shop and the lake. At both places he mostly just binged shows on his phone and told his family he was with friends.

Today the mid-March weather was sunny and warmer than it had been all vacation, and Jake packed food, a blanket, and entertainment so he could spend the whole Saturday by himself. At the lake, he spread out the blanket under the trees, opened a pack of chips and started a movie. When a call came through from his mom, he ignored it, switching notifications to silent.

The sun found breaks in the branches, creating yellow patterns all around him. When he moved his hand, it reflected off his phone's screen and he bounced the light onto the tree trunks, branches, even his jeans. He always carried the sea glass from Ethan in his pocket, and he held it up to see if it would refract light as well. It didn't, but it did shimmer, which gave him an idea for when he came back the next time.

When he arrived home, his mom met him with hands on her hips, demanding where he'd been. Apparently he'd crossed a line. He pulled off his boots, tossing them into the shoe bin, trying to avoid her bad mood. "With friends. It was Anna's birthday. We took her to lunch and then we all went bowling."

"Who's Anna?"

"A friend of Kevin's." His breath caught as he walked out of the room. He should have said Steven Larson. "Anna goes to a different school. You don't know her."

"Who's Kevin?"

He summoned a look of disbelief as he turned to face her. "He's my friend from math. I told you about him. He's really smart."

His mom's face scrunched as she tried to process all the names. She'd never admit to not remembering. "You didn't answer my call."

He looked her in the eye. "Yeah, sorry, I didn't see it until I was on my way home, and I didn't want to text and drive."

"It's really important you tell me where you're going," she said sternly.

He put a hand over his heart. "Right. I know. I totally forgot. Sorry, Mom."

Her tone softened. "I worry about you if I don't know where you are, Jake. Don't forget next time. And don't forget to put your laundry away."

"Yeah, of course. I'll do it right now. I'm so, so sorry, Mom." He turned and ran up the stairs.

All he had to do was say the word "sorry" and she didn't even give him a bad time. Of course, he wasn't really sorry. But he could say the word. It was just as easy as lying.

# 33

## rabbit holes

ON THE LAST NIGHT OF spring break, Jill finally let Henry sleep over at Grandpa's, leaving Sunday morning blissfully quiet. Henry wasn't due home for another hour and then was going to a birthday party. Jake was at an all-day soccer clinic. Their spring break staycation was a nice reprieve from schedules, and she and the boys had had fun together. Definitely an improvement over their disastrous summer trip.

Jake had spent a lot of time with friends, and yesterday he'd been gone all day with a new friend, Kevin, at a girl's birthday party, so hopefully things were looking up and he wasn't as lonely. Skateboarding, soccer, new friends, and homework. Probably a lot of McDonald's. He wasn't great about checking in, but he seemed to be doing well. She was really trying not to worry.

"Hey, Jill, can you come in here?" Matt called from his home office.

She flopped down on the leather couch across from his desk. "What's up?"

He tapped his computer screen. "Have you taken an Uber lately?"

"No."

"I've got three charges on my credit card statement from February."

She moved behind him to look over his shoulder. "Someone's using your card."

"Nothing else looks suspicious. Did you send the kids in an Uber?"

"You know who you're talking to, right? Of course I didn't. You need to cancel your card."

He growled, rubbing the bridge of his nose. "It's such a pain to update everything."

No kidding. It was a pain. She was glad it wasn't hers. Moving back to the couch, she settled into the corner, stretching her legs and pulling a throw pillow onto her lap. "Does it tell you what days?"

"Two of the charges were the same day—February sixth. Another on January thirtieth."

Jill scanned her calendar and then sat up, internal alarms sounding. "Remember that time I told you I thought a woman dropped Jake off at home? I think it was the same day."

Matt leaned back in his chair and chuckled. "Jake's been taking an Uber?"

Her whole body was on alert, and Matt was laughing. "It's not funny. First he was stealing the car and skipping school. Now he's stealing your credit card. Where is he going?"

Matt's grin flickered away.

She massaged her forehead. "There are too many red flags. We've eased off these past months, but it's coming back to bite us. I didn't tell you, but last November I found a paper sack he was hiding in his room."

"What was in it?"

"I don't know. He caught me in there and then it was gone the next time I looked."

"Wait a minute," Matt said, holding up his hands. "I think we're blowing this out of proportion. This is Jake we're talking about. He's a good kid."

Jill raised her brows and her tone. "If he's taking an Uber, he's keeping whatever he's doing a secret from both us and his friends. That's weird, Matt. You know it."

Matt tapped a finger on the desk. "Okay. A stranger may have stolen my card number, or it may have been Jake. How do we confront him?"

She tilted her chin. "Uh, we say, 'Did you take an Uber and charge it to Dad's credit card?'"

"He could easily deny it."

She leaned on her knees, biting her thumbnail. "Where is he going? What's the worst that could be happening?"

"Hang on," said Matt. "Let's start with the likely scenario before jumping to the worst case."

She flashed a sarcastic smirk. "Well, I doubt it's just shakes at McDonald's. I'll text Sam's mom."

Jill picked up her phone:

Hi Lisa. Is Jake there?

Hi, Jill. I haven't seen him.

Three bubbles. Then blank. Finally:

I think they had an argument. Sam's been with
Jeff a lot. Is everything okay?

We're getting it figured out.

She turned her phone face down as if not wanting to see any more bad news. "He and Sam had a fight."

"Is there anyone else he hangs out with?" Matt asked.

"A new friend, Kevin. Says he's really smart in math." Suddenly she had a thought. She did know a Kevin. Kevin in her fourth period. Kevin who was new to the school last year. But Jake wouldn't be hanging out with him. They had nothing in common. Kevin was a teenage smoker. He looked like he was on drugs. Her heart started pounding as the link between Kevin and Jake sounded more likely. Surely not. Kevin wore eye makeup for Chrissakes!

Matt sucked in his cheeks. "He told me the same thing. Said he'd been studying with a kid named Kevin."

Jill was already texting Lisa again:

> Will you ask Sam if Jake is friends with a Kevin and what he knows about him. Be discreet, please.

Lisa sent a thumbs-up in response.

Matt massaged his neck. "Making new friends and studying for math. That's a good thing, right?"

"Taking an Uber and stealing your dad's credit card are not good things."

"Okay, but we don't know that it was him. And if it was, he took an Uber to 'sneak away' to a friend's house to study math. Big deal. He could be doing so much worse."

She stared at him. "You do remember that just because that's what he's telling us he's doing, does not mean that that's what he's actually doing."

Jill's phone pinged.

> I made up a long story about how one of the moms said one of the girls was thinking of asking a new boy named Kevin to Sadie's Dance but none of the moms knew him. Sam said there's a new kid named Carl. But the only Kevin he knows, Jake hung out with at the skatepark last summer. Said he didn't think he was a good kid.

She typed a quick response:

Was Sam more specific?

Nothing. Three bubbles. Nothing. Jill tapped her phone to her knee waiting for Lisa's response. Finally:

That he does drugs.

She held the screen for Matt to see. "Read this."

Matt grunted. "Have you been missing any cash?"

"I don't think so. His college savings?"

"I'll see if there've been any withdrawals from his account."

Jill massaged her temples. "How much do drugs even cost? Can he just use his allowance?"

"I seriously have no idea." Matt closed his eyes.

"Can you Google it?"

He looked at her. "Google *How to buy drugs?* What if the IT department checks my search history?"

"Turn the browsing history to private."

His jaw dropped. "That was quick."

"Fine. I'll do it." She dashed into the kitchen, grabbed her laptop, and settled into the chair. In an instant she'd turned from frantic, overwhelmed mom to a mom with a mission. And she was mad. *Dammit, Jake. Do you want a drug addiction? That's the last thing this family needs.*

She typed, *How much does a joint cost?* "Yikes, here's tons of stuff about pills. Have you checked his search history lately?"

Matt's eyes were wide. "Do I need to check *your* search history? You seem really good at this."

She ignored him. "You search for info about health issues from smoking pot or taking pills. After we confront him, we need to have research to back up why it's bad for him because he'll say we don't know anything."

Matt looked like a scared recruit while the drill sergeant barked out mind-boggling orders. "What am I doing with the research I find?"

"Copy and paste important stuff to a document. Brain development. Lung issues. The impact on future children. Impaired judgment. Addiction. That sort of thing. We'll discuss our concerns backed by research, so when he says, 'everyone does it' and 'it won't hurt him' and 'he's not addicted,' we have facts to refute his excuses."

They worked in silence, heading down a rabbit hole investigating nightmares that kept parents up at night.

Matt closed his laptop. "I just Googled *Red Ribbon Week Facts* and got a slew of information. I forwarded you the doc." He stretched. "Is Henry still at your dad's?"

Her quiet, restorative day had so quickly turned disheartening. Jill checked her watch. "He's bringing him home any time now."

"When should we talk to Jake?"

She saved her document. "Soon—but not until we discuss our approach."

Just then, Henry ran in the front door, yelling, "I'm home!" He dropped his pillow and backpack outside the office and ran to give Jill a hug.

"Hey, bud, did you have a fun sleepover?"

"It was so fun! We stayed awake until midnight! And I didn't brush my teeth!" He jumped up and down.

She realized her dad was standing at the door.

"Hi, Jill! Hi, Matt!"

"Midnight, Dad? You can have fun without staying up so late, you know."

"Can we, Jill?" he asked, winking at Henry.

They chatted while Henry ran upstairs, then came back a few minutes later with a present wrapped in Christmas paper.

"I'm ready for the birthday party! I wrapped Peter's present myself!"

Matt and Jill stood at the same time. "I can take him," she said.

Matt waved her off. "I need to pick up my dry cleaning. Want anything while I'm out?"

Shaking her head, she followed them as far as the kitchen. When Matt and Henry left, she was alone with her dad for the first time in months. He sat on a barstool, so she started washing the three cups and a pot that were soaking in the sink. Her dad just sat there, smiling at her, totally oblivious to the fact that she was having a horrible day and would very much like to be alone right now. "What's on your mind?" she asked, not at all trying to keep the irritation out of her voice.

"Just thinking that it feels pretty good to be sitting here with you."

"Watching me do the dishes?" she sniped.

He jumped up. "I'll do them! You sit."

She waved him down. "No, I'm joking. I'm practically done."

The silence dragged on. She tried to avoid his gaze, focusing on filling the pot with sudsy water. "What?" she finally asked.

He shook his head. "Nothing. Anything on your mind?"

"Nope. Everything's good." She dunked her hands and the scrubber into the water, wiping down the inside of the pot, picking at hardened sauce on the edges. It was the hot water that did it. Warming her hands up through her arms and settling into her chest, softening her resolve not to talk to him. To not give him the satisfaction of opening up and sharing the hard stuff. Before she could stop herself, she was telling him about the credit card and the Uber and that her stupid son was probably sneaking off to do drugs.

"I know where he's been," he casually announced.

She turned her back to put the pot in the cupboard and rearranged the lids. She couldn't stand to look at him while he made up some old-guy explanation of where teenagers hang out these days. He always did like to assume he knew everything. "Where?" she mumbled from the inside of the cabinet.

"My house. He's been working in my shop."

Jill spun around. "Your garage? Doing what?"

"I'm not sure. He comes a couple of times a week."

Blood rushed to her head. "You've been keeping this a secret from me? What the hell, Dad? I've been worried sick! You could have told me he was fine!"

He shrugged. "I wanted to respect his trust. The shop is a safe place, and he wanted to be alone."

"Alone? You weren't with him?"

He shook his head.

She threw her hands in the air. "You don't know a thing about teenagers! What they do these days in private. You bet sitting alone in a comfortable, heated shop is a safe place. A safe place to watch porn! Do you even have filters on your internet? Or do drugs! Skip school. I can think of a million things he could be doing!" She slammed her hand on the counter, the pent-up energy from the last hour coursing through her.

Roger stood up. "Jill, listen," he said, in his stern take-charge voice she hated.

"No, you listen!" she shouted at him. "You think you know everything. You're not his parent. *I'm* his parent. *Me*. You should *not* have kept this a secret from me!"

"Hey . . ." he reached for her elbow.

"No!" She stepped back, stomping her foot, shaking her fists, feeling like she was two years old all over again.

"Everyone is shutting me out." She swallowed so she wouldn't start to cry.

"I'm here for you," he said, putting an arm around her shoulder, pulling her into him.

"I *worried* about him," she said, her body rigid.

"I know," he whispered, squeezing her tight, his flannel shirt encompassing her thin frame. "Because I worry about you."

And finally, she let herself be held by her dad as she cried.

After she'd soaked his shoulder and her tears dried, she let him guide her to the couch. "Jake's a great kid," he said. "You've got nothing to worry about. If you ask me, what he needs is a little understanding."

She rested her head on his arm. "I understand better than anyone how he's feeling. We both lost someone we love."

"Is Connor's death the reason you and Jake are butting heads? Are you sure that's what this is all about?" he asked.

Jill wondered how it couldn't be. Wasn't everything because of Connor? His death had swallowed the importance of anything else. A black hole that would always be gaping at their backs. "Everything was perfect before Connor died."

"Was it?"

A tear ran down her cheek. "Wasn't it?"

"My advice is to sit back and do nothing. Just love him. Teenagers need that from their parents more than anything."

The irony of her dad's advice made her laugh. "Did you seriously just say 'sit back and do nothing'?"

He shrugged. "I think it's the best thing to do."

She swatted his thigh. "Oh, brother. You weren't very good at that when I was growing up. I was grounded half my teenage years."

"And did it help?"

She faced him, adamant. "I turned out pretty good."

"Then why aren't you grounding Jake?"

Her shoulders fell. "He's already sneaking out. It wouldn't change anything." She rested her head back on his shoulder. "Have you ever thought about what you wish you'd done differently?"

Now it was his turn to laugh. "Just about every day of my life. I'm so proud of all you kids. If I'd known then what I see now, I'd have relaxed a lot. I wish I would have smiled more, listened more, lectured less. Just enjoyed that time with everyone at home."

"Oh, please. Parents from your generation were the epitome of 'goodbye and good luck.' We'd walk out the door in the morning and, as long as we were home by sundown, all was well."

Her dad chuckled. "True—when you were children. But as a teenager, many nights you weren't home by curfew. And what about all the times you pretended you were going to bed but then snuck out?" He nudged her.

"You knew?"

He rolled his eyes. "I wasn't born yesterday."

"Why didn't you say anything?"

"You said yourself, you were already grounded half the time. What more could I do?"

Jill curled her legs under her. "If it matters, I wasn't doing drugs."

He nodded, smiling to himself. "Good to know. Assume Jake isn't either."

"I could take his phone. His keys."

"Why?"

"As a consequence for not respecting our family rules. He's got to tell us where he's going." She sighed. "But on the other hand, I don't want to be his chauffeur."

He kissed her on the cheek, then stood. "You've been in his shoes, and now you have the chance to do things differently." He paused before walking away. "You've got a good head on your shoulders, Jill. You'll know what to do."

Jill collapsed into the cushions and pulled a pillow over her face.

When Matt got home, she hadn't moved.

"Are you alive in there?" he asked.

"Barely," was her muffled response.

Matt sank next to her on the couch while she filled him in on the conversation with her dad. That Jake had been spending time in his shop. On snowy days he'd offered to give him a ride home, but Jake said he was getting a ride with a friend. Roger had no idea he was taking an Uber.

"So it was a false alarm." Matt sighed.

Jill closed her eyes. "We still need to have a talk about using your credit card. And find out more about this Kevin kid. But not tonight, I'm exhausted."

"He's fine then, right?" Matt asked.

"I hope so."

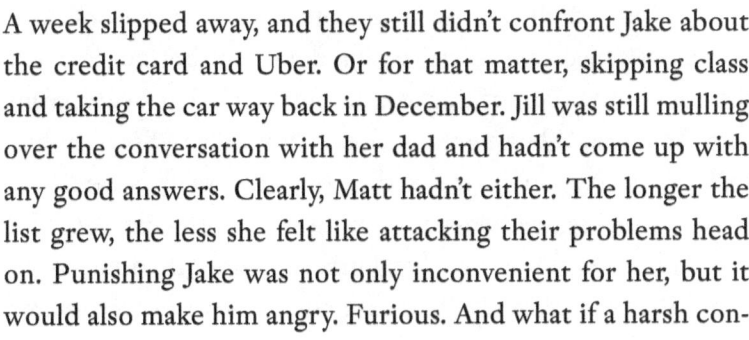

A week slipped away, and they still didn't confront Jake about the credit card and Uber. Or for that matter, skipping class and taking the car way back in December. Jill was still mulling over the conversation with her dad and hadn't come up with any good answers. Clearly, Matt hadn't either. The longer the list grew, the less she felt like attacking their problems head on. Punishing Jake was not only inconvenient for her, but it would also make him angry. Furious. And what if a harsh consequence made him do something drastic? She couldn't take the risk.

Since her dad was hanging out with Jake so much, the least he could do was talk to him about being respectful. Tell him to check in with his parents more often.

On Monday, Vanessa was absent again. Jill had been so preoccupied with Jake the past few months that she hadn't spent any time worrying about her. She had good grades, showed up to class, and in the winter everyone wore sweatshirts. She didn't seem so odd after all.

During January's parent–teacher conferences, Jill fantasized that Vanessa's mom would confide in her that she was worried about her daughter, and Jill would take Vanessa under her wing and make everything better. Of course, it didn't go like that at all. Vanessa was getting an A and wasn't missing any assignments, and with that sterling report, her mom simply said, "Wonderful! Thank you for all you do." She pushed back her chair to leave.

"Mrs. Stuart, do you have any concerns about Vanessa?"

She held Jill's gaze. Seconds passed. Jill was about to smile and wave her off, until she said, "Nothing I can put my finger on. Do *you*?"

*Put her finger on.* Was that a yes? A "yes" that only another mother could interpret? But in that moment, Jill floundered. She couldn't admit she had suspicions. She had no proof. And desperately wanting to make this mom feel better, Jill took the easy route, confirming wholeheartedly what every mom hoped to hear. "She's a great student! Not only in Spanish, but she's in my son's math class and he says she's really smart."

Mrs. Stuart's eyes glazed over and she gave a curt nod. She tucked her notebook into her purse and smoothed her skirt. Her tone was clipped. "I've never been worried about her grades. She's very responsible. Thank you for your time." Her heels tapped across the linoleum floor as she walked away.

Jill sensed she'd crossed a line. From then on, she was hesitant to show Vanessa any extra attention. Jake was right; it was creepy. She had her own moody teen to worry about. But with Jake's secrets on her mind, seeing Vanessa's empty chair today made Jill wonder. Should she be doing something more?

# 34

## vanessa's story

OVER CHRISTMAS BREAK, VANESSA HAD developed a cough. Nothing really noticeable. She just needed to clear her throat more often, but now, three months later, it still hadn't gone away. She'd started using makeup to cover the dark circles under her eyes and the hollows of her cheeks. And she was so tired. What high school kid wasn't? But she was also tired of throwing up.

So she made the decision she wouldn't. Her friends had even commented about how skinny she was, and although she liked being thin, she didn't want any attention. So, for the first time in a long time, instead of excusing herself after lunch, she stayed at the table with her friends.

"Don't you need to go to the bathroom?" Heather asked, sharing a look with Missy.

"No, why?" They couldn't know. It was normal to use the bathroom. So why were they looking at her like that?

"You always run off as soon as you're done eating."

"No, I don't. I mean, sometimes I have to go to the bathroom. I don't think I'm the only one who pees, Heather." She tried to laugh.

They rolled their eyes. "You're not peeing. You're throwing up."

Vanessa's heart raced. "No, I'm not."

They both folded their arms. "We're your friends. You can trust us."

If that was true, why did it feel like they were ganging up on her? "How would you even know?"

"Everyone knows," Heather said.

"Vanessa, we can *hear* you." Missy was never one to beat around the bush.

"You're not in the bathroom with me."

She sighed as if Vanessa was so dense. "Sometimes we are. Sometimes we have to use the bathroom too."

Suddenly Vanessa's stomach started churning. It legitimately hurt now. She sprang up from the table, crumpling the brown paper sack from her lunch. "Now I do feel sick." She covered her mouth, staring the girls down. "But not because of what you're thinking."

Running away, she tried not to let her tears fall. She dashed into a stall and locked the door, willing her stomach to settle.

She turned just in time to be sick, a physical reaction to her friends' accusations. *Everyone knew her secret?* They'd just been pretending they didn't know. She tried to swallow through the gag reflex, but the shame was too much. Was anyone else in here?

It was time to stop.

That night she brought the weighted blanket to bed and, safely smothered under the pressure, let herself cry. She would stop throwing up. She could do it. And stop cutting too. Remembering the looks on her friends' faces, their skeptical, wrinkled brows, brought a moan and sobs that pinched her throat. She couldn't face them tomorrow. She could never go back. If only she could fade away.

She was in the bathroom, holding her secret green glass before she even realized where she was. Her nose was dripping, her face wet with tears. She patted them dry with the bottom of her T-shirt and stared at the girl in the mirror.

By the dim glow of the night-light, the dark circles under her eyes looked black. She ran a finger over the scars on her arms, little crisscross patterns all the way up to her shoulders. She caressed the lines and the bumps as if they were her friends. Slipping off her shorts, she stood in her underwear, touching the purple cuts on her thighs. What seemed artistic before, she now saw as hideous evidence of her brokenness.

Lifting her leg to the edge of the tub, she gripped the shard so tightly it stung her hand. She viciously sliced across her inner thigh. Dark red drops fell like tears onto the white porcelain. She made another cut next to the first one. Then another. Crossing old scars, crossing them off her list. It hardly hurt at all.

She collapsed to the floor. With a stained finger, she wrote her name across her clean leg, then methodically traced over it with the edge of the glass. And then for good measure, cut her arms, and the blood drip, drip, dripped onto the floor. There was so much of it. She was mesmerized watching the puddle grow wider. Then darker.

Finally, she turned away. If she left it too long, it would stain. It was time to clean up.

She pressed tissues onto each leg, but they were saturated immediately. She grabbed a fistful and wiped one arm, then another, but couldn't keep up with the bleeding, so she wrapped herself in a towel. She tried mopping the floor with another towel, but just made more of a mess. Bile filled her mouth and she lunged for the toilet. Acid burned her throat. Her sobs made her choke, then heave, which made her cry harder.

There was a knock at the door. "Vanessa, I need to use the bathroom." Her little brother.

"Use Mom and Dad's. I'm sick," she sputtered.

"Please?"

"No!" she shouted through tears.

Footsteps as he left.

Taking a deep breath, she tried collecting herself. She opened the bottle of alcohol, but the smell made her gag and she dropped it to the floor.

Soaked tissues were everywhere. Her glass shard swam on the edge of the sink in a pool of blood. The stench of vomit filled the room and now the alcohol burned her nose.

Another knock at the door. "I'm sick," she wailed.

"Vanessa, it's Mom. Can I help you?"

She sunk to the floor, cries turning to loud sobs.

"Vanessa," called her mom. "I'd like to help if I can."

She struggled to breathe. "I just need to be alone." But her sobs betrayed her, and she just couldn't get enough air. "Mom, I'm sick."

Silence for a moment. Then, "Unlock the door, honey."

She was so tired. Her mom's voice just outside the door was as soothing as if she were lying next to her, like she had as a little girl.

"V, I'd like to help. Will you unlock the door?"

She curled up in a ball and closed her eyes. "I can't," she moaned.

"Yes, you can. I'm right here. I'm here to help."

Vanessa whispered, "I need help."

"I want to help, Vanessa. I'm here for you. Let me in so I can help."

Her mind was finally settling down. A quiet ebbed through her. "I'm gonna sleep," she mumbled, the soft thrump of her heart serenading her tears.

A soft click and the door began to open, slowly, gently pushing against her.

Through closed eyes she murmured, "I can't move."

Her mom nudged the door. Then again, and again, carefully moving Vanessa's body until she slid through the open space and down to the floor, pulling Vanessa into her arms.

# 35

# broken

MONDAY AFTERNOON JAKE WALKED INTO the kitchen after school, dropped his backpack to the floor and plopped onto a barstool. "You know that girl, Vanessa, who you love so much?"

Reading a Pinterest recipe and measuring spices into a soup pot, Jill had to stop herself from rolling her eyes and playing into whatever this was. "Vanessa, in my Spanish class?" she asked, trying to read the fine print on the spoon. *Did it say half a teaspoon or a quarter?*

"She tried to kill herself."

The set of measuring spoons clattered to the counter. "What happened?"

Jake shrugged. "She slit her wrists or something. They were talking about it in math today."

Jill slammed her laptop shut. "Who was talking about it? What were they saying?"

"Just what I told you. Her friends said she had bulimia, and last Friday they had an intervention at lunch, and that night her mom found her in the bathroom bleeding to death."

Jill's heart pounded. "Is she okay?"

"She's in the hospital."

Tears filled her eyes and she moved to Jake, pulling him into a hug.

He let her linger just a fraction of a second, before moving away and rummaging through the snack cupboard. "So, I guess she's not so great now," he said, his back to her.

Jill's jaw dropped. "What do you mean?"

He turned toward her, a bag of chips in each hand. "You thought she was so perfect, and it turns out she's not."

"I *worried* about her. I don't think any teenager is perfect. No one is. I was trying to show her I cared."

He crunched a Dorito. "That's what parents are for."

Their eyes locked. "I care about you. I hope you know that," Jill said.

"Yeah, whatever." He threw his pack over his shoulder and thumped upstairs.

A riot of unrest swirled inside her. *Vanessa? In the hospital?*

She texted Ellis, the school counselor:

> Can you tell me anything about Vanessa?

Why hadn't she continued reaching out to her? For the past few months she'd practically ignored her. Realizing she was going to be sick, Jill rushed to the bathroom and stood over the commode. No, she was fine. She turned to sit, her heel bouncing up and down. Should she go see her? Reach out to her mom? Had they had a connection? What if her mom blamed her? She nibbled on her thumbnail until she bit through. Why was she in the bathroom? She flicked the nail from her mouth and walked back to the kitchen. The soup. She was in the middle of making soup. She checked her phone. No response from Ellis.

After dinner, the boys turned on a basketball game and she didn't have the energy to remind them that they should be doing homework. She'd been picking up her phone every two minutes, desperate for more information on Vanessa, but she hadn't heard a thing. It was seven thirty already. Henry should be getting ready for bed. Maybe tonight she'd follow her dad's advice and do nothing. Let them all have a break from the schedule.

But she couldn't sit still. The image of Vanessa hurting herself loomed in her mind, worry wringing knots in her stomach. She needed to stay busy. She wandered through each room, cleaning up shoes, papers, used cups, toys, even Nerf bullets, and tossing them into a basket under her arm. *Am I the only one who cares how we live? This place is a junkyard.* She was getting angrier by the minute.

Jill paused in the formal living room—the one room that was clean—and her gaze passed over the couch with its fully fluffed cushions, the coffee table books still wrapped in plastic, and the piano that hadn't been played in almost a year. The brown upright with a chip on its leg seemed to be judging her for not getting the kids back into lessons. *We're taking a break, all right?* Next year they'd start again. She turned to leave but hesitated. Something wasn't right. Scanning the room again, her eyes paused at the end table where a statuette of a family normally sat. The table was empty. Setting the basket down, she crouched on her hands and knees, checking around the furniture. She pulled back the window curtain and discovered the fragile statue on the floor, broken into several pieces.

With the pieces in her hands, she stormed into the kitchen and demanded, "Who broke this?" Matt and the two boys were sitting at the kitchen table, eating cereal. Henry had his face in his bowl, slurping the last of his milk. *Is that chocolate milk in the cereal? This close to bedtime?* Matt and Jake studied the object she was holding, but neither spoke.

"Who broke this?" she asked again, banging the largest piece down in front of them, and then sprinkling broken fragments onto the table from the palm of her hand. It had been a twelve-inch figurine of a mother and father with their arms wrapped around three young boys. A friend gave it to her after Connor died.

Still facing silence and blank stares, Jill put her hands on her hips. "Someone knows what happened and I want the truth. Out with it."

Jake dug back in to his bowl of Cinnamon Toast Crunch. "I have no idea."

Matt turned to Henry, "Do you know what happened?"

"I didn't break it," he said.

Looking back at Jill, Matt shrugged.

"You guys, this didn't break by itself. It was special to me. When you break something, you need to apologize and offer to fix it! That's the polite thing to do."

"If you love it so much, just buy a new one," Jake said, pouring more cereal into his bowl.

It took everything she had not to slap him. "You know what, I could, but that's not the point." Her voice rose. "It was a beautiful *gift*. I liked that it was of our *family*. I liked that it wasn't *broken*. It was special to me and that should count for something!"

Avoiding her eyes, Jake shoveled a huge bite into his mouth and kept talking. "It's a better representation of our family now that its broken." He swallowed. "Maybe karma did it."

She slammed her fist on the table, making Henry's spoon jump. "Are you serious right now? Really, Jake? What is wrong with you?"

Wiping his mouth with his sleeve, he said, "You're the expert on feelings, you tell me."

Jill balled her hands into fists. Her heart raced. "You need to stop right now," she said. "Stop talking."

"What am I even doing wrong? You're the one who's yelling."

"I'm not yelling. I'm being firm."

Jake took a deep breath, folded his hands behind his head and leaned back in his chair. "We were all fine, happily having a snack, and then you barge in raging about a stupid statue and mess it all up!"

Matt jumped in. "Hey, you're crossing a line. You need to stop."

Jake's mouth dropped. "You're defending her? You know it's true. We were fine until she started complaining, like always!"

Jill grabbed Jake by the arm. "I don't call your stuff stupid, and I don't want you calling my stuff stupid. You need to go to your room." She pointed toward the stairs.

He shook his arm free. "I'm finishing my cereal."

Jill shouted at him: "No! I said go to your room! Do as I say!"

He picked a square of cereal from the bowl and popped it into his mouth, mumbling, "Why don't you go to your room? You're the one who's freaking out."

Matt jumped up from the table. "You don't talk to your mom that way!"

Jill yanked Jake's bowl of cereal from him. "Get out of here! Go! Go to your room!" Then she turned on Matt. "I can handle myself. It doesn't help when you jump in!"

Jake threw his spoon toward the sink—a high, arcing toss that crashed on the counter, then bounced onto the floor. They all stared as it rattled on the ground.

"Jacob Knightley Miller. Pick that up right now."

"No."

"Now."

"No." He started walking out.

"Jake, you will be grounded. No car. No friends. No sports."

He stopped, walked backwards, and slowly bent down to pick up the spoon. "How about this?" he said, holding it between them. "I pick up this stupid little spoon, put an end to your stupid little fit over your stupid little statue, and we never speak to each other ever again."

Jill hesitated a split second, then slapped him across the face as hard as she could.

He didn't bring his hand to his cheek. He didn't shout. He didn't cry. He folded his arms, looked her in the eye, and spoke with an even voice that seethed with every syllable: "I hate you. I really, really hate you."

She clenched her sides, fighting the temptation to go at him again.

He glanced at her fists, then back into her eyes. "I dare you," he said.

They glared at each other, his eyes like flint, his jaw hard, until he stalked out of the room and up the stairs.

She considered running after him, wanting to shake some respect into him. He was entitled, disobedient, ungrateful... Before she could act, Matt grabbed her arm.

"Don't touch me," she hissed, shaking herself free.

"Do. Not. Go after him."

She pounded her fist on the counter, then kicked the side of the island, pushing a stool away, toppling it over. "I can't stay in this nightmare one more second!" Storming to the mudroom, she grabbed her purse from the hook, then swung it as hard as she could against the wall, shrieking in frustration.

A sniffle made her turn around. It was Henry, huddled on the mudroom bench, hands clasped over his ears, face buried in his knees. The anger drained out of her, and she collapsed next to him. "Oh, Henry." She tried pulling him to her, but his body went rigid, and he leaned away.

"Henry, buddy, come here, let me give you a hug."

His body tensed at her touch. "Do you hate Jake?" he asked, face still in his knees.

"No! Of course not. I love you guys. I was just angry with how he was speaking to me, and not telling the truth and talking so disrespectfully. We were both mad. I lost my temper."

Mumbling through his hands, he said, "Andrew broke the statue, Mommy. We were playing tag, and he bumped into the table, and it fell onto the floor. I promised I wouldn't tell. I knew it was special, but don't be mad at Andrew. I like playing with him."

Jill banged her head back against the wall, trying to knock sense into her stubborn skull. Jake was right; she was a mess. She was a heinous mom with an out-of-control temper. She'd hit her son. What was wrong with her? Her tears turned to heaving sobs. Pulling her feet onto the bench she buried her head into her own knees.

Henry started to cry as well. "I'm sorry, Mommy." His little hand found hers and she brought it to her chest, holding it against her heart. An image of Connor filled her mind. Connor's hand. He was taken from her in an instant. And at any moment Henry could be too. And even Jake, who was never speaking to her again.

Matt pulled her to him. "I want him back!" she sobbed into his chest. "It's not fair!"

Henry's hand wiggled inside of hers. She took deep breaths, trying to calm herself. She shouldn't be this emotional in front of Henry—it wasn't good for him. She had to get herself under control. She kissed Henry's hand and freed herself from Matt's embrace, announcing she was going to bed.

"I'll help you up," Matt offered.

"No, you stay with Henry."

Squeezing Henry's knee, she tried to smile. "Mommy needs a time-out. Daddy will help you get ready for bed." She stood and kissed the top of his curly head. "I'm sorry I got so mad. Everyone needs a break from Mommy tonight."

Henry reached around her neck clinging to her. "I'm sorry about the statue, Mommy."

His heavy body pulled her down, making it impossible to stand up straight. She drew him close, unwrapped his hands, and kissed them again. "It's okay, bud. I just don't feel well." At the top of the stairs she tiptoed past Jake's closed door and rushed to her room, crumpling onto the bed.

She was a terrible person, a terrible parent. She was messing up her kids. Jake was stubborn—he probably would ignore her forever. With that thought, she cried herself to sleep.

She awoke to Matt gently rubbing her shoulder. Blinking, she tried to focus. The light from the hallway silhouetted Henry holding out the mended statuette. "Daddy and I fixed it," he whispered.

The two big pieces had been glued back together. A head and a broken arm reattached. She took it in her hands. It was essentially intact. Where fragments were missing, they'd tried to fill the gaps with glue. She tried to be grateful, but her heart sagged seeing the perfect family permanently damaged. But she managed to give Henry a hug. "Thank you for fixing it and for telling the truth."

"Should I put it back on the table where it goes?"

"Maybe we should put it up a little higher where it will be safer. How about putting it right there, on the shelf in my room? Daddy can help you."

Matt lifted him up and Henry carefully placed it in the center.

She smiled when they looked at her expectantly, waiting for her approval. "Henry, can you get ready for bed? It's way past your bedtime," she said.

He gave her a double thumbs-up and ran from the room.

"Have you seen Jake?" she asked when Matt sat next to her. She knew she should apologize to Jake, but she couldn't face him. She didn't have the heart for any more contention.

"He left fifteen minutes ago with Sam."

*Wasn't he grounded?* Truthfully, she was relieved he wasn't here. It felt easier that he was gone—less risky. "Did he say where they were going and when he'd be back?"

"Honestly, I didn't have the energy to ask him. It seemed like time with his friends might be good for him." Matt began to massage her foot.

He avoided her eyes, but she could read his train of thought. *Good for me that he was gone.* Matt didn't want to risk another blowup between them either. Her head started to throb and she closed her eyes.

# 36

## checking out

THE NEXT MORNING, JILL FELT a cold coming on. Her head hurt and her neck ached, but she talked herself out of bed and into the shower to get ready for work.

Jake's door was already open as she passed it on her way downstairs. She slowed, trying to see inside from the corner of her eye. Not detecting any movement, she peeked in, but his room was empty. Taking a deep breath, she readied herself to meet him in the kitchen.

Henry and Matt were at the table eating cereal, a horrible déjà vu from last night's fiasco. But it was just the two of them. "Where's Jake?" she asked, sliding into a chair.

"Hasn't come down yet," Matt answered, while scrolling on his phone.

Jill's stomach flipped. "He's not upstairs. His room is empty."

Concern crossed Matt's face. "I'll ping his phone." Seconds later, he replied, "It's off."

Jill darted to the garage. "His car is gone. Henry, have you seen Jake this morning?"

Henry shook his head, eyes wide.

"Did he come home last night?" Jill asked.

"I fell asleep with Henry," Matt said, "then came straight to our room. I don't know."

They ran upstairs. His bed was unmade, pajamas on the floor. "Did he leave extra early this morning?"

Jill felt unbalanced, hovering between panic and fury. Suddenly they heard the front door open and they dashed to the landing. Jake walked in, sweaty, and out of breath. Their eyes connected for a moment, then he broke contact and walked toward the kitchen, ignoring them.

Matt and Jill practically fell over each other getting back downstairs.

"Where have you been?" Jill demanded, unable to keep the anger out of her voice.

Jake pulled the milk from the refrigerator, keeping his back to her. "On a run."

"Where's your car?"

"I don't know."

Matt and Jill looked at each other, shocked. "Has it been stolen?"

Jake was unfazed, calmly drinking straight from the jug as if he did that every day.

"You're late for school!" she yelled at him.

Jake smirked at her, then turned to put the jug back in the fridge.

"Listen," she said, grabbing him by the shoulder and pulling him around to face her. "You may still be mad at me, but you may not be late for school! You have responsibilities."

He leaned away, turning to face his dad. "Dad, sophomores don't have morning classes today because the juniors have testing. I *am* responsible, and I'm not going to be late to school. Sam is picking me up at eleven forty-five."

"Where the hell is the car?" Matt shouted. "The keys aren't on the rack."

Jill massaged the bridge of her nose. "Wait a sec. Wait a sec," she said. "I put the keys in the mailbox yesterday afternoon. Priscilla's husband, Chris, offered to take it into the shop to swap the snow tires for summer... I remember now. We scheduled it for a day Jake didn't have school in the morning. Did anyone see Chris yesterday?"

"Yeah! I did!" exclaimed Henry. "I remember now, too! He said he was here to pick up the car and I opened the garage for him."

Jill exhaled, collapsing onto the kitchen chair.

Jake sat opposite her. "Once again, Mom's freaking out about nothing."

She glared at him. "It's not nothing! You weren't here. We were worried about you!"

He rolled his eyes and turned away. "I'm not speaking to you."

He looked like an idiot craning his neck so hard to avoid looking at her. Jill couldn't stand it. She felt herself losing it, but frankly didn't care anymore. She jumped out of her chair and grabbed him by both shoulders, getting into his face. "Guess what, you have to talk to me. I'm your mother. For the next two years, while you live in this house, you have to listen to me, and we need to communicate."

He tilted his chin toward the ceiling, letting her rant pass by without reacting. He pulled one shoulder out of her grip, stuck his phone between her face and his, tapped the screen and suddenly his obnoxious music started screaming at her.

She wrenched the phone from his fingers and threw it against the wall. The screen shattered.

"Nice," he said, not even flinching. "Guess you can't track me every second anymore. You've made it even easier to disappear." He walked out the front door, slamming it behind him.

Jill cried the whole way to work. She wasn't strong enough or kind enough to rise above this, and now she was going to lose another child. She parked in the faculty parking lot and then dug through her bag as if searching for something so teachers walking past wouldn't notice how disheveled she was. She really did need a Kleenex, though, to wipe her face. Better yet, a towel.

Dabbing her cheeks with her sleeve, she checked herself in the rearview mirror. Her eyes were red and puffy. She couldn't go to school like this. But here she was. *Just pull it together, Jill, and go to work. You can't miss a day when you're feeling fine.* But she wasn't fine. She was a mess. Tears started again. She had to get out of here.

She felt like all eyes were on her as she reversed and left the lot. Well, her kid had died. She deserved a sick day and today she was taking it. She called the office and reported her absence. Her sniffling surely sounded like she had a cold.

She didn't want to go home. What she really wanted was to be alone. She entertained the idea of driving away and never coming back. She would drive away from her world and its expectations. The world where her family relied on her for meals and laundry, where her dad had confidence in her ability to parent, where her students counted on her, where her friends assumed she was hurting or assumed she was healing, where strangers prayed for her recovery. Away from a house with a lifeless room where a bed would forever be neatly made.

She pulled off the freeway when her familiar neighborhood, then town, then city were behind her and drove until she found a park. The trees were dressed in bright pink blooms and groups of yellow daffodils flanked several benches. This far from home, she could sit in silence and anonymity and think.

Three elderly ladies strolled the grassy perimeter, holding each other's arms for balance. A mom caught her toddler at the playground slide, kissing her cheeks each time they met. A young man in sunglasses threw a ball to his dog and over and over the dog ran it back. Obedience. That's what she needed in her family. Respect. Tears started flowing again. She was too sad and it was too cold to be sitting still. She jammed her hands into her pockets and started walking, pumping her arms and legs to occupy her mind and stifle her crying.

She startled when something bumped her leg. The dog, sniffing at her pants. The owner caught up to them, apologizing. "Sorry! He's very friendly."

She waved him off with one hand, wiping tears with the other.

"Is everything okay?" he asked.

"Yes. No. Not really," she said, nodding her head, then shaking it, then finally waving her hand again. "But I'll be fine. Trying to walk it off." She flipped up the collar of her coat as she walked away.

"I'm sorry to disturb you."

She flapped her hand as if trying to indicate everything was okay. Suddenly, she felt so tired. And her head was pounding. Lengthening her stride, she made it around the park and back to her car. She should go home and crawl into bed—she really was feeling sick. But she didn't want her family seeing her like this. She didn't want to cry in front of Jake, especially. But where else could she go? Jill drove off. The thought of not being wanted brought more tears.

Seeing a hotel, she pulled in, not pausing to think it through. With her purse and school bag in hand, she headed to the front desk. Would they wonder why she didn't have luggage? Why her eyes were puffy from crying? *Well, all the busybodies can just slide on down to hell.* She handed over her credit card, took the keycard, and headed up the elevator.

Once in the room, she pulled the curtains closed, stripped off her clothes, and crawled into bed. Burying herself under the covers, she began weeping again, pulling a pillow over her head so her sobs couldn't be heard outside the door. She thought of her son who had died. She thought of her son who hated her. She thought of her child huddling in a corner to protect himself from her anger. Sobs racked her body, causing heaving convulsions. Suddenly, she bolted up, thinking she might vomit. She ran to the bathroom and coughed and choked, but no, she was fine. She stumbled back to bed where she finally fell asleep.

She awoke, groggy but not at all confused. She was in a hotel. She'd left home. She fumbled for her phone to check the time: three in the afternoon. She'd napped for more than four hours. She'd woken multiple times, and each time when she'd registered where she was, tears immediately started again until she cried herself back to sleep. But now, hours later, she felt calm. She stretched to her side and texted Matt:

I think I'm sick.

> Aw, sorry. Should I take the boys out tonight to give you some quiet?

Actually . . .

She paused. What was her plan? She took a breath.

I'm not coming home tonight.

She hit send.

> What's going on? Where are you?

> I'm fine. I'm in a hotel. But after this morning, I just
> need to be alone.

> What can I do?

> Cover for me. Tell the boys I'm out with friends or
> something. And that I'm sick tomorrow morning
> and need to sleep. Just take care of them and
> cover for me.

> You're kind of scaring me.

> I'm ok. But I need this.

She considered turning her phone off. He'd track her location and part of her wanted to be invisible. But another part of her wanted to know someone cared.

Cocooned in the dark in the middle of the day was healing. Being alone, not worrying about every single thing she said or every single thing she did, was healing. But when she thought of Jake and Henry arriving home from school to an empty house and how she was abandoning them, she wept some more. And as soon as she started, the great heaving cries took over again until, once again, she slept.

The next time she woke, it was dark. She texted Ellis, the school counselor:

> Hey, it's Jill Miller.

> Hi, Jill.

> Can I get contact info for those therapists? I think I
> need some help.

# 37

## counseling

WEDNESDAY MORNING IT TOOK JILL a minute to remember she was in a hotel and had basically run away from home. She'd slept off and on for nearly twenty-four hours and finally felt a little better. One of the three therapists she texted yesterday had time to see her today, and in just a few hours, she was scheduled to lie on a couch and admit to all her failings. Hopefully in exchange for the magic words that made teenagers listen to their mothers. Her heart sped up when she thought of it, but her curiosity was piqued as well.

First, she needed to go home to freshen up. The thought of running into Matt or one of the kids filled her with dread. But if everyone was where they were supposed to be—Matt at work and the kids at school—she should be able to avoid them for now.

Matt and Jake's cars were gone, but still Jill held the back door open and waited before entering, listening for the sound of anyone home. Silence. She dashed up the stairs, locked her bedroom door, and hurried to shower and dress.

At noon, she followed a dark-haired woman with a short bob into a bright, sunlit office. The orange poppy brooch she wore on a black tunic sweater and lack of lipstick put Jill at ease. Her clogs made Jill believe she wasn't too judgmental. Plus, she was at least sixty. Jill hoped she was wise. And that she'd raised teenagers.

Cathy indicated a blue velvet couch where Jill could sit, and she took a tan, upholstered club chair for herself. "What can I help you with?" she asked, crossing her legs.

Jill adjusted a green pillow, flattening it behind her back. "Um, well, you know from my text that my son died."

Cathy nodded.

"So, everyone says grief counseling is helpful."

"I agree."

Jill sat up. "You're asking me what I need help with, but I'm not really sure." She tucked her hands under her legs.

"What made you decide to call?"

"Okay, well, yesterday . . . I feel like it was a little out of the blue . . . Not that I haven't been sad or that I haven't cried a lot some days. Because I do. But yesterday, I couldn't stop crying and I wanted to be alone. Not just alone in my room, but alone forever. The thought of seeing another person made me want to scream. Or close my eyes and never wake up."

Jill moved the pillow from behind her, pulling it onto her lap. "I have a teenager, and basically, he hates me. We had a huge fight. Two, actually. Well, we've basically been fighting all year. Yesterday, I left our home and checked into a hotel and cried all day and night. I slept a lot too. But it felt like I'd never stop crying. It was different than when Connor died. Not 'I'm going to be sad for the rest of my life,' but 'I want to be alone for the rest of my life.' And in that moment, it just became really apparent that I needed help. That I needed a professional to help me understand what's wrong with me."

Cathy took a drink from her water bottle. "I'm glad you came to see me."

"So, what do you think happened?" Jill asked.

Cathy raised her brows. "What do *you* think happened?"

The question took Jill aback. She fidgeted with her watch and then folded her arms, trying to think. She massaged the back of her neck. "I think . . . I wonder . . . I've been trying to be strong and move forward. But my teenager is super hard to deal with right now. And him being hard was too much. I sort of lost it."

"How is the rest of your family doing?"

She took a breath. "We're muddling through. Lots of people told us we should go to therapy right after Connor died. But my husband thinks talking about Connor's death with a therapist will make us wallow in grief or keep us living in the past. He'd rather talk about good memories of Connor."

"What do you think?"

"I think that sounds kind of right, but the problem is, when I talk about him, I get mad or sad. So it's easier to just not talk about him."

"And your kids? Do they talk about Connor?"

"My oldest son, Jake, the one who hates me"—she caught Cathy's eye and chuckled, but Cathy's face didn't crack—"we butt heads a lot. Probably normal teenage stuff. I know he loved Connor and misses him. But they were different ages—Jake was getting into the thick of teenage stuff—hanging out with friends all the time, high school, driving soon—you know, growing up. And Connor still liked little kid stuff—playing pretend and Legos. That really wasn't Jake's thing anymore. So I'm not sure how he feels. I'm sure it's not great that when he's in high school, the supposed 'best years of his life,' his family is falling apart."

Another nod. Jill wasn't sure if Cathy agreed or was nodding to say, "I hear you."

"And you have a younger son?"

"Henry. He's six. Connor was always so sweet to him. Like I said, Connor would play little kid games, so that was fun for Henry. He was the perfect big brother. Connor would do whatever Henry wanted."

"How is Henry?"

"Almost totally normal. He talks about Connor—in fact, he told me he talks to Connor and 'answers for him in his head.'" Jill made air quotes. "Most of the time he doesn't seem to be sad at all. Sometimes I wonder if he's just waiting for him to come home. I wonder if he really comprehends how final death is."

Cathy had been taking notes. "I'd like to share some thoughts with you, if that's okay."

"Yes. Of course! That's why I'm here."

"You said you're trying to be strong and move forward. Moms are often in a difficult position when they are grieving. They're missing their child—many describe it as literally feeling like a limb is missing. But they also have the responsibility to care for their other children. This forces them to move on when perhaps they aren't ready. Moving on is a good thing, of course. But our brains—our psyches—are powerful. The emotions we experience need to be felt. We can squash them down temporarily, but at some point, they'll make themselves known. A tipping point. Or a breaking point. I think that's what you experienced."

Jill pulled a tissue from the box next to her. Then two more to wipe her eyes, blow her nose. "I'm sorry," she said, waving her hand in front of her face. "I hate crying in front of people. I'm so sorry. It's just been such an atrocious week. I can't seem to stop."

Cathy sat forward; her voice as soothing as if she'd been Jill's own mother. "It's okay to cry, Jill. It doesn't scare me."

Jill sobbed for several minutes. When she quieted, Cathy asked, "Who do you talk to about the accident?"

Jill immediately felt heat rising in her chest. She unzipped the vest she was wearing to try to cool off. She closed her eyes and rubbed her temples. "I don't think I'm ready to talk about the accident." She peeked to see Cathy's reaction, but there wasn't one. *Is the woman deaf?* "I'd really like to talk about Jake, instead. He's been hiding things from his father and me. He's got a real attitude. I'm hoping to learn how to get him to listen to me."

Cathy nodded. "What are your concerns?"

As Jill launched into all her frustrations about Jake's behavior, her tears dried. She started at the beginning of the school year and remembered how Matt had sided with him, how her dad had harbored him doing who-knows-what in his woodshop, and how she was trying so hard, but no one was listening to her. He was hanging out with a kid who was doing drugs, probably, and ended with how she felt so unequipped to handle his teenage rebellion.

"That *is* hard," Cathy conceded when Jill finally stopped talking. "Let me ask you a question that I think is related to what you see as his rebellion. How often does your family talk about the accident or Connor's death?"

Worn out from revisiting the whole hard year, Jill gave in. "To be honest, I guess with everything going on in the past month, we haven't talked about it too much."

"Before that?"

"Well, at Christmas we tried to have a memorial, but it didn't go over too well. And it seems like we always get sideways with each other at the cemetery."

"It can be a hard thing to talk about."

Jill agreed.

"Are you able to talk about Connor in regular conversation? Do you share memories with one another?"

Jill folded and unfolded her arms. Surely they had. They do. It's Connor. They would never forget about him. He was always on her mind. She looked at the ceiling as a tear fell. "It's just so hard. And I'm just trying to get through each day without being sad."

Cathy was quiet while Jill collected herself, then continued, "It's actually been shown that the more you talk about your son, the likelier you are to find comfortable ways to express your feelings."

"I'm honestly not sure how to do that."

Cathy smiled. "If you come back, and I hope you will, we'll work on it."

Jill looked at her watch and was shocked that their hour was almost up. "But what about Jake? What do I do about him?"

"Let me ask you another question. Would you describe yourself as responsible? Your family and colleagues can depend on you?"

"Absolutely!" This was an area where Jill shined. "I'm a planner. I'm organized. So yeah, I'm known for my dependability. I used to be the person who gets things done, you know?"

"Have you always been this way?" Cathy asked. Jill eagerly nodded. Until Cathy added, "Even in high school?"

That stopped her short. "I was involved in activities and, yes, always followed through on those responsibilities, of course. Well, at home I kind of skirted the rules, but nothing serious. Just typical teenager stuff . . ." Her voice trailed off.

"What I'm hearing is that it was okay for you to skirt some rules at home as a teenager, but you expect more from your son. Is that right?"

Jill squirmed. "I can see what you're getting at. And yes, it makes sense that some of his behavior is 'typical teenager.' But what about drugs? What if he's depressed? I didn't tell you earlier, but I have a student who tried to take her life. And I'm just so worried..."

"That's scary and very real. And I get that you're worried. I wonder if you're also worried about your ability to keep him safe. That it's your responsibility."

Jill nodded, using the wadded-up tissue to dab her eyes again.

"Do you think you'd be able to talk your family into having counseling?

Jill gave a little laugh. "Probably not."

"For now, I can give you tools to help model at home. But it's a big job. Often, I find when families really start to talk and you share what you've learned in therapy, they become more interested in trying it for themselves."

Jill was startled. She'd been thinking she wouldn't tell her family she'd tried therapy. She wasn't excited about revealing she needed help to cope.

Cathy read the stricken look on Jill's face. "It's okay. You don't have to start today. Come see me a few times and then when you're ready, we can talk about the rest of your family."

# 38

## where's mom?

JAKE WAS SO PISSED AT her. *She has a complete freak-out then just disappears? Moms aren't supposed to abandon you, are they?*

At dinner, he refused to give his dad the satisfaction of acting like he cared. He wore his ball cap at the table, slurped his milk, and totally enjoyed no one bugging him about talking with his mouth full. His dad had ordered pizza, so he was clearly mad at her too. Mom hated pizza on weeknights.

But Henry was too young to read the room. "Where's Mom?" he asked.

*Should Moms ditch their families when one of them's just a little kid? Geez. He's only six.*

His dad's tie was still cinched, sleeves buttoned at his wrists. He smiled at Henry. "She has a meeting at school and has to work late tonight. It's a guys' night!"

Jake knew that wasn't true. First of all, his dad certainly wasn't getting comfortable on their guys' night. And secondly, his friend told him there was a sub in Spanish class. His mom had skipped school. And now his dad was lying. *Interesting.*

After dinner, his dad told Henry to get his homework. Usually, Mom helped Henry while Dad and Jake did the dishes. But tonight, the plates sat in the sink and his dad sat next to Henry. Well, Jake certainly wasn't going to do the dishes. But he didn't want to miss any more clues either, so he opened his laptop and sat next to them to work on his English assignment instead of going to his room like he normally did.

After his dad pronounced Henry's spelling practice as perfect, Henry zipped his homework into his backpack, and instead of going upstairs to get ready for bed, he plopped on the couch and turned on the TV. "I'm going to wait for Mommy."

"You need to go to bed before she gets home, kiddo. She's got a late night." His dad started rinsing dishes and loading the dishwasher. "Go get in the bath and I'll come up and help you wash your hair."

"No! You never do it right!" Henry screamed. "You always get soap in my eyes!" He didn't even take his eyes off the TV. "I want Mommy!"

His dad didn't react. Just picked up the milk and put it in the fridge. "It's just me tonight, buddy. I'll do my best to keep the soap out. Head on up."

Jake suddenly wanted to be helpful. "You gotta remember to use a washrag to cover your eyes, Henry. That's why you think Mom does it better. She just reminds you to use the washrag."

Henry stomped his foot and stuck out his tongue as he walked toward the stairs. "I hate you, Jake. Just shut up."

Jake caught his dad's eye and made a "what's got into him" smirk to share, but his dad just looked away and started scrubbing the counters.

At two in the morning, Jake woke up and snuck down the hall to his parents' room. He cracked open the door and peeked in. Even in the dark, it was clear there was only one person in the bed. His dad was alone. He softly pulled the door shut and tiptoed back to his room. Did he care? He wasn't sure.

In the morning, Dad put orange juice and a bowl of cereal in front of Henry, who was as surly as ever. He folded his arms like a tiny mob boss and leveled his gaze at him. "Did Mom go on a trip without us?"

Jake studied his dad, searching for a sign that he knew where she was. He sat between them and took a bite of Cheerios. "No trip," he answered, mouth full. "She's just extra busy right now."

Henry didn't let up. "When is she going to be home?" he demanded.

Jake caught the pause. His dad pretended to chew even though he'd already swallowed. "Tonight, like normal."

"She better be. She reads stories way better than you do." He popped out of his chair, leaving his bowl on the counter. If their mom were here, she'd scold him for not putting it into the sink. Henry grabbed his backpack and threw it over one shoulder like he was heading off to high school, not first grade, and called, "I'm waiting for Cole outside!" Jake noticed Henry's shoes were on the wrong foot.

"You'd better get going too," his dad said in a monotone, looking at his watch. Jake grabbed his keys, and before he went out the garage door, he glanced back at his dad sitting at the counter in his gray suit and tie, pathetically eating Cheerios alone.

His mom did come home that night, just as they were finishing dinner. Jake thought for sure she'd start in on his dad for making a box of macaroni and cheese with no vegetables for sides. But she was pretty quiet.

"Mommy!" Henry shouted and ran to her when she came in. She gave him a hug and smiled at Jake. But he looked away, staring into his empty milk glass. Henry pulled out his homework and climbed up to the counter and she sat next to him. "Show me what you've got," she said.

When she was upstairs for Henry's bath, Jake heard Henry shriek, "You got soap in my eyes!" So, she wasn't having better luck either. Jake was on edge all evening, wondering if she'd try to talk to him. When he went up to his room, he could hear her reading to Henry. He locked his bedroom door, restlessly working on homework for an hour, dreading a knock. But when Jake got ready for bed, the crack under Henry's door was dark. She'd probably fallen asleep with him. He turned out his own light much earlier than normal, relieved he'd avoided her tonight.

The next day, Jake was in math class when she texted him:

Can we talk after school?

She'd still been in bed when he'd left for school, and when he sneaked a look in her classroom before third period, he saw a sub. So, she'd stayed home again. Ever since she left, he'd been feeling jittery again. Maybe clearing the air would be a good thing. He texted back:

sure

On the drive home after school, he was eager to get all this behind him. He hated the tightness in his chest he'd had for the past few days. It felt a lot like that bad day on the soccer field, and he hoped hearing whatever his mom had to say would make him feel better.

Henry wouldn't be home for another hour. Maybe he'd take him for ice cream after dinner. He'd been promising him a brothers' trip but hadn't done it yet. His mom would think that was a pretty cool thing to do. Jake was starting to feel better already.

His mom was waiting for him on the small leather couch in their home office. Several framed family pictures hung on the walls. Would they ever take another one? Or would he forever be immortalized at fifteen and Henry at six? In an instant decision of goodwill, Jake sat next to her.

"I'm sorry I was so upset," she said, touching his knee. "I was way out of line with how I reacted."

Jake studied the floor. *Yes*, he thought. *Yes you were.*

"It's normal to have disagreements," she continued, "and I wish I had talked to you calmly and listened to how you felt. I care about how you're feeling."

Jake's mouth went dry. He didn't want to talk about his feelings. He just wanted to feel better. Didn't she have anything at all she could say to help him out?

"Do you have anything *you* want to say about our disagreement?" she asked.

His mind raced. What was he supposed to say? *Everything's okay?* Or *You're forgiven?* The way she'd acted wasn't okay. And he didn't forgive her. He went with the line she always used when he apologized as a kid: "Um, thanks for saying, 'I'm sorry'?"

She didn't respond.

He glanced up, which was unfortunate because she was just staring at him, and now he was trapped in her gaze, and it was impossible to look away. He squirmed.

"Do you want to say you're sorry too?"

Her question took him by surprise. He didn't have anything to be sorry about. She's the one who accused him of breaking the statue when he didn't. Accused him of lying, when he didn't. She's the one who slapped him. He hadn't even yelled or anything. What did she expect him to apologize for? He wiped his sweaty palms on his pants.

She didn't wait for a response. Instead, she leaned toward him and continued, her voice low, "Ever since Connor died, people have been telling me to see a therapist. I didn't want to. How would it be helpful? They don't know us. They don't know Connor. But after . . . " She swallowed. "After what happened between you and me, I did see one. Yesterday."

This was interesting. And upsetting. He scratched his neck wondering when this would be over.

"I liked it," she said. "She was a good listener." His mom touched his knee again. "Jake, would you ever want to talk to her? I think it could be really helpful."

His head shot up. "What? Why? I don't need to see a psychiatrist!" He jumped up. "You're trying to turn this on me! I don't have anything to be sorry for! You're the one who freaked out!"

She held up her hands. "You're right. I *am* the one who freaked out. I totally freaked out. And I'm not saying you have to talk to her if you don't want to. I just wanted to offer."

He was breathing hard. "Are we done yet?"

His mom took a deep breath. "No, not yet. There's something else I want to ask you about."

He folded his arms, looking past her to a picture on his dad's desk. Henry was a new baby. Everyone laughing. He remembered the photographer talking in baby talk with a dumb stuffed animal trying to get Henry to look at the camera and Connor to smile. It was so lame. Jake didn't want to laugh at the time, but he couldn't help it.

"Somebody used Dad's credit card three times for an Uber. Do you know anything about that?"

Oh geez. He was so stupid. Why did he think they wouldn't find out? It was snowing a couple of times when he wanted to go to Grandpa's shop, so he couldn't skate. He thought he was being clever.

Before he could respond, she added, "And Grandpa told me you've been spending time in his shop."

His mouth dropped. "He told you? That was supposed to be private!"

She spoke fast. "I was worried because I don't know where you are half the time, and he told me to ease my mind. It was the right thing to do."

Jake's chest tightened as his eyes welled up. How could Grandpa tell? Why couldn't everyone just mind their own business?"

"Jake, I also know that this Kevin you've been spending time with might... Well, Jake, have you been experimenting with drugs?"

"What?" The tightness in his chest exploded. He clenched his fists, shaking them at her. "I'm just trying... I'm trying so hard to do everything right and you think I'm such a bad kid!" He started sobbing. "I don't do drugs!" he screamed. He started pacing. "What's the point? I can't do this! I hate this. I hate it so bad!"

His mom reached out her hand, but he swatted it away. She stood and tried to put her arm around him, but he dodged out of her embrace. "No! I hate you! I hate you so much!" He bent over, hands on his legs, whispering, "Don't touch me. Please, don't touch me." He couldn't breathe. Taking shallow gasps, he tried to regain control. "I need to get out of here. I can't do this anymore." He faced her. "You of all people understand this." He grabbed his backpack, ran up to his room, and slammed the door. He dumped his bag out onto his bed—books, pens, crumpled homework assignments, wrappers, energy bars—

his mom was always handing him a Clif Bar just in case he needed a snack. Well, finally she was good for something. He put those back in. He packed long johns and a sweatshirt and stuffed them in too. Warm socks.

He slipped out of his sneakers and swapped them for boots, then pulled on his coat.

His mom caught up to him when he was headed out the back door. "Jake, just tell me where you're going."

He glared at her and then yanked the door shut, patting the flip phone in his pocket, the old one his dad had activated for him when his mom destroyed his iPhone. No GPS. That would show her.

He threw his backpack into the passenger seat, and as he started the car, he noticed the bin of camping gear. He jumped back out, pulled a sleeping bag off the shelf, then opened the bin and rummaged around, finding a headlamp and a pocket-knife. Perfect. He screeched out of the garage, determined to never come home again.

# 39

## escape room

WHEN MATT WALKED IN THE door, the smell of dinner welcomed him home. All the dishes had been washed and the kitchen was spotless. Henry was on the couch watching TV. Vacuum lines traced the floor in the family room. Jill had been busy. She must be feeling better. Maybe things were finally getting back to normal.

Matt sat next to Henry, kissing the top of his head. "Hey, bud, where's Mom?"

"Don't know," he said, not turning from the screen.

"What are you watching?"

"Dad, shhh! I'm trying to watch a show!"

Matt walked to the hall. "Jill!" he called. Hearing movement, he called again, climbing the stairs, "Jill, are you up here?"

"Laundry room."

Neat stacks of folded clothes sat on the counter. As he approached, he admired her from the back. Her hair had grown longer, and it was pulled into a braid. He loved her strong shoulders, the faded jeans she wore so well. He even loved her need to fold the towels with perfect symmetry. "Hey," he said, wrapping his arms around her. Tilting his head over her shoulder, he tried to kiss her cheek but stopped when he saw the tears. "What's wrong?" he asked.

She didn't stop folding. "I screwed up."

Moving to see her face clearly, he saw bloodshot eyes, ruddy cheeks, and tears running down her chin.

She blinked rapidly, crying and folding at the same time. Taking the towel from her, he laid it on the counter, pulling her into him. "It's going to be okay. What happened?"

"Jake."

"What'd he do?" he asked with a sigh.

"He's gone."

Matt froze. *Nothing to worry about.* He took a deep breath and hugged her tighter. "Gone where?"

"I don't know." She started sobbing. "Matt, I totally screwed up."

His stomach clenched. It seemed this despair would be his constant companion every day for the rest of his life. He wasn't sure how long he could take it. He was, quite frankly, the only sane person in this house. "Tell me what happened."

She pulled away, sinking to the laundry room floor, so he, too, sat crisscross next to her and held her hand.

"I asked Jake to come home after school so we could talk. So we could clear the air."

"Did he come?"

"Yes, straight away. I apologized for getting so upset. He didn't say much. Then I told him we needed to talk about some other stuff." Jill sniffed, wiping her eyes on her sleeve.

Matt thought he knew what was coming.

"I asked him about the Uber and his friend Kevin, and then point blank asked if he was experimenting with drugs. I thought it was the right thing to do!" She started crying again. "I mean, we're supposed to talk to our kids about these things. Everyone says so. There are *billboards* about it!"

"And what did he say?"

"He was shocked, and I think genuinely hurt. He started crying and pacing and saying he's just trying to do everything right and no one believes him. I apologized, but he completely brushed me off. He said he hated me. Then he stopped shouting and got quiet and said he needed to get out of here. He was crying, but he was also so calm. It was really scary. I'm scared that he might hurt himself." As soon as she said it out loud, she started sobbing again, heaving and gasping, gulping for breath.

Matt wiped tears from his own eyes, then rubbed his arms. It was all too much. One thing after another. How did anyone ever survive a tragedy? Was it even possible?

An image of his family came to mind. Five smiling faces from the family photo in his office. He had his arm around Jill, her hand was on Connor's shoulder, the two of them enjoying their perfect life with their three perfect boys. He had a great job and a great home. Watching over and providing for these four people whom he loved so much had been easy.

But now . . . He wanted to fold up that image, the photo. The reminder hurt too much. Fold it up and put it in the back of a drawer where he never had to see it again. The moment would be safely stored away, but not a constant reminder. He imagined shutting the drawer and, instead of being sad, relieved. There in the laundry room he wiped his hands on his pants as if ridding himself of any trace that the picture, his family, existed. *My God, who was he?*

"Okay, listen," he said, swallowing and taking a breath. "He just needs to blow off steam." He stood and held out his hand to help Jill to her feet. "It's totally normal for a teenager to need some space. He's going to be fine." He only half-believed what he was saying because if he was honest, he wanted to escape from here too.

# 40

# dirty laundry

ALL NIGHT LONG, JILL LAY awake, straining to hear the back door open, soft steps in the hall or the creak of a stair. She counted the seconds and minutes as they crept by. When light finally began to brighten the room, she turned over and realized Matt wasn't there. She thought she hadn't slept, but she'd never heard him leave. In the hallway, she saw Jake's bedroom door was wide open. She ran downstairs and found Matt in his office, hoping Jake would be there too. But when she ran in, eyes wide, Matt shook his head.

"He just needs space," he assured her.

She fed Henry breakfast, made his lunch, and hugged him when he left for the bus stop. She taught four classes of Spanish. Peeked in Jake's sixth period and only saw his empty desk. Stopped at the market after school and bought frozen lasagna for dinner. When she arrived home, there was no car in Jake's side of the garage. His room dark. Still no word.

Dinner was quiet, practically silent. They didn't even try to make small talk. They told Henry that Jake was at a friend's house. He barely acknowledged them, one hand propping his head up, staring at his plate, eating without comment. He pushed his dish away and laid his head on the table. Matt picked him up and carried him to bed.

When he came back down, Matt asked, "Have you texted Jake's friends' parents?"

Jill had tried to compose a text, rewriting it a million times. Why was it embarrassing reaching out to friends?

She remembered the time she lost Henry in Macy's at the mall when he was three. One minute he was holding her hand and the next she couldn't find him anywhere. A security guard was at the door, not twenty feet away, yet she couldn't bring herself to ask for help. Henry was obviously here somewhere. No reason to cause panic. Or invite the judgment of others. She searched inside racks of clothes and under dressing stalls, hesitating to call his name, not wanting to draw attention to herself for losing her child.

Fifteen minutes later, however, she was convinced that someone really, truly had taken him. She ran to the security guard, no longer caring what anyone thought and shouted, "I've lost my son!"

A crackly announcement was made, outside doors were locked, and guests and employees walked around together calling, "Henry!" Minutes later, in the arms of a stranger in high heels, there he was, beaming and sucking on a green lollipop. After Jill stopped hugging him and kissing his head, smelling his (not clean) hair, the glamorous saleslady explained how she'd found him under the sunglasses counter, curled up on a shelf. Turns out he'd swiped a sucker from the candy display and hid, so he wouldn't be found out.

Jill profusely apologized, thanking the small crowd that had gathered to see the happy ending. Joyful at the reunion, everyone lingered, laughing at their own stories of lost children and ensuing panic. The finder was treated like a hero by security, onlookers and, of course, Jill.

Maybe that was the reason asking for help was so hard. You were giving up—admitting that you needed someone else to be the hero of your story.

She hated airing their dirty laundry, but she was doing an appalling job of parenting on her own. If it came down to exposing her weaknesses or saving Jake, she chose Jake. Jill started texting:

> Jake is missing. Will you ask your boys if they've heard from him?

By ten that night, she'd heard back from a dozen friends with no luck. Several moms said they'd talked with their kids about the seriousness of the situation and the importance of being honest. But still, no information.

Their only clue was from her dad. Jake had stopped by yesterday and picked up a brown bag he'd been keeping in the shop.

"What was in it?" Jill asked.

"I never looked," he replied.

*Oh, Dad.*

That night in bed, lying next to Matt but neither sleeping, Jill whispered, "I think we should call the police tomorrow."

Matt's hand found her fingers and folded them into his.

She woke the next morning to Matt sitting on her side of the bed, gently rubbing her shoulder and calling her name. She bolted upright. "Is he okay?"

Matt held out his phone so she could read their exchange:

> I just need to know you're ok.

> Ya

Jill gasped, pulling her knees to her chest and bowing her head. Had she even cried this much after Connor died? Matt wrapped her in his arms. "I've done everything wrong," she said.

"No," he replied, rubbing her back.

"Yes, I have. I thought I was doing an okay job of holding it together this year. But I wasn't. I assume I know what everyone wants, what they need. My dad used to do the same thing, and I hated that about him. Now I'm the same way. The exact same way."

"Often you *do* know what everyone needs. You care so much. I love that about you."

"The boys don't. I've been so focused on trying to keep my shit together so my grief doesn't drown Henry and Jake. So I wouldn't lose them too. But it's happening anyway."

"It's okay to lose your shit once in a while. My parents sure as hell did. Your dad did. And we still love them."

Jill gave him a side-eye. "Sort of."

He nudged her. "You don't mean that. Your dad is one of your best friends, even if you're mad at him right now. Do my parents annoy me sometimes? Yes. But I know they care about me. And I've relied on that. More than I ever admit."

Jill laid her head on his shoulder. "I don't think I'll ever be able to stop crying." Quiet settled between them. They were staring over a chasm that had opened the past year, and instead of crossing it, they hadn't moved an inch. "I went to see a therapist on Wednesday."

She expected Matt to be shocked. But instead, he just nodded. She guessed that after this week, nothing would surprise him.

"What was it like?"

"Nice. I sort of expected her to help me with Jake. I'd tell her all the things he does wrong, and she'd give me some magic words to get him to be more respectful and put him in his place."

Matt's breathing was slow, steady. Jill continued, "Obviously, that didn't happen. She's probably going to fire me as a patient for being so hopeless when she hears about this."

He sighed. "I think she'll be excited she's going to make so much money off us."

"Probably true."

"Do you want to tell me what you talked about?"

"I'd feel better talking about it if I hadn't completely screwed up," she said, taking a breath. "Later, okay?"

Matt nodded.

"I promised Henry I'd take him to the Children's Museum soon, and I'd like to take him today. I think it would be a good distraction for both me and him. You'll come too, I hope?"

Matt squeezed her hand. "Would you mind if I didn't go? I could use the day in the office to catch up. I haven't been super productive lately."

Jill sighed. "That's my fault."

He squeezed her hand. "Are you sure you'll be okay on your own?"

"Yes. Of course. But you'll text me if you hear anything more from him, right?"

# 41

## anywhere but here

MATT WASN'T GOING INTO THE office this morning. He still couldn't focus on spreadsheets or act passionate about tax code. Or shoot the breeze with Gary, who always worked weekends. He was tired of fake laughing at his crude jokes. *Read the room, Gary. I have a wife and kids. I'm not your guy,* he wanted to shout.

He put on his coat, and when Jill was distracted with Henry, grabbed his boots from the front closet and shouted goodbye from the hall. He was headed to the lake.

This was the third time he'd gone by himself. A month ago when the lake was frozen, he'd been determined to walk across the ice to their beach. He'd take his time, skid his feet carefully, and basically skate to Connor's spot. Well, the cove. Where Connor died.

With his very first step he slipped in his damn loafers. And what was he thinking, only wearing a thin sweater? February was freezing. He couldn't even see the inlet from this side of the lake. He trudged back to his car, slipping so much on the uphill that he must have looked every bit like the fool that he felt.

Going back had been on his mind ever since then, when he could prepare for the weather and have the time to stay as long as he wanted. To be all alone and really think.

Today, when he arrived, the lake was mostly still frozen except for the middle, even at the end of March. The ice shone under the sun's glare. He adjusted his Ray-Bans and scanned the opposite shore, the brightness making his eyes water, as if he were staring at the sun. He squeezed his eyes shut and turned away.

Leaning on a wooden post, he kicked a rock near his toe. It skittered off the dock, onto the frozen lake. *How solid was the ice? Would it hold him?* He picked up another rock, and side-armed it. As it glided across the ice, the reverberations created a one-note song. Matt had never heard ice make music before. Lying on his stomach, he leaned over the edge and reached for another stone, stretching until it was in his fingers. He tossed it, and just like before, it cried a long, lonely wail.

What if Connor's body had sunk and they weren't able to find him? What if he'd been trapped under this ice? Matt shuddered. He'd drive himself mad searching, trying to break through and free his son.

Instead, he experienced a different kind of horror—holding the lifeless body of his little boy. He hadn't comprehended how much he loved him until that moment. And adding to the insult, the doctors had pronounced him dead without Matt's consent. Before he could even see for himself. He felt sure he could have brought him back. He was his father, after all.

After the doctor told them he'd died, Jill collapsed to the floor. Gina rushed to her side, so Matt left her, pushing past the doctor and running into Connor's room, ready to fix everything the doctors missed. He would pump his chest, expel the water, restart his breathing. But instead, the sight of Connor's face, blue and rigid, was a gut-punch. He looked so unlike Connor that he thought surely they'd made a mistake.

Matt was still gasping for air, trying to hold himself upright, when Jill entered, crying a tortured strangle that rattled him in a way that still echoed. It pierced his heart, and at the same time, reminded him that he'd left her when she fell. Abandoned her at the worst possible time.

He'd picked Connor up, trying to hold him. But it was no longer his boy, and he was ashamed to admit that it sickened him, and he had to lay him back down. Now he lived with the fact that he'd turned his back not only on his wife, but on the last chance he had to physically love his son.

Jill had flung her body over Connor's, howling. And at that moment, Matt just wanted out. He wanted to cover Connor's head with the sheet, leave the room, and find a place to sit down. More than anything else, he wanted to be alone. A buzz started in his head that scared him. Because if he acted on what he was feeling, he'd yell for Jill to shut up, to just shut the hell up. He wanted to cover his ears and drown out her cries and scream at her to be quiet for just a damn second so he could think. But he swallowed and swallowed and stuffed those feelings down as far as he could. He clamped his mouth shut so nothing monstrous came out, clenching and unclenching his fists, letting his tears lighten the weight.

He realized he was crying now, which surprised him. He hadn't cried—*really* cried—in months. Thought he'd cried himself out at the funeral.

He had so many questions about the accident that were never adequately answered. He wanted a minute-by-minute understanding of what happened. He and Jill had talked about the details just once. He'd said, "But back up to where you were before. After you had Henry and you'd swum back to shore. Could you see your dad?"

She'd responded, "Yes, he was swimming and then did CPR."

Again, he asked, "But between those times, when they swam to shore, then what?"

Jill had balked. "You want the minute-by-minute version?"

"Yes, I do," he said.

She gave a short laugh, got a faraway look like she was trying to remember, and then skipped to the part where the other boat was coming to rescue them.

It felt like she was keeping secrets from him. Keeping the last few minutes of their son's life to herself. He wanted her to share them, but she would not.

And now she was seeing a therapist, probably talking about him and everything he was doing wrong. And once again Jill was the center of attention. No one ever said, "How are you, Matt?" No one cared that he was the father of the boy who died. That he also loved him and read to him and taught him to ride a bike and throw a ball and actually liked listening to him tell all about his dreams every morning.

Jill would roll her eyes and sometimes even say, "Wrap it up, Connor. It was just a dream."

But Matt loved hearing what went on in his head while he slept—awestruck at his little mind making up such vivid stories. He appreciated that he wasn't a teenager yet and still loved talking and talking and talking to his mom and dad. He missed him so much. So much. His heart would never be right. It had been smashed and then turned to shale—hard as stone, but oh, so fragile. Every once in a while, something touched it that hurt so much, like a piece had been sheared off, leaving a pain that reverberated in his every extremity, as if a hammer had smashed not his thumb, but his heart, shattering off another fragment.

People brought meals "to ease Jill's burden" and sent flowers "to give her light." Numerous friends dropped off treats for the boys and even some toys for Henry. A group of girls made a poster for Jake, and he said he didn't even know them that well.

But who did the dishes after they ate? He did. Who did the laundry those first few weeks after the funeral when he wondered if Jill would ever get out of bed again? He did. Who heard Henry crying and lay with him night after night until he fell asleep? He did. Who made breakfast, mowed the lawn, and worked from home for a month so Jill could recuperate? He did. And he wished so badly he could say it was because he loved her. That he was trying to be strong so she could heal. But, no, he resented her for it. Because did anyone ever think he'd like to stay in bed and pull the covers over his head for two weeks? Or two days? Or even two hours? No. Because no one cares if the dad is okay.

And now even the therapist would be on her side. And he was sure she'd make him out to be the bad guy.

He scanned the frozen landscape. They'd already lost one child. And now, was it happening again? *Jake, where are you? Time to come home, son.*

# 42

## out on the town

WHEN JAKE LEFT ON THURSDAY night, he stopped at
McDonald's and bought ten burgers for twenty bucks, hoping
they'd last him for a while. He didn't have a plan, just knew he
needed to be alone. Camping at the lake under his trees was
the only place where that seemed possible.

By the time he arrived, the sky was orange, but he knew
his way well enough to get down to the beach without much
light, making the descent easily even while carrying his backpack, sleeping bag, blanket, and food.

The trees made a good tent, and the pine needles a soft
bed. With the blanket on top, it was downright cozy. He
pushed his pants to the bottom of the bag and put on long
johns and wool socks, zipped his coat up to his chin, and slid
inside. After a minute he climbed out to get two burgers, then
put the rest in his backpack, wondering if there were bears
nearby. He didn't think so. He hoped not. He was about to
Google it, but remembered he only had an old flip phone.
Which meant he didn't have any movies, music, or social

media either. He was furious at his mom all over again, stuck in the middle of nowhere without any entertainment.

After eating, his eyes were heavy, even though it was only seven in the evening. He imagined his family eating dinner without him. Were they worried or glad he was gone? He turned off his phone. The good thing about only having a flip phone is that no one could discover where he was. Served them right. He scooted deeper into the bag and fell asleep.

A couple of times he woke up to turn over and once to pull the beanie over his eyes because it was getting light. When the sun was too bright and his bag too hot, he turned on his phone and saw it was nine in the morning. A solid fourteen hours. He'd never slept that long in his life. He was starving and very, very thirsty and grateful a convenience store wasn't too far away.

He tossed his bag and blanket over a branch, threw his backpack over his shoulder, and ran up the hill, reveling in the knowledge that he was perfectly capable of fending for himself. Not long after, he left the store with a smoothie, a six-pack of Cokes, two bags of chips, a large package of cookies, and two extra-large bottles of water.

Back at the beach, he sat on the log, sipping a Coke and staring across the water. The middle of the lake had melted, changing from frozen white around the perimeter to intense black in the center. The depth of the dark area seemed like the entrance to another galaxy hiding just below the surface, and he desperately wanted to be a part of it.

Shuffling onto the ice, he took little steps to keep his balance. The wind bit at his face and ears, his stomach clenched, and the cold pricked its way to his brain. Strolling on a frozen lake wasn't as carefree as he'd imagined it would be. Each step was precarious, especially with his hands tucked into his sleeves to stay warm. He only made it ten yards, to where the cliff-jumping rocks loomed over him.

In the summer, the water was much higher, and it was easy to find footholds to climb to the top of the lower level of the cliff, then leap into the water. He and Connor could both scramble up easily. It would be epic to sit there now and check out the lake from up high. But even though the rocks weren't icy like earlier in the year, they were still bitter cold to the touch, so he ran back to camp to get gloves.

When he returned, he saw a wide crack running up the beach side of the massive outcrop to a higher shelf they'd never reached before, and the crack was big enough for him to get inside. It was taller than he could reach, but if he could build some sort of bridge, he could make it.

A pile of driftwood had accumulated on the opposite edge of the beach. Tossing smaller branches to the side, he uncovered two big logs—about six inches around and six feet long. Holding an end in each arm, he dragged these across the beach and propped the ends near the crack, creating a ladder of sorts. He found enough holds to climb the rest of the way through the crevice and pulled himself out on top.

Low, gray clouds flattened the landscape, sucking the color and life from everything as far as he could see, except for the mysterious darkness in the center of the lake. He imagined it was a black hole swallowing everything good around it. A place that wouldn't allow happiness to exist. For a short time you'd think you were happy, but then you'd discover it was just a mirage and nothing would ever be the same again. He shivered.

No one ever talked about the accident and exactly what had happened at the cove. Once he overheard his mom say Grandpa was driving too fast. But Jake refused to believe Grandpa had done anything wrong. He imagined the boat flipping. Did they scream? Did it hurt? He wanted to talk and talk about Connor. About that day. There was so much he didn't understand. He'd only overheard his mom and dad talk about it once. His mom mentioned the waves, the rain, nearly hitting rocks, and needing to turn the boat around.

That part Jake knew. Then the boat flipped. And everyone was in the water. His dad had asked, "Could you see Connor? Was he swimming when the boat turned over?"

And his mom began calmly, "I was on the other side of the boat."

"How did you get on one side and your dad on the other?"

"I don't know."

"Did you jump from the boat, or did you fall?"

"I'm not sure. No, we fell. And I saw Henry and I was so scared. I was able to swim to him and grab him by the life jacket."

"You need to talk to your dad."

"Why?"

"To understand what happened."

"We know what happened. Connor died."

"Yes, but how?"

"It won't change anything. We can't bring him back! I've relived it and relived it. I know I should have swum to him. But my dad said he had him. I assumed he was telling the truth."

"Could you hear your dad? Did he say he needed help and you misheard him?"

She'd tilted her head and didn't speak for several seconds. That's when Jake had stopped pretending to be reading and had looked up. She had caught his eyes and then turned away. "Believe me, I beat myself up over it every day and never stop wishing I'd done things differently. I know you both blame me too."

"I don't blame you," his dad had said.

"Mmmm."

Once Jake had asked her, "Did Connor hit his head?" But she just looked away as if she hadn't heard him.

Jake crawled to the edge of the cliff and looked over. From up here he could tell that the ice was thin—that the dusky water spread far beyond the center. If he jumped, would it be quiet under there? Would his heart's constant racing finally slow down? His mom and dad would probably be relieved if he never came back. Well, at least his mom would. She hated him. Tears welled up in his eyes and his chest began to burn. A jump through thin ice would create the most satisfying snap.

He let his feet dangle. How long would it take to die? And if he died, would he see Connor again?

He lay on his back, letting the cold seep through him. A cold that hurt so much even his eyes started to burn. He pushed away from the edge. If he died, would Henry miss him? He *knew* Grandpa would miss him. He might even be so sad that he'd have a heart attack. Then Gina would be all alone and Henry would grow up without a grandpa.

As if in warning, a hawk shrieked overhead. His warm sleeping bag in his hideout under the trees beckoned to him. He shimmied down from the rocks, ran back to camp, curled into his bag, and napped.

When he opened his eyes, he lay still, mesmerized by patterns made by the sun. Shadows and light danced around him, and he imagined he was in an alternative universe—where he was the only person on the planet. He dozed again, and in this dreamy state, remembered the sea glass wind chime that was in his pocket. Wrapping the sleeping bag around him, he stood to hang the chime over a branch, then lay down again to watch it sway in the soft breeze.

Before leaving yesterday, he'd stopped at Grandpa's to get his paper sack. Mostly because he didn't want anyone snooping through it. Also, because if they did snoop, he knew they'd think what they found was dumb. They'd probably think he was cooler if he was doing drugs instead of making stupid wind chimes, like a kindergarten craft. But he remembered Ethan. Ethan wasn't stupid. He was nice, and he was proud of his art.

In addition to making a few wind chimes in Grandpa's shop, he'd tried designing other things with the sea glass too—little towers or decorative arrangements—imagining becoming an artist when he grew up. Sometimes he drew plans, trying to remember projects he saw at the Woodworkers' Festival. But most often, while in the shop, he read or did homework or just slept in the old green chair.

He opened the bag. He didn't have glue, but he had plenty of fishing line. He wrapped it multiple times around a pale aqua piece, then looped the end through and made a knot. Leaving two inches of space between the next stone, he wrapped an emerald-green one, alternating colors until he had a chain of five. He tied it to a branch near the longer chain, close enough so they touched when they moved. The branch waved in the light breeze as if showing off her new bracelets.

He spent the rest of the afternoon working on his chimes until the sun set. He reluctantly cleaned up. Wrapped in his blanket, he ate three cold burgers in the dark, the twinkly music of his chimes keeping him company, along with the high of creating something that was actually pretty cool.

Sometime later he jerked awake, a hamburger still in his hand. Had he heard rustling? He held his breath, but his heart thumping in his ears drowned out all other noises.

The ground was lumpy, and he reached under the sleeping bag, tossing aside several pinecones. Still unable to get comfortable, he turned on his phone to check for messages. It was 2:00 a.m., hours before it would get light. He pushed deeper into his bag and checked his texts. He had several from Sam. They started out normal enough:

> whats up
> any plans tonight

Then:

> my mom said your mom is looking for you

And finally:

> are you ok everyone is worried

He had similar notes from soccer friends.

His face grew hot thinking of his mom starting a freaking-out-mom group text. She was so embarrassing, dragging the whole world into her drama. Now how would he be able to face everyone when he went back home? He rolled over. *Am I going back home?*

Just then, the phone buzzed, and a new message came in from his dad:

> Just need to know you're okay.

Jake imagined his dad lying awake, just like he was now. A tear escaped. Was he okay? He'd felt calm all day. The quiet felt good. But now he wasn't so sure. After the fight with his mom, he wanted her to be mad. It made him happy that she was angry. But did he really hate her?

He just wanted his old mom back. The one who listened. The one who drove him and his friends places. The one who actually liked being with him.

Why would no one talk to him about the accident? Grandpa would probably answer his questions, but every time he thought about asking him, it felt disloyal to his mom.

Finally, he cried. He missed Connor. He missed his mom. He missed his mom and dad loving each other. He didn't like the feeling he had when his dad took his side. At first, he did. But it wasn't supposed to work that way and now it was scary. Were his parents going to get a divorce?

He texted his dad a single word:

Ya

Then he turned his phone off again.

He lay awake most of the night, or at least he thought he did, but it was late morning when he came to. By the afternoon, he was bored. He missed his bed. He missed his house. He even missed his family. He was mortified that everyone knew he'd run away. But he did love his wind chimes. In fact, he envisioned making a lot more. And he was pretty sure he knew who would like them too.

After midnight, Jake carefully opened the door to their home, assuming everyone would be asleep, planning to sneak straight to his room. Earlier in the evening, he'd packed up camp, then drove around listening to music. He found a bookstore and flipped through magazines for a while, then went to the children's section, sat on the floor, and read *Harry Potter* until they closed. He stopped at Walmart, just to kill time, and wandered the aisles. Then finally, he drove home.

He tiptoed to the stairs but startled when his mom called his name from the dark family room. She was on the couch. "Jake, is that you?"

He paused. "Yeah."

Her voice was quiet. "I've been worried about you."

"I know. I'm sorry."

"I'm the one who's sorry. I'm glad you're home and you're safe. Are you headed to bed?"

"Yeah."

"Sleep well. I missed you."

He stepped onto the first step then stopped. "Mom?"

"Yeah?"

"I missed you too."

# 43

## i want answers

SUNDAY MORNING, JILL WOKE TO Henry's nose touching hers. "Mommy, Jake's home."

She scooped him onto the couch where she'd fallen asleep and spooned him close to her under the blanket. A tear escaped as she thought of two other boys she used to snuggle on Sunday mornings. She'd taken those cozy mornings for granted and the familiar feeling of regret started to settle in her gut. She squeezed Henry to her, exhaling the negative self-talk. *No, I will not let despair get the better of me today.* Cuddling your child was taking advantage of moments. She wished she had more, yes. But kids grow up. Even Connor would have been too old to be snuggling right now. She closed her eyes, trying to imprint this moment on her spirit forever.

"How do you know?" she asked. "Did you peek in his room this morning?"

"He slept in my bed last night."

Jill's breath caught at the thought of Jake wanting—needing—to be close to his little brother. She replayed his deep voice saying, *I missed you too.* "Was he still sleeping when you woke up?"

"Kind of. He tried to tickle me, but I got away."

Jill's whole body relaxed, relishing the image.

"Should we get up and make him breakfast in bed? Is it a special day, Mommy?"

She kissed Henry's cheek. "You have really good ideas, bud. Do you think he'll like pancakes?"

Fifteen minutes later, they had a stack of pancakes and sliced oranges on a plate, with two Swedish Fish added by Henry.

As they headed up the stairs, Jill suddenly felt nervous. Waking a teenager on a Sunday morning rarely delivered good results. She didn't want Henry to be disappointed. She didn't want to be disappointed. "Let's make sure to wake him up quietly. Okay?"

Henry scoffed. "Duh, Mom, I know!"

Tiptoeing into the room, Henry climbed onto his twin bed and curled up near Jake's face. "Jake!" he loudly whispered. "We made you breakfast in bed. I'll bet you're pretty hungry, right?"

Jake stretched. "Yeah, I'm pretty hungry all right." He opened one eye, grinning at Henry.

Jill sat down on the bed next to them, holding out the tray. "Henry said it felt like a special day."

Jake sat up. "Pancakes with Swedish Fish? Wow! Thanks, Henry."

Henry chewed on his thumbnail. "Do you think we should share the fish, Jake?"

Jake dropped one in Henry's outstretched palm and popped the other in his own mouth.

Henry jumped off the bed. "I'll go tell Daddy we're having a special morning." He ran out of the room and then suddenly was back, hanging onto the doorframe. "Wait. Mom, what do we call it when we're all together? Are we having a unioning?"

"Are you thinking of 'reunion'?"

His curly head bobbed up and down. "Yeah, yeah. That's it. I'll tell Daddy to come for the reunion!"

The silence between Jake and Jill was heavy. He cut a bite of pancake and chewed for an exceptionally long time.

Jill scratched his back. "I'm glad you're home."

Jake nodded, taking another bite, his eyes locked on the plate.

"I'm sorry I hurt your feelings. That it seems like I don't trust you. I think you're an amazing kid. I haven't been a very good listener."

Jake took a shaky breath, then another bite.

Jill rubbed her arms. "I just worry. I guess I imagine the worst things that can happen, and I panic instead of talking to you." She touched his shoulder. "Jake, I care about you. That's the most important thing I want you to know. I care about you."

He wiped his eyes with the palms of his hands, "Mom, we've never talked about what happened during the accident."

"What do you mean?" she asked.

"I just have so many questions. There's so much I don't understand."

"Oh." Jill's heart began its familiar drumming. She swallowed.

"I think we should talk about that day."

"Yes, of course. What's your question?"

Jake leaned toward her. "Mom, not one question, *all* the questions. I want to know the whole thing, from getting to the beach to what he looked like in the hospital."

Jill's breath caught and her head started to spin. She massaged her temples. She'd just committed to listening to him, hadn't she? She slid her two clenched fists under her thighs. Hopefully out of sight.

Jake continued talking, excitement building in his voice. "I've been thinking about it, and I think we should have Grandpa and Gina there too. You know, when we talk about it."

Jill felt sick. She closed her eyes. "Have we not done that before?" She'd relived that day so many times, she couldn't imagine that everyone else hadn't done the same. The images and sounds haunted her. One minute, she'd be sitting in traffic and suddenly she'd be on a boat that was tipping and would have to literally shudder to suppress the memory and square herself back into reality. But of course, Jake and Matt hadn't been there.

Was not knowing equally hard? She thought she'd been protecting them. So many people had asked, over and over, "What happened?" They'd told their family, the medical personnel, the police. Then the neighbors, strangers, and everyone else. They'd told the story so many times, it was impossible to think there was more to say. But now she realized it was a summarized version. They'd never spoken about details. She didn't know how she could face it, but maybe this was a way she could save her family. She put her arms around him. "Yes, Jake, of course."

"Do you have your phone?" he asked, bouncing on the bed. "Let's call Grandpa, right now and make a plan. So we don't forget!"

# 44

## questions and answers

JILL'S HANDS WERE SHAKING BY the time the doorbell rang. She'd looked at her watch a million times in the last hour, dreading the start of reliving the past. Dreading the pain they'd all tried so hard to put behind them. Dreading revealing her failures—not only from the day of the accident but from the past year. She'd seesawed between two prevailing emotions over the past week since Jake came home—knee-buckling euphoria that he was safe, and abject melancholy for the wretched mother she'd become.

They sat in the formal living room—Jill and Matt on the blue couch across from her dad and Gina, and Jake and Henry in the stiff, high-back chairs, completing their circle—like an uncomfortable intervention where no one knew how to begin.

She'd assumed just the adults and Jake would meet. But Henry begged to join them, saying he had lots of questions too. She was sick thinking of him trying to work out the accident on his own for the past year, while she'd assumed his happy demeanor meant he was preternaturally resilient—or not old enough to be truly upset. It broke her heart that she hadn't seen the truth.

Jill caught Matt's eye, gesturing with raised brows for him to take the lead. He smiled back at her, not taking the hint. Like a twelve-year-old, she turned toward her dad, hoping he'd bail her out.

But it was Jake who spoke first. "I think we should start from the moment Dad and I were dropped off at the dock. We all know what happened up to that point."

"I don't," Gina interjected. "I've never understood why only Roger and Jill returned to the beach to collect us. I know you all considered waiting out the storm at the marina and then changed your minds. But why weren't Matt and Jake on the boat on the return trip?"

Before Jill could confess that she'd been the one to convince her dad to go back out, he spoke. He rubbed his arms as though nervous, but his voice was strong. "The dock was closer than the beach, and I wanted to get off the water as quickly as possible while there was lightning." He nodded, as if reminding himself that it was indeed the right decision, and Jill was grateful that he didn't call her out in a play-by-play review of terrible decision making.

"I wanted to come with you when you decided to go back out," Matt said. "I was trying to jump back on board, but you took off too fast." Jill was surprised to see him wipe his eyes. "I could have helped. Maybe I could have saved him." His voice was tight, wretched.

Her dad shook his head. "There was nothing you could have done. He was already gone."

Jill took Matt's hand, wondering how they were ever going to get through this.

"How did the boat flip over?" Jake asked. "Did you know it was going to tip and you jumped? Or did you just suddenly end up in the water?"

Roger rubbed his face. He started to speak, then stopped, put a hand to his heart and took a deep breath, and began again, nodding, as if convincing himself to go ahead and say it out loud. "This is the part I go over and over..." He glanced at Jill, then at the floor. "I obsess over what I could have done differently. I went too fast. I know that. I was worried about hitting the rocks, and we *were* very, very close. So I gunned it, never imagining that the boat would flip. I just didn't think."

He composed himself. "I'm not even sure what happened next. We shot into the air and the boat was sideways. It was different than a big bounce over a big wave. It was just the craziest feeling. That's probably when Connor hit his head on the tower. Jill, could you tell we were flipping?"

"It just happened so fast. Henry dropped into me, we both crashed onto the side, and then we were in the water."

"I was scared," Henry said, his little body dwarfed in the big chair.

"So was I," Jill said, patting her legs, indicating a space for him.

He squeezed between her and Matt, resting his head on her arm. "I love you, Mommy. I'm glad you're a good swimmer."

She wrapped her arms around him and let her tears fall. "I was clutching Henry and searching for Connor." She turned toward her dad. "I asked if you had him, and you said yes."

Her dad swallowed. "I did."

Squeezing Henry, she whispered, "It feels like you lied to me."

Her dad leaned toward her. "Jill, I could see him. I *almost* had him. But the waves and the wind took him further away.

It was hard to hear and hard to yell. I felt like 'yes' or 'no' were the only options. And 'yes' seemed accurate. Also . . ." He faltered, closing his eyes and gripping his thighs.

"What?"

"If I'd said I needed your help, you'd try to get to us, and it wouldn't have changed the outcome." He clasped his hands. "It may have made it worse."

She closed her eyes, trying to shut out the memories and the people around her as she cried. "Did you swim as fast as you could? Did you try as hard as I would have tried?"

And then he was next to her, pulling her into his soft flannel shirt, whispering into her hair. "I promise you, I gave all that I could until I reached him, then even more as we swam to shore. You and I both know CPR. It never crossed my mind that we couldn't bring him back. Oh, Jill," he said, sniffling through his own tears, "I loved Connor every bit as much as I love you."

"I know I should say thank you," Jill said, groaning, "and I want to say it's okay, but those words don't feel right. And I can't think of any others."

There was silence until their crying eased.

"Roger," Matt murmured, "was he unresponsive when you got to him?"

"He was face down."

Silence again while everyone imagined the unimaginable but needing to visualize it to put their minds at rest. "I knew time was urgent," he continued. "It was never a question that I had to hurry."

"In our rush to get on the boat, I'd left my bag on the beach," Gina said. "But it turned out to be a blessing because my phone was in it and I could call 911." She turned to Matt. "Not knowing what was happening must have been terrifying. Where were you waiting?"

"In the diner, where we were out of the rain but could see the dock. I figured when the boat came in, we'd run back to help tie her up. But instead, an ambulance arrived." His face was full of pain. "Not knowing why was torture."

Jill closed her eyes, remembering the chaos of the rain, the wind and the waves, her panic in the lake, their desperate attempts to save her son. How strange that, at the same time, Matt and Jake were waiting in the lively marina diner, unaware of the catastrophe unfolding, as far away as if they'd been on the opposite side of the world.

"What happened when you got Connor to the beach?" Jake asked. "Who gave him CPR? Did he ever start breathing? How badly was his head bleeding?"

Her dad answered. "His head was bleeding, but we hardly noticed. Perhaps the cold water made a difference."

Jill took over the telling. "Grandpa unbuckled his life jacket and started CPR, Gina massaged his feet, and I held his head."

Henry whispered, "I held his hand."

"Did you?" Jill asked, kissing his cheek.

"Yes. He wanted me close."

"Did you hear him talk to you, Henry?" she asked, wondering if it was possible.

He shrugged. "I just knew that's what he wanted," he said.

Jill rested her chin on his head as her heart broke in a whole new way—her little boy holding his big brother's hand as he died.

Her dad finished, "I'm not sure how long it was before the other boat showed up, but it was only a ten-minute ride back to the dock. By then, the storm had quieted. And you know what happened from there."

Jill closed her eyes. "There's just one more thing." Her voice shook as her throat closed, trying to stop her from speaking. Trying to give her an out. "I never should have insisted that we go back to the beach. I should have listened to you when you said we should wait. To both of you." She wished she could avoid looking in Matt's eyes, but she needed to acknowledge the pain her decision had caused. He was crying, but he didn't turn away. She clutched his hand. "I was wrong and I'm so sorry," she said. "All I could think of at the time was how I just wanted my boys safe in my arms."

Jake's sobs filled the room. A chill ran through Jill. This had been a bad idea. The pain was too much. And in the end, what was the point? Nothing had changed. They couldn't bring Connor back.

Before she could move, her dad was at Jake's side, enveloping him in the strong embrace Jill knew so well. Jill joined their hug, wrapping her arms around them both. She felt Matt's arms around her and then Gina and Henry.

"I miss Connor so much," Jake cried. "And I've had so many questions. But last week when I was alone, I realized the most important thing is that we don't lose anyone else in our family."

# 45

## hungover

AFTER ALL THE TEARS AND hugs, and after Gina and Grandpa left, their too-small family of four lingered in a stupor for several minutes until Henry broke their reverie. "Did everyone forget about dessert?"

Matt cuddled him while carrying him to the kitchen table, then helped Jill serve brownies and ice cream. Jake talked about his physics class and how much he liked it, possible summer camps he'd Googled, and even college. When Henry cracked a joke, making everyone laugh, he beamed from ear to ear. They were an ad-worthy happy family, and later, as Matt drifted off to sleep, spooning Jill to him, her head under his chin, he felt a peace he hadn't experienced in a long time.

But when the alarm rang, jolting him from unconsciousness, he felt the loss of Connor as strongly as ever. He hit the snooze button. Last night was good. Really good. But today, Connor was still gone.

Eventually Matt dragged himself from bed, but as he dressed for work, it was as if weights were strapped to his knees, and he was struggling to breathe, creating a smothering despair that was new to him.

As he descended the stairs, Jake and Jill's voices met him, seemingly as animated as last night. He entered the kitchen trying to match their enthusiasm.

"Hey, Henry." He rubbed his head. "Sleep well?"

"Not really. I miss Connor."

Matt tried to be honest. "Yeah, me too." But still, the knot in his throat was choking him. During breakfast he smiled on cue, rubbed a shoulder to show affection, guffawed at a joke, and desperately longed to creep back into bed.

The boys left for school, Matt put his cereal bowl in the sink, gave Jill a kiss on the cheek, and picked up his briefcase.

"Hey, is everything okay?" she asked.

He paused, not sure why he was feeling off. "Yeah, I'm great," he said, forcing himself to look at her so she'd believe it was true. Then he winked and headed out.

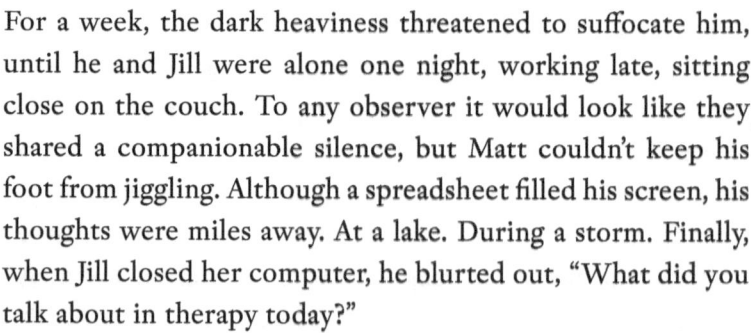

For a week, the dark heaviness threatened to suffocate him, until he and Jill were alone one night, working late, sitting close on the couch. To any observer it would look like they shared a companionable silence, but Matt couldn't keep his foot from jiggling. Although a spreadsheet filled his screen, his thoughts were miles away. At a lake. During a storm. Finally, when Jill closed her computer, he blurted out, "What did you talk about in therapy today?"

He tracked her in his peripheral vision, but faced his computer screen, preemptively hiding his embarrassment at what she might reveal.

"I really like it," she said, tucking her legs under her. "It's been good for me."

When she didn't offer anything more, he glanced up. "I guess you talk about Connor and stuff?" He deleted a cell, bolded another. Highlighted a column. Distracting himself with a mess of Excel nonsense.

"A little bit."

That surprised him. It seemed like they would be talking about Connor quite a lot.

She touched his arm. "I'd like to tell you about it, if you're interested."

His heart raced. Did she have a list of all the things the therapist said he was doing wrong? Sighing louder than he intended, he shut his laptop and set it on the cushion next to him. "I haven't had a great day," he said, surprising himself for saying it out loud.

"Is everything okay at work?"

"It's not work." He fidgeted and wiped his forehead. Oh God, was he going to cry? "Jill . . ." He swallowed, suppressing the onslaught of emotion. He folded his hands behind his neck to gain control. "I'm not sure why it's been a bad day. Nothing in particular." He pushed down his feelings and smiled. "Yes, I'm curious. Tell me about your therapy."

She looked away, thankfully allowing him privacy. "It's so much different than I expected. I went in hoping for an ally, I guess. Someone to give me the magic words I needed to make everyone do what I felt they should be doing—Jake especially. You know, learn how to get a teenager to obey his parents." She chuckled. "But instead, when I tell her something I'm frustrated with, she just asks, 'Why?' She asks 'Why?' a lot."

He frowned. "How is that helpful?"

"Right?" She opened her hands as if commiserating with him. He'd missed this—their dynamic. "It doesn't sound helpful at all. But, for example, when something someone said or did made me feel sad, or annoyed, or worried, when I recall it with her, she asks me *why* I felt that way, and I have to really think it through. She calls it 'owning my feelings.' Instead of tossing blame like, 'someone said this, and it made me mad, and everything is their fault,' I'm thinking about why what they said made me mad, or sad, or whatever, and I have these aha moments about myself. Like 'it seemed like they weren't really hearing what I was saying.'"

He drummed his fingers on the side of his leg. "Do you lay down on a couch?"

"No! It's not like in the movies. I just sit on a normal couch, and she sits in her chair. Not even behind a desk or anything. Just a comfy chair. And I talk about whatever's on my mind, and she asks, 'Why?' and I try to figure it out. My brain actually hurts when I'm done because I'm working so hard to figure it out. It's like being in school again."

"Do you ever cry?"

"Sometimes. But not big, huge crying. Just tears. She doesn't react like I'm scaring her, or that she's worried she made me sad, or that she needs to fix me, or anything like that. She just keeps letting me talk. It's kind of nice to be with someone who is so professional. I feel safe with her—like her training means she is prepared for me and my emotions, so I don't have to feel like I'm overwhelming her." She touched his arm. "Would you ever consider coming with me?"

He laughed. "So you ladies could tell me what I've been doing all wrong?"

She grabbed his hand. "It's not like that. At first, I wondered if it would be. But I've learned that therapy is about me understanding myself so I can improve my reactions—so I can respond instead of react. You can talk about whatever you want with her. Especially Connor. Even me. I would love for us to go together."

Matt nodded, but a knot took hold in his chest.

~

At their first appointment, Cathy greeted him warmly. It was kind of bizarre. Surely they'd talked about him. What had Jill said? She wasn't the most reliable narrator. He felt defensive just walking into their territory.

"It's so nice to meet you," she said as they got settled. "Tell me, what brings you here?"

"Oh. Um. Jill wanted me to come with her."

Cathy smiled pleasantly and didn't respond, apparently waiting for him to say more.

"I was curious too, I guess."

"What do you hope to get out of therapy, Matt?"

He squirmed. *Ugh, therapy.* "Well, Jill said talking to you was helping her feel better. So yeah, that's important to me too."

"To feel better?"

"Yeah."

"How have you been feeling, Matt?"

The heat from Jill's arm, just a few inches away, seemed to burn him. He glanced at her and could tell she was trying to suppress a grin. She thought his discomfort was funny. But before he could stand up and walk out, she took his hand and squeezed it, rubbing her thumb along his, and suddenly his eyes welled with tears. He pulled away to press his palms into his eyes. He did not want to cry in front of this stranger or his wife, who was friends with this stranger.

Jill spoke up. "I told Matt that you and I talked about how sometimes it's hard to know how we're feeling. I feel mad, but if I have a chance to step back, I see that I'm actually sad. And sometimes I'm just tired after a regular day and I'll find myself crying, and suddenly it's because of Connor, not because it

320 The Things They Didn't See

was a lousy day. My emotions are so mixed up. It's hard to put a name on them."

Matt exhaled, folding his arms across his chest. "Yeah, me too. Sometimes I'm so relieved to be going home from work—to be under the same roof with my family—hang out, watch TV, talk. And then I walk in the door and find out Jake is out late with friends or has a ton of homework and is in his room all night, and I get mad. But really, I'm just disappointed. I think I feel disappointed a lot."

An hour later, as they left her office, Matt felt lighter. He liked that Cathy didn't say "I'm sorry" all the time or look upset, like so many people he talked to this past year. He liked that when he talked about feeling mad or confused, she said that was normal. He liked being told he was normal.

# 46

## goodbye

JAKE SKIPPED FIFTH PERIOD—HE SIMPLY wasn't in the mood to go. It was a gorgeous April day, the sun finally out after weeks of rain. He putzed around at home, then figured he'd skip the rest of school and go to the lake—hang the wind chimes he'd made over the weekend. By the time he arrived, it was already three in the afternoon, and his mom would be texting soon if he didn't check in.

He tapped his phone against his leg, considering what to do. It had been a month since that weekend when he'd run away. Since then, things had been almost normal—good normal—between them, but he'd never told her where he'd been and was shocked she hadn't bugged him about it. She did ask if he'd been somewhere safe. He said he had, and that was it.

He texted:

Just letting you know I'm with friends.

Then he turned his phone off and climbed out of his car. As he walked down the hill, a low rumble made him look up. He hadn't noticed the gathering dark clouds and the spring shower didn't wait. Picking up his pace, he slipped and slid through the rest of the brush and made a run for the trees.

It was mostly dry inside the protected grove, so he took his time deciding where to hang the chimes. The eight he'd hung earlier still looked perfect. He placed seven more on another branch. It was starting to look like an inside-out Christmas tree.

With another rumble of thunder, the shower turned into a downpour, and now the trees weren't keeping him dry, so he climbed out. The lake had thawed and was heaving in the storm. Waves crashed onto shore and lightning flashed in the distance. The rain poured from his wet hair into his face, and he backed against a tree, hoping to quiet his trembling.

A dark shape bobbing in the water caught his eye. It rolled on a wave then disappeared. He held his breath until he saw it again. It was probably just driftwood. But when it disappeared again, he ran toward it. Running across the sand was like running in slow motion—like running in a dream where the unseen held you back. *It's just a stick*, he repeated over and over, trying to stay calm. It wasn't working.

When he was ankle deep in the water, he searched the waves. Where had it gone? He splashed up to his knees. "Connor!" he screamed until his voice was hoarse. "Come back!" But the stick had vanished.

Back at his car, he chucked his shoes and socks on the floor, rolled up his drenched pant legs, and turned up the heat. His whole body was numb. He couldn't feel his fingers to properly drive and wasn't sure if his freezing bare feet could press the pedals. The windshield wipers swished back and forth, while he leaned his head against the seat and cried.

When he got home, he let the door slam behind him.

"Where have you been?" his mom asked, catching him before he could get upstairs. She was at the counter, rifling through mail.

"With friends."

"In the rain?"

"Yeah. We were outside."

He started toward his bedroom.

"We're eating in an hour," his mom called.

He stopped. He couldn't be here. Not today. But he didn't have the energy to fight. "Mom," he called from the stairs.

"Yeah?"

"I'm working on a project for homework and we're meeting right now—I just came home to get dry clothes. I can't stay for dinner. Is that okay?"

He held his breath. Dinner was generally nonnegotiable.

She was quiet.

*Just today*, he thought. *Just today.*

"Um, yeah. Okay. Want me to heat something up for you before you go?"

Relief washed over him. And exhaustion. "No. No, I'm good. Thanks, Mom." He ran up the stairs, tossed his wet clothes on the floor and pulled on sweats, a sweatshirt, dry shoes, and raced out the door before his mom could change her mind.

"Hey," he called as he let himself in Grandpa's front door. Grandpa and Gina waved from the kitchen table. He forgot they ate dinner early.

"Do you want to join us?" Gina asked.

"No, I'm good. I have something I want to do. Is it okay . . .?" He pointed toward the shop.

"Of course." Grandpa stood. "We won't bother you. But I do want a hug." He wrapped his arms around him.

He let himself relax into Grandpa's arms. He was shaking. "Are you cold?"

"I got caught in the rain. I changed clothes, but I'm still a little chilly."

Grandpa rubbed his arms, then his back. "Love you, Jake."

"I love you too, Grandpa."

Grandpa released him. "Have you eaten? Want me to bring you a plate?"

"Thanks, but I'm not hungry right now. I'm just going to get to work."

An hour later, warmed from the space heater set close to his legs, he wandered back into the house. "Grandpa, I need some kind of glue that's extra strong and can get wet."

"If you have time to go to the hardware store tomorrow, I can show you different options. You've really been working hard. Are you happy with how your project is turning out?"

Jake nodded, shuffling his feet. "If you want, I can show you what I've been doing."

Grandpa squeezed his shoulder and followed him into the shop.

Jake spread out the wind chimes, and eager to finally share his surprise, let loose. "Remember the wood show? That's where I got the idea to make something from Connor's sea glass collection. I brought it here and the first time I just poured them out onto the table, pushed them around a little bit, ran my hand through them. Kind of got to know them, you know?"

Roger did know.

"I wasn't sure how to make chimes and didn't know how to make them extra special. But I experimented and my first one was pretty neat. I made a few more but wasn't sure what I was going to do with them—like what was the point, you know? Then one day, I figured it out. It was just so cool how these ideas sort of came to me. At first, I had nothing, and then slowly the idea got more developed until I knew exactly what I wanted. And it's turned out really cool!"

Grandpa held up a chime and put his other arm around Jake. "They're really beautiful. And you made them from Connor's glass, so they're meaningful too. Thanks for sharing them with me, Jake. Will you tell your family or are you keeping it private?"

"I'm waiting until I get it just right. I could use your help on one last thing, not my wind chimes, something else I've been researching. It's what I need the glue for. And when that's finished, I'll show my family too. I think everyone will really like it."

# 47

## see me too

ON A WARM MAY AFTERNOON, Jill was relaxing on the patio furniture, devouring the scent of trees in bloom and freshly cut grass as she read. Next to her was a book about grief and another about parenting teenagers, but she was reading a mystery. It had been a long time since she'd picked up a book for fun. Almost a year.

She and Matt had been going to therapy once a week as a couple and another day on their own. They were communicating better, rediscovering the person they'd fallen in love with. But she was also crying in Cathy's office more often, trying to work through her guilt for taking pleasure in life and her marriage, when it felt like being happy was betraying the acute grief she felt over losing Connor. But talking about it helped. Therapy helped. Matt holding her helped.

Last week, with the emotional strength she was building, she'd tackled another hard task that had been weighing on her. She'd talked it through with Cathy, then immediately after her appointment, before she could talk herself out of it, she drove to Vanessa's home. Vanessa was currently living in a residential center for the treatment of bulimia and self-harm. It was Vanessa's mom Jill hoped to apologize to.

The conversation went well. Jill hadn't expected to leave with a new best friend; she just wanted to tell her that she was sorry. Sorry that even though she'd suspected something was wrong, she'd dismissed it, really, really wanting to believe that everything was okay. She apologized for not speaking up. Mrs. Stuart let her hold her hand, bravely swallowed back tears, and acknowledged that it was hard to know the difference between helping and interfering. Vanessa was getting help and was feeling optimistic, and the whole family was benefitting from group therapy at the center.

"Us too," Jill had said. Which wasn't exactly true. She'd found a children's support group that Henry was enjoying. But Jake wasn't interested yet. However, therapy was definitely helping the rest of them.

Jill realized she'd been dozing when she heard Jake calling her name.

"Mom, can I talk to you about something?"

She patted the seat next to her, moving the books to give him space. Her heart skipped a beat. *Don't assume the worst,* she reminded herself, thinking she really should spend more time with the parenting book.

"I've been going to the lake," he said.

She blinked and blinked again, as if her eyes were having little spasms. Her mind went blank. There was a pond the kids used to fish in on the other side of the park. "Which lake?"

"Lake Koda." His eyes didn't leave hers.

She fluttered her lashes to keep the sudden tears away. "Alone?"

He nodded.

"It's so far. You shouldn't be driving that far without permission."

"I've been going all winter. I told you I wanted to go, and you said no. So I went by myself. I've been a bunch of times."

Her mind buzzed trying to think of what he'd even do there. "I don't want you going there. It isn't safe."

His eyes narrowed. "I'm trying to share something with you and you're just getting mad at me! It feels like you don't even care about me!"

She threw up her arms.

He stood, as if leaving. "See? Here we go."

Jill grabbed his hand. "No, not 'here we go.' I'm not mad at you—I'm mad at myself for reacting like this. I can see what you're saying. But I need a minute to think." She took a breath and patted the seat next to her again. "Sit down, please. I want to listen."

Jake sat but kept his head down. She waited. When he didn't say anything more, she tried again. "You really wanted to go to the lake, and when I refused, you went on your own."

He nodded.

"You didn't tell me because you knew I'd be upset."

"Yes, and you'd tell me I couldn't go." He shrugged. "But I like being there. I'm not doing anything wrong. It's just a good place to be by myself and think."

"I do care about you. But when you keep secrets from me, I worry that it's because you're doing something you know you shouldn't be doing. But I'm hearing that I need to trust you and not let my worries take precedence. You want some independence. And you're right, you deserve that."

He wiped his eyes.

"I think you know I've been seeing a therapist. And Dad's come with me a few times too. I offered you therapy that day, not because I didn't want to listen, but because the therapist had helped me so much. I wanted you to get that same help because I know I don't always say the right things. I thought she would be more helpful than I could be, and I want that for you."

"But you're my mom."

"I do want you to feel like you can talk to me. But I might not always say the right thing."

"You probably will."

She wanted to weep at his continued trust despite all she'd put them through. "I'll try at least. I want you to know I care about you and Henry more than anything else in the world. Nothing can come close to how much I love you two. I'm sorry if my actions didn't show that."

"I know, Mom."

She held his hand and looked at him steadily. "I really do care, Jake."

He pointed to her book. "I have that book too."

"This mystery?"

"No, that one on grief." He pulled his cap further over his eyes and started to bite his fingernail.

*He'd picked up his own book on grief? Her sweet sixteen-year-old was that resourceful?* "Tell me more."

"I have this friend, Kevin. I met him at the skatepark, but he goes to our school. His little sister died a few years ago, and when he heard about Connor and we got to know each other, he gave me the book. His family read it together and he said they really liked it, and I probably would too. Why are you crying?"

"Kevin, in my fourth period, who was new last year?"

"Yeah. I know he looks kinda sketchy, but he's actually a really nice guy."

"Do you hang out with him very much?"

"No. I was kinda embarrassed after he gave me the book, and then school started, and I haven't really talked to him since. I feel like kind of a jerk."

"It's never too late to tell someone you're thinking of them. My dad always says that."

Jake smiled. "Yeah, he's told me that too." He stood. "So, I'd like to go to the lake today. Is that okay? I might be late for dinner."

She nodded. "Thanks for telling me. Jake, have you read any of the book yet?"

"A little. I keep it in a bag over at Grandpa's shop."

# 48

# testing the waters

FROM HER BENCH NEAR THE pool at the recreation center, Jill pretended to adjust her swim goggles, but really, she was just stalling. She was evaluating which of the other swimmers she wouldn't mind sharing a lane with. Her therapist suggested she start exercising again—she hadn't been on more than a walk since Connor died—but Jill's sport of choice had always been swimming, and it was something she never wanted to do again.

Cathy said it would be good to face the new fear, to which Jill responded that Cathy was being heartless. But it was also possible that as she got to know Jill better, Cathy knew a kick in the pants was often what she needed—what Old Jill needed. Was she ready to be Old Jill again?

The steamy smell of chlorine was a surprising analgesic, flooding her with nostalgia for her youth and hours spent on the school swim team. She fiddled with her swim cap, tucking her braid inside, then changed her mind and let it hang. She hadn't had a haircut in over a year.

Three blue lane markers ran twenty-five meters to the other end of the pool. It wasn't far. It was easy, in fact. She could swim one length without taking a breath if she wanted. She could get to the other side and back in less than a minute if she went all out. And that would count, wouldn't it? She could say she swam and decide sixty seconds was enough for one day. It was up to her. But even so, she was having difficulty willing herself into the pool.

Before, she'd loved gliding through the warm water, the predictable rhythm of one, two, three strokes, then a breath, along with the smell of chlorine that lingered on her skin and in her hair. She loved the full-body ache after working out. The strength she felt the rest of the day.

Seven other swimmers swam at different paces. Some flipped when they got to the opposite end, others just turned around. An older woman made a slow sidestroke, keeping her head above water the whole time, bobbing imperceptibly forward. A young man's cadence was beautiful to watch as he kicked and pulled in perfect rhythm.

In the only lane with just one swimmer, a woman about Jill's age stood in the shallow end, coughing as she poured water from her goggles. She caught Jill watching her, smiled slightly, then swam away—if that's what you could call her chaotic splashing—zigzagging from one side of the lane to the other. Jill sighed, dispirited at having to share a lane with her.

As a child, she'd practiced different strokes with her dad. He tossed quarters in the deep end to train her to dive and hold her breath. She got bonuses when she collected two at a time, then three, then four.

Todd and Cara looked for excuses to skip his lessons or would end up splashing each other and everyone else until their dad sent them inside. But Jill loved following his meticulous instructions, working on precision with her dad's undivided attention. She loved when he bragged about "what a little fish" she was. How he'd tell her that when she was in high school, she'd beat his best time, he was sure of it. "I was a darn good swimmer," he'd say. "But Jill? She's great."

He was at every meet, stopwatch in hand, volunteering to time races so he could be on the front row. He not only kept stats for the team, but he also tracked her main competitors and the times she needed to beat them.

She adored her swim coach and his enthusiasm, but she relished recapping races with her dad, discussing tips for moving faster, and techniques he used for motivating himself—how to get out of your head and cut seconds off times.

As she got stronger, she did break a high school record. And her name was up on the wall of state champs, right next to his.

Two lifeguards were sitting in their tall chairs overlooking each end of the community pool. They looked young, yet Jill knew how capable they had to be. Every summer during high school and college, she renewed her lifesaving and CPR certificates so she could work at the club pool. Not once did she have to jump in the water to help a struggling child—or adult. She'd blown her whistle plenty at kids who were roughhousing, and she'd cleared the pool on several occasions when it had become . . . contaminated, but that was the extent of her lifesaving career.

Until it really mattered.

She and her therapist had talked about her guilt—for the decision she made to go back into the storm. She'd truly thought it was the right thing to do. Now the *if only, if only, if only* warped her belief that she could ever again be a good mother. They worked on strategies to manage her grief without the need to constantly be "doing." Like a shark who has to keep swimming to breathe.

As she learned to give herself grace, the anger she felt toward her dad dissipated as well. She had practiced, with her therapist, thanking her dad for his help in rescuing Connor. For his swimming skills, even in a storm, in bringing Connor back to shore. For not giving up. For teaching her how to swim so she could rescue Henry and herself. For knowing how to do CPR.

She was surprised at how well the affirmations helped. Detailing all that she had to be grateful for actually helped her feel grateful. She was able to start forgiving her dad. Forgiving herself. Forgiving the other families who got to keep their children.

She put in her ear plugs and fixed her swim cap. The splashy lady was still the only one with an empty spot in her lane and had just flipped around at the opposite end of the pool. Jill sat on the edge, letting her feet dangle in the water. She'd make eye contact when she returned to signal she was sharing the lane. It was an unspoken rule that two could share, but it was polite to acknowledge each other.

Jill stretched her arms above her head, behind and to her side, taking deep breaths to expand her lungs. She'd done this thousands of times.

As the lady neared, instead of reaching for the wall, she popped up with a cough and a ragged breath and turned to flounder her way back. Exasperated, Jill waited for her to get halfway across, then pushed off.

She started out slow, counting three strokes, then a breath. Before the end of the lap, she'd caught up to her lane mate who stopped to hold on to the wall. To avoid accidently running into her, Jill didn't flip, just turned and sped to the other end.

When they passed each other again, the lady was kicking so vigorously that Jill inhaled water and choked. She dog-paddled while she coughed to clear her lungs, and when she finally caught her breath, she directed silent, evil thoughts toward her lane mate.

*It's a miracle there's any water left in the pool*, Jill thought, uncharitably. And it was pretty selfish of her that she didn't hug the side of her lane so Jill could pass easily. How would she feel if she knew Jill had lost her son in a drowning accident? Jill was trying to get over PTSD, for crying out loud, and this lady was making it worse, the way she flailed her arms and legs as if she herself were drowning.

Jill swam harder. She even imagined smacking the woman as she flipped around. Of course, she wouldn't. But what if she did? Could she pull it off as an accident? She flipped again, taking a long glide before surfacing to breathe. She showed off, hoping to scare off this rookie swimmer from ever coming back.

Finally, the tussle was over, and the lady sat on the edge, stretching. Should Jill stop to explain pool etiquette? She pretended to catch her breath, but as soon as she stopped, the woman spoke. "I'm sorry for nearly hitting you back there. I haven't been swimming in years. I'm afraid I'm not any good."

Her British accent was disarming. So was her apology. "It's okay. I'm fine," Jill replied.

"You're an incredible swimmer."

Jill lifted her goggles so she would seem more amiable. "I've been swimming all my life. Kudos for trying—it's great exercise." She turned, assuming the conversation was over.

"Yeah. My therapist thinks it's good for me too."

Jill couldn't hide her curiosity. "Really? How come?"

She daintily pressed her manicured fingers to her lips. "I'm talking too much. I shouldn't keep you from your swim, but my husband is sick. I've been caring for him, but apparently, I need to fit *self-care* into my day."

Jill's heart softened. "My goodness. I'm so sorry."

The woman looked toward the floor-to-ceiling windows brightening the far end of the pool. "I feel guilty for exercising—that I'm able to move my arms and legs. I usually run, but my therapist suggested I try something different—a challenge that might help mitigate some of the misplaced guilt I feel for leaving my husband behind. For being able to move when he can't."

"Is it working?" Jill asked, genuinely interested.

The woman gave a quiet laugh. "The swimming is as challenging as the guilt."

"I'd be happy to give you some tips," Jill offered.

Her look told Jill she'd hoped to be done for the day.

Jill held up a finger. "Just one small change for one lap. Try keeping your head neutral and your eyes on the bottom of the pool. I'll meet you at the other end."

She smiled in resignation. "I'm Lily, by the way."

Jill swam to the opposite end to watch her progress. Lily's line was already much straighter, and Jill couldn't resist encouraging her to lift her chin to the side, not forward, to breathe.

When they met back at the shallow end, Lily cheered for herself, and Jill gave her a high five. Lily's positive energy was contagious.

"Will you be here again tomorrow?" Jill asked.

"No, the day after," Lily replied, clumsily pulling herself out of the water.

"Are you thinking '*if* I come back'?" Jill asked.

"Ha. Exactly!"

"Come. I've got my own stuff I'm trying to 'swim out.' Knowing you're expecting me will help get me here."

"Would you forgive me if I didn't show?"

Jill grinned. "I'm not the very forgiving type, but that's one of the things I'm working on. So, yes. But I do hope to see you again."

Jill looked at her watch. She'd only been swimming for twenty minutes, but now that she was here, she didn't want to quit.

# 49

## *it was here*

"PULL OVER RIGHT THERE," JAKE said, pointing to a narrow shoulder of road ahead of them. They were on a hill overlooking the lake, surrounded by wilderness. For, as well as Jill thought she knew Lake Koda, this road circumnavigating the lake was one she'd never travelled before.

Summer was officially a week away, but boats were already cruising around the water. From her vantage point, they looked like a colorful collection of bathtub toys, but up close they held families who were blissfully unaware how one decision—even made with the best intentions—could change everything.

Jake hopped over the guardrail and the rest of them followed him down the hill through the brush on a rough path worn bare by his frequent trips.

Jill helped Henry navigate over a rock and Matt held back a wayward branch. And then Jake called, "We're here!" as the trail opened to a wide beach—their beach. The soft gray log, the rocky cliff, and the water shimmering a blue so exquisite it was like an embrace. A pain grasped at Jill's throat, and she couldn't hold back tears. She clasped Matt's hand in hers, knowing he was fragile too.

Jake was showing Henry how to climb on top of the log and as Jill and Matt approached, concern wrinkled Jake's face, but Jill quickly reassured him. "I'm happy to be here," she said. "I really am. I just... It just makes me cry too. But I'm okay." She hugged him. "Thank you for bringing us."

After a moment, he tried to pull back, but she squeezed him tighter. "I just need to hold you for another minute. Do you know how much I care about you?"

Giving in, he returned the hug and let her linger.

Finally, she let go, kissing him on the forehead. She gazed into his eyes, hoping that the depth of her caring would find a way to his heart and burrow into a lasting spot on his soul, to somehow sustain him through everything life pitched at him.

Breaking away, Jake exclaimed, "I want to show you some of my favorite things! If you lean back on this branch, you can relax your head and close your eyes and not even fall off. You can even lay down. And here"—he pointed to where Henry was sitting—"can you tell what these are?"

Everyone peered closer at letters carved into the log. In the middle was the letter C with a heart around it. "Does this stand for Connor?" Jill asked. She traced the outlines of a J, H, M, and another J. "Our family's initials."

Matt put his arm around Jake. "Really cool, son."

Jill thought she could hear music. She spun around looking for the source.

"You can hear it, can't you?" Jake said, beaming. "Come and see."

He led them to a grove of pines at the back of the beach. He stepped over low branches and ducked to maneuver around others. The three of them followed until they came into an open space that literally sparkled. Hundreds of glittering blue and green jewels were suspended in midair. And they were singing. Transfixed, Jill turned in a slow circle.

"Wow!" Henry said wide-eyed.

Jill looked closer, and saw they were pieces of sea glass strung together with fishing line, hanging on branches at various heights. They clinked as they touched in the breeze, creating magical music, like a fairy song.

She held one in her palm. Each strand was made up of five or more small pieces in varying shades—teal, aqua, milky white, bright green, baby blue. Not only did they sing, but as they caught wisps of sunlight, the shine bounced around the clearing.

"You did all this?" she asked.

Jake nodded.

"It's Connor's sea glass," Henry said in awe. "Can I share it with you?"

"Of course! I made it for all of us. Lots of the chimes are made with five pieces, one for each member of our family. Do you want to stretch out? There's room for all of us." They lay on the bed of pine needles and watched the colors swirling around them.

Jill closed her eyes. If she could keep her family snuggled next to her, she would spend the night here too.

After a while, Jake sat up. "I've got one more thing to show you."

They brushed the needles from their backs and then crawled out of the trees, with the chimes serenading them.

Jake led them to the edge of the beach. "Wait here," he said, disappearing behind the cliff.

Jill searched across the water for the opposite shore. It seemed impossible that this same serene lake could have been so angry that it flipped their boat. If someone else was telling the story, she would have never believed conditions could change that fast.

Jake called to them, but she couldn't see him. When he shouted again, she spotted him sitting on top of the highest cliff, waving his arms. She caught her breath. He was so high, so close to the edge.

"Come on!" he shouted.

"You want us to come up there?" Matt yelled back.

"Yeah, I have something to show you!"

Jill knitted her brows. "How? Can we get Henry up?"

Henry was already running over. "Where, Jake? Where do I go?"

"Between the rocks. You'll see it!"

A crack between the rocks was wide enough for a person and narrow enough to give support as they made their way to the top.

Jill was nervous about Henry climbing so high. Nervous there wouldn't be room at the top for all of them. Worried that someone would fall.

But Matt scrambled up the makeshift ladder quickly. Henry made it a few feet before asking his mom for help. She boosted his bottom, encouraging him to reach just a little further until he could grasp Matt's hand, who pulled him up and out of Jill's sight.

She easily found the footholds to make her way up, and nearing the top, Matt's hand again appeared, his firm grip helping her the rest of the way.

Henry and Jake were huddled over something Jill couldn't see until she crouched next to them. A square stone plaque was affixed to the rocks with an etching of Connor's face smiling back at them.

"I got the idea from a crafting site I follow and glued it with a special glue Grandpa helped me find," Jake said. "He said it would last a long time in all kinds of weather."

"Grandpa has been here with you?"

"Just once, a few weeks ago, when I placed the plaque. But everything else I did by myself, alone in his shop."

As a kid, Jill never liked the shop because the lathe was noisy, and dust covered everything. But her dad always said it was a good place to think.

"Do you help Grandpa turn bowls?" she asked.

"No. I said it wasn't my favorite and he said we each have to find our own thing."

So, she and her dad were both learning. Instead of forcing his interests on Jake, her dad pivoted to help Jake with the things he enjoyed. Why was it so hard to give up our expectations for our children and simply love what they loved?

Jill leaned closer to examine the photo. She recognized it, but it wasn't one from a frame. He must have gone through the family photo albums to find it. Connor's face was tilted toward the sky. It looked like hope. Her smiling boy, untouchable now by waves and storms, sheltered from disagreements, disappointments, and heartache.

But her heart ached at all the good he was missing out on too, and it would never stop aching, wishing she could watch him grow up—see how tall he'd be. How he'd fix his hair and style his clothes. The jokes that would make him laugh. The girl he'd fall in love with. She had a feeling he'd have always been sweet.

That Jake had created all of this took her breath away. He'd been so constructive with his anger and grief, when she feared he was up to something dangerous. So many nights she'd imagined the worst. This year might have been so different if she'd simply trusted him—if she'd listened to him rather than searched for clues to confirm her misguided suspicions. What other good had she missed?

But before she could sink into regrets, she watched Jake and Henry standing side by side—Jake pointing to something on the lake, Henry glowing from his brother's attention, his boyish smile transformed by two new permanent teeth. With his other hand, Jake held Henry's shoulder, preventing his little brother from getting too close to the edge. Jill remembered countless days that she had done the same—spotting beauty and sharing it with her boys, but also protecting them whenever she could.

In spite of her shortcomings, she recognized she'd influenced the strong young man Jake was choosing to be. Her failings over the past year didn't define her. For sixteen years she'd held him when he cried and snuggled him to sleep. She'd sung him songs when he was a baby and surprised him with donut runs as a teen. She'd taught him to skip rope in the driveway and cheered for him on the soccer field. She laughed at his jokes and cooked his favorite meals. She'd held his hand when they crossed the street but encouraged him when it was time to walk on his own. Every day of his whole life, she strived to show him that he was loved.

This year she had swum out of her lane, but it was never too late to self-correct. Starting today. She didn't have to be perfect to be a good mom. She'd finally realized that wasn't the goal.

"I want to show you something," Jake called, interrupting her thoughts.

Jill reached for Matt to help him up and they smiled at each other through their tears. With his hand in hers, they moved closer to their boys to see all the things they saw.

# acknowledgments

WRITING THIS BOOK HAS BEEN a decade-long experience with many people to thank along the way. I'm starting from the very beginning, because surely, I'm not the only person who appreciates a good backstory.

After eighteen amazing years as a stay-at-home mom to four children, I started to feel like something was missing. Yes, my oldest had just moved away to college. But it was more than that. I'd become so consumed with volunteering, I'd forgotten that before becoming a mother, I'd dreamed of writing a book.

At first, getting involved in my children's schools and activities was a way to help out, use my talents and make new friends; but, the need for volunteers are limitless: fundraising committees, PTA committees, room parent, team parent, teaching church classes, organizing organizations, endless meetings and even a stint refereeing kindergarten soccer because no one else would do it. (I knew so little about the sport that I had to look to parents on the sidelines to tell me if it was a corner or goal kick. To their credit, no one complained.)

Like Jill, I look forward to fresh starts on Mondays, January, and new school years. But my goals had morphed into accomplishing long to-do lists. I still loved being a full-time mom; but after twenty years, I was exhausted with my other unintentional full-time job as a person who always said *yes*.

Through much self-reflection I recalled my aspirations to be a writer. I started journaling again, writing personal essays, and tackling daily writing prompts from the book, *Pen on Fire*, by Barbara DeMarco-Barrett. I found it on my front porch one morning, tied up with a ribbon. Thank you, Steph Bywater for the inspired surprise.

I mapped a path toward a master's degree in creative writing until one serendipitous afternoon, Jody Matsumori dropped by to borrow a child's lacrosse stick. While chatting on the front porch—the boardroom for many mothers—I learned she had an MFA and was a college English instructor. She advised me that if I wanted to learn to write, write. And consider enrolling in a professional program. She also gave constructive feedback on my very amateur first chapter in 2018. Two thank-yous, Jody.

UCLA Extension's online creative writing program offered the learning and collaborative peer workshops I'd been craving. After several years of classes, I *finally* mustered the courage to enroll in the first of five courses on novel writing.

I began the class with zero story ideas and wondered if they would come. I didn't even know the difference between a protagonist and an antagonist. But I was missing my dad who had recently died and thinking a lot about our relationship and how differently everyone who loved him was experiencing grief. After a writing exercise exploring those emotions, the seed of my novel was planted. My first chapter was thirty pages, and the head-hopping was atrocious, but I would learn more about refinement and POV later. Most importantly, my novel was born. Thank you to UCLA and Paul Witcover for the direction.

Leslie Bringhurst was one of my first confidantes (as hair stylists often are) after she divulged that she was also a writer. She introduced me to NaNoWriMo (National Novel Writing Month) and was a constant inspiration by sharing her story ideas and the love she had for her writing community. She gave gentle nudges, but also acceptance when I let my pages lie dormant.

After writing chapter one, my book had its first experience of sitting on the shelf for over a year. But in 2019 I committed to November's NaNoWriMo, and a month later, I'd written 50,000 words and pants'd a first draft.

During the pandemic, several online writing workshops were indispensable for making progress in learning, if not in actual writing. And I discovered how expansive the writing community was outside of formal classes.

Chris Terry taught our Novel 2 class to *get your butt in the chair and write*, but even better, challenged us to create writing groups. I took a chance, reaching out to several classmates who impressed me with their prose and feedback. They said yes, and we created, WorD, my dearest writing friends whom I've never actually met in person.

Our friendship was instantaneous. I treasured sharing work with Sherry Yang, Jacqui Swedberg and Anne Maxwell, also our random texts that had nothing to do with writing. Thank you for your fierce friendship, wise feedback, all the laughs, and most of all, belief.

All the while, parenting remained my first priority. As each of my children started the inevitable process of untying apron strings, I discovered I needed help through therapy to navigate that transition. Thanks to Tom Bunnell, LCSW, for listening, asking "why?," and for noticing that the challenge of writing a book made me so happy. Thanks also for your insight on the Vanessa chapters.

I'm so appreciative to my beta readers for all the sticky notes, your invaluable critiques, flagging loose ends, and most of all, your encouragement: Robyn Bechthold, Josh Burgoyne, Chad Christensen, KT Janke and Jo Ellen Shaeffer.

Extra thanks, KT, for listening to the lives of my characters as if they were real people during all our hikes. And Josh, for your detailed copy editing. Your comments in the margins asking for more scene detail, fixing grammar and semantics, or a little tear emoji letting me know I struck the right emotion, were fantastic motivation. I'm so impressed with your talent and can't wait to read what you write someday.

Andrea Hurst, Jessica Strawser, and Tiffany Yates-Martin were all very helpful in different phases of developmental editing and proofreading. DaMonza was fantastic to work with for cover design and detailed proofreading (again and again and again). Thank you to Shelly Coleman for creating the custom cover art—I saw her raindrop paintings and fell in love. Many thanks to Paula Fitzgerald for even more proofreading and Author Imprints for the interior formatting that was so pretty, I wept, and their guidance through the final mile.

All my love to my mom and sisters who have always been my biggest cheerleaders. I'm blessed with a big family of brothers, sisters, parents, stepparents, in-laws, children, nieces and nephews and countless friends whose genuine interest matters more than anyone can imagine.

Thanks to my kids for their enthusiastic support. Often while I worked a scene at the kitchen table, Chris and Nick gave valuable expertise with things like skateboarding terms and texting like a teenager. Courtney, Marty, Michael, and Lizzie read one of the early-final versions (yes, that's a thing) and gave their stamp of approval. All of them made me feel so amazing for writing a book. Thanks guys. You'll all know soon enough how much it means when your kids are proud of you.

My dad and father-in-law both passed away the year before I started writing *The Things They Didn't See*. Both believed in my dream that I would someday write a book. And both, when I confided parenting worries, so often said, "Just love them."

To Dan, for everything. And especially for saying yes to making dinners.

*about the author*

ANGELA SHAEFFER is a mother to four grown children, two children-in-law, and Grammy to two adorable granddaughters. She lives in Utah with her husband when they're not escaping to Colorado's San Juan Mountains or exploring New York City. She loves to hike, road bike and travel but also cherishes solitary hours to read and write. *The Things They Didn't See* is her debut novel.